Cinder

in the Lunar Chronicles.

Coming soon from Marissa Meyer:

Scarlet

2013

Cress

2014

Winter

2015

Cinder

Book One

The Lunar Chronicles

WRITTEN BY

Marissa Meyer

SQUARE FISH

Feiwel and Friends

NEW YORK

For my grandma, Samalee Jones,
with more love than could ever fit into these pages.

An Imprint of Macmillan

 Printed in the United States of America by
R. R. Donnelley & Sons Company, Harrisonburg, Virginia. For information,
address Square Fish, 175 Fifth Avenue, New York, NY 10010.

Library of Congress Cataloging-in-Publication Data Available
ISBN 978-1-250-00720-9

Originally published in the United States by Feiwel and Friends
First Square Fish Edition: January 2013
Square Fish logo designed by Filomena Tuosto
Book designed by Barbara Grzeslo
macteenbooks.com

12 14 16 18 20 19 17 15 13 11

AR: 5.1 / LEXILE: 790L

BOOK One

While her sisters were given beautiful dresses and fine slippers, Cinderella had only a filthy smock and wooden shoes.

One

THE SCREW THROUGH CINDER'S ANKLE HAD RUSTED, THE engraved cross marks worn to a mangled circle. Her knuckles ached from forcing the screwdriver into the joint as she struggled to loosen the screw one gritting twist after another. By the time it was extracted far enough for her to wrench free with her prosthetic steel hand, the hairline threads had been stripped clean.

Tossing the screwdriver onto the table, Cinder gripped her heel and yanked the foot from its socket. A spark singed her fingertips and she jerked away, leaving the foot to dangle from a tangle of red and yellow wires.

She slumped back with a relieved groan. A sense of release hovered at the end of those wires—freedom. Having loathed the too-small foot for four years, she swore to never put the piece of junk back on again. She just hoped Iko would be back soon with its replacement.

Cinder was the only full-service mechanic at New Beijing's

weekly market. Without a sign, her booth hinted at her trade only by the shelves of stock android parts that crowded the walls. It was squeezed into a shady cove between a used netscreen dealer and a silk merchant, both of whom frequently complained about the tangy smell of metal and grease that came from Cinder's booth, even though it was usually disguised by the aroma of honey buns from the bakery across the square. Cinder knew they really just didn't like being next to *her.*

A stained tablecloth divided Cinder from browsers as they shuffled past. The square was filled with shoppers and hawkers, children and noise. The bellows of men as they bargained with robotic shopkeepers, trying to talk the computers down from their desired profit margins. The hum of ID scanners and monotone voice receipts as money changed accounts. The netscreens that covered every building and filled the air with the chatter of advertisements, news reports, gossip.

Cinder's auditory interface dulled the noise into a static thrumming, but today one melody lingered above the rest that she couldn't drown out. A ring of children were standing just outside her booth, trilling—"Ashes, ashes, we all fall down!"—and then laughing hysterically as they collapsed to the pavement.

A smile tugged at Cinder's lips. Not so much at the nursery rhyme, a phantom song about pestilence and death that had regained popularity in the past decade. The song itself made her squeamish. But she did love the glares from passersby as the giggling children fell over in their paths. The inconvenience of having to swarm around the writhing bodies stirred grumbles from the shoppers, and Cinder adored the children for it.

"Sunto! *Sunto!*"

Cinder's amusement wilted. She spotted Chang Sacha, the baker, pushing through the crowd in her flour-coated apron. "Sunto, come here! I told you not to play so close to—"

Sacha met Cinder's gaze, knotted her lips, then grabbed her son by the arm and spun away. The boy whined, dragging his feet as Sacha ordered him to stay closer to their booth. Cinder wrinkled her nose at the baker's retreating back. The remaining children fled into the crowd, taking their bright laughter with them.

"It's not like wires are contagious," Cinder muttered to her empty booth.

With a spine-popping stretch, she pulled her dirty fingers through her hair, combing it up into a messy tail, then grabbed her blackened work gloves. She covered her steel hand first, and though her right palm began to sweat immediately inside the thick material, she felt more comfortable with the gloves on, hiding the plating of her left hand. She stretched her fingers wide, working out the cramp that had formed at the fleshy base of her thumb from clenching the screwdriver, and squinted again into the city square. She spotted plenty of stocky white androids in the din, but none of them Iko.

Sighing, Cinder bent over the toolbox beneath the worktable. After digging through the jumbled mess of screwdrivers and wrenches, she emerged with the fuse puller that had been long buried at the bottom. One by one, she disconnected the wires that still linked her foot and ankle, each spurting a tiny spark. She couldn't feel them through the gloves, but her retina display helpfully informed her with blinking red text that she was losing connection to the limb.

With a yank of the last wire, her foot clattered to the concrete.

The difference was instant. For once in her life, she felt . . . weightless.

She made room for the discarded foot on the table, setting it up like a shrine amid the wrenches and lug nuts, before hunkering over her ankle again and cleaning the grime from the socket with an old rag.

THUD.

Cinder jerked, her head smacking the underside of the table. She shoved back from the desk, her scowl landing first on a lifeless android that sat squat on her worktable and then on the man behind it. She was met with startled copper-brown eyes and black hair that hung past his ears and lips that every girl in the country had admired a thousand times.

Her scowl vanished.

His own surprise was short-lived, melting into an apology. "I'm sorry," he said. "I didn't realize anyone was back there."

Cinder barely heard him above the blankness in her mind. With her heartbeat gathering speed, her retina display scanned his features, so familiar from years spent watching him on the netscreens. He seemed taller in real life and a gray hooded sweatshirt was like none of the fine clothes he usually made appearances in, but still, it took only 2.6 seconds for Cinder's scanner to measure the points of his face and link his image to the net database. Another second and the display informed her of what she already knew; details scribbled across the bottom of her vision in a stream of green text.

PRINCE KAITO, CROWN PRINCE OF THE EASTERN COMMONWEALTH

ID #0082719057

BORN 7 APR 108 T.E.

FF 88,987 MEDIA HITS, REVERSE CHRON

POSTED 14 AUG 126 T.E.: *A PRESS MEETING IS TO BE HOSTED BY CROWN PRINCE KAI ON 15 AUG TO DISCUSS THE ONGOING LETUMOSIS RESEARCH AND POSSIBLE LEADS FOR AN ANTIDOTE—*

Cinder launched up from her chair, nearly toppling over when she forgot about her missing limb. Steadying herself with both hands on the table, she managed an awkward bow. The retina display sank out of sight.

"Your Highness," she stammered, head lowered, glad that he couldn't see her empty ankle behind the tablecloth.

The prince flinched and cast a glance over his shoulder before hunching toward her. "Maybe, um . . ."—he pulled his fingers across his lips—"on the Highness stuff?"

Wide-eyed, Cinder forced a shaky nod. "Right. Of course. How—can I—are you—" She swallowed, the words sticking like bean paste to her tongue.

"I'm looking for a Linh Cinder," said the prince. "Is he around?"

Cinder dared to lift one stabilizing hand from the table, using it to tug the hem of her glove higher on her wrist. Staring at the prince's chest, she stammered, "I-I'm Linh Cinder."

Her eyes followed his hand as he planted it on top of the android's bulbous head.

"*You're* Linh Cinder?"

"Yes, Your High—" She bit down on her lip.

"The mechanic?"

She nodded. "How can I help you?"

Instead of answering, the prince bent down, craning his neck so that she had no choice but to meet his eyes, and dashed a grin at her. Her heart winced.

The prince straightened, forcing her gaze to follow him.

"You're not quite what I was expecting."

"Well you're hardly—what I—um." Unable to hold his gaze, Cinder reached for the android and pulled it to her side of the table. "What seems to be wrong with the android, Your Highness?"

The android looked like it had just stepped off the conveyer belt, but Cinder could tell from the mock-feminine shape that it was an outdated model. The design was sleek, though, with a spherical head atop a pear-shaped body and a glossy white finish.

"I can't get her to turn on," said Prince Kai, watching as Cinder examined the robot. "She was working fine one day, and the next, nothing."

Cinder turned the android around so its sensor light faced the prince. She was glad to have routine tasks for her hands and routine questions for her mouth—something to focus on so she wouldn't get flustered and lose control of her brain's net connection again. "Have you had problems with her before?"

"No. She gets a monthly checkup from the royal mechanics, and this is the first real problem she's ever had."

Leaning forward, Prince Kai picked up Cinder's small metal foot from the worktable, turning it curiously over in his palms. Cinder tensed, watching as he peered into the wire-filled cavity, fiddled with the flexible joints of the toes. He used the too-long sleeve of his sweatshirt to polish off a smudge.

"Aren't you hot?" Cinder said, instantly regretting the question when his attention returned to her.

For the briefest moment, the prince almost looked embarrassed. "Dying," he said, "but I'm trying to be inconspicuous."

Cinder considered telling him it wasn't working but thought better of it. The lack of a throng of screaming girls surrounding her booth was probably evidence that it was working better than she suspected. Instead of looking like a royal heartthrob, he just looked crazy.

Clearing her throat, Cinder refocused on the android. She found the nearly invisible latch and opened its back panel. "Why aren't the royal mechanics fixing her?"

"They tried but couldn't figure it out. Someone suggested I bring her to you." He set the foot down and turned his attention to the shelves of old and battered parts—parts for androids, hovers, netscreens, portscreens. Parts for cyborgs. "They say you're the best mechanic in New Beijing. I was expecting an old man."

"Do they?" she murmured.

He wasn't the first to voice surprise. Most of her customers couldn't fathom how a teenage girl could be the best mechanic in the city, and she never broadcast the reason for her talent. The fewer people who knew she was cyborg, the better. She was sure she'd go mad if *all* the market shopkeepers looked at her with the same disdain as Chang Sacha did.

She nudged some of the android's wires aside with her pinkie. "Sometimes they just get worn out. Maybe it's time to upgrade to a new model."

"I'm afraid I can't do that. She contains top-secret information. It's a matter of national security that I retrieve it . . . before anyone else does."

Fingers stalling, Cinder glanced up at him.

He held her gaze a full three seconds before his lips twitched. "I'm just joking. Nainsi was my first android. It's sentimental."

An orange light flickered in the corner of Cinder's vision. Her optobionics had picked up on something, though she didn't know what—an extra swallow, a too-quick blink, a clenching of the prince's jaw.

She was used to the little orange light. It came up all the time.

It meant that someone was lying.

"National security," she said. "Funny."

The prince listed his head, as if challenging her to contradict him. A strand of black hair fell into his eyes. Cinder looked away.

"Tutor8.6 model," she said, reading the faintly lit panel inside the plastic cranium. The android was nearly twenty years old. Ancient for an android. "She looks to be in pristine condition."

Raising her fist, she thunked the android hard on the side of its head, barely catching it before it toppled over onto the table. The prince jumped.

Cinder set the android back on its treads and jabbed the power button but nothing happened. "You'd be surprised how often that works."

The prince let out a single, awkward chuckle. "Are you sure you're Linh Cinder? The mechanic?"

"Cinder! I've got it!" Iko wheeled out of the crowd and up to the worktable, her blue sensor flashing. Lifting one pronged hand, she slammed a brand-new steel-plated foot onto the desk, in the shadow of the prince's android. "It's a huge improvement over the old one, only lightly used, and the wiring looks compatible as is. Plus, I was able to get the dealer down to just 600 univs."

Panic jolted through Cinder. Still balancing on her human leg, she snatched the foot off the table and dropped it behind her. "Good work, Iko. Nguyen-shìfu will be delighted to have a replacement foot for his escort-droid."

Iko's sensor dimmed. "Nguyen-shìfu? I don't compute."

Smiling through locked teeth, Cinder gestured at the prince. "Iko, please pay your respects to our customer." She lowered her voice. "His Imperial Highness."

Iko craned her head, aiming the round sensor up at the prince, who towered more than three feet above her. The light flared as her scanner recognized him. "Prince Kai," she said, her metallic voice squeaking. "You are even more handsome in person."

Cinder's stomach twisted in embarrassment, even as the prince laughed.

"That's enough, Iko. Get in the booth."

Iko obeyed, pushing aside the tablecloth and ducking under the table.

"You don't see a personality like that every day," said Prince Kai, leaning against the booth's door frame as if he brought androids to the market all the time. "Did you program her yourself?"

"Believe it or not, she came that way. I suspect a programming error, which is probably why my stepmother got her so cheap."

"I do not have a programming error!" said Iko from behind her.

Cinder met the prince's gaze, was caught momentarily dazzled by another easy laugh, and ducked her head back behind his android.

"So what do you think?" he asked.

"I'll need to run her diagnostics. It will take me a few days, maybe a week." Tucking a strand of hair behind one ear, Cinder sat down, grateful to give her leg a rest while she examined the android's innards. She knew she must be breaking some rule of etiquette, but the prince didn't seem to mind as he tipped forward, watching her hands.

"Do you need payment up front?"

He held his left wrist toward her, embedded with his ID chip, but Cinder waved a gloved hand at him. "No, thank you. It will be my honor."

Prince Kai looked about to protest but then let his hand fall. "I don't suppose there's any hope of having her done before the festival?"

Cinder shut the android's panel. "I don't think that will be a problem. But without knowing what's wrong with her—"

"I know, I know." He rocked back on his heels. "Just wishful thinking."

"How will I contact you when she's ready?"

"Send a comm to the palace. Or will you be here again next weekend? I could stop by then."

"Oh, yes!" said Iko from the back of the booth. "We're here every market day. You should come by again. That would be lovely."

Cinder flinched. "You don't need to—"

"It'll be my pleasure." He dipped his head in polite farewell, simultaneously pulling the edges of the hood farther over his face. Cinder returned the nod, knowing she should have stood and bowed, but not daring to test her balance a second time.

She waited until his shadow had disappeared from the tabletop before surveying the square. The prince's presence among the harried crowd seemed to have gone unnoticed. Cinder let her muscles relax.

Iko rolled to her side, clasping her metal grippers over her chest. "Prince Kai! Check my fan, I think I'm overheating."

Cinder bent over and picked up her replacement foot, dusting it off on her cargo pants. She checked the plating, glad that she hadn't dented it.

"Can you imagine Peony's expression when she hears about this?" said Iko.

"I can imagine a lot of high-pitched squealing." Cinder allowed one more wary scan of the crowd before the first tickle of giddiness stirred inside her. She couldn't wait to tell Peony. *The prince himself!* An abrupt laugh escaped her. It was uncanny. It was unbelievable. It was—

"Oh, *dear*."

Cinder's smile fell. "What?"

Iko pointed at her forehead with a pronged finger. "You have a grease splotch."

Cinder jerked back and scrubbed at her brow. "You're kidding."

"I'm sure he hardly noticed."

Cinder dropped her hand. "What does it matter? Come on, help me put this on before any other royalty stops by." She propped her ankle on the opposite knee and began connecting the color-coordinated wires, wondering if the prince had been fooled.

"Fits like a glove, doesn't it?" Iko said, holding a handful of screws while Cinder twisted them into the predrilled holes.

"It's very nice, Iko, thank you. I just hope Adri doesn't notice. She'd murder me if she knew I'd spent 600 univs on a foot." She tightened the last screw and stretched out her leg, rolling her ankle forward, back, wiggling the toes. It was a little stiff, and the nerve sensors would need a few days to harmonize with the updated wiring, but at least she wouldn't have to limp around off-kilter anymore.

"It's perfect," she said, pulling on her boot. She spotted her old foot held in Iko's pincers. "You can throw that piece of junk awa—"

A scream filled Cinder's ears. She flinched, the sound peaking in her audio interface, and turned toward it. The market silenced. The children, who had switched to a game of hide-and-seek among the clustered booths, crept out from their hiding spots.

The scream had come from the baker, Chang Sacha. Baffled, Cinder stood and climbed on top of her chair to peer over the crowd. She spotted Sacha in her booth, behind the glass case of sweet breads and pork buns, gawking at her outstretched hands.

Cinder clamped a hand over her nose at the same moment realization skittered through the rest of the square.

"The plague!" someone yelled. "She has the plague!"

The street filled with panic. Mothers scooped up their

children, masking their faces with desperate hands as they scrambled to get away from Sacha's booth. Shopkeepers slammed shut their rolling doors.

Sunto screamed and rushed toward his mother, but she held her hands out to him. *No, no, stay back.* A neighboring shopkeeper grabbed the boy, tucking the child under his arm as he ran. Sacha yelled something after him, but the words were lost in the uproar.

Cinder's stomach churned. They couldn't run or Iko would be trampled in the chaos. Holding her breath, she reached for the cord at the booth's corner and yanked the metal door down its rail. Darkness cloaked them but for a single shard of daylight along the ground. The heat rose up from the concrete floor, stifling in the cramped space.

"Cinder?" said Iko, worry in her robotic voice. She brightened her sensor, washing the booth in blue light.

"Don't worry," Cinder said, hopping down from the chair and grabbing the grease-covered rag from the table. The screams were already fading, transforming the booth into its own empty universe. "She's all the way across the square. We're fine here." But she slipped back toward the wall of shelves anyway, crouched down and covered her nose and mouth with the rag.

There they waited, Cinder breathing as shallowly as possible, until they heard the sirens of the emergency hover come and take Sacha away.

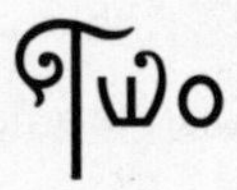

THE EMERGENCY SIRENS HADN'T FADED BEFORE THE HUM OF another engine rumbled into the square. The market's silence was split by feet thumping on the pavement and then someone spitting commands. Someone else's guttural response.

Slinging her messenger bag across her back, Cinder crept across the dusty floor of her booth and pushed past the tablecloth that draped her work desk. She slipped her fingers into the gap of light beneath the door and inched it open. Pressing her cheek to the warm, gritty pavement, she was able to make out three sets of yellow boots across the square. An emergency crew. She peeled the door open farther and watched the men—all wearing gas masks—as they doused the interior of the booth with liquid from a yellow can. Even across the square, Cinder wrinkled her nose at the stench.

"What's happening?" Iko asked from behind her.

"They're going to burn Chang-jiě's booth." Cinder's eyes swept along the square, noting the pristine white hover planted near the corner. Other than the three men, the square was abandoned. Rolling onto her back, Cinder peered up into Iko's sensor, still glowing faintly in the dark. "We'll leave when the flames start, when they're distracted."

"Are we in trouble?"

"No. I just can't be bothered with a trip to the quarantines today."

One of the men spouted an order, followed by shuffling feet. Cinder turned her head and squinted through the gap. A flame was thrown into the booth. The smell of gasoline was soon met with that of burned toast. The men stood back, their uniforms silhouetted against the growing flames.

Reaching up, Cinder grabbed Prince Kai's android around its neck and pulled it down beside her. Tucking it under one arm, she slid the door open enough to crawl through, keeping her eyes on the men's backs. Iko followed, scooting against the next booth as Cinder lowered the door. They darted along the storefronts—most left wide open during the mass exodus—and turned into the first skinny alley between shops. Black smoke blotted the sky above them. Seconds later, a horde of news hovers buzzed over the buildings on their way to the market square.

Cinder slowed when they'd put enough distance between them and the market, emerging from the maze of alleys. The sun had passed overhead and was descending behind the skyscrapers to the west. The air sweated with August heat, but an occasional warm breeze was funneled between the buildings, picking up whirlwinds of garbage from the gutters. Four blocks from the market, signs of life appeared again on the streets—pedestrians pooling on the sidewalks and gossiping about the plague outbreak in the city center. Netscreens implanted into building walls showed live feeds of fire and smoke in downtown New Beijing and panicked headlines in which the toll of infected mounted by the second—even though only one person had been confirmed sick so far as Cinder could tell.

"All those sticky buns," Iko said as they passed a close-up shot of the blackened booth.

Cinder bit the inside corner of her cheek. Neither of them had ever sampled the acclaimed sweets of the market bakery. Iko didn't have taste buds, and Chang Sacha didn't serve cyborgs.

Towering offices and shopping centers gradually melded with a messy assortment of apartment buildings, built so close that they became an unending stretch of glass and concrete. Apartments in this corner of the city had once been spacious and desirable but had been so subdivided and remodeled over time—always trying to cram more people into the same square footage—that the buildings had become labyrinths of corridors and stairwells.

But all the crowded ugliness was briefly forgotten as Cinder turned the corner onto her own street. For half a step, New Beijing Palace could be glimpsed between complexes, sprawling and serene on the cliff that overlooked the city. The palace's pointed gold roofs sparkled orange beneath the sun, the windows glinting the light back at the city. The ornate gables, the tiered pavilions that teetered dangerously close to the cliff's edge, the rounded temples stretching to the heavens. Cinder paused longer than usual to look up at it, thinking about someone who lived beyond those walls, who was up there perhaps this very second.

Not that she hadn't *known* the prince lived there every time she'd seen the palace before, but today she felt a connection she'd never had before, and with it came an almost smug delight. She had met the prince. He had come to her booth. He knew her name.

Sucking in a breath of humid air, Cinder forced herself to turn away, feeling childish. She was going to start sounding like Peony.

She shifted the royal android to her other arm as she and Iko ducked beneath the overhang of the Phoenix Tower apartments. She flashed her freed wrist at the ID scanner on the wall and heard the clunking of the lock.

Iko used her arm extensions to clop down the stairs as they descended into the basement, a dim maze of storage spaces caged with chicken wire. As a wave of musty air blew up to meet them, the android turned on her floodlight, dispersing the shadows from the sparse halogens. It was a familiar path from the stairwell to storage space number 18-20—the cramped, always chilly cell that Adri allowed Cinder to use for her work.

Cinder cleared a space for the android among the worktable's clutter and set her messenger bag on the floor. She swapped her heavy work gloves for less grungy cotton ones before locking up the storage room. "If Adri asks," she said as they made their way to the elevators, "our booth is nowhere near the baker's."

Iko's light flickered. "Noted."

They were alone in the elevator. It wasn't until they stepped out onto the eighteenth floor that the building became a crawling hive—children chasing each other down the corridors, both domestic and stray cats creeping tight against the walls, the ever-constant blur of netscreen chatter spilling from the doorways. Cinder adjusted the white-noise output from her brain interface as she dodged the children on her way to the apartment.

The door was wide open, making Cinder pause and check the number before entering.

She heard Adri's stiff voice from the living room. "Lower neckline for Peony. She looks like an old woman."

Cinder peered around the corner. Adri was standing with one hand on the mantel of the holographic fireplace, wearing a chrysanthemum-embroidered bathrobe that blended in with the collection of garish paper fans that covered the wall behind her—reproductions made to look antique. With her face shimmering with too much powder and her lips painted horrifically bright, Adri almost looked like a reproduction herself. Her face was made up as if she'd been planning to go somewhere, although she rarely left the apartment.

If she noticed Cinder loitering in the doorway, she ignored her.

The netscreen above the heatless flames was showing footage from the market. The baker's booth had been reduced to rubble and the skeleton of a portable oven.

In the center of the room, Pearl and Peony each stood swathed in silk and tulle. Peony was holding up her dark curly hair while a woman Cinder didn't recognize fidgeted with her dress's neckline. Peony caught sight of Cinder over the woman's shoulder and her eyes sparked, a glow bursting across her face. She gestured at the dress with a barely silenced squeal.

Cinder grinned back. Her younger stepsister looked angelic, her dress all silver and shimmering, with hints of lavender when caught in the fire's light.

"Pearl." Adri gestured at her older daughter with a twirling finger, and Pearl spun around, displaying a row of pearl buttons down her back. Her dress matched Peony's with its snug bodice and flouncy skirt, only it was made of stardust gold. "Let's take in her waist some more."

Threading a pin through the hem of Peony's neckline, the stranger started at seeing Cinder in the doorway but quickly turned away. Stepping back, the woman removed a bundle of sharp pins from between her lips and tilted her head to one side. "It's already very snug," she said. "We want her to dance, don't we?"

"We want her to find a husband," said Adri.

"No, no," the seamstress tittered even as she reached out and pinched the material around Pearl's waist. Cinder could tell Pearl was sucking in her stomach as much as she could; she detected the edges of ribs beneath the fabric. "She is much too young for marriage."

"I'm seventeen," Pearl said, glaring at the woman.

"Seventeen! See? A child. Now is for fun, right, girl?"

"She is too expensive for *fun,*" said Adri. "I expect results from this gown."

"Do not worry, Linh-jiě. She will be lovely as morning dew." Stuffing the pins back into her mouth, the woman returned her focus to Peony's neckline.

Adri lifted her chin and finally acknowledged Cinder's presence by swiping her gaze down Cinder's filthy boots and cargo pants. "Why aren't you at the market?"

"It closed down early today," said Cinder, with a meaningful look at the netscreen that Adri didn't follow. Feigning nonchalance, Cinder thrust a thumb toward the hall. "So I'll just go get cleaned up, and then I'll be ready for my dress fitting."

The seamstress paused. "Another dress, Linh-jiě? I did not bring material for—"

"Have you replaced the magbelt on the hover yet?"

Cinder's smile faltered. "No. Not yet."

"Well, none of us will be going to the ball unless that gets fixed, will we?"

Cinder stifled her irritation. They'd already had this conversation twice in the past week. "I need money to buy a new magbelt. 800 univs, at least. If income from the market wasn't deposited directly into your account, I would have bought one by now."

"And trust you not to spend it all on your frivolous toys?" Adri said *toys* with a glare at Iko and a curl of her lip, even though Iko technically belonged to her. "Besides, I can't afford both a magbelt *and* a new dress that you'll only wear once. You'll have to find some other way of fixing the hover or find your own gown for the ball."

Irritation hardened in Cinder's gut. She might have pointed out that Pearl and Peony could have been given ready-made rather than custom dresses in order to budget for Cinder's as well. She might have pointed out that they would only wear their dresses one time too. She might have pointed out that, as she was the one doing the work, the money should have been hers to spend as she saw fit. But all arguments would come to nothing. Legally, Cinder belonged to Adri as much as the household android and so too did her money, her few possessions, even the new foot she'd just attached. Adri loved to remind her of that.

So she stomped the anger down before Adri could see a spark of rebellion.

"I may be able to offer a trade for the magbelt. I'll check with the local shops."

Adri sniffed. "Why don't we trade that worthless android for it?"

Iko ducked behind Cinder's legs.

"We wouldn't get much for her," said Cinder. "Nobody wants such an old model."

"No. They don't, do they? Perhaps I will have to sell both of you off as spare parts." Adri reached forward and fidgeted with the unfinished hem of Pearl's sleeve. "I don't care how you fix the hover, just fix it before the ball—and cheaply. I don't need that pile of junk taking up valuable parking space."

Cinder tucked her hands into her back pockets. "Are you saying that if I fix the hover and get a dress, I can really go this year?"

Adri's lips puckered slightly at the corners. "It will be a miracle if you can find something suitable to wear that will hide your"—her gaze dropped to Cinder's boots—"*eccentricities.* But, yes. If you fix the hover, I suppose you can go to the ball."

Peony flashed Cinder a stunned half smile, while her older sister spun on their mother. "You can't be serious! *Her?* Go with *us*?"

Cinder pressed her shoulder into the door frame, trying to hide her disappointment from Peony. Pearl's outrage was unnecessary. A little orange light had flickered in the corner of Cinder's vision—Adri had not meant her promise.

"Well," she said, attempting to look heartened. "I guess I'd better go find a magbelt then."

Adri flourished her arm at Cinder, her attention once again captivated by Pearl's dress. A silent dismissal.

Cinder cast one more look at her stepsisters' sumptuous gowns before backing out of the room. She had barely turned toward the hallway when Peony squealed.

"Prince Kai!"

Freezing, Cinder glanced back at the netscreen. The plague

alerts had been replaced with a live broadcast from the palace's pressroom. Prince Kai was speaking to a crowd of journalists—human and android.

"Volume on," said Pearl, batting the seamstress away.

". . . research continues to be our top priority," Prince Kai was saying, gripping the sides of a podium. "Our research team is determined to find a vaccine for this disease that has now taken one of my parents and threatens to take the other, as well as tens of thousands of our citizens. The circumstances are made even more desperate in the face of the outbreak that occurred today within the city limits. No longer can we claim this disease is relegated to the poor, rural communities of our country. Letumosis threatens us all, and we will find a way to stop it. Only then can we begin to rebuild our economy and return the Eastern Commonwealth to its once prosperous state."

Unenthusiastic applause shifted through the crowd. Research on the plague had been underway since the first outbreak had occurred in a small town in the African Union over a dozen years ago. It seemed that very little progress had been made. Meanwhile, the disease had surfaced in hundreds of seemingly unconnected communities throughout the world. Hundreds of thousands of people had fallen ill, suffered, died. Even Adri's husband had contracted it on a trip to Europe—the same trip during which he'd agreed to become the guardian of an eleven-year-old orphaned cyborg. One of Cinder's few memories of the man was of him being carted away to the quarantines while Adri raved at how he could not leave her with *this thing.*

Adri never talked about her husband, and few memories of him lingered in the apartment. The only reminder that he'd even existed was found in a row of holographic plaques and carved medallions that lined the fireplace's mantel—achievement awards and congratulatory prizes from an international technology fair, three years running. Cinder had no idea what he'd invented. Evidently, whatever it was hadn't taken off, because he'd left his family almost no money when he had died.

On the screen, the prince's speech was interrupted when a stranger stepped onto the platform and handed a note to Prince Kai. The prince's eyes clouded over. The screen blackened.

The pressroom was replaced with a desk before a blue screen. A woman sat behind it, expressionless but with whitened knuckles atop the desk.

"We interrupt His Imperial Highness's press conference with an update on the status of His Imperial Majesty Emperor Rikan. The emperor's physicians have just informed us that His Majesty has entered into the third stage of letumosis."

Gasping, the seamstress pulled the pins from her mouth.

Cinder pressed herself against the door frame. She had not even thought to give Kai her condolences, or wishes for the emperor's return of health. He must think her so insensitive. So ignorant.

"We are told that everything is being done to ensure His Imperial Majesty's comfort at this time, and palace officials tell us that researchers are working nonstop in their search for a vaccine. Volunteers are still urgently needed for antidote testing, even as the cyborg draft continues.

"There has been much controversy regarding the 126th Annual Peace Festival due to the emperor's illness, but Prince Kaito has told the press that the festival will continue as scheduled and that he hopes it might bring some joy in this otherwise tragic time." The anchor paused, hesitating, even with the prompter before her. Her face softened, and her stiff voice had a warble when she finished. "Long live the emperor."

The seamstress murmured the words back to the anchor. The screen went black again before returning to the press conference, but Prince Kai had left the stage, and the audience of journalists was in upheaval as they reported to their individual cameras.

"I know a cyborg who could volunteer for plague testing," said Pearl. "Why wait for the draft?"

Cinder leveled a glare at Pearl, who was nearly six inches shorter than she was despite being a year older. "Good idea," she said. "And then *you* could get a job to pay for your pretty dress."

Pearl snarled. "They reimburse the volunteers' families, wirehead."

The cyborg draft had been started by some royal research team a year ago. Every morning, a new ID number was drawn from the pool of so many thousand cyborgs who resided in the Eastern Commonwealth. Subjects had been carted in from provinces as far-reaching as Mumbai and Singapore to act as guinea pigs for the antidote testing. It was made out to be some sort of honor, giving your life for the good of humanity, but it was really just a reminder that cyborgs were not like everyone else. Many of them had been given a second chance at life by the generous hand of scientists and therefore owed their very existence to those who had created them. They were lucky to have lived this long, many thought. It's only right that they should be the first to give up their lives in search for the cure.

"We can't volunteer Cinder," said Peony, bunching her skirt in her hands. "I need her to fix my portscreen."

Pearl sniffed and turned away from both of them. Peony scrunched her nose at her sister's back.

"Stop bickering," said Adri. "Peony, you're wrinkling your skirt."

Cinder stepped back into the hallway as the seamstress returned to her work. Iko was already two steps ahead of her, eager to escape Adri's presence.

She appreciated Peony coming to her defense, of course, but she knew in the end it wouldn't matter. Adri would never volunteer her for the testing, because that would be the end of her only income, and Cinder was sure her stepmother had never worked a day in her life.

But if the draft chose her, no one could do anything about it. And it seemed that lately a disproportionate number of those chosen were from New Beijing and the surrounding suburbs.

Every time one of the draft's victims was a teenage girl, Cinder imagined a clock ticking inside her head.

Three

"YOU'RE GOING TO THE BALL!" IKO TAPPED HER GRIPPERS together in an imitation of clapping. "We have to find you a dress, and shoes. I will not allow you to wear those awful boots. We'll get some new gloves and—"

"Could you bring that light over here?" Cinder said, yanking out the top drawer of her standing toolbox. She riffled through it, spare bolts and sockets jangling as Iko scooted closer. A wash of bluish light dispersed the dimness of the storage room.

"Think of the food they'll have," said Iko. "And the dresses. And music!"

Cinder ignored her, selecting an assortment of varying tools and arranging them on Iko's magnetic torso.

"Oh, my stars! Think about Prince Kai! You could dance with Prince Kai!"

This made Cinder pause and squint into Iko's blinding light. "Why would the prince dance with me?"

Iko's fan hummed as she sought an answer. "Because you won't have grease on your face this time."

Cinder fought down a chuckle. Android reasoning could be so simplistic. "I hate to break this to you, Iko," she said, slamming in the drawer and moving on to the next, "but I'm not going to the ball."

Iko's fan stopped momentarily, started up again. "I don't compute."

"For starters, I just spent my life savings on a new foot. But even if I did have money, why would I spend it on a dress or shoes or gloves? What a waste."

"What else could you have to spend it on?"

"A complete set of wrenches? A toolbox with drawers that don't stick?" She slammed in the second drawer with her shoulder to emphasize her point. "A down payment on my own apartment where I won't have to be Adri's servant anymore?"

"Adri wouldn't sign the release documents."

Cinder opened the third drawer. "I know. It would cost a lot more than a silly dress anyway." She grabbed a ratchet and a handful of wrenches and set them on top of the toolbox. "Maybe I'd get skin grafting."

"Your skin is fine."

Cinder glanced at Iko from the corner of her eye.

"Oh. You mean your cyborg parts."

Shutting the third drawer, Cinder grabbed her messenger bag from the work desk and shoveled the tools into it. "What else do you think we'll—oh, the floor jack. Where'd I put that?"

"You're being unreasonable," said Iko. "Maybe you can trade for a dress or get one on consignment. I've been dying to go into that vintage dress store on Sakura. You know the one I mean?"

Cinder shuffled around the random tools that had collected beneath the worktable. "It doesn't matter. I'm not going."

"But it does matter. It's the ball. And the prince!"

"Iko, I'm fixing an android for him. It's not like we're friends now." Mentioning the prince's android sparked a memory, and a moment later Cinder pulled the floor jack out from behind its tread. "And it doesn't matter because Adri will never let me go."

"She said if you fixed the hover—"

"Right. And after I fix the hover? What about Peony's portscreen that's always acting up? What about—" She scanned the room and spotted a rusty android tucked away in the corner. "What about that old Gard7.3?"

"What would Adri want with that old thing? She doesn't have a garden anymore. She doesn't even have a balcony."

"I'm just saying that she has no real intention of letting me go. As long as she can come up with things for me to fix, my 'chores' will never be done." Cinder shoved a couple jack stands into her bag, telling herself that she didn't care. Not really.

She wouldn't fit in at a formal ball anyway. Even if she did find dress gloves and slippers that could hide her metal monstrosities, her mousy hair would never hold a curl, and she didn't know the first thing about makeup. She would just end up sitting off the dance floor and making fun of the girls who swooned to get Prince Kai's attention, pretending she wasn't jealous. Pretending it didn't bother her.

Although she was curious about the food.

And the prince did know her now, sort of. He had been kind to her at the market. Perhaps he would ask her to dance. Out of politeness. Out of chivalry when he saw her standing alone.

The precarious fantasy crashed down around her as quickly as it had begun. It was impossible. Not worth thinking about.

She was cyborg, and she would never go to the ball.

"I think that's everything," she said, masking her disappointment by adjusting the messenger bag over her shoulders. "You ready?"

"I don't compute," said Iko. "If fixing the hover won't convince Adri to let you go to the ball, then why are we going to the junkyard? If she wants a magbelt so bad, why doesn't she go dig through the trash to find one?"

"Because ball or no, I *do* believe she would sell you off for pocket change if given a reason. Besides, with them off to the ball, we'll have the apartment to ourselves. Doesn't that sound nice?"

"It sounds great to me!"

Cinder turned to see Peony heaving herself through the doorway. She still wore her silver ball gown, but now the hems along the neck and sleeves were finished. A hint of lace had been added at her cleavage, accentuating the fact that, at fourteen, Peony had already developed curves that Cinder couldn't begin to hope for. If Cinder's body had ever been predisposed to femininity, it had been ruined by whatever the surgeons had done to her, leaving her with a stick-straight figure. Too angular. Too boyish. Too awkward with her heavy artificial leg.

"I'm going to strangle Mom," said Peony. "She's making me loony. 'Pearl needs to find a husband,' 'My daughters are such a drain,' 'No one appreciates what I do for them,' yap yap yap." She wobbled her fingers in the air in mockery of her mother.

"What are you doing down here?"

"*Hiding.* Oh, and to ask if you could look at my portscreen." She pulled a handheld screen from behind her back, offering it to Cinder.

Cinder took it, but her eyes were on the bottom of Peony's skirt, watching as the shimmering hem gathered dust bunnies around it. "You're going to ruin that dress. Then Adri will really be a tyrant."

Peony stuck out her tongue but then gathered up her skirt in both fists, hiking the hem up to her knees. "So what do you think?" she said, bouncing on the balls of her bare feet.

"You look amazing."

Peony preened, wrinkling the fabric more in her fingers. But then her cheeriness faltered. "She should have had one made for you too. It's not fair."

"I don't really want to go." Cinder shrugged. Peony's tone had such sympathy that she didn't bother to argue. She was usually able to ignore the jealousy she had toward her stepsisters—how Adri doted on them, how soft their hands were—especially when Peony was the only human friend she had. But she could not swallow the twitch of envy at seeing Peony in that dress.

She brushed the topic away. "What's wrong with the port?"

"It's doing that gibberish thing again." Peony pushed some tools off a stack of empty paint bins, choosing the cleanest spot before sitting down, her full skirts flouncing around her. She swung her feet so that her heels beat steadily against the plastic.

"Have you been downloading those stupid celeb apps again?"

"No."

Cinder raised an eyebrow.

"One language app. That's it. And I needed it for class. Oh—before I forget, Iko, I brought you something."

Iko rolled to Peony's side as she pulled a velvet ribbon from her bodice, leftover trim from the seamstress. The light in the room brightened when Iko saw it.

"Thank you," said the android as Peony tied the ribbon around her skinny wrist joint. "It's lovely."

Cinder set the portscreen on the work desk, next to Prince Kai's android. "I'll look at it tomorrow. We're off to find a mag-belt for Her Majesty."

"Oh? Where are you going?"

"The junkyard."

"It's going to be a bundle of fun," said Iko, scanning the makeshift bracelet with her sensor again and again.

"Really?" said Peony. "Can I come?"

Cinder laughed. "She's kidding. Iko's been practicing her sarcasm."

"I don't care. Anything's better than going back into that stuffy apartment." Peony fanned herself and absently leaned back against a stack of metal shelving.

Reaching out, Cinder pulled her back. "Careful, your dress."

Peony surveyed her skirt, then the grime-covered shelves, then waved Cinder's concern away. "Really, can I? Sounds exciting."

"It sounds dirty and stinky," said Iko.

"How would you know?" said Cinder. "You don't have scent receptors."

"I have a fantastic imagination."

Smirking, Cinder half shoved her stepsister toward the door. "Fine, go get changed. But be quick. I have a story to tell you."

Four

PEONY SLUGGED CINDER IN THE SHOULDER, NEARLY PUSHING her into a pile of bald android treads. "How could you wait so long to tell me? You've only been home for, what, *four hours*?"

"I know, I know, I'm sorry," said Cinder, rubbing her shoulder. "There wasn't a good time, and I didn't want Adri to know. I don't want her taking advantage of it."

"Who cares about what Mom thinks? *I* want to take advantage of this. Good stars, the prince. In your booth. I can't believe I wasn't there. Why wasn't I there?"

"You were busy being fitted in silk and brocade."

"Ugh." Peony kicked a broken headlight out of her path. "You should have commed me. I would have been there in two seconds, unfinished ball gown and all. *Ugh.* I hate you. It's official, I *hate* you. Are you going to see him again? I mean, you'll have to, right? I might be able to stop hating you if you *promise* to bring me with you, all right, deal?"

"Found one!" Iko called from ten yards ahead. Her

floodlight targeted the body of a rusted hover, entrenching the piles of debris behind it in shadows.

"So? What was he like?" Peony said, keeping pace as Cinder hurried toward the earthbound vehicle, as if being near her was now on par with being near His Imperial Highness himself.

"I don't know," said Cinder, unlatching the vehicle's hood and lifting it up on the prop-rod. "Ah, good, it hasn't been scavenged."

Iko scooted out of Cinder's way. "He was polite enough not to point out the giant grease stain on her forehead."

Peony gasped. "Oh, you didn't!"

"What? I'm a mechanic. I get dirty. If he wanted me to get all gussied up, he should have commed ahead. Iko, I could use some light in here."

Iko tilted her head forward, illuminating the engine compartment. On Cinder's other side, Peony clucked her tongue. "Maybe he thought it was a mole?"

"That makes me feel much better." Cinder pulled a pair of pliers from her bag. The night sky was clear, and though the lights from the city blocked out any stars, the sharp crescent moon lurked near the horizon, a sleepy eye squinting through the haze.

"Is he as handsome in real life as he looks on the netscreens?"

"Yes," said Iko. "Even more handsome. And awful tall."

"Everyone's tall to you." Peony leaned against the front bumper, arms folded. "And I want to hear Cinder's opinion."

Cinder stopped poking the pliers around the engine as the

memory of his easy smile rushed into her. Though Prince Kai had long been one of Peony's favorite topics—she was probably in every one of his net fangroups—Cinder had never imagined that she might share the admiration. In fact, she'd always thought Peony's celebrity crush was a little silly, a little preadolescent. *Prince Kai this, Prince Kai that.* An impossible fantasy.

But now . . .

Something in Cinder's face must have said enough, because Peony suddenly shrieked and lunged at her, wrapping her arms around Cinder's waist and hopping up and down. "I knew it! I *knew* you liked him too! I can't believe you actually met him! It's not fair. Did I mention how much I hate you?"

"Yes, yes, I know," said Cinder, prying Peony's arms off her. "Now go be giddy somewhere else. I'm trying to work."

Peony made a face and skipped away, twirling amid the piles of junk. "What else? Tell me everything. What did he say? What did he do?"

"Nothing," said Cinder. "He just asked me to fix his android." She peeled away the spiderwebs from what had once been the hover's solar generator but was now little more than a plastic shell. A cloud of dust kicked up into her face and she pulled away, coughing. "Ratchet?"

Iko plucked the ratchet from her torso and handed it to Cinder.

"What kind of android is it?" asked Peony.

Cinder pried the generator from the compartment with a grunt and set it on the ground beside the hover. "An old one."

"Tutor8.6," said Iko. "Older than me. And he said he would come back to the market next weekend to pick it up."

Peony kicked a rusted oil can out of the path before bending over the engine. "The news said the market's going to be shut down next week because of the outbreak."

"Oh—I hadn't heard that." Cinder wiped her hands on her pants, peering down into the engine's lower compartment. "I guess we'll have to drop it off at the palace then."

"Yes!" Peony jigged in place. "We'll go together and you can introduce me and—and—"

"Aha!" Cinder beamed. "Magbelt."

Peony cupped her cheek in her palm, raising her voice. *"And then* he'll recognize me at the ball, and I'll dance with him and—Pearl will be *livid*!" She laughed, as if angering her older sister were life's greatest accomplishment.

"If the android's even done before the ball." Cinder selected a wrench from the tool belt slung around her hips. She didn't want to inform Peony that Prince Kai probably wouldn't be the one signing for deliveries at the palace.

Peony whisked her hand through the air. "Well, or whenever."

"I want to go to the ball," said Iko, gazing up at the horizon. "It's prejudice not to let androids attend."

"Petition the government then. I'm sure Peony will be happy to take your cause direct to the prince himself." Cinder clamped onto Iko's spherical head and forced her to aim the light back into the hood. "Now hold still. I've just about got this end detached."

Cinder stuck the wrench to Iko, then pried the magbelt from its bracket, letting it clatter to the ground below. "One side down, one to go." She led the way around the hover, clearing a path through the garbage so Iko's treads wouldn't get stuck.

Peony followed and climbed on top of the hover's trunk, folding her legs beneath her. "You know, some people are saying he's going to be looking for a bride at the ball."

"A bride!" said Iko. "How romantic."

Cinder lowered herself onto her side behind the hover's back bumper and took a small flashlight from her tool belt. "Hand me that wrench again?"

"Didn't you hear me? A *bride*, Cinder. As in, a princess."

"As in, not going to happen. He's only, what? Nineteen?" Tucking the flashlight between her teeth, Cinder took the wrench from Iko. The bolts in the back had less rust on them, better protected from the overhanging trunk, and took only a few quick turns to loosen.

"Eighteen and a half," said Peony. "And it's true. All the gossip links are saying so."

Cinder grunted.

"I would marry Prince Kai in a heartbeat."

"Me too," said Iko.

Cinder spit out the flashlight and shuffled to the fourth corner. "You and every other girl in the Commonwealth."

"Like you wouldn't," said Peony.

Cinder didn't answer as she loosened the final bolt gripping the magbelt. It released and fell to the ground with a clang. "There we go." She slid out from beneath the car and tucked the wrench and flashlight into her calf compartment before standing. "See any other hovers worth scavenging while we're here?" Pulling the magbelt out from beneath the hover, she folded it at its hinges, forming a less cumbersome metal rod.

"I did see something over there." Iko swished the light around the stacks. "Not sure what model."

"Great. Lead the way." Cinder nudged the android with the belt. Iko took off, muttering about being stuck in junkyards while Adri was all clean and cozy at home.

"Besides," said Peony, hopping off the trunk, "the rumor that he's looking for a bride at the ball is a lot better than what the *other* rumors are saying."

"Let me guess. Prince Kai is actually a martian? Or no, no—he had an illegitimate child with an escort, didn't he?"

"Escort-droids can have *children*?"

"No."

Peony huffed, blowing a curl off her brow. "Well, this is even worse. They say there's been talk of him marrying . . ." She dropped her voice to a harsh whisper. "Queen Levana."

"*Queen—*" Cinder froze and clamped a gloved hand over her mouth, glancing around as if someone could be lurking in the piles of garbage, listening. She pulled her hand away but kept her voice down. "Honestly, Peony. Those tabloids are going to rot your brain."

"I don't want to believe it either, but they're all saying it. That's why the queen's witchy ambassador has been staying at the palace, so she can secure an alliance. It's all very political."

"I don't think so. Prince Kai would never marry her."

"You don't know that."

But she did know. Cinder may not know much about intergalactic politics, but she knew Prince Kai would be a fool to marry Queen Levana.

The lingering moon caught Cinder's attention, and a shock of goose bumps covered her arms. The moon had always given her a sense of paranoia, like the people who lived up there could be watching her, and if she stared for too long, she might draw their attention. Superstitious nonsense, but then everything about Lunars was eerie and superstitious.

Lunars were a society that had evolved from an Earthen moon colony centuries ago, but they weren't human anymore. People said Lunars could alter a person's brain—make you see things you shouldn't see, feel things you shouldn't feel, do things you didn't want to do. Their unnatural power had made them a greedy and violent race, and Queen Levana was the worst of all of them.

They said she knew when people were talking about her even thousands of miles away. Even down on Earth.

They said she'd murdered her older sister, Queen Channary, so she could take the throne from her. They said she'd had her own husband killed too so she would be free to make a more advantageous match. They said she had forced her stepdaughter to mutilate her own face because, at the sweet age of thirteen, she had become more beautiful than the jealous queen could stand.

They said she'd killed her niece, her only threat to the throne. Princess Selene had only been three years old when a fire caught in her nursery, killing her and her nanny.

Some conspiracy theorists thought the princess had survived and was still alive somewhere, waiting for the right time to reclaim her crown and end Levana's rule of tyranny, but Cinder knew it was only desperation that fueled these rumors. After all, they'd found traces of the child's flesh in the ashes.

"Here." Iko raised her hand and knocked on a slab of metal jutting from a huge mound of junk, startling Cinder.

She shoved the thoughts aside. Prince Kai would never marry that witch. He could never marry a Lunar.

Cinder pushed a few rusted aerosol cans and an old mattress aside before she was able to clearly make out the hover's nose. "Good eye."

Together they shuffled enough junk out of the way so that the full front of the vehicle could be seen. "I've never seen one like this," Cinder said, running a hand over the pitted chrome insignia.

"It's hideous," said Peony with a sneer. "What an awful color."

"It must be really old." Cinder found the latch and pulled open the hood. She drew back, blinking at the mess of metal and plastic that greeted her. "*Really* old." She squinted into the front corner of the engine, but the undercarriage hid the magbelt clamps from view. "Huh. Point the light over there, would you?"

Cinder lowered herself to the dirt. She tightened her ponytail before squirming under the hover, shoving aside the jumble of old parts that had been left to rust in the weeds beneath it.

"Stars," she muttered when she was able to look up into its belly. Iko's light filtered down from above, through cables and wires, ducts and manifolds, nuts and bolts. "This thing is ancient."

"It is in a junkyard," said Peony.

"I'm serious. I've never seen anything like it." Cinder ran a hand along a rubber cable.

The light flashed back and forth as Iko's sensor scanned the engine from above. "Any useful parts?"

"Good question." Cinder's vision tinted blue as she connected to her netlink. "Could you read me the VIN by the windshield?" She searched the number as Peony read it to her and had the hover's blueprint downloaded in minutes, the display creating an overlaid image on top of the engine above her. "Seems to be fairly intact," she murmured, running her fingertips along a cluster of wires over her head. She followed them with her eyes, tilting her head to trace the path from hoses to pulleys to axles, trying to decipher how it all fit together. How it all worked.

"This is so cool."

"I'm bored," said Peony.

Sighing, Cinder searched for the magbelt on the blueprint, but a green error message flashed in her vision. She tried just *magnet,* and then just *belt,* finally receiving a hit. The blueprint lit up a rubber band wrapped around a series of gears, encapsulated by a metal cover—something called a timing belt. Frowning, Cinder reached up and felt for the bolts and lock washers that attached the cover to the engine block.

She thought timing belts hadn't been used since internal combustion had become obsolete.

Gasping, she craned her neck to the side. In the deep shadows beneath the vehicle, she could make out something round beside her, connected to the bars overhead. A wheel.

"It's not a hover. It's a car. A gasoline car."

"Seriously?" said Peony. "I thought real cars were supposed to be . . . I don't know. Classy."

Indignation flared in Cinder's chest. "It has character," she said, feeling for the tire's treads.

"So," said Iko a second later, "does this mean we can't use any of its parts?"

Ignoring her, Cinder hungrily scanned the blueprint before her. Oil pan, fuel injectors, exhaust pipes. "It's from the second era."

"Fascinating. *Not,*" said Peony. She suddenly screeched, launching herself back from the car.

Cinder started so fast she whapped her head on the front suspension. "Peony, what?"

"A rat just came out of the window! A big hairy fat one. Oh, *gross.*"

Groaning, Cinder settled her head back into the dirt, massaging her forehead. That made two head injuries in one day. At that rate, she was going to have to buy a new control panel too. "It must have been nesting in the upholstery. We probably scared it."

"*We* scared *it?*" Peony's voice carried a shudder with it. "Can we go now, please?"

Cinder sighed. "Fine." Dismissing the blueprint, she squirmed out from beneath the car, accepting Iko's offered grippers to stand. "I thought all the surviving gasoline cars were in museums," she said, brushing the cobwebs from her hair.

"I'm not sure I would label it a 'survivor,'" said Iko, her sensor darkening with disgust. "It looks more like a rotting pumpkin."

Cinder shut the hood with a bang, sending an impressive dust cloud over the android. "What was that about having a fantastic imagination? With some attention and a good cleaning, it could be restored to its former glory."

She caressed the hood. The car's dome-shaped body was a yellow-orange shade that looked sickly under Iko's light—a color that no one in modern times would choose—but with the antique style of the vehicle it bordered on charming. Rust was creeping up from the hollow beneath the shattered headlights, arching along the dented fender. One of the back windows was missing, but the seats were intact, albeit mildew covered and torn and probably home to more than just rodents. The steering wheel and dash seemed to have suffered only minor damage over the years.

"Maybe it could be our escape car."

Peony peered into the passenger's side window. "Escape from what?"

"Adri. New Beijing. We could get out of the Commonwealth altogether. We could go to Europe!" Cinder rounded the driver's side and scrubbed the dirt from the window with her glove. On the floor inside, three pedals winked up at her. Though hovers were all controlled by computer, she had read enough about old technology to know what a clutch was and even had a basic idea of how to operate one.

"This hunk of metal wouldn't get us to the city limits," said Peony.

Stepping back, Cinder dusted off her hands. They were probably right. Maybe this wasn't a fantasy vehicle, maybe it wasn't their key to salvation, but somehow, someday, she would leave New Beijing. She would find a place where no one knew who she was—or what she was.

"Plus, we couldn't afford the gasoline," continued Iko. "We could trade in your new foot and still not be able to afford enough fuel to get out of here. Plus, the pollution fines. Plus, I'm not getting in this thing. There's probably decades' worth of rat droppings under those seats."

Peony cringed. "*Ew.*"

Cinder laughed. "All right, I get it. I won't make you guys push the car home."

"Whew, you had me worried," said Peony. She smiled because she hadn't really been worried and flipped her hair off her shoulder.

Cinder's eye caught on something—a dark spot below Peony's collarbone, visible just above the collar of her shirt. "Hold still," she said, reaching forward.

Peony did the opposite, panicking and swiping at phantoms on her chest. "What? What is it? A bug? A spider?"

"I said, hold still!" Cinder grabbed Peony by the wrist, swiped at the spot—and froze.

Dropping Peony's arm, she stumbled back.

"What? What is it?" Peony tugged on her shirt, trying to see, but then spotted another spot on the back of her hand.

She looked up at Cinder, blood draining from her face. "A . . . a rash?" she said. "From the car?"

Cinder gulped and neared her with hesitant footsteps, holding her breath. She reached again for Peony's collarbone and pulled the fabric of her shirt down, revealing the entire spot in the moonlight. A splotch of red, rimmed with bruise purple.

Her fingers trembled. She pulled away, meeting Peony's gaze.

Peony screamed.

Five

PEONY'S SHRIEKS FILLED THE JUNKYARD, SEEPING INTO THE cracks of broken machinery and outdated computers. Cinder's auditory interface couldn't protect her from the shrill memory, even as Peony's voice cracked and she dissolved into hysteria.

Cinder stood trembling, unable to move. Wanting to comfort Peony. Wanting to run away.

How was this possible?

Peony was young, healthy. She couldn't be sick.

Peony cried, brushing repeatedly at her skin, the spots.

Cinder's netlink took over, as it did in moments when she couldn't think for herself. Searching, connecting, feeding information to her she didn't want.

Letumosis. The blue fever. Worldwide pandemic. Hundreds of thousands dead. Unknown cause, unknown cure.

"Peony—"

She tentatively reached forward, but Peony stumbled back,

swiping at her wet cheeks and nose. "Don't come near me! You'll get it. You'll all get it."

Cinder retracted her hand. She heard Iko at her side, fan whirring. Saw the blue light darting over Peony, around the junkyard, flickering. She was scared.

"I said, get back!" Peony collapsed to her knees, hunching over her stomach.

Cinder took two steps away, then lingered, watching Peony rock herself back and forth in Iko's spotlight.

"I . . . I need to call an emergency hover. To—"

To come and take you away.

Peony didn't respond. Her whole body was rattling. Cinder could hear her teeth chattering in between the wails.

Cinder shivered. She rubbed at her arms, inspecting them for spots. She couldn't see any, but she eyed her right glove with distrust, not wanting to remove it, not wanting to check.

She stepped back again. The junkyard shadows loomed toward her. The plague. It was here. In the air. In the garbage. How long did it take for the first symptoms of the plague to show up?

Or . . .

She thought of Chang Sacha at the market. The terrified mob running from her booth. The blare of the sirens.

Her stomach plummeted.

Was this her fault? Had she brought the plague home from the market?

She checked her arms again, swiping at invisible bugs that

crawled over her skin. Stumbled back. Peony's sobs filled her head, suffocating her.

A red warning flashed across her retina display, informing her that she was experiencing elevated levels of adrenaline. She blinked it away, then called up her comm link with a writhing gut and sent a simple message before she could question it.

EMERGENCY, TAIHANG DISTRICT JUNKYARD. LETUMOSIS.

She clenched her jaw, feeling the painful dryness of her eyes. A throbbing headache told her that she should be crying, that her sobs should match her sister's.

"Why?" Peony said, her voice stammering. "What did I do?"

"You didn't do anything," said Cinder. "This isn't your fault."

But it might be mine.

"What should I do?" Iko asked, almost too quiet to be heard.

"I don't know," said Cinder. "A hover is on its way."

Peony rubbed her nose with her forearm. Her eyes were rimmed in red. "You n-need to go. You'll catch it."

Feeling dizzy, Cinder realized she'd been breathing too shallowly. She took another step away before filling her lungs. "Maybe I already have it. Maybe it's my fault you caught it. The outbreak at the market today . . . I-I didn't think I was close enough, but . . . Peony, I'm so sorry."

Peony squeezed her eyes and buried her face again. Her brown hair was a mess of tangles hanging across her shoulders, stark against her pale skin. A hiccup, followed by another sob. "I don't want to go."

"I know."

It was all Cinder could think to say. Don't be scared? It will be all right? She couldn't lie, not when it would be so obvious.

"I wish there was something..." She stopped herself. She heard the sirens before Peony did. "I'm so sorry."

Peony swiped at her nose with her sleeve, leaving a trail of mucus. Then kept crying. She didn't respond until the wails of the sirens reached her ears and her head snapped up. She stared into the distance, the entrance of the junkyard somewhere beyond the trash heaps. Eyes rounded. Lips trembling. Face blotchy red.

Cinder's heart shriveled in on itself.

She couldn't help herself. If she was going to catch it, she already had.

She fell to her knees, wrapping Peony up in both arms. Her tool belt dug into her hip, but she ignored it as Peony grasped at her T-shirt, sobs renewed.

"I'm so sorry."

"What will you tell Mom and Pearl?"

Cinder bit her lips. "I don't know." Then, "The truth, I guess."

Bile rose in her mouth. Maybe it was a sign. Maybe stomach sickness was a symptom. She looked down at her forearm, embracing Peony to her. Still no spots.

Peony shoved her away, scooting back in the dirt. "Stay

away. You might not be sick yet. But they would take you. You have to get out of here."

Cinder hesitated. She heard the crunch of treads over scattered aluminum and plastic. She didn't want to leave Peony, but what if she really hadn't caught it yet?

She sat back on her heels, then clambered to her feet. Yellow lights were nearing them from the shadows.

Cinder's right hand was sweating in its glove. Her breathing had shallowed again.

"Peony . . ."

"Go! Go away!"

Cinder stepped back. Back. Had the bleary sense to stop and pick up the folded magbelt. She moved toward the exit, her human leg as numb as the prosthesis. Peony's sobs chased after her.

Three white androids met her around a corner. They had yellow sensors and red crosses painted on their heads and two were pushing a hovering gurney between them.

"Are you the letumosis victim?" one asked in a neutral voice, holding up an ID scanner.

Cinder hid her wrist. "No. My sister, Linh Peony. She-she's that way, to the left."

The med-droids with the gurney wheeled away from her, down the path.

"Have you had direct contact with the victim in the past twelve hours?" the remaining android asked.

Cinder opened her mouth, hesitated. Guilt and fear curdled in her gut.

She could lie. There was no proof she had it yet, but if they took her to the quarantines, she didn't stand a chance.

But if she went home, she could infect everyone. Adri. Pearl. Those screeching, laughing children rushing through the hallways.

She could barely hear her own voice. "Yes."

"Are you showing symptoms?"

"N-no. I don't know. I feel lightheaded, but not—" She stopped herself.

The med-droid neared her, its treads grating on the dirty ground. Cinder stumbled away from it, but it said nothing, only inched closer until Cinder's calves were pressed against a rotting storage crate. It held up the ID scanner in one pronged hand, and then a third arm appeared from within its torso—a syringe in place of grippers.

Cinder shuddered but didn't resist as it grabbed her right wrist and inserted the needle. She flinched, watching as dark liquid, almost black in the android's yellow light, was pulled up into the syringe. She was not afraid of needles, but the world began to tilt. The android removed it just in time for her to slump down onto the crate.

"What are you doing?" she whispered.

"Initiating blood scan for letumosis-carrying pathogens." Cinder heard a motor start up inside the android, faint beeps announcing each step. The android's light dimmed as its power source was diverted.

She held her breath until her control panel kicked in and forced her lungs to contract.

"ID," said the android, holding the scanner out to her. A red light passed over her wrist and the scanner beeped. The android stashed it away in its hollow torso.

She wondered how long it would take for it to finish the scan and determine that she was a carrier, confirming that she was at fault. For everything.

The sound of treads approached along the path. Cinder turned her head as the two androids appeared with Peony atop their gurney. She was sitting up with her hands wrapped around her knees. Swollen eyes wildly darted around the junkyard as if searching for an escape. As if she'd stumbled into a nightmare.

But she didn't try to run. No one ever put up a fight when being taken to the quarantines.

Their eyes met. Cinder opened her mouth but nothing came out. She tried to plead forgiveness with her eyes.

The faintest of smiles touched Peony's lips. She raised a hand and waved with only her fingers.

Cinder returned it, knowing it should be her.

She had already outlived fate once. She should be the one being carted away. She should be the one dying. It should be her.

It was about to be her.

She tried to speak, to tell Peony she would be right behind her. She wouldn't be alone. But then the android beeped. "Scan complete. No letumosis-carrying pathogens detected. Subject is urged to stand fifty feet back from infected patient."

Cinder blinked. Relief and dread both squirmed inside her.

She wasn't sick. She wasn't going to die.

She wasn't going with Peony.

"We will alert you via comm when Linh Peony enters the subsequent stages of the disease. Thank you for your cooperation."

Cinder wrapped her arms around herself and watched Peony lay down as she was carted away, curling up like a child on the gurney.

Six

CINDER SLINKED THROUGH THE BALMY NIGHT, THE SOUND of her boots shuffling across the concrete, as if both legs were made of steel. The empty night was a chorus of muted sounds in her head: the sandy crunching of Iko's treads, the sputtering of street lamps above them, the constant hum of the magnetic superconductor beneath the street. With every step, the wrench inside Cinder's calf clanked. It all dulled in comparison to the video replaying in her mind.

Her interface did that sometimes—recording moments of strong emotion and replaying them over and over. Like déjà vu or when the last words of a conversation linger in the air long after silence has settled in. Usually, she could make the memory stop before it drove her crazy, but tonight she didn't have the energy.

The black splotch on Peony's skin. Her scream. The med-droid's syringe dragging Cinder's blood from the flesh of her elbow. Peony, small and trembling on the gurney. Already dying.

She stopped, clutching her stomach as nausea roiled up. Iko paused a few paces ahead, shining her spotlight on Cinder's scrunched face.

"Are you all right?"

The light darted down the length of Cinder's body, and she was sure Iko was searching for bruise-like rings even though the med-droid had said she wasn't infected.

Instead of answering, Cinder peeled off her gloves and shoved them into her back pocket. Her faintness passing, she leaned her shoulder against a street lamp and drank in the humid air. They'd made it home, almost. The Phoenix Tower apartments stood on the next corner, only the top floor catching the faint light from the crescent moon, the rest of the building cast in shadow. The windows were black but for a handful of lights and some bluish white glares from flickering netscreens. Cinder counted floors, finding the windows to the kitchen and Adri's bedroom.

Though dim, a light was still on somewhere in the apartment. Adri wasn't a night person, but perhaps she'd discovered that Peony was still out. Or perhaps Pearl was awake, working on a school project or comming friends late into the night.

It was probably better this way. She didn't want to have to wake them.

"What am I going to tell them?"

Iko's sensor was on the apartment building for a moment, then the ground, picking up the shuffled debris across the sidewalk.

Cinder rubbed her sweaty palm on her pants and forced

herself onward. Try as she might, suitable words would not come to her. Explanations, excuses. How do you tell a woman her daughter is dying?

She swiped her ID and entered through the main door this time. The gray lobby was decorated only with a netscreen that held announcements for the residents—a rise in maintenance fees, a petition for a new ID scanner at the front door, a lost cat. Then the elevator, loud with the clunking of old machinery. The hallway was empty, save the man from apartment 1807 snoozing on his doorstep. Cinder had to tuck in his splayed arm so Iko wouldn't crush it. Heavy breathing and the sweet aroma of rice wine wafted up.

She hesitated in front of apartment 1820, heart pounding. She couldn't recall when the video of Peony had stopped repeating in her head, eclipsed by her harsh nerves.

What was she going to say?

Cinder bit her lip and held up her wrist for the scanner. The small light switched to green. She opened the door as quietly as possible.

Brightness from the living room spilled into the dark hallway. Cinder caught a glimpse of the netscreen, still showing footage of the market from earlier that day, the baker's booth going up in flames again and again. The screen was muted.

Cinder entered the room, but halted mid-step. Iko bumped against her leg.

Facing her from the middle of the living room were three androids with red crosses painted on their spherical heads. Emergency med-droids.

Behind them, Adri in her silk bathrobe stood against the mantel although the holographic fire was turned off. Pearl was still fully clothed, sitting on the sofa with her knees pulled up to her chin. They were both holding dry washcloths over their noses and eyeing Cinder with a mixture of repulsion and fear.

Cinder's stomach clenched. She drew a half step back into the hallway, wondering which of them was sick, but she quickly realized that neither of them could be. The androids would have taken them immediately. They wouldn't be protecting their breath. The entire building would be on lockdown.

She noticed a small bandage on Adri's elbow. They'd already been tested.

Cinder shifted her messenger bag, setting it on the ground, but kept the magbelt.

Adri cleared her throat and lowered the cloth to her sternum. She looked like a skeleton in the pale lighting, mealy skin and jutting bones. Without makeup, dark circles swelled beneath her bloodshot eyes. She'd been crying, but now her lips were set in a stiff line.

"I received a comm an hour ago," she said once the silence had congealed in the room. "It informed me that Peony was picked up in the Taihang District junkyard and taken—" Her voice broke. She dropped her gaze, and when she looked up again, her eyes were flashing. "But you know that already, don't you?"

Cinder shifted, trying not to look at the med-droids.

Without waiting for Cinder's answer, Adri said, "Iko, you

can begin disposing of Peony's things. Anything she wore in the past week can go into waste collection—but take it to the alley yourself, I don't want it clogging up the chutes. I suppose everything else can be sold at the market." Her voice was sharp and steady, as if this list had been repeating in her head from the moment she'd received the news.

"Yes, Linh-jiě," said Iko, wheeling back into the hallway. Cinder stayed, frozen, both hands clutching the magbelt like a shield. Though the android was incapable of ignoring Adri's commands, it was clear from her slowness that she didn't want to leave Cinder alone so long as the med-droids were watching with their hollow yellow sensors.

"Why," said Adri, wringing the washcloth, "was my youngest daughter at the Taihang District junkyard this evening?"

Cinder drew the magbelt against her, lining it up from shoulder to toe. Made of the same steel as her hand and equally tarnished, it felt like an extension of her. "She came with me to look for a magbelt." She drew in a heavy breath. Her tongue felt swollen, her throat closing in. "I'm so sorry. I didn't—I saw the spots, and I called the emergency hover. I didn't know what to do."

Tears puddled in Adri's eyes, briefly, before she blinked them away. She dropped her head, staring down at the twisted cloth. Her body sagged against the mantel. "I wasn't sure that you would come back here, Cinder. I expected to receive another comm at any minute, telling me that my ward had also been taken." Adri pulled her shoulders back, lifting her gaze. The weakness passed, her dark eyes hardened. "These med-droids tested Pearl and myself. The plague has not yet spread to either of us."

Cinder started to nod, relieved, but Adri continued. "Tell me, Cinder. If Pearl and I are not carrying the disease, where did Peony get it from?"

"I don't know."

"You don't know? But you *did* know about the outbreak in the market today."

Cinder's lips parted. Of course. The cloths. The med-droids. They thought she was infected.

"I don't understand you, Cinder. How could you be so *selfish*?"

She jerked her head, no. "They tested me too, at the junkyard. I don't have it. I don't know where she got it from." She held out her arm, showing the bruise blooming on her inner elbow. "They can check again if they want to."

One of the med-droids showed its first sign of life, shining the light at the small red spot where the needle had pricked her. But they didn't move, and Adri didn't encourage them. Instead, she turned her attention to a small framed portscreen on the mantel, shuffling through pictures of Pearl and Peony in their childhood. Pictures at their old house, the one with the garden. Pictures with Adri, before she'd lost her smile. Pictures with their father.

"I'm so sorry," said Cinder. "I love her too."

Adri squeezed the frame. "Don't insult me," she said, sliding the frame closer to her. "Do your kind even know what love is? Can you feel anything at all, or is it just . . . programmed?"

She was talking to herself, but the words stung. Cinder risked a glance at Pearl, who was still sitting on the sofa with her face half-hidden behind her knees, but she was no longer holding the washcloth to her face. When she saw Cinder looking at her, she turned her gaze to the floor.

Cinder flexed her fingers against the magbelt. "Of course I know what love is." And sadness too. She wished she could cry to prove it.

"Good. Then you will understand that I am doing what a mother must do, to protect my children." Adri turned the frame facedown on the mantel. On the couch, Pearl turned her face away, pressing her cheek against her knees.

A tendril of fear curled in Cinder's stomach. "Adri?"

"It has been five years since you became a part of this household, Cinder. Five years since Garan left you to me. I still don't know what made him do it, don't know why he felt obligated to travel to Europe, of all places, to find some . . . mutant to take care of. He never explained it to me. Perhaps he would have someday. But I never wanted you. You know that."

Cinder pursed her lips. The blank-faced med-droids leered up at her.

She did know it, but she didn't think Adri had ever put it so clearly.

"Garan wanted you to be taken care of, so I've done my best. Even when he died, even when the money ran out, even when . . . everything fell apart." Her voice cracked, and she pressed one palm firmly against her mouth. Cinder watched her shoulders tremble, listened to the short gasps of breath as she tried to stifle the sobs. "But Garan would have agreed. Peony comes first. *Our girls come first.*"

Cinder started at the raised voice. She could hear the justification in Adri's tone. The determination.

Don't leave me with this thing.

She shuddered. "Adri—"

"If it weren't for you, Garan would still be alive. And Peony—"

"No, it's not my fault." Cinder spotted a flash of white, saw Iko loitering in the hallway, uncertain. Her sensor had gone nearly black.

Cinder searched for her voice. Her pulse was throbbing, white spots flickering across her vision. A red warning flickered in the corner of her eye—a recommendation that she calm down. "I didn't ask to be made like this. I didn't ask for you or anybody to adopt me. This isn't my fault!"

"It isn't my fault either!" Adri lashed out, shoving the netscreen off its brackets with one shove. It fell and crashed, taking two of her husband's achievement plaques down with it. Bits of plastic ricocheted across the worn carpet.

Cinder jumped back, but the frenzy fled as fast as it had come. Adri's ragged breath was already slowing. She was always so careful not to disturb the neighbors. Not to be noticed. Not to cause a commotion. Not to do anything that could ruin their reputation. Even now.

"Cinder," said Adri, chafing her fingers with the washcloth

as if she could erase her lost temper. "You will be going with these med-droids. Don't make a scene."

The floor shifted. "What? Why?"

"Because we all have a duty to do what we can, and you know what a high demand there is for . . . your type. Especially now." She paused. Her face had gone pink and mottled. "We can still help Peony. They just need cyborgs, to find a cure."

"You volunteered me for plague research?" Her mouth could barely form the words.

"What *else* was I to do?"

Cinder's jaw hung. She shook her head, dumbly, as all three yellow sensors focused on her. "But . . . nobody survives the testing. How could you—"

"Nobody survives the *plague*. If you care for Peony as much as you claim to, you'll do as I say. If you hadn't been so selfish, you would have volunteered yourself after you left the market today, before coming here and ruining my family. Again."

"But—"

"Take her away. She is yours."

Cinder was too stunned to move as the nearest android held a scanner up to her wrist. It beeped and she flinched back.

"Linh Cinder," it said in its metallic voice, "your voluntary sacrifice is admired and appreciated by all citizens of the Eastern Commonwealth. A payment will be made to your loved ones as a show of gratitude for your contribution to our ongoing studies."

Her grip tightened on the magbelt. "No—*that's* what this is really about, isn't it? You don't care about Peony, you don't care about me, you just want the stupid payout!"

Adri's eyes widened, her temples pulling taut against her skull.

She crossed the room in two steps, the back of her hand whipping across Cinder's face. Cinder fell against the door frame and pressed a hand to her cheek.

"Take her," said Adri. "Get her out of my sight."

"I didn't volunteer. You can't take me against my will!"

The android was unperturbed. "We have been authorized by your legal guardian to take you into custody through the use of force if necessary."

Cinder curled her fingers, balling a fist against her ear.

"You can't force me to be a test subject."

"Yes," said Adri, her own breathing labored. "I can. So long as you are under my guardianship."

"You don't really think this will save Peony, so don't pretend this is about her. She has *days.* The chances of them finding a cure before—"

"Then my only mistake was in waiting too long to be rid of you," Adri said, running the washcloth between her fingers. "Believe me, Cinder. You are a sacrifice I will never regret."

The treads of one of the med-droids clattered against the carpet. "Are you prepared to come with us?"

Cinder pursed her lips and lowered her hand from her face. She glared at Adri, but she could find no sympathy in her stepmother's eyes. A new hatred boiled up inside her. Warnings flashed in her vision. "No. I'm not."

Cinder swung the magbelt, smacking it hard against the android's cranium. The robot fell to the floor, treads spinning midair. "I won't go. Scientists have done enough to me already!"

A second android rolled toward her. "Initiating procedure 240B: forcible removal of cyborg draft subject."

Cinder sneered and shoved the end of the magbelt at the android's sensor, shattering the lens and thrusting it onto its back.

She spun around to face the last android, already thinking how she would run from the apartment. Wondering if it would be too risky to call a hover. Wondering where to find a knife for cutting out her ID chip, otherwise they were sure to track her. Wondering if Iko would be fast enough to follow. Wondering if her legs could carry her all the way to Europe.

The med-droid approached too fast. She stumbled, changing the trajectory of the magbelt, but the android's metal pinchers grasped her wrist first. Electrodes fired. Electricity sizzled through Cinder's nervous system. The voltage overwhelmed her wiring. Cinder's lips parted, but the cry stuck in the back of her throat.

She dropped the magbelt and collapsed. Red warnings flashed across her vision until, in an act of cyborg self-preservation, her brain forced her to shut down.

Seven

DR. DMITRI ERLAND DRAGGED HIS FINGER ACROSS THE portscreen, scanning the patient's records. Male. Thirty-two years old. He had a child but no mention of a spouse. Unemployed. Turned cyborg after a debilitating work-related accident three years ago, no doubt spent most of his savings on the surgery. He'd traveled all the way from Tokyo.

So many strikes against him, and Dr. Erland couldn't explain that to anybody. Sticking his tongue out between his teeth, he raspberried his disappointment.

"What do you think, doctor?" asked today's assistant, a dark-skinned girl whose name he could never recall and who was taller than he was by at least four inches. He liked to give her tasks that kept her seated while she worked.

Dr. Erland filled his lungs slowly, then released them all at once, changing the display to the more relevant diagram of the patient's body. He had a mere 6.4 percent makeup—his right foot, a bit of wiring, and a thumbnail-size control panel imbedded in his thigh.

"Too old," he said, tossing the port onto the countertop before the observation window. On the other side of the glass, the patient was laid out on the lab table. He looked peaceful but for madly tapping fingers against the plastic cushions. His feet were bare, but skin grafting covered the prosthesis.

"Too old?" said the assistant. She stood and came to the window, waving her own portscreen at him. "Thirty-two is too old now?"

"We can't use him."

She bunched her lips to one side. "Doctor, this will be the sixth draft subject you've turned away this month. We can't afford to keep doing this."

"He has a child. A son. It says so right here."

"Yeah, a child who'll be able to afford dinner tonight because his daddy was lucky enough to fit our subject profile."

"To fit our profile? With a 6.4 percent ratio?"

"It's better than testing on people." She dropped the portscreen beside a tray of petri dishes. "You really want to let him go?"

Dr. Erland glared into the quarantine room, a growl humming in the back of his throat. Pulling his shoulders back, he tugged down on his lab coat. "Placebo him."

"Pla—but he's not sick!"

"Yes, but if we don't give him anything, the treasury will wonder what we're doing down here. Now, give him a placebo and submit a report so he can be on his way."

The girl huffed and went to grab a labeled vial from a shelf. "What *are* we doing down here?"

Dr. Erland held up a finger, but the girl gave him such an irritated look that he forgot what he'd been about to say. "What's your name again?"

She rolled her eyes. "Honestly. I've only been your assistant every Monday for the past four months."

She turned her back on him, her long black braid whipping against her hip. Dr. Erland's eyebrows drew together as he stared at the braid, watching as it wound itself up, curling in on itself. A shiny black snake rearing its head. Hissing at him. Ready to strike.

He slammed shut his eyes and counted to ten. When he opened them again, the braid was just a braid. Shiny black hair. Harmless.

Pulling off his hat, Dr. Erland took a moment to rub at his own hair, gray and considerably less full than his assistant's.

The visions were getting worse.

The door to the lab room opened. "Doctor?"

He jolted and stuffed his head back into the hat. "Yes?" he said, grabbing his portscreen. Li, another assistant, lingered with his hand on the doorknob. Dr. Erland had always liked Li—who was also tall but not as tall as the girl.

"There's a volunteer waiting in 6D," said Li. "Someone they brought in last night."

"A volunteer?" said the girl. "Been a while since we had one of those."

Li pulled a portscreen from his breast pocket. "She's young too, a teenager. We haven't run her diagnostics yet, but I think she's going to have a pretty high ratio. No skin grafting."

Dr. Erland perked up, scratching his temple with the corner of his port. "A teenage girl, you say? How . . ." He fumbled for an appropriate descriptor. *Unusual? Coincidental? Lucky?*

"Suspicious," said the girl, her voice low. Dr. Erland turned, found her glower bearing down on him.

"Suspicious? Whatever do you mean?"

She perched against the edge of the counter, diminishing her height so she was eye level, but she still seemed intimidating with her folded arms and unimpressed scowl. "Just that you're always more than willing to placebo the male cyborgs that come in, but you perk right up when you catch word of a girl, especially the *young* ones."

He opened his mouth, closed it, then started again. "The younger, the healthier," he said. "The healthier, the fewer complications we'll have. And it isn't *my* fault that the draft keeps picking on females."

"Fewer complications. Right. Either way, they're going to die."

"Yes, well. Thank you for the optimism." He gestured to the man on the other side of the glass. "Placebo, please. Come join us when you've finished."

He stepped out of the lab room, Li at his side, and cupped a hand around his mouth. "What is her name again?"

"Fateen?"

"Fateen! I can never remember that. One of these days, I'll be forgetting my own name."

Li chuckled, and Dr. Erland was glad he'd made the joke.

People seemed to overlook an old man losing his mind if he occasionally made light of it.

The hallway was empty save for two med-droids lingering by the stairwell, awaiting orders. It was a short walk to lab room 6D.

Dr. Erland pulled a stylus from behind his ear and tapped at his port, downloading the information Li had sent him. The new patient's profile popped up.

LINH CINDER, LICENSED MECHANIC

ID #0097917305

BORN 29 NOV 109 T.E.

0 MEDIA HITS

RESIDENT OF NEW BEIJING, EASTERN COMMONWEALTH. WARD OF LINH ADRI.

Li opened the door to the lab. Tucking the stylus back behind his ear, Dr. Erland entered the room with twitching fingers.

The girl was lying on the table on the other side of the viewing window. The sterile quarantine room was so bright he had to squint into the glare. A med-droid was just capping a plastic vial filled with blood and plunking it onto the chute, sending it off to the blood lab.

The girl's hands and wrists had been fastened with metal bands. Her left hand was steel, tarnished and dark between the joints as if it needed a good cleaning. Her pant legs had been rolled up her calves, revealing one human leg and one synthetic.

"Is she plugged in yet?" he asked, slipping his port into his coat pocket.

"Not yet," said Li. "But look at her."

Dr. Erland grunted, staving off his disappointment. "Yes, her ratio should be impressive. But it's not the best quality, is it?"

"Not the exterior maybe, but you should have seen her wiring. Autocontrol and four-grade nervous system."

Dr. Erland quirked an eyebrow, then lowered it just as fast. "Has she been unruly?"

"The med-droids had trouble apprehending her. She disabled two of them with a . . . a belt, or something, before they were able to shock her system. She's been out all night."

"But she volunteered?"

"Her legal guardian did. She suspects the patient has already had contact with the disease. A sister—taken in yesterday."

Dr. Erland pulled the microphone across the desk. "Wakey, wakey, sleeping beauty," he sang, rapping on the glass.

"They stunned her with 200 volts," said Li. "But I expect her to be coming around any minute now."

Dr. Erland hooked his thumbs on his coat pockets. "Well. We don't need consciousness. Let's go ahead and get started."

"Oh, good," Fateen said in the doorway. Her heels clipped against the tile floor as she entered the lab room. "Glad you found one to suit your tastes."

Dr. Erland pressed a finger to the glass. "Young," he said, eyeing the metallic sheen of the girl's limbs. "Healthy."

With a sneer, Fateen claimed a seat before a netscreen that projected the cyborg's records. "If thirty-two is old and decrepit, what does that make you, old man?"

"Very valuable in the antique market." Dr. Erland lowered his lips to the mic. "Med? Ready the ratio detector, if you please."

Eight

SHE WAS LYING ON A BURNING PYRE, HOT COALS BENEATH her back. Flames. Smoke. Blisters burbling across her skin. Her leg and hand were gone, leaving stumps where the surgeons had attached her prostheses. Dead wires dangled from them. She tried to crawl but was as useless as an upended turtle. She reached out with her one hand, trying to drag her body from the fire, but the bed of coals stretched off into the horizon.

She'd had this dream before, a hundred times. This time though, it was different.

Instead of being all alone, like usual, she was surrounded. Other crippled victims writhed among the coals, moaning, begging for water. They were all missing limbs. Some were nothing more than a head and a torso and a mouth, pleading, pleading. Cinder shrank away from them, noticing bluish splotches on their skin. Their necks, their stump thighs, their shriveled wrists.

She saw Peony. Screaming. Accusing Cinder. She had done

this to her. She had brought the plague to their household. It was all her fault.

Cinder opened her mouth to beg for forgiveness, but she stopped when she caught sight of her one good hand. Her skin was covered in blue spots.

The fire began to melt the diseased skin away, revealing metal and wires beneath the flesh.

She met Peony's gaze again. Her sister opened her mouth, but her voice sounded awkward, deep. "Ready the ratio detector, if you please."

The words hummed like bees in Cinder's ears. Her body jolted, but she couldn't move. Her limbs were too heavy. The smell of smoke lingered in her nostrils, but the heat from the flames was dying away, leaving only her sore, burning back. Peony faded away. The pit of coals melted into the ground.

Green text scrolled along the bottom corner of Cinder's vision.

Beyond the darkness, she heard the familiar rumble of android treads. Iko?

DIAGNOSTICS CHECK COMPLETE. ALL SYSTEMS STABILIZED. REBOOTING IN 3 . . . 2 . . . 1 . . .

Something clattered above her head. The hum of electricity. Cinder felt her finger twitch, the closest thing to a flinch her body was capable of.

The darkness began to warm, a subtle crimson brightness beyond her eyelids.

She forced her eyes open, squinting into harsh fluorescents.

"Ah! Juliet awakens."

She shut her eyes again, let them adjust. She tried to bring her hand up to cover them, but something had her locked in place.

Panic raced along her nerves. She opened her eyes again and turned her head, straining to see who had spoken.

A mirror filled the wall. Her own face stared wild-eyed back at her. Her ponytail was a mess: dull, tangled, in need of a wash. Her skin was too pale, almost translucent, as if the voltage had drained her of more than energy.

They'd taken her gloves and her boots and rolled her pant legs up. She was not looking at a girl in the mirror. She was looking at a machine.

"How are you feeling, Miss, uh . . . Miss Linh?" said a disembodied voice in an accent she couldn't pinpoint. European? American?

She wet her parched lips and craned her neck to peer at the android behind her. It was fidgeting with a small machine on a countertop, amid a dozen other machines. Medical equipment. Surgical toys. IVs. Needles. Cinder realized she was attached to one of the machines by wired sensors on her chest and forehead.

A netscreen hung on the wall to her right, displaying her name and ID number. Otherwise the room was empty.

"If you will just hold still and cooperate, we won't take up too much of your time," said the voice.

Cinder scowled. "Very funny," she said, forcibly straining against the metal bands. "I didn't sign up for this. I didn't volunteer for your stupid tests."

A silence. Something beeped behind her. Peering overhead, she saw the android pulling two prongs attached to thin cables out of a machine. A chill crawled up her spine.

"Keep that thing away from me."

"This won't hurt a bit, Miss Linh."

"I don't care. Stay out of my head. I'm not one of your lemming volunteers."

The voice clucked. "I have a signature here from a Miss Linh Adri. You must know her?"

"She's not my mother! She's just—" Her heart lurched.

"Your legal guardian?"

Cinder thumped her head against the padded exam table. Tissue paper crinkled beneath her. "This isn't right."

"Don't fret, Miss Linh. You are doing your fellow citizens a great service by being here."

She glared at the mirror, hoping she was glaring at the jerk on the other side. "Yeah? And what'd they ever do for me?"

Instead of answering, he said simply, "Med, please proceed."

Treads wheeled toward her. Cinder jerked away, twisting her neck in an effort to avoid the cold prongs, but the android gripped her scalp with mechanical strength and forced her right cheek to the tissue paper. She thrashed her arms and legs, but it was useless.

Perhaps if she fought hard enough they would knock her out again. She wasn't sure if that would be better or worse, but the memory of the pit of burning embers halted her struggling.

Her heart galloped as the android undid the latch in the back of her head. She shut her eyes, trying to imagine herself anywhere but this cold, sterile room. She didn't want to think about the two metal prongs being inserted into her control panel—her brain—but it was impossible not to think about it as she heard them being maneuvered into place.

Nausea. She swallowed back the bile.

She heard the click of the prongs. She couldn't feel anything—there were no nerve endings. But a shudder ripped through her, sending goose bumps down her arms. Her retina display informed her that she was now connected to **RATIO DETECTOR 2.3. SCANNING . . . 2% . . . 7% . . . 16% . . .**

The machine hummed on the table behind her. Cinder imagined a subtle current of electricity slipping along her wires. She felt it most where the skin joined with metal, a tingle where the blood had been cut off.

63% . . .

Cinder clenched her jaw. Someone had been there before—in her head. A fact never forgotten, always ignored. Some surgeon, some stranger, opening her skull and inserting their made-up system of wires and conductors while she had lain helpless beneath them. Someone had altered her brain. Someone had altered her.

78% . . .

She choked on the scream that tried to burble out of her. It was painless. Painless. But someone was in her head. Inside her. An invasion. A violation. She tried to jerk away, but the android held her firm.

"Get out!" The scream echoed back to her off the cold walls.

SCAN COMPLETED.

The med-droid disconnected the prongs. Cinder lay trembling, her heart crushed against her ribcage.

The med-droid didn't bother to close the panel in the back of her head.

Cinder hated it. Hated Adri. Hated the mad voice behind the mirror. Hated the nameless people who had turned her into this.

"Thank you for that stellar cooperation," said the disembodied voice. "It will take just a minute for us to record your cybernetic makeup, and then we'll proceed. Please make yourself comfortable."

Cinder ignored him, face turned away from the mirror. It was one of those rare moments she was glad to have no tear ducts, otherwise she was sure she'd be a sniveling disaster, and she would have hated herself all the more for it.

She could still hear voices over the speakers, but their words consisted of muttered scientific lingo she didn't understand. The med-droid was bustling around behind her, putting the ratio detector away. Readying her next instrument of torture.

Cinder opened her eyes. The netscreen on the wall had changed, no longer showing her life stats. Her ID number was still at the top, headlining a holographic diagram.

Of a girl.

A girl full of wires.

It was as if someone had chopped her down the middle, dividing her front half from her back half, and then put her cartoonish image into a medical textbook. Her heart, her brain, her intestines, her muscles, her blue veins. Her control panel, her synthetic hand and leg, wires that trailed from the base of her skull all the way down her spine and out to her prosthetic limbs. The scar tissue where flesh met metal. A small dark square in her wrist—her ID chip.

But those things she had known. Those things she had expected.

She had not known about the metal vertebrae along her spine, or the four metal ribs, or the synthetic tissue around her heart, or the metal splints along the bones in her right leg.

The bottom of the screen was labeled:

RATIO: 36.28%

She was 36.28 percent not human.

"Thank you for your patience," came the voice, startling her. "As you've no doubt noticed, you are quite the exemplary model of modern science, young lady."

"Leave me alone," she whispered.

"What's going to happen next is that the med-droid is going to inject you with a one-tenth solution of letumosis microbes. They've been magnetically tagged and so will appear bright green on the holographic diagram, in real time. Once your body enters into the first stage of the disease, your immune system will kick in and try to destroy the microbes, but it will fail. Your body will then proceed to stage two of the disease, which is of course where we see the bruise-like spots on your skin. At that point, we will inject you with our most recent batch of antibodies, which, if we've succeeded, will permanently disable the pathogens. Abracadabra, you'll be home in time for dumplings. Are you ready?"

Cinder stared at the holograph and imagined watching herself die. In real time.

"How many different batches of antibodies have you gone through?"

"Med?"

"Twenty-seven," said the med-droid.

"But," said the foreign voice, "they die a little slower each time."

Cinder crinkled the tissue paper beneath her fingertips.

"I believe we're all ready. Med, please proceed with syringe A."

Something clattered on the table, and then the android was beside her. A panel was open in its torso, revealing a third arm ending in a syringe, like those in the emergency androids.

Cinder tried to pull away, but she had nowhere to go.

Imagining the headless voice on the other side of the mirror, watching, laughing at her vain struggles, she froze and tried her best to hold still. To be strong. To not think about what they were doing to her.

The android's prongs were cold as they gripped Cinder's elbow, still bruised from having blood taken twice in the past twelve hours. She grimaced, muscles pulling taut to her bones.

"It is easier to find the vein if you are relaxed," the android said in a hollow voice.

Cinder tensed her arm's muscles until they were shaking. A snort came through the speakers, as if the disembodied voice was amused by her antics.

The android was well-programmed. Despite her rebellion, the needle punctured her vein on the first try. Cinder gasped.

A pinch. Just a pinch. The fight drained out of her as the clear liquid ran in.

BOOK Two

There was no bed for her, and at night

when she had worked herself weary,

she had to sleep by the hearth in the ashes.

Nine

"SUCCESSFUL TRANSMITTAL OF THE CARRIERS," SAID LI. "ALL reactions appear normal. Blood pressure stabilizing. Signs of stage two expected around 0100 tomorrow morning." He clapped his hands and spun in his chair to face Dr. Erland and Fateen. "That means we can all go home and take naps, right?"

Dr. Erland sniffed. He traced his finger along the screen before him, slowly turning the holographic image of the patient. Twenty little green lights were flickering along her bloodstream, spreading slowly through her veins. But he had seen that before, dozens of times. It was the rest of her that held his interest now.

"Have you ever seen anything like her before?" said Fateen, standing beside him. "The sales from her control panel alone will cover the family payoff."

Dr. Erland tried to give her an unimpressed glare, but it was less than effective when he had to tilt his head back to look up at her. Snarling, he scooted away and turned back to the holograph. He tapped on the top of the glowing spine, where two metal vertebrae connected, and enlarged the image. What had been a small shadow before now appeared too substantial, too geometric.

Fateen crossed her arms and bent down. "What is that?"

"I'm not sure," said Erland, rotating the image for a better view.

"It looks like a chip," said Li, getting up to join them.

"On her spine?" said Fateen. "What good would that do her?"

"I'm just saying that's what it looks like. Or maybe they messed up on the vertebrae and had to reweld it or something."

Fateen pointed. "This is more than just welding though. You can see the ridges here, like it's plugged into . . ." She hesitated.

They both faced Dr. Erland, whose eyes were following a small green dot that had just floated into the holograph's viewing range. "Like a vicious green firefly," he muttered to himself.

"Doctor," said Fateen, snapping his attention back to her, "why would she have a chip plugged into her nervous system?"

He cleared his throat. "Perhaps," he said, pulling spectacles from his breast pocket and sliding them onto his nose, "her nervous system experienced traumatic damage."

"From a hover accident?" said Li.

"Spinal injuries used to be quite common before computer-operated navigation took over." Dr. Erland scratched his nail across the screen, pulling the holograph back to show her whole torso. He squinted into the lenses, his fingers flittering over the image.

"What are you looking for?" asked Fateen.

Dr. Erland dropped his hand and glanced at the immobile girl on the other side of the window. "Something is missing."

The scar tissue around her wrist. The dull sheen of her synthetic foot. The grease beneath her fingertips.

"What?" said Li. "What's missing?"

Dr. Erland stepped closer to the window and pressed a sweating palm against the counter. "A little green firefly."

Behind him, Li and Fateen traded glances, before spinning back to the holograph. They each began their count, him silently, her out loud, but Fateen paused on number twelve with a gasp.

"One just disappeared," she said, pointing to an empty spot on the girl's right thigh. "A microbe, it was right here, I was looking right at it, and now it's gone."

As they watched, two more dots flickered and disappeared, like burned-out lightbulbs.

Li grabbed his portscreen off a desk and pounded his fingers against it. "Her immune system is going berserk."

Dr. Erland leaned into the microphone. "Med, please draw another blood sample. Quickly." The girl jolted to attention at the sound of his voice.

Fateen joined him at the window. "We haven't given her the antidote yet."

"No."

"So how . . ."

Dr. Erland bit down on a thumbnail to tame the rush of giddiness. "I need to go get that first blood sample," he said, backing away, almost afraid to take his eyes from the cyborg girl. "When all the microbes have disappeared, have her taken into lab four."

"Lab four isn't set up for quarantine," said Li.

"Indeed. She won't be contagious." Dr. Erland snapped his fingers, halfway out the door. "And perhaps have the med untie her."

"Untie—" Fateen's face contorted with disbelief. "Are you sure that's such a good idea? She was violent with the med-droids, remember?"

Li folded his arms. "She's right. I know I wouldn't want to be on the other side of that fist if she got angry."

"In that case, you have nothing to fear," said Dr. Erland. "I'll be meeting with her in private."

Ten

CINDER STARTED WHEN THE MYSTERY VOICE FILLED THE room again, demanding another blood sample from the sacrificial lamb. She glared at the mirror, ignoring the med-droid as it prepared a new needle with robotic efficiency.

She fought down a gulp, moistening her throat. "How long before I get the pretend antidote?"

She waited, but there was no answer. The android clipped its metal claws around her arm. She flinched at the cold, then again as the needle poked into her sore elbow.

The bruise would last for days.

Then she remembered that tomorrow she would be dead. Or dying.

Like Peony.

Her stomach twisted. Maybe Adri was right. Maybe it was for the best.

A shudder wracked her body. Her metal leg clanked hard against her restraints.

Maybe not, though. Maybe the antidote would work.

She filled her lungs with the cool, sterile air of the lab and watched as the holograph on the wall mimicked her. Two green dots lingered by her right foot.

The med-droid pulled out the needle and used a cotton ball to stopper the wound. The vial filled with her blood was set into a metal box attached to the wall.

Cinder thumped her head against the lab table. "I asked you a question. Antidote? Any day now? You are going to at least *try* to save my life, right?"

"Med," said a new voice, a female. Cinder snapped her head around to look at herself in the mirror again. "Disconnect the patient from the monitoring machines and escort her into lab room 4D."

Cinder dug her fingernails into the tissue paper beneath her. Lab room 4D. Is that where they sent you so they could watch you die?

The android snapped shut her head panel and removed the nodes from her chest. The heart rate machine flatlined.

"Hello?" said Cinder. "Could you tell me what's going on?"

No answer. A green light flickered beside the android's sensor, and the door opened into a room's white tiled hallway. The med-droid wheeled Cinder's exam table out of the lab, past the mirror. The corridor was empty and smelled of bleach, and one of the table's wheels squeaked in time with the android's treads.

Cinder craned her head but was unable to meet the

med-droid's sensor. "I think I have some oil in my calf if you'd like me to fix that wheel."

The android remained silent.

Cinder pressed her lips. Numbered white doors slid past them. "What's in lab room 4D?"

Silence.

Cinder drummed her fingers, listening to the crinkle of tissue paper and the wheel that was sure to give her a twitch. She caught the sound of voices somewhere far away, down another corridor, and half expected to hear screams coming from behind the closed doors. Then one of the doors opened, and the android pushed her past a black 4D. The room was almost an exact duplicate of the other but without the observation mirror.

Cinder was wheeled alongside another exam table, upon which sat a familiar pair of boots and gloves. Then, to Cinder's surprise, her shackles released with a simultaneous whistle of air.

She jerked her hands and feet out of the opened metal rings before the android could realize it had made a mistake and bind her again, but the android showed no reaction as it retreated to the hall without comment. The door clanked shut behind it.

Shivering, Cinder sat up and searched the room for hidden cameras, but nothing struck her as obvious. A counter along one wall held the same heart-rate machines and ratio detectors as the other had. One netscreen to her right sat blank. The door. Two exam tables. And her.

She swung her legs over the side and snatched up her

gloves and boots. While lacing up her left boot, she remembered the tools she'd stashed in her leg before leaving the junkyard, what seemed like eons ago. She unlatched the compartment and was relieved to find it hadn't been raided. With a steadying breath, she grabbed the largest, heaviest tool she had—a wrench—before closing the compartment and tying off her boot.

With her synthetic limbs covered and a weapon in hand, she felt better. Still tense, but not as vulnerable as before.

More confused than ever.

Why give her stuff back if they were going to kill her? Why take her to a new lab?

She rubbed the cool wrench against the bruise on the eye of her elbow. It almost looked like a spot from the plague. She pressed on it with her thumb, glad to feel the dull pain that proved it wasn't.

Again she scanned the room for a camera, half expecting a small army of med-droids to stampede the room before she could destroy all the lab equipment, but no one came. The hallway outside betrayed no footsteps.

Sliding off the exam table, Cinder went to the door and tested the handle. Locked. An ID scanner was inserted into the frame, but it stayed red when she flashed her wrist before it, so it must have been coded to select personnel.

She went to the cabinets and fiddled with the row of drawers, but none opened.

Tapping the wrench against her thigh, she turned on the

netscreen. It blazed to life, a holographic image jumping out at her. It was her again, her medical diagram spliced in half.

She swiped the wrench through the holograph's abdomen. It flickered, then returned to normal.

Behind her, the door whooshed open.

Cinder spun, tucking the wrench against her side.

An old man in a gray newsboy cap stood before her, holding a portscreen in his left hand and two blood-filled vials in the other. He was shorter than Cinder. A white lab coat hung from his shoulders as it would a model skeleton. Lines drawn into his face suggested he had spent many years thinking very hard over very difficult problems. But his eyes were bluer than the sky and, at that moment, they were smiling.

He reminded her of a child salivating over a sticky bun.

The door shut behind him.

"Hello, Miss Linh."

Her fingers tightened on the wrench. The strange accent. The disembodied voice.

"I am Dr. Erland, the leading scientist of the royal letumosis research team."

She forced her shoulders to relax. "Shouldn't you be wearing a face mask?"

His gray eyebrows lifted. "Whatever for? Are you sick?"

Cinder clenched her teeth and pressed the wrench into her thigh.

"Why don't you sit down? I have some important things to discuss with you."

"Oh, *now* you want to talk," she said, inching toward him. "I was under the impression you didn't care too much about the opinions of your guinea pigs."

"You are a bit different than our usual volunteers."

Cinder eyed him, the metal tool warming in her palm. "Maybe that's because I *didn't volunteer*."

In a fluid motion, she raised her arm. Targeted his temple. Envisioned him crumpling to the floor.

But she froze, her vision blurring. Her heart rate slowed, the spike of adrenaline gone before her retina display could warn her about it.

Thoughts came to her, sharp and clear amid the syrupy confusion of her brain. He was a simple old man. A frail, helpless old man. With the sweetest, most innocent blue eyes she'd ever seen. She did not want to hurt him.

Her arm trembled.

The little orange light clicked on and she dropped the wrench in surprise. It clattered to the tile floor, but she was too dazed to worry about it.

He hadn't said anything. How could he be lying?

The doctor didn't even flinch. His eyes beamed, pleased with Cinder's reaction. "Please," he said, fanning his fingers toward the exam table. "Won't you sit?"

Eleven

CINDER BLINKED RAPIDLY, TRYING TO DISPEL THE FOG FROM her brain. The orange light in the corner of her vision disappeared—she still had no idea what had caused it.

Maybe the earlier shock to her system had messed with her programming.

The doctor brushed past her and gestured at the holographic image that jutted from the netscreen. "You no doubt recognize this," he said, sliding his finger along the screen so that the body spun in a lazy circle. "Let me tell you what is peculiar about it."

Cinder tugged her glove up, pulling the hem over her scar tissue. She scooted toward him. Her foot bumped the wrench, sending it beneath the exam table. "I'd say about 36.28 percent of it is pretty peculiar."

When Dr. Erland did not face her, she bent and picked the wrench up. It seemed heavier than before. In fact, everything felt heavy. Her hand, her leg, her head.

The doctor pointed to the holograph's right elbow. "This is where we injected the letumosis-carrying microbes. They were tagged so that we could monitor their progress through your body." He withdrew the finger, tapping his lip. "Now you see what is peculiar?"

"The fact that I'm not dead, and you don't seem concerned about being in the same room with me?"

"Yes, in a way." He faced her, rubbing his head through his wool hat. "As you can see, the microbes are gone."

Cinder scratched an itch on her shoulder with the wrench. "What do you mean?"

"I mean they are gone. Disappeared. Poof." He exploded his hands like fireworks.

"So . . . I don't have the plague?"

"That's correct, Miss Linh. You do not have the plague."

"And I'm not going to die."

"Correct."

"And I'm not contagious?"

"Yes, yes, yes. Lovely feeling, isn't it?"

She leaned against the wall. Relief filled her, but it was followed by suspicion. They had given her the plague, but now she was healed? Without any antidote?

It felt like a trap, but the orange light was nowhere to be seen. He was telling her the truth, no matter how unbelievable it seemed. "Has this happened before?"

An impish grin spread across the doctor's weathered face. "You are the first. I have some theories about how it could be possible, but I'll need to run tests, of course."

He abandoned the holograph and went to the counter, lying out the two vials. "These are your blood samples, one taken before the injection, one after. I am *very* excited to see what secrets they contain."

She slid her eyes to the door, then back to the doctor. "Are you saying you think I'm *immune*?"

"Yes! That is precisely what it seems. Very interesting. Very special." He gripped his hands together. "It is possible that you were born with it. Something in your DNA that predisposed your immune system to fight off this particular disease. Or perhaps you were introduced to letumosis in a very small amount some time in your past, perhaps in your childhood, and your body was able to fight it off, therefore building an immunity to it which you utilized today."

Cinder shrank back, uncomfortable under his eager stare.

"Do you recall anything from your childhood that could be connected to this?" he continued. "Any horrible sicknesses? Near brushes with death?"

"No. Well . . ." She hesitated, stuffing the wrench into a side cargo pocket. "I guess, maybe. My stepfather died of letumosis. Five years ago."

"Your stepfather. Do you know where he could have contracted it?"

She shrugged. "I don't know. My step—my guardian, Adri, always suspected he got it in Europe. When he adopted me."

The doctor's hands trembled, as if his clutched fingers alone were keeping him from combusting. "You're from Europe then."

She nodded, uncertainly. It felt odd to think she was from a place she had no memory of.

"Were there many sick people in Europe that you recall? Any notable outbreaks in your province?"

"I don't know. I don't actually remember anything from before the surgery."

His eyebrows rose, his blue eyes sucking in all the light of the room. "The cybernetic operation?"

"No, the sex change."

The doctor's smile faltered.

"I'm joking."

Dr. Erland reassembled his composure. "What do you mean when you say you don't remember anything?"

Cinder blew a wisp of hair from her face. "Just that. Something about when they installed the brain interface, it did some damage to my . . . you know, whatever. The part of the brain that remembers things."

"The hippocampus."

"I guess."

"And how old were you?"

"Eleven."

"Eleven." He released his breath in a rush. His gaze darted haphazardly around the floor as if the reason for her immunity was written upon it. "Eleven. Because of a hover accident, was it?"

"Right."

"Hover accidents are nearly impossible these days."

"Until some idiot removes the collision sensor, trying to make it go faster."

"Even so, it wouldn't seem that a few bumps and bruises would justify the amount of repairs you had."

Cinder tapped her fingers against her hip. *Repairs*—what a very cyborg term.

"Yeah, well, it killed my parents and threw me through the windshield. The force pushed the hover off the maglev track. It rolled a couple times and pinned me underneath. Afterward some of the bones in my leg were the consistency of sawdust." She paused, fiddling with her gloves. "At least, that's what they told me. Like I said, I don't remember any of it."

She only barely remembered the drug-induced fog, her mushy thoughts. And then there was the pain. Every muscle burning. Every joint screaming. Her body in rebellion as it discovered what had been done to it.

"Do you have any trouble retaining memories since then, or forming new ones?"

"Not that I know of." She glared. "Is this relevant?"

"It's fascinating," Dr. Erland said, dodging the question. He pulled out his portscreen, making some notation. "Eleven years old," he muttered again, then, "You must have gone through a lot of prosthetic limbs growing into those."

Cinder twisted her lips. She *should* have gone through lots of limbs, but Adri had refused to pay for new parts for her freak stepdaughter. Instead of responding, she cast her eyes to the door, then at the blood-filled vials. "So . . . am I free to go?"

Dr. Erland's eyes flashed as if injured by her question. "Go? Miss Linh, you must realize how valuable you've become with this discovery."

Her muscles tensed, her fingers trailing along the hard outline of the wrench in her pocket. "So I'm still a prisoner. Just a valuable one now."

His face softened, and he tucked the port out of sight. "This is much bigger than you realize. You have no idea how important . . . no idea of your worth."

"So what now? Are you going to inject me with even more lethal diseases, to see how my body fares against those?"

"Stars, no. You are much too precious to kill."

"You weren't exactly saying that an hour ago."

Dr. Erland's gaze flickered to the holograph, brow furrowed as if considering her words. "Things are quite different than they were an hour ago, Miss Linh. With your help, we could save hundreds of thousands of lives. If you are what I think you are, we could—well, we could stop the cyborg draft, to start with." He settled his fist against his mouth. "Plus, we would pay you, of course."

Hooking her thumbs into the belt loops of her pants, Cinder leaned against the counter that held all the machines that had seemed so threatening before.

She was immune.

She was *important*.

The money was tempting, of course. If she could prove her self-sufficiency, she might be able to annul Adri's legal guardianship over her. She could buy back her freedom.

But even that insight dulled when she thought of Peony.

"You really think I can help?"

"I do. In fact, I think every person on Earth could soon find themselves immensely grateful to you."

She gulped and lifted herself onto an exam table, folding both legs beneath her. "All right, just so long as we're clear—I *am* here on a volunteer basis now, which means I can leave at any point I want to. No questions, no arguments."

The doctor's face brightened, eyes shining like lanterns between the wrinkles. "Yes. Absolutely."

"And I do expect payment, like you said, but I need a separate account. Something my legal guardian can't access. I don't want her to have any idea I've agreed to do this, or any access to the money."

To her surprise, he didn't hesitate. "Of course."

She sucked in a steadying breath. "And one other thing. My sister. She was taken to the quarantines yesterday. If you do find an antidote, or anything that even holds promise as an antidote, I want her to be the first one to get it."

This time, the doctor's gaze faltered. He turned away and paced to the holograph, rubbing his hands down the front of his lab coat. "*That,* I'm afraid I cannot promise."

She squeezed her fists together. "Why not?"

"Because the emperor must be the first to receive the antidote." His eyelids crinkled with sympathy. "But I *can* promise your sister will be second."

Twelve

PRINCE KAI WATCHED THROUGH THE GLASS AS A MED-DROID inserted an IV into his father's arm. Only five days had passed since the emperor had shown the first signs of the blue fever, but it felt like a lifetime. Years' worth of worry and anguish rolled into so few hours.

Dr. Erland had once told him of an old suspicion that bad things always came in threes.

First, his android Nainsi had broken before she could communicate her findings.

And now his father was sick, with no hope for survival.

What would happen next? What could be worse than this?

Perhaps the Lunars would declare war.

He cringed, wanting to take back the thought the second he had it.

Konn Torin, his father's adviser and the only other human allowed to see the emperor in such a state, clapped a hand on Kai's shoulder. "It will be all right," he said, without emotion, in that peculiar way he had of reading another person's thoughts.

Kai's father moaned and opened swollen eyes. The room was quarantined on the seventh floor of the palace's research wing, but the emperor had been made as comfortable as possible. Numerous screens lined the walls so he might enjoy music and entertainment, so he might be read to. His favorite flowers had been brought in droves from the gardens—lilies and chrysanthemums filling the otherwise sterile room. The bed was dressed in the finest silks the Commonwealth had to offer.

But none of it made much of a difference. It was still a room made to keep the living separate from the dying.

A clear window separated Kai from his father. He was squinting up at Kai now, but his eyes were empty as glass.

"Your Majesty," said Torin. "How are you feeling?"

The emperor's eyes crinkled at their corners. He was not an old man, but the illness had aged him quickly. His complexion was yellow and pallid, and black and red splotches stippled his neck.

His fingers lifted from the blankets, the closest thing he could manage to a wave.

"Is there anything you need?" Torin asked. "A glass of water? Food?"

"An Escort5.3?" Kai suggested.

Torin cast the prince a disapproving glare, but the emperor wheezed a small chuckle.

Kai felt his eyes misting and had to look away, down at fingertips pressed into the windowsill.

"How much longer?" he said, quiet so his father wouldn't hear.

Torin shook his head. "Days, if that."

Kai could feel Torin's gaze on him, understanding but also harsh.

"You should be grateful for the time you have with him. Most people don't get to see their loved ones when they're taken away."

"And who wants to see their loved ones like this?" Kai looked up. His father was struggling to stay awake, his eyelids twitching. "Med, bring him water."

The android rolled to the emperor's side and lifted his backrest, guiding a glass of water to his lips and wiping away the dribble with a white cloth. He did not drink much but seemed refreshed when he had sunk again into the pillows.

"Kai . . ."

"I'm here," Kai said, his breath fogging the glass.

"Be strong. Trust . . ." His words broke into a cough. The med-droid held a towel to his mouth, and Kai caught a glimpse of blood against the cotton. He shut his eyes, measuring his breath.

When he opened them again, the med-droid was filling the IV with clear liquid, something to ease the pain. Kai and Torin watched as the emperor sank into a motionless sleep. Like watching a stranger. Kai loved him but couldn't quite connect the sick man before him with the vibrant father he'd had a week ago.

One week.

A shudder ran through him, and Torin squeezed his shoulder. Kai had forgotten his hand was there.

"Your Highness."

Kai said nothing, staring at his father's chest as it rose and fell.

The fingers on his shoulder tightened briefly, then fell away. "You are going to be emperor, Your Highness. We must begin to prepare you. We've already put it off too long."

Too long. One week.

Kai pretended not to hear him.

"As His Majesty said, you must be strong. You know I will help in any way I can." Torin paused. "You're going to be a fine leader."

"No. I'm not." Kai tugged a hand through his hair, pulling it back from his scalp.

He was going to be emperor.

The words rang hollow.

The true emperor was there, in that bed. *He* was an imposter.

"I'm going to go talk to Dr. Erland," he said, stepping back from the glass.

"The doctor is busy, Your Highness. You shouldn't keep distracting him."

"I just want to ask if there've been any developments."

"I'm sure he will tell you immediately if there are."

Kai set his jaw and fixed his gaze on Torin, the man who had been his father's adviser since before Kai was born. Even now, standing in the same room with Torin made him feel like a child, gave him a peculiar urge to be unruly. He wondered if he would ever get over that.

"I need to feel like I'm doing *something,*" he said. "I can't just stand here watching him die."

Torin's eyes dropped. "I know, Your Highness. It's hard for all of us."

It's not the same, Kai wanted to say, but held his tongue.

Torin turned away from him, facing the window, and bowed his head. "Long live the emperor."

Kai repeated the words, whispering around the dryness in his throat. "Long live the emperor."

They were silent leaving the visitors room and walking down the hallway to the elevators.

A woman was waiting for them. Kai should have expected it—she was always nearby these days, when she was the last person on Earth he wanted to see.

Sybil Mira. Head thaumaturge to the Lunar Crown. Exceptionally beautiful, with waist-length black hair and warm, honeyed skin. She wore the uniform befitting her rank and title: a long white coat with a high collar and bell-shaped sleeves, embroidered along the hems with runes and hieroglyphs that meant nothing to Kai.

Five paces behind her stood her ever-present, ever-silent guard. He was a young man as handsome as Sybil was beautiful, with blond hair pulled into a low ponytail and sharp features that Kai had yet to see an expression on.

Sybil's lips curved as Kai and Torin approached, but her gray eyes remained cold.

"Your Imperial Highness," she said with a graceful dip of her head. "How fares the honorable Emperor Rikan?"

When Kai didn't respond, Torin answered, "Not well. Thank you for your concern."

"I am most displeased to hear that." She sounded about as displeased as a cat who'd just cornered a mouse. "My mistress sends her condolences and a wish for a speedy recovery."

She fixed her eyes on the prince, and her image seemed to shudder before him like a mirage. Whispers filled his head. Respect and admiration, compassion and concern.

Kai tore his gaze from her, silencing the voices. It took a moment for his racing pulse to steady.

"What do you want?" he said.

Sybil gestured toward the elevators. "A word with the man who will soon be emperor... should the fates deem it so."

Kai glanced at Torin, but the face that met him was unsympathetic. Tact. Diplomacy. Always. Especially when it came to the cursed Lunars.

Sighing, he half turned to the waiting android. "Third floor."

The sensor flashed. "Please proceed to elevator C, Your Highness."

They boarded the elevator, Sybil floating into it like a feather upon a breeze. The guard entered last, staying by the door and facing the three of them as if the thaumaturge were in mortal danger. His icy gaze made Kai uncomfortable, but Sybil seemed to forget the guard was even there.

"This is a tragic time for His Majesty to fall ill," she said.

Kai gripped the rail and faced her, pressing his hatred

into the polished wood. "Would next month have been more convenient for you?"

Her patience didn't falter. "I speak, of course, of the alliance discussions my mistress has been engaged in with Emperor Rikan. We are most eager for an agreement that will suit both Luna and the Commonwealth."

Watching her made him feel dizzy, off balance, so he tore his gaze away and watched the numbers above the doors descend. "My father has been attempting to secure an alliance with Queen Levana since she first took the throne. *She* has always declined."

"He has yet to meet her sensible demands."

Kai locked his teeth.

Sybil continued, "My hope is that, as emperor, you will be better able to see reason, Your Highness."

Kai was silent as the elevator passed floors six, five, four. "My father is a wise man. At this time, I have no intention of altering any of his previous decisions. I do hope we will be able to come to an agreement, but I'm afraid your *mistress* will need to lower her very sensible demands."

Sybil's smile had frozen on her face.

"Well," she said as the doors opened to the third floor, "you are young."

He dipped his head, pretending she'd given him a compliment, then faced Torin. "If you have a minute to spare, perhaps you could walk with me to Dr. Erland's office? You may have questions I've not thought of."

"Of course, Your Highness."

Neither of them acknowledged the thaumaturge or her guard as they left the elevator, but Kai heard her sugared voice behind them—"Long live the emperor"—before the doors shut.

He growled. "We should have her incarcerated."

"A Lunar ambassador? That's hardly a show of peace."

"It's better treatment than they would give us." He raked a hand through his hair. "Gah—*Lunars*."

Realizing that Torin had stopped following, Kai dropped his hand and turned around. Torin's gaze was heavy. Worried.

"What?"

"I know this is a difficult time for you."

Kai felt his hackles rise in self-defense and tried to nudge them back down. "This is a difficult time for everyone."

"Eventually, Your Highness, we will have to discuss Queen Levana and what you intend to do about her. It would be wise to have a plan."

Kai stepped closer to Torin, ignoring a group of lab technicians that were forced to swarm around them. "I have a plan. My plan is to *not* marry her. Diplomacy be damned. There. End of discussion."

Torin's jaw flexed.

"Don't look at me like that. She would destroy us." Kai lowered his voice. "She would turn us into slaves."

"I know, Your Highness." His sympathetic eyes diffused Kai's mounting anger. "Please believe me when I say I would not ask it of you. Just as I never asked it of your father."

Kai backed away and slumped against the corridor wall. Scientists bustled past in their white coats, android treads whirred on the linoleum, but if anyone noticed the prince and his adviser, they didn't show it.

"All right, I'm listening," he said. "What's our plan?"

"Your Highness, this is not the place—"

"No, no, you have my attention. Please, give me something to think about other than this stupid disease."

Torin took a calculated breath. "I don't think we need to rewrite our foreign affairs policy. We'll follow your father's example. For now, we'll hold out for a peace agreement, a treatise."

"And if she won't sign it? What if she gets tired of waiting and decides to follow through on her threats? Can you imagine a war right now, with the plague, and the economy, and . . . she would destroy us. And she knows that."

"If she wanted to start a war, she would have done it by now."

"Unless she's just biding her time, waiting for us to get so weak we won't have any choice but to surrender." Kai scratched at the back of his neck, watching the bustle of the corridor. Everyone so busy, so determined in their search for an antidote.

If there were an antidote.

He sighed. "I should have married. If I'd already married, Queen Levana wouldn't even be an issue. She'd *have* to sign a peace treaty . . . if she wanted peace."

At Torin's silence, he forced himself to look back at the adviser, surprised to find a rare warmth in his face.

"Perhaps you'll meet a girl at the festival," said Torin. "Have a whirlwind romance, a happily ever after, and have no more worries for the rest of your days."

Kai tried to glare at him but couldn't maintain it. Torin so rarely joked. "Brilliant idea. Why didn't I think of it?" He turned, bracing his shoulder against the wall, and folded his arms over his chest. "Actually, maybe there's one option that you and my father haven't considered yet. Something that's been on my mind lately."

"Do tell, Your Highness."

He lowered his voice. "Lately, I've been doing a little research." He paused, before proceeding. "On . . . on the Lunar heir."

Torin's eyes widened. "Your Highness—"

"Just hear me out," Kai said, raising his hands to silence Torin before he could be chastised. He already knew what Torin would say: Princess Selene, Queen Levana's niece, was dead. She had died in a fire thirteen years ago. There was no Lunar heir.

"There are rumors every day," Kai continued. "Sightings, people claiming they helped her, theories . . ."

"Yes, we've all heard the theories. You know as well as I there's no substance to them."

"But what if they're true?" Kai crossed his arms and ducked his head toward Torin, voice trailing to a whisper. "What if there's a girl out there who could usurp Levana? Someone even stronger?"

"Are you listening to yourself? Someone *stronger* than Levana? You mean someone like her sister, who had her favorite seamstress's feet chopped off so she would have nothing better to do than sit and make her fine dresses?"

"We're not talking about Queen Channary."

"No, we're talking about her *daughter.* Kai, the entire bloodline, every last one of them has been greedy, violent, corrupted by their own power. It's in their blood. Believe me when I say that Princess Selene, even if she were alive, would be no better."

Kai realized his arms were aching from squeezing them so hard, his skin gone white around his fingertips. "She can't very well be worse," he said. "And who knows? If the rumors are right, and she has been on Earth all this time, maybe she *would* be different. Maybe she would be sympathetic to us."

"You're basing this wishful thinking on *rumors.*"

"They never found a body. . . ."

Torin pursed his lips in a thin line. "They found what was left of one."

"It couldn't hurt to do some research, could it?" said Kai, beginning to feel desperate. His heart had been set on the idea for so long, his research harbored so close to his heart. He couldn't bear to think it had all been just wishful thinking, although the possibility had always lingered in the back of his mind.

"Yes, it *could* hurt," said Torin. "If Levana were to find out you were considering this, it would destroy our chance at procuring a treaty. We shouldn't even be talking about this here—it's dangerous."

"Now who's listening to rumors?"

"Your Highness, this is the end of this discussion. Your

objective right now must be to prevent a war, not worrying about phantom Lunar princesses."

"What if I *can't* prevent it?"

Torin opened his palms, looking weary after the argument. "Then the Union will fight."

"Right. Excellent plan. I'm so comforted now that we've had this talk."

He turned away and marched blindly toward the labs.

Sure, the Earthen Union would fight. But against Luna, they would lose.

Thirteen

"YOUR CONTROL PANEL IS MARVELOUSLY COMPLEX. SOME OF the highest technology I've ever seen in a cyborg." Dr. Erland spun the holograph one way and then the other. "And look at this wiring along your spine. It melds almost perfectly with your central nervous system. Pristine workmanship. And ah! Look here!" He pointed to the holograph's pelvis. "Your reproductive system is almost untouched. You know, lots of female cyborgs are left infertile because of the invasive procedures, but from the looks of it, I don't suspect you will have any problems."

Cinder sat on one of the exam tables, chin settled atop both palms. "Lucky me."

The doctor wagged a finger at her. "You should be grateful your surgeons took such care."

"I'm sure I'll feel much more grateful when I find a guy who thinks complex wiring in a girl is a turn-on." She kicked her heels against the metal base of the table. "Does this have anything to do with my immunity?"

"Maybe, maybe not." The doctor took a pair of spectacles from his pocket and slid them onto his face, still staring at the holograph.

Cinder tilted her head. "Don't they pay you enough for corrective eye surgery?"

"I like the way these feel." Dr. Erland dragged the holograph down, revealing the inside of Cinder's head. "Speaking of eye surgery, do you realize you're missing tear ducts?"

"What? Really? And I thought I was just emotionally withdrawn." She pulled her feet up, hugging her knees. "I'm also incapable of blushing, if that was going to be your next brilliant observation."

He turned around, his eyes magnified behind their spectacles. "Incapable of blushing? How so?"

"My brain monitors my body temperature, forces me to cool down if I get too warm, too fast. I guess just sweating like a normal human being wasn't enough."

Dr. Erland pulled his portscreen out, punched something in. "That's really quite smart," he muttered. "They must have been worried about your system overheating."

Cinder strained her neck, but couldn't see the little screen on his port. "Is that important?"

He ignored her. "And look at your heart," he said, gesturing at the holograph again. "These two chambers are made primarily of silicon, mixed with bio tissue. Amazing."

Cinder pressed her hand against her chest. Her heart. Her brain. Her nervous system. What *hadn't* been tampered with?

Her hand moved to her neck, tracing the ridges of her spine as her gaze traveled over the metal vertebrae, those metallic invaders. "What's this?" she asked, stretching forward and pointing at a shadow on the diagram.

"Ah, yes, my assistants and I were discussing that earlier." Dr. Erland scratched his head through the hat. "It looks to be made of a different material than the vertebrae, and it's right over a central cluster of nerves. Perhaps it was meant to correct a glitch."

Cinder wrinkled her nose. "Great. I have glitches."

"Has your neck ever bothered you?"

"Only when I've been under a hover all day."

And when I'm dreaming. In her nightmare, the fire always seemed to be hottest beneath her neck, the heat trickling down her spine. The unrelenting pain, like a hot coal had gotten beneath her skin. She shuddered, remembering Peony in last night's dream, crying and screaming, blaming Cinder for what had become of her.

Dr. Erland was watching her, tapping his portscreen against his lips.

Cinder squirmed. "I have a question."

"Yes?" said the doctor, pocketing the screen.

"You said before that I wasn't contagious after my body got rid of those microbes."

"That's correct."

"So . . . if I had contracted the plague naturally, say . . . a couple days ago, how long before I was no longer contagious?"

Dr. Erland puckered his lips. "Well. One can imagine that your body is more efficient at ridding itself of the carriers every time it comes in contact with them. So if it took twenty minutes to defeat them all this time . . . oh, I would think it would have taken no longer than an hour the time before that. Two at the most. Hard to say, of course, given that every disease and every body works a little differently."

Cinder folded her hands in her lap. It had taken a little more than an hour to walk home from the market. "What about . . . can it cling to, say, clothing?"

"Only briefly. The pathogens can't survive long without a host." He frowned at her. "Are you all right?"

She fiddled with the fingers of her gloves. Nodded. "When do we get to start saving lives?"

Dr. Erland adjusted his hat. "I'm afraid we can't do much until I've had a chance to analyze your blood samples and map your DNA sequencing. But first I wanted to get a better grasp on your body makeup, in case it could affect the results."

"Being cyborg can't change your DNA, can it?"

"No, but there have been studies suggesting that human bodies develop different hormones, chemical imbalances, antibodies, that sort of thing, as a result of the operations. Of course, the more invasive the procedure, the more—"

"You think it has something to do with my immunity? Being cyborg?"

The doctor's eyes glowed, giddy, unnerving Cinder. "Not exactly," he said. "But like I said before . . . I do have a theory or two."

"Were you planning on sharing any of those theories with me?"

"Oh, yes. Once I know I am correct, I plan on sharing my discovery with the world. In fact, I have had a thought about the mystery shadow on your spine. Would you mind if I tried something?" He took off the spectacles and slid them back into his pocket, beside the portscreen.

"What are you going to do?"

"Just a little experiment, nothing to worry about."

She twisted her head as Dr. Erland walked around the table and placed the tips of his fingers on her neck, pinching the vertebrae just above her shoulders. She stiffened at the touch. His hands were warm, but she shivered anyway.

"Tell me if you feel anything . . . unusual."

Cinder opened her mouth, about to announce that *any* human touch felt unusual, but her breath hiccupped.

Fire and pain ruptured her spine, flooding her veins.

She cried out and fell off the table, crumpling to the floor.

Fourteen

RED LIGHT PIERCED HER EYELIDS. GOING HAYWIRE, HER retina display was sending a skein of green gibberish against the backdrop of her lids. Something was wrong with her wiring—her left fingers kept twitching, pulsing uncontrollably.

"Calm down, Miss Linh. You're perfectly all right." This voice, calm and unsympathetic in its strange accent, was followed by one much more panicked.

"Perfectly all right? Are you crazy? What *happened* to her?"

Cinder groaned.

"Only a little experiment. She's going to be fine, Your Highness. See? She's waking up now."

Another strangled protest before she could pry her eyes open. The lab's whiteness would have blinded her but for the two shadows cutting through it. Her eyes focused the shapes into Dr. Erland's wool hat and sky blue eyes, and Prince Kai with strands of black hair hanging unkempt across his brow.

As the retina display began running the basic diagnostic test for the second time that day, she shut her eyes again, faintly worried that Prince Kai would notice the green light at the base of her pupil.

At least she had her gloves on.

"Are you alive?" Kai said, pushing her mussed hair back from her forehead. His fingers felt hot and clammy against her skin before she realized that she was the one who was feverish.

Which shouldn't have been possible. She couldn't blush, couldn't have a fever.

Couldn't overheat.

What had the doctor done to her?

"Did she hit her head?" Kai asked.

The twitching stopped. Cinder pressed her hands against her body in an instinctual effort to hide them.

"Oh, she's *fine,*" Dr. Erland said again. "Had a bit of a scare—but no harm done. I am sorry for that, Miss Linh. I didn't realize you would be so sensitive."

"What did you do?" she said, careful not to slur her words.

Kai slipped an arm beneath her and helped her sit up. She flinched against him and tugged down her pant leg in case the metal gleam of her shin was visible.

"I was merely adjusting your spine."

Cinder squinted at the doctor, not needing the little orange light to tell her he was lying, but it popped up anyway.

"What's wrong with her spine?" Kai's hand slid down to her lower back.

Cinder sucked in a breath, a shiver racing along her skin. She feared the pain would come back, that the prince's touch would somehow override her system like Dr. Erland's had—but nothing happened, and soon Kai lessened the pressure of his touch.

"Nothing is wrong with it," said Dr. Erland. "But the spinal region is where many of our nerves congregate before sending messages up to our brains."

Cinder watched Dr. Erland with wild eyes. She could already imagine how quickly Kai would pull away from her when the doctor told him he was supporting a cyborg.

"Miss Linh was complaining of a bothersome pain in her neck . . ."

She squeezed her fists together until her fingers began to ache.

". . . and so I gave her a bit of an adjustment. It's called *chiropractic,* a very old practice, and yet amazingly effective. She must have been more out of alignment than I realized, and so the sudden realigning of the vertebrae created a temporary shock to her system." He grinned at the prince, eyes devoid of concern. The orange light persisted.

Cinder gaped, waiting for the doctor to continue, to move past his inane lie and start telling the prince all of her secrets. She was a cyborg, she was immune to the plague, she was his new favorite guinea pig.

But Dr. Erland said nothing else, only smiled at her with mischievous eyes that filled her with suspicion.

Feeling Kai's gaze upon her, Cinder turned to him, meaning to shrug as if Dr. Erland's explanation made no more sense to her than it did to him, but the intensity of Prince Kai's gaze snatched away her words.

"I hope he's telling me the truth, because it would be a shame for you to die when we've just had the pleasure of meeting." His eyes glinted, as if sharing a secret joke, and she forced the fakest laugh she'd ever heard from her own lips. "Are you all right?" he said, taking her hand into his—one arm still around her back. "Can you stand?"

"I think so."

He helped her to her feet. Not a sign of the excruciating pain remained.

"Thank you." She backed away from him, brushing herself off, even though the lab floor was immaculate. Her thigh bumped the exam table.

"What are you doing here?" he asked, hands falling to his sides and hanging awkwardly for a second before finding their way into his pockets.

Cinder opened her mouth, but was interrupted by Dr. Erland clearing his throat.

"You two have met?" he asked, bushy eyebrows disappearing into his cap.

Kai answered. "We met yesterday. At the market."

Cinder shoved her hands into her pockets, mirroring Kai, and discovered the wrench. "I'm, um, here . . . because . . . uh—"

"One of the med-droids was acting up, Your Highness,"

interrupted Dr. Erland. "I requested that she come take a look at it. Her mechanic business has exceptional ratings."

Kai began to nod, but stopped and scanned the room. "What med-droid?"

"It isn't here anymore, of course," said Dr. Erland, his voice chipper as if lying were a fun game. "It's probably off drawing blood as we speak."

"R-right," said Cinder, forcing her jaw to stop hanging open like an idiot's. "I already fixed it. Good as new." She pulled out the wrench and twirled it over her fingers like hard evidence.

Though Kai appeared confused, he nodded as if the story wasn't worth questioning. Cinder was grateful that the doctor had so easily devised a story, but it also unnerved her. What reason did he have to keep secrets from the Crown Prince, especially when he could be nearing a breakthrough on plague research? Didn't Kai deserve to know about it? Didn't everyone?

"I don't suppose you've had a chance to look at Nainsi?" Kai asked.

Cinder stopped twirling the wrench and clutched it with both hands to keep herself from fidgeting. "No, not yet. I'm sorry. It's been . . . the last twenty-four hours . . ."

He shrugged her words away, but the gesture was stiff on him. "You probably have a client list a mile long. I shouldn't expect royal treatment." His mouth twitched. "Although I guess I do anyway."

Cinder's heart tripped as his grin caught her by surprise,

every bit as charming and unexpected as it had been at the market. Then her eye spotted the holograph behind him, still showing her inner workings—from the metal vertebrae to her bunched wires to her perfectly intact ovaries. She snapped her gaze back to Kai, pulse racing.

"I promise to take a look at it as soon as I can. Before the festival. Definitely."

Kai turned, following her gaze to the holograph. Cinder squeezed her fists together, nerves twisting in the base of her stomach, as Kai recoiled from the image.

A girl. A machine. A freak.

She bit her lip, resigning herself to never receiving another of the prince's heart-stopping smiles, when Dr. Erland stepped toward the holograph and turned the netscreen off with a flick. "My apologies, Your Highness, patient confidentiality. That was from today's draft subject."

Another lie.

Cinder strangled the wrench, equal parts gratitude and suspicion filling her.

Kai shook off his surprise. "That's actually why I came down here. I was wondering if you've made any progress."

"Hard to say at this point, Your Highness, but we may have found a potential lead. I'll of course keep you posted on any developments." He smiled innocently, first at Kai, then at Cinder. The look was clear—he would not tell Kai anything.

She just couldn't understand why.

Clearing her throat, Cinder backed toward the exit. "I should go then, let you get back to work," she said, tapping the wrench against her palm. "I guess . . . um . . . I'll be back to make sure the med is performing properly? Say . . . tomorrow?"

"Perfect," said the doctor. "I also have your ID number in case I ever need to find you." His smile darkened, just barely, as if to say that Cinder's "volunteer" status would only last so long as she did return voluntarily. She was valuable now. He had no intention of letting her walk out forever.

"I'll see you out," said the prince, flashing his wrist by the scanner. The door breezed open.

Cinder held up her gloved hands, the wrench locked in her grip. "No, no, that's fine. I can find my way."

"Are you sure? It's no trouble."

"Yes. Positive. I'm sure you have very important . . . royal . . . government . . . research things. To discuss. But thank you. Your Highness." She attempted an awkward bow, glad that at least this time she had both feet firmly attached.

"All right. Well, it was nice to see you again. A pleasant surprise."

She laughed ironically, surprised to find his expression serious. His eyes warm upon her, and a little curious.

"Y-you too." She backed out the door. Smiling. Trembling. Praying there were no grease spots on her face. "I'll comm you, then. When your android is ready."

"Thank you. Linh-mèi."

"You can call me Cin—" The door shut between them. "—der. Cinder. Would be fine. Your Highness." She sagged against the corridor wall, thumping her knuckles against her forehead. *"I'll comm you. You can call me Cinder,"* she mimicked, then bit down on her lip. "Don't mind the babbling girl."

He was the fantasy of every girl in the country. He was so far out of her realm, her *world,* that she should have stopped thinking about him the second the door had closed. Should stop thinking about him immediately. Should never think about him again, except maybe as a client—and her prince.

And yet, the memory of his fingers against her skin refused to fade.

Fifteen

CINDER HAD TO DOWNLOAD A MAP OF THE PALACE'S RESEARCH wing to find her way to the exit. Her nerves were on edge, with the prince, with Peony, with *everything*. She felt like an imposter roaming the slick white halls with her head bent, avoiding eye contact with the scientists and white-plated androids. Even if she really was a volunteer now. A valuable one.

She passed a waiting room—complete with two netscreens and three cushioned chairs—and froze, her gaze catching on the window.

The view.

The city.

From ground level, New Beijing was a mess—too many buildings crammed into too little space, the streets untended, power lines and clotheslines strung across every alley, intruding vines scurrying up every concrete wall.

But from here, atop the cliff and three stories up, the city was beautiful. The sun was high, and its light sang off of glass skyscrapers and gold-tinted roofs. Cinder could see the constant movement of huge netscreens and flashing hovers as they darted between the buildings. From here, the city hummed with life—but without all the technochatter.

Cinder sought out the cluster of slender blue glass and chrome buildings that stood sentry over the market square, then tried to trace the roads north, searching for the Phoenix Tower apartments, but they were tucked behind too much city and too many shadows.

Her awe slipped away.

She had to go back. Back to the apartment. Back to her prison.

She had to fix Kai's android. She had to protect Iko, who wouldn't last a week before Adri got the idea in her head to dismantle her for scrap metal, or worse—replace her "faulty" personality chip. She'd been complaining about the android being too opinionated since the day Cinder had come to live with her.

Besides, she had nowhere else to go. Until Dr. Erland was able to figure out how to deposit the payment into Cinder's account without Adri finding out, she had no money and no hover, and her only human friend was a prisoner herself in the quarantines.

She balled her fists.

She had to go back. But she wouldn't stay long. Adri had made it quite clear that she saw Cinder as worthless, a burden. She'd had no qualms dismissing her when she found a lucrative means to do it, a way that could keep her free of guilt because, after all, they needed to find an antidote. Peony needed an antidote.

And maybe she'd been right to do it. Maybe it was Cinder's duty as a cyborg to sacrifice herself so all the normal humans could be cured. Maybe it did make sense to use the ones who had already been tampered with. But Cinder knew she would never forgive Adri for it. The woman was supposed to be the one to protect *her*, to help *her.* If Adri and Pearl were her only family left, she would be better off alone.

She had to get away. And she knew just how she was going to do it.

THE LOOK ON ADRI'S FACE WHEN CINDER ENTERED THE apartment almost made the whole ghastly ordeal worthwhile.

She'd been sitting on the sofa, reading on her portscreen. Pearl was at the far end of the room, playing a holographic board game in which the game pieces were modeled after the girls' favorite celebrities—including three Prince Kai look-alikes. It had long been her and Peony's favorite, but Pearl was now battling strangers over the net and looked both bored and miserable about it. When Cinder walked in, both Pearl and Adri gaped at her, and a miniature version of the prince fell onto his virtual opponent's long sword. Pearl paused the game too late.

"Cinder," said Adri, setting her portscreen on a side table. "How are you—?"

"They ran some tests and decided I wasn't what they

wanted. So they sent me back." Cinder pulled up a tight-lipped smile. "Don't worry, I'm sure they'll still recognize your noble sacrifice. Maybe they'll send you a thank-you comm."

Eyeing Cinder with disbelief, Adri stood. "They can't send you back!"

Cinder peeled off her gloves and stuffed them into her pocket. "You'll have to file an official complaint, I guess. So sorry to barge in. I can see you were very busy running your household. If you'll excuse me, I'd better go try to earn my keep so you might actually blink an eye the next time you find a convenient way to get rid of me."

She marched into the hallway. Iko was poking her shiny head out of the kitchen, her blue sensor bright with astonishment. Cinder was amazed at how quickly her emotions switched from bitter to relieved. For a time, she'd thought she would never see Iko again.

The momentary joy faded when Adri bustled into the hallway behind her. "Cinder, stop."

Though tempted to ignore her, Cinder did stop and turn back to face her guardian.

They stared at each other, Adri's jaw working as she stumbled over her surprise. She looked old. Years older than she had before.

"I will be contacting the research facility to check your story and make sure you aren't lying about this," she said. "If you did something . . . if you ruined this one chance I had to help my daughter—" The anger in Adri's voice broke, then rose into shrill yelling. Cinder could hear her burying tears beneath her words. "You cannot be that useless!" She pulled her shoulders back, gripping the doorjamb.

"What else do you want me to do?" Cinder yelled back, flailing her hands. "Fine, contact the researchers! I didn't do anything wrong. I went there, they ran some tests, and they didn't want me. I'm so sorry if they didn't ship me home in a cardboard box, if that's what you were hoping for."

Adri pulled her lips taut. "Your position in this household has not changed, and I do not appreciate being spoken to in such a disrespectful manner by the *orphan* that I accepted into my home."

"Really?" said Cinder. "Would you like me to list all the things *I* didn't appreciate being done to me today? I've had needles poked at me and prongs stuck in my head and poisonous microbes—" She caught herself, not wanting Adri to know the truth. Her true value. "Honestly, I don't care so much what you do and don't appreciate right now. You're the one who betrayed me, when I've never done anything to you."

"That is enough. You know very well what you've done to me. To this family."

"Garan's death wasn't my fault." She turned her head away, angry white spots flecking in her vision.

"Fine," said Adri, her voice losing none of its superiority. "So you've returned. Welcome home, Cinder. But so long as you continue to live in my home, you will continue to obey my orders. Do you understand?"

Cinder planted her cyborg hand against the wall, fingers splayed out, grounding herself. "Obey your orders. Right. Like, 'Do the chores, Cinder. Get a job so I can pay *my* bills, Cinder. Go play lab rat for these deranged scientists, Cinder.' Yes, I understand you perfectly." She glanced back over her shoulder, but Iko had ducked back into the kitchen. "As I'm sure *you* will understand that I just lost half a day of perfectly good work hours, and I'd better borrow your Serv9.2 to get caught up. You don't mind, do you?" Without waiting for a response, she stormed back to her closet of a bedroom and slammed the door behind her.

She stood with her back against the door until the warning text on her retina had gone away and her hands stopped shaking. When she opened her eyes, she found that the old netscreen, the one Adri had shoved off the wall, had been heaped on the pile of blankets she called a bed. Bits of plastic had spilled over onto her pillow.

She hadn't noticed if Adri had already bought them a new one or if the living room wall was empty.

Sighing, she changed her clothes, eager to be rid of the smell of antiseptic that lingered on them. She shoved the spare plastic pieces into her toolbox and tucked the screen beneath one arm before venturing back out into the apartment. Iko hadn't moved, half-hidden in the kitchen doorway. Cinder cocked her head toward the front of the apartment, and the android followed.

She did not look into the living room as she passed, but she thought she heard the strangled sound of Prince Kai dying from Pearl's game.

They had barely stepped out into the main corridor—fairly

quiet for once with the neighbor children off at school—when Iko wrapped her gangly arms around Cinder's legs. "How is this possible? I was sure you'd be killed. What happened?"

Cinder handed the toolbox to the robot and headed for the elevators. "I'll tell you everything, but we have work to do." She waited until they were alone and on their way to the basement before filling Iko in on all that had happened, leaving out only the part about Prince Kai coming in and finding her unconscious on the floor.

"You mean you have to go back?" said Iko as they stepped out into the basement.

"Yes, but it's fine. The doctor said I'm not in any danger now. Plus, they're going to pay me, and Adri won't know about it."

"How much?"

"I'm not sure, but a lot, I think."

Iko grabbed Cinder's wrist just as Cinder opened the chicken wire door to her workroom. "You realize what this means?"

Cinder held the door open with her foot. "Which part?"

"It means you can afford a pretty dress—*prettier* than Pearl's! You can go to the ball, and Adri won't be able to say anything to stop you!"

Cinder pressed her lips together like she'd just bitten a lemon and pulled her wrist from Iko's grip. "Really, Iko?" she said, examining her mess of tools and spare parts. "You really think Adri's going to let me go now just because I can buy my own dress? She would probably tear it off me and try to resell the buttons."

"Well—fine, we won't tell her about the dress or about going to the ball. You don't have to go with them. You're better than them. You're *valuable.*" Iko's fan was whirring like mad as if her processor could barely keep up with all these revelations. "Immune to letumosis. My stars, you could be a celebrity because of this!"

Cinder ignored her, stooping to prop the netscreen against the shelving unit. Her gaze had landed on a pile of silver fabric crumpled in the far corner, barely shimmering in the dusty light. "What's that?"

Iko's fan calmed to a slow hum. "Peony's ball gown. I . . . I couldn't bring myself to throw it away. I didn't think anyone would ever come down here again, what with you . . . so I just thought I'd keep it. For myself."

"That was bad, Iko. It could have been infected." Cinder hesitated only for a moment before walking to the dress and picking it up by the pearl-dotted sleeves. It was smudged with dirt and covered in wrinkles, and there *was* a chance it had been exposed to letumosis, but the doctor had said the disease wouldn't survive long on clothing.

Besides, nobody was ever going to wear it now.

She draped the gown over the welder and turned away. "We're not using this money on a dress," she said. "We're still not going to the ball."

"Why not?" Iko said, a distinct whine in her robotic voice.

Approaching her desk, Cinder swung her leg up and started unloading the stashed tools from her calf. "You remember that car we saw at the junkyard? The old gasoline one?"

Iko's speakers made a coarse grumbling noise, the closest she could get to a groan. "What about it?"

"It's going to take all our time and money to fix it up."

"No. Cinder! Tell me you're joking."

Cinder was recording a mental list as she shut the storage compartment and rolled down her pant leg. The words scrolled across her vision. **GET CAR. ASSESS CONDITION. FIND PARTS. DOWNLOAD WIRING BLUEPRINT. ORDER GASOLINE.**

She spotted Kai's android on her worktable. **FIX ANDROID.** "I am serious."

She pulled her hair back into its tight ponytail, strangely excited. Marching to the standing toolbox in the corner, she started fishing for things that might come in handy—bungee cords and chains, rags and generators, anything to help get that car cleaned up and ready for fixing. "We're going to go back tonight. Get it to the parking garage if we can, otherwise we might have to fix it at the yard. Now, I need to go back to the palace tomorrow morning and take a look at the prince's android tomorrow afternoon, but if we're diligent, I think I could have it fixed in a couple weeks, maybe less. Depending on what it needs, of course."

"But *why?* Why are we fixing it?"

Cinder shoved the tools into her messenger bag. "Because that car is going to get us out of here."

Sixteen

NIGHTSHIFT NURSES AND ANDROIDS PLASTERED THEMSELVES to the walls as Prince Kai barreled through the corridor. He had run all the way from his bedroom on the sixteenth floor of the palace's private wing, pausing to catch his breath only when he was forced to wait for the elevator. He burst through the door to the visiting room and came to a halt all at once, still gripping the door's handle.

His mad eyes found Torin, arms crossed as he leaned against the far wall. The adviser tore his gaze from the glass window and met Kai's panicked expression with one of resignation.

"I heard—" Kai started, pulling back his shoulders. Wetting his dry mouth, he came into the room. The door clicked behind him. The small sitting room was lit only by a table lamp and the bright fluorescents in the quarantine.

Kai peered into the sickroom just as a med-droid pulled a white cloth over his father's closed eyes. His hammering heart plummeted. "I'm too late."

Torin stirred. "It happened only minutes ago," he said,

forcing himself away from the wall. Kai took in the adviser's lined face and sleepless eyes, and a cup of untouched tea that sat beside his portscreen. He'd stayed late to work, rather than return to his own home, his own bed.

The exhaustion caught up to Kai all at once and he pressed his burning forehead against the cool glass. He should have been there too.

"I will set up a press conference." Torin's voice was hollow.

"A *press* conference?"

"The country needs to know. We will mourn together." Torin seemed shaken for a rare moment—he covered it with a measured breath.

Kai squeezed his eyes shut and chafed them with his fingers. Even knowing that it was coming, that his father was sick with this incurable disease, it still made no sense. All that had just been lost, taken so quickly. Not just his father. Not just the emperor.

His youth. His freedom.

"You will be a good emperor," said Torin. "As he was."

Kai flinched away from him. He did not want to think about it, all of his own inadequacies. He was too young, too stupid, too optimistic, too naive. He couldn't do this.

The screen behind them pinged, followed by a sweetly feminine voice: "Incoming communication for Crown Prince Kaito of the Eastern Commonwealth from Queen Levana of Luna."

Kai spun toward the netscreen, blank but for a spinning globe in the corner, signaling an available comm. Any threat of tears vanished into an oncoming headache. The air thickened, but neither of them moved.

"How could she know? So soon?" said Kai. "She must have spies."

From the corner of his eye, he saw Torin level a glare at him. A warning not to start in on the conspiracy theories just yet. "Perhaps the thaumaturge or her guard saw you," he said. "Running through the castle in the middle of the night. What else could it mean?"

Locking his jaw, Kai drew himself to his full height, hailing the screen like an enemy. "I guess our mourning period is over," he murmured. "Screen, accept comm."

The screen brightened. Kai bristled at the sight of the Lunar Queen, her head and shoulders draped in an ornate cream-colored veil, like a perpetual bride. All that could be seen beneath the shroud was a hint of long dark hair and the ghost of her features. The explanation told by the Lunars was that their queen's beauty was a gift not to be seen by undeserving Earthens, but Kai had heard that in reality the queen's glamour—her ability to make people see her as divinely beautiful by manipulating their brain waves—could not translate over the netscreens, therefore she never allowed herself to be seen over them.

Whatever the reason, looking at the white-swathed figure for too long always made Kai's eyes sting.

"My dear Prince Regent," Levana said in a saccharine voice, "may I be the first to offer my condolences on the loss of your father, the good Emperor Rikan. May he forever rest in peace."

Kai cast a cool glare at Torin. *Spies?*

Torin did not return the look.

"Though the occasion is tragic, I do look forward to continuing the talk of an alliance with you, as the new leader of Earth's Eastern Commonwealth. As I see no reason to defer these conversations until your coronation, whensoever that shall be, I do think it appropriate to plan a meeting as soon as is convenient in your time of mourning. My shuttle is prepared. I can depart as soon as your next sunrise and come to offer both my sympathies and my congratulations in the flesh. I will alert my thaumaturge to expect my arrival. She can ensure that accommodations are adequately prepared. I ask that you do not concern yourself with my comfort. I am sure you will have many other concerns during this tragic time. My sympathies are with you and the Commonwealth." She finished her message with a tilt of her head and the screen blackened.

Jaw hanging, Kai faced Torin. He squeezed his fists against his sides before they could start to shake. "She wants to come *here*? Now? It hasn't even been fifteen minutes!"

Torin cleared his throat. "We should discuss this in the morning. Before the press conference, I suppose."

Kai turned away, thunking his head against the window. Beyond the glass, the peaks of his father's body were obscured beneath the white sheet, not unlike the queen and her veil. The emperor had lost so much weight in the past weeks that his form seemed more like a mannequin's than a man's.

His father was no longer there. Unable to protect Kai. Unable to offer advice. Unable to lead his country ever again.

"She thinks I'm weak," Kai said. "She's going to try and persuade me to accept the marriage alliance now, while everything is in chaos." He kicked the wall, biting back a cry of pain when he remembered he wasn't wearing shoes. "Can't we tell her no? Tell her she's not welcome here?"

"I'm not sure that would be the indication of peace your father had been striving for."

"*She's* the one who's been threatening war for the last twelve years!"

Torin pursed his lips, and the haunting worry in his gaze quelled Kai's anger. "Discussions must go two ways, Your Highness. We will listen to her requests, but she must listen to ours as well."

Kai's shoulders drooped. He turned around, craning his head back and staring at the shadowed ceiling. "What did she mean, her thaumaturge will prepare her accommodations?"

"Removing the mirrors, I suspect."

Kai squeezed his eyes shut. "Mirrors. Right. I forgot." He massaged his forehead. What was it about the Lunars? And not just any Lunar. Queen Levana. On Earth. In his country, his *home.* He shivered. "The people aren't going to like this."

"No." Torin sighed. "Tomorrow will be a dark day for the Commonwealth."

Seventeen

A PING DARTED THROUGH CINDER'S HEAD, FOLLOWED BY A message scrolled across the blackness of sleep.

COMM RECEIVED FROM NEW BEIJING DISTRICT 29, LETUMOSIS QUARANTINE. LINH PEONY ENTERED THIRD STAGE OF LETUMOSIS AT 04:57 ON 17 AUG 126 T.E.

It took a minute to shake off the grogginess of sleep and make sense of the scrawling words. She opened her eyes to the windowless bedroom and sat up. All her muscles ached from the midnight trip to the junkyard. Her back hurt so bad it felt as though that old car had run her over, rather than sat in neutral while she and Iko pushed and pulled it through the back roads. But they had succeeded. The car was hers, moved to a dark corner of the apartment's underground parking garage, where she'd be able to work on it every spare moment. As long as no one complained about the smell, it would remain her and Iko's little secret.

When they'd finally returned home, Cinder had crashed like someone had hit her power button. For once, she'd had no nightmares.

At least, no nightmares until the message woke her.

The thought of Peony all alone in the quarantines spurred her out of her pile of blankets with a stifled groan. She pulled on a pair of gloves, stole a green brocade blanket from the linen closet in the hall, and passed Iko—set to conservation mode and connected to a charging station in the living room. It felt strange leaving without the android, but she planned on going straight to the palace afterward.

In the apartment corridor, she could hear someone pacing on the next floor and a netscreen mumbling the morning news. Cinder commed a hover for the first time in her life, and it was ready for her by the time she got down to the street. She scanned her ID and gave it the quarantine's coordinates before settling into the far back. Cinder netlinked so she could trace the hover's path to the quarantine. The map that overlaid her vision indicated it was in the industrial district, fifteen miles outside the city limits.

The city was all shadows, blurry, sleepy apartments and empty sidewalks. The buildings grew shorter with more space between them as the heart of the city was left behind. Pale sunlight crawled down the streets, sending long shadows across the pavement.

Cinder knew they'd reached the industrial district without the map's help. She blinked it away and watched the factories roll by alongside squat concrete warehouses with gigantic roll-up doors that could accommodate even the largest hover. Probably even cargo ships.

Cinder scanned her ID as she exited so the hover could debit her nearly depleted account, then ordered it to wait for her. She headed toward the nearest warehouse where a group of androids stood by the door. Above the door was a brand-new netscreen flashing,

LETUMOSIS QUARANTINE. PATIENTS AND ANDROIDS ONLY BEYOND THIS POINT.

She draped the blanket over her forearms and tried to look confident as she walked, wondering what she would say if the androids questioned her. But the med-droids must not have been programmed to deal with *healthy* people coming into the quarantines; they hardly even noticed her as she passed. She hoped it would be as easy to leave. Perhaps she should have asked Dr. Erland for a pass.

The stench of excrement and rot reached out to her as she stepped into the warehouse. She reeled back, cupping her palm over her nose as her stomach churned, wishing her brain interface could dull odors as easily as it could noise.

Sucking in a breath through her glove and holding it, she forced herself into the warehouse.

It was cooler inside, the concrete floor untouched by the sun. Opaque green plastic covered a thin row of windows near the high ceilings, swathing the building in a dingy haze. Gray lightbulbs hummed overhead, but they did little to dispel the darkness.

Hundreds of beds were lined up between the distant walls, covered in mismatched blankets—donations and scraps. She was glad to have brought a nice one for Peony. Most of the beds sat empty. This quarantine had been hastily constructed in just the past weeks as the sickness crept closer to the city. Still, the flies had already caught on and filled the room with buzzing.

The few patients Cinder passed were sleeping or staring blankly up at the ceiling, their skin covered in a blue-black rash. Those who still had their senses were hunkered over portscreens—their last connection to the outside world. Glossy eyes looked up, following Cinder as she hurried by.

More med-droids moved between the beds, supplying food and water, but none of them stopped Cinder.

She found Peony asleep, tangled in a baby blue blanket. Cinder wasn't sure she would have recognized her if it hadn't been for the chestnut curls draped over the pillow. The purplish blotches had spread up her arms. Though she was shivering, her forehead glistened with sweat. She looked like an old woman, just this side of death.

Cinder removed her glove and placed the back of her hand against Peony's forehead. Warm to the touch and damp. The third stage of letumosis.

She spread the green blanket over Peony, then stood, wondering if she should wake her or if it was better to let her rest.

Rocking back on her heels, she looked around. The bed behind her was empty. The one on the opposite side of Peony was occupied by a petite form turned away from her, curled in a fetal position. A child.

Cinder started as she felt a tug on her left wrist. Peony was gripping her steel fingers, squeezing with the little strength she had left. Her eyes watched Cinder, pleading. Afraid. Awed, as if Peony were seeing a ghost.

Cinder swallowed hard and sat down on the bed. It was almost as hard as the floor in her own bedroom.

"Take me home?" Peony said, her voice scratching at the words.

Cinder flinched. She covered Peony's hand. "I brought you a blanket," she said, as if it explained her presence.

Peony's gaze fell from her. Her free hand traced the texture of the brocade. They said nothing for a long time, until a shrill scream reached them. Peony's hands clenched as Cinder spun around, searching, sure someone was being murdered.

A woman four aisles away was thrashing in her bed, screeching, begging to be left alone as a calm med-droid waited to inject her with a syringe. A minute later, two more androids arrived to hold the woman still, forcing her down on the bed, holding her arm out to receive the shot.

Feeling Peony curl up beside her, Cinder turned back. Peony was shaking.

"I'm being punished for something," Peony said, shutting her eyes.

"Don't be ridiculous," Cinder said. "The plague, it's just . . . it isn't fair. I know. But you didn't do anything wrong."

She patted the girl's hand.

"Are Mom and Pearl . . . ?"

"Heartbroken," said Cinder. "We all miss you so much. But they haven't caught it."

Peony's eyes flickered open. She scanned Cinder's face, her neck. "Where are your spots?"

Lips parting, Cinder rubbed absently at her throat, but Peony didn't wait for an answer. "You can sleep there, right?" she said, gesturing to the empty bed. "They won't give you a bed far away?"

Cinder squeezed Peony's hands. "No, Peony, I'm not . . ." She looked around but no one was paying them any attention. A med-droid two beds away was helping a patient take a drink of water. "I'm not sick."

Peony listed her head. "You're here."

"I know. It's complicated. You see, I went to the letumosis research center yesterday, and they tested me and . . . Peony, I'm immune. I can't get letumosis."

Peony's tense brow melted. She scanned Cinder's face, neck, arms again, as if her immunity were something visible, something that should have been apparent. "Immune?"

Cinder rubbed Peony's hand more quickly, anxious now that she'd told someone her secret. "They asked me to go back again today. The head doctor thinks he might be able to use me to find an antidote. I told him that if he finds anything,

anything at all, you have to be the first person to get it. I made him promise."

She watched, amazed, as Peony's eyes began to fill with tears. "Really?"

"Absolutely. We're going to find one."

"How long will it take?"

"I-I'm not sure."

Peony's other hand found her wrist and squeezed. Her long nails dug into Cinder's skin, but it took her a long time to register the pain. Peony's breath had grown rapid. More tears pooled in her eyes, but some of the instant hope had faded, leaving her wild with desperation. "Don't let me die, Cinder. I wanted to go to the ball. Remember? You were going to introduce me to Prince—" She turned her head, scrunching her face up in a vain attempt to hold in the tears, or hide them, or squeeze them out faster. Then a harsh cough burst from her mouth, along with a thin trail of blood.

Cinder grimaced, then reached forward and swiped the blood off Peony's chin with the corner of the brocade blanket. "Don't give up, Peony. If I'm immune, then there has to be a way to defeat it. And they're going to find it. You're still going to the ball." She considered telling Peony that Iko had managed to save her dress, but realized that would require telling her that everything else she'd ever touched was gone. She cleared her throat and stroked Peony's hair off her temple. "Is there anything I can do to make you more comfortable?"

Peony shook her head against the worn pillow, holding the

blanket against her mouth. But then she raised her eyes. "My portscreen?"

Cinder flinched with guilt. "I'm sorry. It's still broken. But I'll look at it tonight."

"I just want to comm Pearl. And Mom."

"Of course. I'll bring it to you, as soon as I can." *Peony's portscreen. The prince's android. The car.* "I'm so sorry, Peony, but I need to go."

The small hands tightened.

"I'll be back as soon as I can. I promise."

Peony took in a shaky breath, sniffed, then released her. She dug her frail hands beneath the blanket, burying herself up to her chin.

Cinder stood and untangled Peony's hair with her fingers. "Try to get some sleep. Reserve your strength."

Peony followed Cinder with her watery gaze. "I love you, Cinder. I'm glad you're not sick."

Cinder's heart tightened. Pursing her lips, she bent over and placed a kiss against Peony's damp forehead. "I love you too."

She struggled to breathe as she forced herself to walk away, trying to trick herself into being hopeful. There was a chance. A chance.

She didn't look at any of the other patients as she made her way to the quarantine's exit, but then she heard her name. She paused, thinking that the sandpaper voice had been nothing more than her imagination mixed with too many hysterical cries.

"Cin-der?"

She turned and spotted a familiar face half-covered by an age-bleached quilt.

"Chang-jiě?" She neared the foot of the bed, nose wrinkling at the pungent odor wafting from the woman's bed. Chang Sacha, the market baker, was barely recognizable with her swollen eyelids and sallow skin.

Trying to breathe normally, Cinder rounded the bed.

The quilt that rested across Sacha's nose and mouth shifted with her belabored breathing. Her eyes were glossy, as wide as Cinder had ever seen them. It was the only time she could remember Sacha looking at her without disdain. "You too? Cinder?"

Instead of answering, Cinder said, uncertainly, "Can I do anything for you?"

They were the kindest words that had ever passed between them. The blanket shifted, inching down Sacha's face. Cinder bit back a gasp at seeing the blue-ringed splotches on the woman's jaw and down her throat.

"My son," she said, wheezing each word. "Bring Sunto? I need to see him."

Cinder didn't move, remembering how Sacha had ordered Sunto away from her booth days before. "Bring him?"

Sacha snaked one arm out from beneath the blankets and reached toward Cinder, grasping her wrist where skin met metal. Cinder squirmed, trying to pull away, but Sacha held tight. Her hand was marked by bluish pigment around her yellowed fingernails.

The fourth and final stage of the blue fever.

"I will try," she said. She reached up, hesitated, then pet Sacha on the knuckles. The blue fingers released her and sank to the bed.

"Sunto," Sacha murmured. Her gaze was still locked on Cinder's face, but the recognition had faded. "Sunto."

Cinder stepped back, watching as the words dried up. The life dulled in Sacha's black eyes.

Cinder convulsed, tying her arms around her stomach. She looked around. None of the other patients were paying any attention to her or the woman—the corpse—beside her. But then she saw the android rolling toward them. The med-droids must be linked somehow, she thought, to know when someone dies.

How long did it take for the notification comm to be sent to the family? How long would it be before Sunto knew he was motherless?

She wanted to turn away, to leave, but she felt rooted to the spot as the android wheeled up beside the bed and took Sacha's limp hand between its grippers. Sacha's complexion was ashen but for the bruised blotches on her jaw. Her eyes were still open, turned toward the heavens.

Perhaps the med-droid would have questions for Cinder. Perhaps someone would want to know the woman's final words. Her son might want to know. Cinder should tell someone.

But the med-droid's sensor did not turn toward her.

Cinder licked her lips. She opened her mouth but could think of nothing to say.

A panel opened in the body of the med-droid. It reached

in with its free prongs and pulled out a scalpel. Cinder watched, mesmerized and disgusted, as the android pressed the blade into Sacha's wrist. A stream of blood dripped down Sacha's palm.

Cinder shook herself from her stupor and stumbled forward. The foot of the bed pressed into her thighs. "What are you doing?" she said, louder than she'd meant to.

The med-droid paused with the scalpel buried in Sacha's flesh. Its yellow visor flashed toward Cinder, then dimmed. "How can I help you?" it said with its manufactured politeness.

"What are you doing to her?" she asked again. She wanted to reach out and snatch the scalpel away, but feared she misunderstood. There must be a reason, something logical. Med-droids were all logic.

"Removing her ID chip," said the android.

"Why?"

The visor flashed again, and the android returned its focus to Sacha's wrist. "She has no more use for it." The med-droid traded the scalpel for tweezers, and Cinder heard the subtle click of metal on metal. She grimaced as the android extracted the small chip. Its protective plastic coating glistened scarlet.

"But . . . don't you need it to identify the body?"

The android dropped the chip into a tray that opened up in its plastic plating. Cinder saw it fall into a bed of dozens of other bloodied chips.

It drew the tattered blanket over Sacha's unblinking eyes. Instead of answering her question, it said simply, "I have been programmed to follow instructions."

Eighteen

A MED-DROID ROLLED INTO CINDER'S PATH AS SHE EXITED the warehouse, blocking her way with outstretched spindly arms. "Patients are strictly forbidden from leaving the quarantine area," it said, nudging Cinder back into the shadows of the doorway.

Cinder swallowed her panic and halted the robot with a palm against its smooth forehead. "I'm not a patient," she said. "I'm not even sick. Here." She held out her elbow, displaying a small bruise from being stuck with too many needles the past two days.

The android's innards hummed as it processed her statement, searching its database for a logical reaction. Then a panel opened in its torso and the third arm, the syringe arm, extended toward Cinder. She flinched, her skin tender, but tried to relax as the android drew a fresh sample of blood. The syringe disappeared into the android's body and Cinder waited, rolling her sleeve down over the hem of her glove.

The test seemed to take longer than at the junkyard, and a sinking panic was crawling up Cinder's spine—what if Dr. Erland had been wrong?—when she heard a low beep and the android backed away, clearing her path.

She released her breath and did not look back at the robot or any of its companions as she crossed the hot asphalt. The hover was still waiting for her. Settling into the backseat, she told it to take her to New Beijing Palace.

Having been unconscious the first time she'd been brought to the palace, Cinder found herself plastered to the hover's window as she was taken up the steep winding road to the top of the harsh cliffs that bordered the city. Her netlink fished for information, telling her that the palace had been built after World War IV, when the city was little more than rubble. It was designed in the fashion of the old world, with hearty dosages of both nostalgic symbolism and state-of-the-art engineering. The pagoda-style roofs were made of gold-tinged tiles and surrounded by *qilin* gargoyles, but the tiles were actually galvanized steel covered with tiny solar capsules that created enough energy to sustain the entire palace, including the research wing, and the gargoyles were equipped with motion sensors, ID scanners, 360-degree cameras, and radars that could detect approaching aircrafts and hovers within a sixty-mile radius. All that was invisible, though, the technology hidden in the ornately carved beams and tiered pavilions.

What captured Cinder's eye was not modern technology but a cobblestoned road lined with cherry blossom trees. Bamboo screens framing the garden entrances. Through a peep window, a steadily trickling stream.

The hover did not stop at the main entrance with its crimson pergolas. Instead, it rounded to the northern side of the palace, nearest the research wing. Though this part of the palace was more modern, less nostalgic, Cinder still noticed a squat Buddha sculpture with a cheery face off the pathway. As she paid for the hover and walked toward the automatic glass door, a subtle pulse tugged at her ankle—Buddha scanning visitors for weapons. To her relief, the steel in her leg did not set off any alarms.

Inside, she was greeted by an android who asked for her name and told her to wait in the elevator bank. The research center was a hive of activity—diplomats and doctors, ambassadors and androids, all roaming the halls on their separate missions.

An elevator opened and Cinder stepped into it, glad to be alone. The doors began to close, but then paused and opened again. "Please hold," said the mechanical voice of the elevator operator.

A moment later, Prince Kai darted through the half-open doors. "Sorry, sorry, thanks for hold—"

He saw her and froze. "Linh-mèi?"

Cinder pushed herself off the elevator wall and fell into the most natural bow she could, simultaneously checking that her left glove was pulled up over her wrist. "Your Highness." The words were a rush, spit out automatically, and she felt the need to say something more, to fill the space of the elevator, but nothing came.

The doors closed; the box began to rise.

She cleared her throat. "You should, um, just call me Cinder. You don't have to be so—" *Diplomatic.*

The corner of the prince's lip quirked, but the almost smile didn't reach his eyes. "All right. Cinder. Are you following me?"

She frowned, hackles rising before she realized he was teasing her. "I'm just going to check on the med-droid. That I looked at yesterday. To ensure it doesn't have any remaining bugs or anything."

He nodded, but Cinder detected a shadow lingering behind his eyes, a new stiffness to his shoulders. "I was on my way to talk to Dr. Erland about his progress. I heard through the grapevine that he may have made progress with one of the recent draft subjects. I don't suppose he said anything to you?"

Cinder fidgeted with her belt loops. "No, he didn't mention anything. But I'm just the mechanic."

The elevator came to a stop. Kai gestured for her to exit first and then joined her as they made their way to the laboratories. She watched the white floor pass beneath her feet.

"Your Highness?" interrupted a youngish woman with black hair that hung in a tight braid. Her gaze was fixed on Prince Kai, all sympathy. "I am so sorry."

Cinder's gaze shifted to Kai, who tipped his head at the woman. "Thank you, Fateen." And kept walking.

Cinder frowned.

Not a dozen steps later, they were halted again by a man carrying a handful of clear vials in his fists. "My condolences, Your Highness."

Cinder shivered as her feet came to a pause beneath her.

Kai stopped and peered back at her. "You haven't seen the net this morning."

A heartbeat later, Cinder was accessing her netlink, pages flashing across her eyesight. The EC news page, a half-dozen pictures of Emperor Rikan, two pictures of Kai—the prince regent.

She clapped a hand to her mouth.

Kai seemed surprised, but the look quickly faded. He ducked his head, his black bangs falling into his eyes. "Good guess."

"I'm so sorry. I didn't know."

He tucked his hands into his pockets and gazed down the hallway. Only now did Cinder notice the faint rim of red around his eyes.

"I wish my father's death were the worst of it."

"Your Highness?" Her netlink was still scanning for information, but nothing seemed worse than Emperor Rikan having passed away last night. The only other noteworthy tidbit was that Prince Kai's coronation had been scheduled for the same evening of the Peace Festival, to take place before the ball.

He met her gaze, surprised, as if he'd forgotten who he was speaking with. Then, "You can call me Kai."

She blinked. "Excuse me?"

"No more 'Your Highness.' I get enough of that from... everyone else. You should just call me Kai."

"No. That wouldn't be—"

"Don't make me turn it into a royal command." He hinted at a smile.

Cinder scrunched her shoulders up by her ears, suddenly embarrassed. "All right. I suppose."

"Thank you." He cocked his head toward the hall. "We should go, then."

She had nearly forgotten that they were in the research hall, surrounded by people, everyone politely ignoring them as if they were not even there. She started down the hallway, wondering if she'd spoken out of place, and awkward beside the prince who was suddenly *just Kai.* It didn't feel right.

"What was wrong with the android?"

She scratched at an oil stain on her glove. "Oh, I'm sorry. She's not done yet. I'm working on her, I swear."

"No, I meant the med-droid. That you fixed for Dr. Erland?"

"Oh. Oh, right. Um. It was... it had... a... dead wire. Between its optosensor and... control panel." Kai lifted an eyebrow and she wasn't sure that she'd convinced him. She cleared her throat. "You, uh, said something was worse? Before?"

When Kai said nothing for an awkward moment, she shrugged. "Never mind. I didn't mean to pry."

"No, it's all right. You'll find out soon enough." He lowered his voice, inclining his head toward her as they walked. "The Lunar queen informed us this morning that she is coming to the Commonwealth on a diplomatic mission. Supposedly."

Cinder nearly tripped, but Kai kept walking. She stumbled after him. "The Lunar queen is coming here? You can't be serious."

"I wish I weren't. Every android in the palace has spent the morning taking down every reflective surface in the guest wing. It's ridiculous—like we have nothing better to do."

"Reflective surfaces? I always thought that was just superstition."

"Evidently not. Something about their glamour . . ." He twirled a finger around his face, then stopped. "It doesn't really matter."

"When is she coming?"

"Today."

Cinder's stomach plummeted. The Lunar queen? Coming to New Beijing? A chill crawled down her arms.

"I'll be making an announcement in half an hour."

"But why would she come now, when we're in mourning?"

A grim smile. "*Because* we're in mourning."

Kai paused. With a glance around the hallway, he inched toward Cinder, lowering his voice. "Look, I really appreciate your helping with the med-droids, and I'm sure the best mechanic in the city has a million jobs to prioritize, but at the risk of sounding like a spoiled prince, could I ask that you move Nainsi to the top of your list? I'm starting to get anxious about getting her back. I—" He hesitated. "I think I could use the moral support of my childhood tutor right now. You know?" The intensity in his eyes did not try to hide his true meaning. He wanted her to know he was lying. This had nothing to do with moral support or childhood attachments.

The panic behind the prince's eyes spoke volumes. What information could that android have that was so important? And what did it have to do with the Lunar queen?

"Of course, Your Highness. Sorry, Prince Kai. I'll take a look at her as soon as I get home."

She thought she spotted gratitude hidden somewhere beneath all his worry. Kai gestured at a door beside him, labeled DR. DMITRI ERLAND. He opened the door and ushered her in.

Dr. Erland was sitting at a lacquered desk, poring over a screen set into the surface. When he spotted Kai, he leaped to his feet, simultaneously snatching up his wool cap and rounding the desk toward them.

"Your Highness—I am so sorry. What can I do to help you?"

"Nothing, thank you," said Kai, a practiced reaction. Then he pulled his shoulders back, reconsidering. "Find a cure."

"I will, Your Highness." He pulled his hat on. "Of course I will." The conviction in the doctor's face was almost startling, but also comforting. Cinder immediately wondered if he'd found something new in the hours since she'd last seen him.

She thought of Peony, alone in the quarantine. Though it was an awful thing to think, and she immediately chastised herself for it, she couldn't help it—with Emperor Rikan dead, Peony was the first in line for an antidote.

Kai cleared his throat. "I found your pretty new mechanic down in the lobby, and she tells me she's here to check on the med-droids again. You know I could get you funding for some upgraded models if you require it."

Cinder started at that simple word—*pretty*—but neither Kai nor Dr. Erland looked at her. Teetering on her feet, she scanned the room. A floor-to-ceiling window captured a perfect view of the lush palace gardens and the city beyond. Open shelves were filled with objects both familiar and unusual, new and ancient. A stack of books—not portscreens, but solid, paper books. Jars filled with leaves and dried flowers, jars filled with finely labeled liquids, jars filled with animal specimens and formaldehyde. A series of rocks and metals and ores, all finely labeled.

It was the office of a witch doctor as much as an acclaimed royal scientist.

"No, no, they only needed a touch of maintenance," Dr. Erland was saying, lying as smoothly as he had the day before. "Nothing to worry about, and I would hate to have to program a new model. Besides, if we didn't have any malfunctioning androids, what excuse would we have for asking Miss Linh back to the palace from time to time?"

Cinder glared at the doctor, half-mortified, but the start of a smile grew on Kai's face.

"Doctor," said Kai, "I heard a rumor that you've made some sort of a breakthrough in the past few days. Is it true?"

Dr. Erland pulled the spectacles from his pocket and set to cleaning them with the hem of his lab coat. "My prince, you should know better than to ask after rumors like that. I hate to give you hope before I know anything concrete. But when I do have solid information, you will be the first to see the report." He slid the glasses onto his nose.

Kai tucked his hands into his pockets, seemingly satisfied. "Right. In that case, I'll leave you be and hope to see a report cross my desk any day now."

"That could be difficult, Your Highness, considering you do not have a desk."

Kai shrugged and turned to Cinder. His eyes softened a little with a polite bow of his head. "I hope our paths will cross again."

"Really? In that case, I guess I'll keep following you." She regretted the joke for half a breath before Kai laughed. A real laugh, and her chest warmed.

Then the prince reached for her hand—her cyborg hand.

Cinder tensed, terrified that he would feel the hard metal, even through her gloves, and yet even more afraid to pull away lest he find it suspicious. She mentally urged the robotic limb to go soft, to be pliant, to be *human*, as she watched Kai lift the hand and kiss the back of it. She held her breath, overwhelmed and embarrassed.

The prince released her, bowed—his hair falling into his eyes again—and left the room.

Cinder stood frozen, her wired nerves humming.

She heard Dr. Erland grunt in curiosity, but the door opened again as soon as it had closed.

"Gracious," Dr. Erland muttered as Kai stepped back inside.

"Pardon me, but might I have one more brief word with Linh-mèi?"

Dr. Erland flicked his wrist toward her. "By all means."

Kai turned to her, still in the doorway. "I know this sounds like very poor timing, but trust me when I say my motives are based on self-preservation." He inhaled a sharp breath. "Would you consider being my personal guest at the ball?"

The floor dissolved beneath Cinder. Her mind blanked. Surely, she hadn't heard correctly.

But he just stood, patient, and after a long moment raised both his eyebrows in a mute prompt.

"E-excuse me?"

Kai cleared his throat. Stood straighter. "I assume you are going to the ball?"

"I-I don't know. I mean, no. No, I'm sorry, I'm not going to the ball."

Kai drew back, confused. "Oh. Well . . . but . . . maybe you would change your mind? Because I am, you know."

"The prince."

"Not bragging," he said quickly. "Just a fact."

"I know." She gulped. The ball. Prince Kai was asking her to the ball. But that was the night she and Iko would be running away, if the car was fixed in time. The night she would escape.

Besides, he didn't know who, what, he was asking. If he knew the truth . . . how mortified would he be if anyone found out?

Kai shifted on his feet, casting a nervous glance toward the doctor.

"I-I'm sorry," she stammered. "Thank you—I . . . Thank you, Your Highness. But I must respectfully decline."

He blinked. His eyes fell as he processed her response. Then he lifted his chin and attempted a grin that was almost painfully dejected. "No, it's all right. I understand."

Dr. Erland leaned back against his desk. "My sincerest condolences, Your Highness. In more ways than one, it seems."

Cinder cast him a frosty glare, but he focused his attention on cleaning his spectacles again.

Kai scratched behind his neck. "It was nice to see you again, Linh-mèi."

She flinched at the return of the formality and made to speak, her voice catching at apologies, explanations, but the prince didn't wait for them. The door was already shutting behind him.

She snapped her jaw shut, thoughts sparking in her head. Dr. Erland clucked his tongue, and Cinder prepared to rail at him with those budding explanations, but he turned away before she could and paced back to his seat.

"What a shame you cannot blush, Miss Linh."

Nineteen

DR. ERLAND HELD BOTH HANDS TOWARD A CHAIR ON THE other side of his desk. "Please sit down. I only need to finish up a few notes, and then I will tell you some things I've learned since yesterday afternoon."

Cinder sat down, glad to get off her weak legs. "The prince just . . ."

"Yes. I was standing right here." Dr. Erland reclaimed his own seat and tapped at the screen in his desk.

Cinder leaned back against the chair, gripping its arms to quell her shaking. Her mind was replaying the conversation while her retina scanner informed her that her body was producing mass amounts of endorphins and she should try to calm down.

"What do you think he meant by his motives being based on self-preservation?"

"He probably doesn't want to be mauled by all the young ladies at the ball this year. You know there was nearly a stampede a couple years back."

She bit her lip. Of all the girls in the whole city, she was . . .

The most convenient.

She forced these words to resonate, to stick. She was here and she seemed to be sane and she was a safe bet for him to ask to the ball. That was all it could be.

Besides, he was in mourning. He wasn't thinking straight.

"Emperor Rikan is dead," she said, snatching for anything else to think about.

"Indeed. Prince Kai was close to his father, you know."

She lowered her gaze to the screen Dr. Erland was hunched over. She could see only a small diagram of a human torso, surrounded by boxes of dense text. It did not appear to be hers.

"I would be lying," Dr. Erland continued, "if I said that I had not harbored secret hopes of finding an antidote in time to save His Majesty, though I knew from the moment the diagnosis was made that it was unlikely. Nevertheless, we must proceed with our work."

She nodded in agreement, thinking of Peony's little hand gripping hers. "Doctor, why haven't you told the prince about me? Don't you want him to know that you've found someone who's immune? Isn't that important?"

He pressed his lips, but he didn't look up at her. "Perhaps I should. But it would be his responsibility to share the news with the country, and I don't think we're ready to draw attention to this. When we have solid evidence that you are . . . as valuable as I hope, then we will share our news with the prince. And the world."

She picked up a portscreen stylus that was lying abandoned

on the desk and examined it like a scientific mystery. Twirling it like a pinwheel over her fingers, she murmured, "You also didn't tell him I'm cyborg."

The doctor made eye contact now, his crow's-feet crinkling. "Ah. And that is what you're most concerned about?"

Before she could confirm or deny, Dr. Erland waved his hand as if to dismiss her defensiveness. "Do you think I *should* tell him you're a cyborg? I will if you want me to. But I frankly didn't see that it was any of his business."

Cinder dropped the stylus into her lap. "No, that isn't—I just—"

Dr. Erland snorted. He was laughing at her.

Cinder huffed in irritation and glared out the window. The city was almost blindingly bright in the morning sun. "Not like it matters. He'll find out eventually."

"Yes, I suppose he will. Especially if he continues to show, erm, *interest* in you." Dr. Erland pushed his chair back from the desk. "There. Your DNA sequencing has been completed. Shall we make our way to the lab room?"

She followed him into the sterile hallway. It was a short walk to the labs, and they entered lab room 11D this time, which looked exactly like lab room 4D: netscreen, built-in cabinets, a single exam table. No mirror.

Cinder sat down on the exam table without being told. "I went to the quarantines today . . . to visit my sister."

The doctor paused, his hand on the netscreen's power button. "That was something of a risk. You understand that people aren't supposed to *leave* once they arrive, don't you?"

"I know. But I had to see her." She swung her legs, beating her feet against the table's legs. "One of the med-droids ran a blood test on me before I left, and I was clear."

The doctor fiddled with the netscreen's controls. "Indeed."

"I just thought you should know, in case that might affect something."

"It doesn't." He stuck his tongue out the corner of his mouth. A second later, the screen blazed to life. His hands skimmed across the screen, pulling up Cinder's file. It was more complex today, filled with information even she didn't know about herself.

"And I saw something," she said.

The doctor grunted, more focused on the screen than her.

"One of the med-droids took an ID chip from a victim. After she died. The med-droid said it was programmed to take it. It had *dozens* of them."

Dr. Erland turned back to her with a mildly interested expression. He seemed to ponder this a moment, then his face slowly relaxed. "Well."

"Well what? Why would it do that?"

The doctor scratched his cheek, where a fine beard had started to grow across his leathery face. "It's a common practice in rural parts of the world—where letumosis has been claiming lives for much longer than it has in the cities. The chips are extracted from the deceased and sold off. Illegally, of course, but I understand they can fetch a high price."

"Why would anyone want to buy someone else's ID chip?"

"Because it is difficult making a living without one—money accounts, benefits, licenses, they all require an identity." He stitched his eyebrows. "Although, that brings up an interesting point. With all the letumosis fatalities the past few years, one would think the market is saturated with unneeded ID chips. It's curious that they would still be in demand."

"I know, but when you already *have* one . . ." She paused as his words sank in. Would it really be that easy to steal a person's identity?

"Unless you want to become someone else," he said, reading her thoughts. "Thieves. Fugitives of the law." The doctor rubbed his head through the hat. "The rare Lunar. They, of course, do not have ID chips to begin with."

"There aren't any Lunars on Earth. Well, other than ambassadors, I guess."

Dr. Erland's gaze filled with pity, as if she were a naive child. "Oh, yes. To Queen Levana's endless dismay, *not* all Lunars are so easily brainwashed into mindless contentment, and many have risked their lives to escape Luna and relocate here. It's difficult to leave the moon, and I'm sure many more die attempting it than succeed, especially as more restrictions are put on Lunar ports, but I'm sure it still happens."

"But . . . that's illegal. They're not supposed to be here at all. Why haven't we stopped them?"

For a moment, it looked as if Dr. Erland might laugh. "Escaping from Luna is difficult—getting to Earth is the easy part. Lunars have ways of cloaking their spacecrafts and making their way into Earth's atmosphere without detection."

Magic. Cinder fidgeted. "You make it sound like they're escaping from a prison."

Dr. Erland raised both eyebrows at her. "Yes. That seems exactly right."

Cinder kicked her boots against the lab table. The thought of Queen Levana coming to New Beijing had twisted her stomach—the thought of dozens, maybe even hundreds of Lunars living on Earth and impersonating Earthens nearly had her running for the sink. Those savages—with a programmed ID chip and their ability to brainwash people, they could be anyone, *become* anyone.

And Earthens would never know they were being manipulated.

"Don't look so frightened, Miss Linh. They mostly stick to the countrysides, where their presence is more likely to go unnoticed. The chances that you have ever crossed paths with one is extremely unlikely." He smiled, a teasing, close-lipped smile.

Cinder sat up straighter. "You sure seem to know a lot about them."

"I am an old man, Miss Linh. I know a lot about a lot of things."

"All right, here's a question. What's with Lunars and mirrors? I always thought it was just a myth that they're afraid of them, but . . . is it true?"

The doctor's eyebrows knit together. "It has some element of truth. You understand how Lunars make use of their glamours?"

"Not really."

"Ah. I see," he said, rocking back on his heels. "Well . . . the Lunar gift is nothing more than the ability to manipulate bioelectric energy—the energy that is naturally created by all living things. For example, it is the same energy that sharks use to detect their prey."

"Sounds like something Lunars would do."

The lines around the doctor's mouth crinkled. "Lunars have the unique ability to not only detect bioelectricity in others, but to also control it. They can manipulate it so that people see what the Lunar wishes them to see, and even feel what the Lunar wishes them to feel. A glamour is what they call the illusion of themselves that they project into the minds of others."

"Like making people think you're more beautiful than you really are?"

"Precisely. Or . . ." He gestured at Cinder's hands. "Making a person see skin where there is really metal."

Cinder self-consciously rubbed her cyborg hand through the glove.

"It is why Queen Levana is so striking to look at. Some talented Lunars, such as the queen, keep their glamour up all the time. But just as she cannot trick the netscreens, neither can she trick a mirror."

"So they don't like mirrors because they don't want to see themselves?"

"Vanity is a factor, but it is more a question of control. It is easier to trick others into perceiving you as beautiful if you can convince yourself you *are* beautiful. But mirrors have an uncanny way of telling the truth." Dr. Erland peered at her, as if amused. "And now a question for you, Miss Linh. Why the sudden interest in Lunars?"

Cinder lowered her gaze to her hands and realized she was still carrying the stylus stolen off his desk. "Something Kai said."

"His Highness?"

She nodded. "He told me Queen Levana is coming to New Beijing."

The doctor drew back. He gaped at her, bushy eyebrows nearly touching the brim of his hat, then stepped back against the cabinets. For the first time that day, his focus was entirely on her. "When?"

"She's supposed to arrive today."

"*Today?*"

She jumped. She could not have imagined Dr. Erland raising his voice before. He spun away from her, scratching his hat, pondering.

"Are you all right?"

He waved away the question. "I suppose she would have been waiting for this." He pulled off his hat, revealing a bald spot surrounded by thin, messy hair. He shuffled his hand through it a few times, glaring at the floor. "She is hoping to prey on Kai. His youth, his inexperience." He blew out a furious breath and replaced the hat.

Cinder splayed her fingers out on her knees. "What do you mean, prey on him?"

He turned back to her. His face was pulled taut, his eyes turbulent. The stare he pinned on Cinder made her shrink away.

"You should not be worried about the prince, Miss Linh."

"I shouldn't?"

"She is coming today? That is what he told you?"

She nodded.

"Then you must leave. Quickly. You can't be here when she arrives."

He shooed her off the table. Cinder hopped down, but made no move toward the door. "What does this have to do with me?"

"We have your blood samples, your DNA. We can do without you for now. Just stay away from the palace until she's gone, do you understand?"

Cinder planted her feet. "No, I don't."

The doctor looked from her to the netscreen still showing her stats. He appeared confused. Old. Frazzled. "Screen, display current newsfeed."

Cinder's stats vanished, replaced by a news anchor. The headline above him announced the emperor's death. ". . . Highness is preparing to make a speech in just a few minutes on the death of His Imperial Majesty and the upcoming coronation. We will be broadcasting live—"

"Mute."

Cinder folded her arms. "Doctor?"

He turned pleading eyes to Cinder. "Miss Linh, you must listen very carefully."

"I'll turn my audio interface volume to max." She leaned back against the cabinets, disappointed when Dr. Erland didn't so much as blink at her sarcasm.

Instead he blew out a disgruntled sigh. "I am not sure how to say this. I thought I would have more time." He rubbed his hands together. Paced back toward the door. Squared his shoulder and faced Cinder again. "You were eleven when you had your operation, correct?"

The question was not what she'd been expecting. "Yes . . ."

"And before that, you don't remember anything?"

"Nothing. What does this have to do with—"

"But your adoptive parents? Surely they must have told you something about your childhood? Your background?"

Her right palm began to sweat. "My stepfather died not long after the accident, and Adri doesn't like to talk about it, if she even knows anything. Adopting me wasn't exactly her idea."

"Do you know anything about your biological parents?"

Cinder shook her head. "Just their names, birth dates . . . whatever was in my files."

"The files on your ID chip."

"Well . . ." Irritation burst inside her. "What's your point?"

Dr. Erland's eyes softened, trying to comfort, but the look only unnerved her.

"Miss Linh, from your blood samples I have deduced that you are, in fact, Lunar."

The word washed over Cinder as if he were speaking a different language. The machine in her brain kept ticking, ticking, like it was working through an impossible equation.

"Lunar?" The word evaporated off her tongue, almost nonexistent.

"Yes."

"Lunar?"

"Indeed."

She pulled back. Looked at the walls, the exam table, the silent news anchor. "I don't have magic," she said, folding her arms in defiance.

"Yes, well. Not *all* Lunars are born with the gift. They're called shells, which is a slightly derogatory connotation on Luna, so . . . well, bioelectrically challenged doesn't sound much better, does it?" He chuckled awkwardly.

Cinder's metal hand clenched. She briefly wished she did have some sort of magic so she could shoot a bolt of lightning through his head. "I'm not Lunar." She wrenched her glove off and waved her hand at him. "I'm *cyborg.* You don't think that's bad enough?"

"Lunars can be cyborgs as easily as humans. It's rare, of course, given their intense opposition of cybernetics and brain-machine interfaces—"

Cinder faked a gasp. "*No.* Who would be opposed to *that*?"

"But being Lunar and being cyborg are not mutually exclusive. And it isn't altogether surprising that you were brought here. Since the instatement of the non-gifted infanticide under Queen Channary, many Lunar parents have attempted to rescue their shell children by bringing them to Earth. Of course, most of them die and are executed for the attempt, but still . . . I believe this was the case with you. The rescuing part. Not the execution part."

An orange light flickered in the corner of her vision. Cinder squinted at the man. "You're lying."

"I am not lying, Miss Linh."

She opened her mouth to argue—which part? What exactly had he said that triggered the lie detector?

The light went away as he continued speaking.

"This also explains your immunity. In fact, when you defeated the pathogens yesterday, your being Lunar was the first possibility to cross my mind, but I didn't want to say anything until I'd confirmed it."

Cinder pressed her palms against her eyes, blocking out the blaring fluorescents. "What does this have to do with immunity?"

"Lunars are immune to the disease, of course."

"No! Not *of course.* This is not common knowledge." She strung her hands back against her ponytail.

"Oh. Well, but it is common sense when you know the history." He wrung his hands. "Which, I suppose, most people don't."

Cinder hid her face, gasping for air. Perhaps she could rely on the man being insane and not have to believe anything he said after all.

"You see," said Dr. Erland, "Lunars are the original carrier hosts for letumosis. Their migration to the rural areas of Earth, mostly during the reign of Queen Channary, brought the disease into contact with humans for the first time. Historically, it's a common situation. The rats that brought the bubonic plague to Europe, the conquistadors who brought smallpox to the

Native Americans. It sounds so second era that Earthens take their immunities for granted now, but with the migration of the Lunars, well . . . Earthen immune systems just weren't prepared. Once even a handful of Lunars arrived, bringing the disease with them, it began spreading like wildfire."

"I thought I wasn't contagious."

"You aren't *now,* because your body has developed means of ridding itself of the disease, but you may have been at one point. Besides, I suspect that Lunars have different levels of immunity—while some can rid their bodies of the disease entirely, others carry it around without ever developing outward symptoms, spreading it everywhere they go and being none the wiser of the trouble they're causing."

Cinder waved her hands before him. "No. You're wrong. There's some other explanation. I can't be—"

"I understand this is a lot to take in. But I need you to understand why you cannot be present when the Her Majesty arrives. It's far too dangerous."

"No, you *don't* understand. I am not one of *them*!"

To be cyborg *and* Lunar. One was enough to make her a mutant, an outcast, but to be *both*? She shuddered. Lunars were a cruel, savage people. They murdered their shell children. They lied and scammed and brainwashed each other because they *could.* They didn't care who they hurt, so long as it benefitted themselves. She was not one of them.

"Miss Linh, you must listen to me. You were brought here for a reason."

"What, to help you find a cure? You think this is some sort of twisted gift of fate?"

"I am not talking fate or destiny. I am talking survival. You *cannot* let the queen see you."

Cinder shrank against the cabinet, more baffled by the second. "Why? Why would she care about me?"

"She would care very much about you." He hesitated, his sea-blue eyes wild with panic. "She . . . she hates Lunar shells, you see. Shells are immune to the Lunar glamour." He twirled his hands through the air, searching. "Their *brainwashing*, as it were. Queen Levana can't control shells, which is why she continues to have them exterminated." His lips hardened. "Queen Levana will stop at nothing to ensure her control, to terminate any resistance. That means killing those who could resist her—people like you. Do you understand me, Miss Linh? If she were to see you, she would kill you."

Gulping, Cinder pressed her thumb against her left wrist. She couldn't feel her ID chip, but she knew it was there.

Extracted from the deceased.

If Dr. Erland were right, then everything she knew about herself, her childhood, her parents, was wrong. A made-up history. A made-up girl.

The idea that Lunars were fugitives no longer sounded so odd.

She turned toward the netscreen. Kai was there now, in the pressroom, talking at a podium.

"Miss Linh, somebody went through a great deal of trouble

to bring you here, and now you are in extreme danger. You cannot jeopardize yourself."

She barely heard, watching as text began to scroll along the bottom of the screen.

JUST ANNOUNCED: LUNAR QUEEN LEVANA TO COME TO THE EASTERN COMMONWEALTH FOR PEACE ALLIANCE DISCUSSIONS. JUST ANNOUNCED: LUNAR QUEEN LEVANA . . .

"Miss Linh? Are you listening to me?"

"Yeah," she said. "Extreme danger. I heard you."

Twenty

THE LUNAR SPACECRAFT DID NOT APPEAR MUCH DIFFERENT from Earthen spacecrafts, except that its body shimmered as if inlaid with diamonds, and a string of gold runes encircled its hull in an unbroken line. The ship was too bright in the afternoon sun and Kai had to squint against the glare. He did not know if the runes were magic or if they were only meant to seem so. He did not know if the ship was made out of some fancy, glittery material, or if they'd just painted it that way. He did know it hurt to look at.

The ship was larger than the personal shuttle the queen's head thaumaturge, Sybil, had come to Earth on and yet still relatively small for all the importance it carried: smaller than most passenger ships and smaller than any cargo ship Kai had seen. It was a private ship, meant only for the Lunar queen and her entourage.

The ship landed without a jolt. Heat rose up from the concrete in blistering waves. The fine silk of Kai's shirt was clinging to his back and a trickle of sweat had begun down his neck—in the evening the welcome pad would be sheltered by the palace's stone walls, but now it was under full assault by the late August sun.

They waited.

Torin, at Kai's side, did not fidget. His face was impassive, expectant. His calmness only unsettled Kai even more.

On Kai's other side, Sybil Mira stood dressed in her official white coat with its embroidered runes, similar to those on the ship. The material seemed lightweight, yet it covered her from the top of her throat to the knuckles of each hand, and the flared tails hung past her knees. She must have been sweltering, but she looked fully composed.

A few steps behind her stood the blond guard, hands clasped behind his back.

Two of Kai's own royal guards stood at either side of the platform.

That was all. Levana had insisted that no one else greet her at the pad.

Kai dug his nails into his palms in an attempt to keep the sneer from his face, and waited while the heat plastered his bangs to his forehead.

Finally, when the queen seemed to have grown tired of making them suffer, the ramp of the ship descended, revealing silver-furnished stairs.

Two men alighted first—both tall, both muscular. One was pale with wildly unkempt orange hair and was dressed in the same warrior-like body armor and weaponry that Sybil's guard wore. The other man was dark as a night sky, with no hair at all, and wore a coat like Sybil's with its bell sleeves and embroidery. His, however, was crimson, announcing that he was beneath Sybil, a second-tier thaumaturge. Kai was glad he knew enough about the Lunar court to recognize *that,* at least.

He watched the two men as they surveyed the pad, the surrounding walls, and the assembled group with stoic expressions before standing to either side of the ramp.

Sybil slinked forward. Kai swallowed a breath of stifling air.

Queen Levana appeared at the top of the stairs. She still wore her long veil, blindingly bright beneath the relentless sun. Her white dress whispered around her hips as she glided down the steps and accepted Sybil's hand.

Sybil dipped to one knee and touched her forehead to her queen's knuckle. "Our separation was insufferable. I am pleased to be in your service once more, my Queen." Then she stood and with a single graceful motion lifted the veil back from Levana's face.

The hot air caught in Kai's throat, choking him. The queen paused just long enough to seem as though she were letting her eyes adjust to the bright daylight of Earth—but Kai suspected she really just wanted him to see her.

She was indeed beautiful, as if someone had taken the scientific measurements of perfection and used them to mold a single ideal specimen. Her face was slightly heart-shaped, with high cheekbones barely flushed. Auburn hair fell in silken ringlets to her waist and her unblemished ivory skin shimmered like mother-of-pearl in the sunshine. Her lips were red red red, looking like she'd just drunk a pint of blood.

A chill shook Kai from the inside out. She was unnatural.

Kai risked a glance at Torin and saw that he held Levana's gaze without outward emotion. Seeing his adviser's resolve sent a jolt of determination through Kai. Reminding himself that it was only an illusion, he forced himself to look at the queen again.

Her onyx eyes glittered as they swept over him.

"Your Majesty," Kai said, folding a fist to his heart, "it is my greatest honor to welcome you to my country and planet."

Her lips curled. A sweetness lit up her face—an innocence to match a child's. It unsettled him. She did not bow or even nod but instead held out her hand.

Kai hesitated, staring at the pale, translucent skin, wondering if just touching her was all it would take to destroy a man's mind.

Bracing himself, he took her hand and brushed a quick kiss against her fingers. Nothing happened.

"Your Highness," she said in a lilting voice that thrummed along Kai's spine. "It is my greatest honor to be thus welcomed. Might I again offer my sincerest condolences on the loss of your father, the great Emperor Rikan."

Kai knew she was not at all sorry for his father's death, but neither her expression nor her tone hinted at a thing.

"Thank you," he replied. "I hope everything meets your expectations during your visit."

"I look forward to the Eastern Commonwealth's famed hospitality."

Sybil stepped forward, eyes respectfully averted from Queen Levana. "I inspected your quarters myself, my Queen. They are subpar to our accommodations on Luna, but I think they will be adequate."

Levana did not acknowledge her thaumaturge, but her gaze softened, and the world changed. Kai felt that the ground lurched beneath him. That the air had been sucked from the earth's atmosphere. That the sun had gone black, leaving the ethereal queen the only source of light in the galaxy.

Tears pricked at the back of his eyes.

He loved her. He needed her. He would do anything to please her.

He jabbed his fingernails into his palms as hard as he could, nearly yelping from the pain, but it worked. The queen's control disintegrated, leaving only the beautiful woman—not the desperate adoration of her.

He knew that she was aware of the effect she'd had on him as he struggled to soothe his ragged breathing, and though he wanted to detect cold haughtiness in her black eyes, he saw nothing. Nothing at all.

"If you will follow me," he said, his voice slightly hoarse, "I will show you to your rooms."

"That will not be necessary," said Sybil. "I am quite familiar with the guest wing and can take Her Majesty myself. We would like a moment to speak in private."

"Of course," said Kai, hoping that his relief didn't show.

Sybil led the way, the second thaumaturge and the two guards marching behind. They paid Kai and Torin no heed as they passed, but Kai didn't doubt they would snap his neck in a second if he made any suspicious movements.

He released a shaky breath when they had gone. "Did you feel her?" he asked, barely above a whisper.

"Of course," said Torin. His eyes were drawn to the ship, but he could have been staring at Mars for all the focus in his eyes. "You resisted her well, Your Highness. I know it was difficult."

Kai brushed his hair off his forehead, seeking a breeze, any breeze, but it didn't come. "It wasn't so hard. It was only for a moment."

Torin's eyes met his. It was one of the few times Kai had seen true sympathy in that gaze. "It will get harder."

BOOK Three

"You want to go to the festival,

all covered in dust and dirt?

But we would only be ashamed of you!"

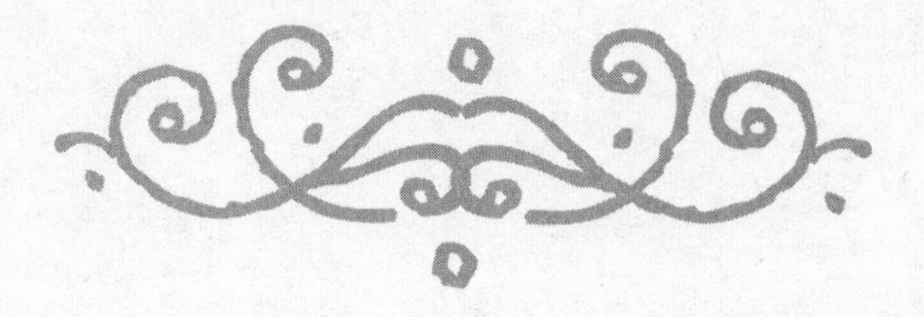

Twenty-One

CINDER SLUMPED DOWN AT HER WORK DESK, RELIEVED TO finally be out of that stifling apartment. Not only was the air system down—*again*—with maintenance nowhere to be seen, but the awkwardness between her and Adri bordered on unbearable. They'd been tiptoeing around each other since she'd returned home from the lab two days before, Adri trying to remind Cinder of her superiority by ordering her to defrag their apartment's entire mainframe and update all the software that they didn't even use anymore, while at the same time lurking around as if she were—almost, kind of—ashamed of what she'd done to Cinder.

But Cinder was probably imagining that last part.

At least Pearl had been gone all day and had only shown up when Cinder and Iko were on their way out to work on the car.

Another long day. Another late night. The car was going to take more work than she'd realized—the entire exhaust system needed to be replaced, which meant manufacturing a lot of parts herself, which created any number of headaches. She had a feeling she wasn't going to get much sleep if they were going to have it road ready by the night of the ball.

She sighed. *The ball.*

She didn't regret saying no when the prince had asked her, because she knew how badly that would end. Any number of things were sure to go wrong—from tripping on the stairs and flashing the prince a sexy metal thigh, to running into Pearl or Adri or someone from the market. People would talk. The gossip channels were sure to look into her past, and pretty soon the whole world would know that the prince had taken a cyborg to his coronation ball. He would be mortified. *She* would be mortified.

But it didn't make it any easier when she wondered, what if she were wrong? What if Prince Kai wouldn't care? What if the world were different and nobody cared if she was cyborg . . . and on top of that, Lunar?

Yeah. Wishful thinking.

Spotting the broken netscreen on the carpet, she peeled herself off her chair and kneeled before it. The black screen was just reflective enough for her to see the outline of her face and body, the tanned skin of her arms contrasted with the dark steel of her hand.

Denial had run its course until it had nowhere else to go. She was Lunar.

But she was not afraid of the mirrored surface, not afraid of her own reflection. She couldn't understand what Levana and her kind, *their* kind, found so disturbing about it. Her mechanical parts were the only disturbing thing in Cinder's reflection, and that had been done to her on Earth.

Lunar. And cyborg.

And a fugitive.

Did Adri know? No, Adri never would have housed a Lunar. If she'd known, she would have turned Cinder in herself, probably expecting payment.

Had Adri's husband known?

That was a question Cinder would probably never know the answer to.

Nevertheless, she was confident that so long as Dr. Erland didn't say anything, her secret would be safe. She would just have to go on as if nothing had changed.

In many ways, nothing had. She was every bit an outcast as ever.

A white blob caught her eye in the screen's surface—Kai's android, its lifeless sensor staring down at her from its perch on top of her desk. Its pear-shaped body was the brightest thing in the room and probably the cleanest. It reminded her of the sterile med-droids in the labs and the quarantines, but this machine did not have scalpels and syringes hidden in its torso.

Work. Mechanics. She needed the distraction.

Returning to her desk, she turned on her audio interface for some tranquil background music. Kicking off her boots, she gripped both sides of the android and wheeled it toward her. After a quick examination of its external plating, she tipped the android over, laying it horizontal so that it balanced on the edge of its treads.

Cinder opened the back panel and inspected the wiring throughout the cylindrical frame. It was not a complicated android. The interior was mostly hollow, a shell for housing a minimum of hard drives, wires, chips. Tutor androids required little more than a central processing unit. Cinder suspected that the android would have to be wiped and reprogrammed, but she had a feeling that wasn't a viable option. Despite Kai's nonchalance, it was clear this android knew something important, and after their conversation in the research hall, she had an uneasy feeling it had something to do with Lunars.

War strategies? Classified communications? Evidence for blackmail? Whatever it was, Kai clearly thought it would help, and he'd trusted Cinder to save it.

"No pressure or anything," she muttered, gripping a flashlight between her teeth so she could see inside the android. She grabbed a pair of pliers and coerced the wires from one side of its cranium to the other. Its configuration was similar to Iko's, so Cinder felt a familiarity with its parts, knew exactly where to find all the important connections. She checked that the wire connectors were sound, that the battery held power, that no important pieces were missing, and everything seemed fine. She cleaned out the noise translator and adjusted the internal fan, but Nainsi the android remained a lifeless statue of plastic and aluminum.

"All dressed up with nowhere to go," said Iko from the doorway.

Cinder spit out the flashlight with a laugh and glanced down at her oil-stained cargo pants. "Yeah, right. All I need is a tiara."

"I was talking about me."

She spun her chair around. Iko had draped a strand of Adri's pearls around her bulbous head and smeared cherry lipstick beneath her sensor in a horrible imitation of lips.

Cinder laughed. "Wow. That's a great color on you."

"Do you think?" Iko wheeled her way into the room and paused before Cinder's desk, trying to catch her reflection in the netscreen. "I was imagining going to the ball and dancing with the prince."

Cinder rubbed her jaw with one hand and mindlessly tapped the table with the other. "Funny. I've found myself imagining that exact thing lately."

"I knew you liked him. You pretend to be immune to his charms, but I could see the way you looked at him at the market." Iko rubbed at the lipstick, smearing it across her blank white chin.

"Yeah, well." Cinder pinched her metal fingers with the pliers' nose. "We all have our weaknesses."

"I know," said Iko. "Mine is shoes."

Cinder tossed the tool onto her desk. Something like guilt was beginning to grow in her when Iko was around. She knew she should tell Iko about being Lunar, that Iko more than anyone would understand what it was like to be different and unwanted. But somehow she couldn't bring herself to say it out loud. *By the way, Iko, it turns out I'm Lunar. You don't mind, do you?*

"What are you doing down here?" she asked instead.

"Just seeing if you need help. I'm supposed to be dusting the air vents, but Adri was in the bath."

"So?"

"I could hear her crying."

Cinder blinked. "Oh."

"It was making me feel useless."

"I see."

Iko was not a normal servant android, but she did retain one prominent trait—uselessness was the worst emotion they knew.

"Well, sure, you can help," Cinder said, rubbing her hands together. "Just don't let her catch you with those pearls."

Iko lifted the beaded necklace up with her prongs, and Cinder noticed she was wearing the ribbon Peony had given her. She pulled back, as if she'd been stung. "How about some light?"

The blue sensor brightened, shedding a spotlight into Nainsi's interior.

Cinder twisted up her lips. "Do you think it could have a virus?"

"Maybe her programming was overwhelmed by Prince Kai's uncanny hotness."

Cinder flinched. "Can we please not talk about the prince?"

"I don't think that will be possible. You're working on his android, after all. Just think about the things she knows, the things she's seen and—" Iko's voice sputtered. "Do you think she's seen him in the nude?"

"Oh, for heaven's sake." Cinder yanked off her gloves and tossed them onto the table. "You're not helping."

"I'm just making conversation."

"Well stop." Crossing her arms over her chest, Cinder pushed her chair back from the worktable and swung both legs up to rest on top of it. "It has to be a software issue."

She sneered to herself. Software issues usually came down to reinstallation, but that would turn the android into a blank slate. She didn't know if Kai was concerned with the android's personality chip, which had probably developed into something quite complicated after twenty years of service, but she did know Kai was concerned with something in this android's hard drive, and she didn't want to risk wiping whatever it was.

The only way to determine what was wrong and if a reboot was necessary was to check the android's internal diagnostics, and that required plugging in. Cinder hated plugging in. Connecting her own wiring with a foreign object had always felt hazardous, like if she wasn't careful, her own software could be overridden.

Chastising herself for being squeamish, she reached for the panel in the back of her head. Her fingernail caught the small latch and it swung open.

"What's that?"

Cinder stared at Iko's outstretched prong. "What's what?"

"That chip."

Cinder dropped her feet to the floor and leaned forward. She squinted into the far back of the model, where a row of tiny chips stood like soldiers along the bottom of the control panel. There were twenty plugs in all, but only thirteen of them were full; manufacturers always left plenty of room for add-ons and updates.

Iko had spotted the thirteenth chip, and she was right. Something was different about it. It was tucked far enough behind the other chips that it was easy to miss with a cursory glance, but when Cinder targeted it with the flashlight, it gleamed like polished silver.

Cinder shut the panel in the back of her head and called up the digital blueprint of the android's model on her retina. According to the manufacturer's original plans, this model only came with twelve chips. But surely, after twenty years, the android would have received at least one add-on. Surely, the palace had access to the newest, finest programs available. Still, Cinder had never seen a chip quite like that.

She pressed a fingernail into the release switch and gripped the edge of the silver chip with the pliers. It slid like grease from its plug.

Cinder held it up for closer inspection. With the exception of the pearlescent, shimmering finish, it looked like every other program chip she'd ever seen. Flipping it over, she saw the letters D-COMM engraved on the other side.

"Is that so?" She lowered her arm.

"What is it?" asked Iko.

"A direct communication chip."

Cinder furrowed her brow. Almost all communication was done through the net—direct communication that bypassed the net entirely was practically obsolete, as it was slow and had a tendency to lose connection in the middle of a link. She supposed paranoid types who required absolute privacy would find direct comms appealing, but even then, they would use a port or netscreen—a device that was set up for it. Using an android as one side of the link didn't make any sense.

Iko's light dimmed. "My database informs me that androids

have not come equipped with direct communication abilities since 89 T.E."

"Which would explain why it didn't work with her programming." Cinder held the chip toward Iko. "Can you run a material scan, see what it's made out of?"

Iko backed away. "Absolutely not. Having a mental breakdown is not on my list of things to do today."

"It doesn't seem like it would have caused her to malfunction, though. Wouldn't the system have just rejected it?" Cinder angled the chip back and forth, mesmerized by how its reflective surface caught Iko's light. "Unless she tried to send information over the direct link. It could have jammed up the bandwidth."

Standing, Cinder strolled across the storage space toward the netscreen. Though its frame had been shattered, the screen and controls seemed undamaged. She slid the chip in and pressed the power button, having to jab it harder than usual before a pale green light came to life beside the drive and the screen flared bright blue. A spiral in the corner announced that it was reading the new chip. Cinder released her breath and folded her legs beneath her.

A second later the spiral disappeared, replaced with text.

INITIATING DIRECT LINK WITH UNKNOWN USER.

PLEASE WAIT . . .

INITIATING DIRECT LINK WITH UNKNOWN USER.

PLEASE WAIT . . .

INITIATING DIRECT LINK WITH UNKNOWN USER.

PLEASE WAIT . . .

Cinder waited. And wiggled her foot. And waited. And drummed her fingers against her knee. And began to wonder if she were wasting her time. She'd never heard of a direct communication chip hurting anything, even if the technology was archaic. This wasn't helping her solve the problem.

"I guess no one's home," said Iko, rolling up behind her. Her fan turned on, blowing warm air on Cinder's neck. "Oh, drat, Adri is comming me. She must be out of the bath."

Cinder tilted her head back. "Thanks for your help. Don't forget to take those pearls off before you see her."

Tilting forward, Iko pressed her flat, cool face to Cinder's brow, no doubt leaving a smudge of lipstick. Cinder laughed.

"You'll find out what's wrong with His Highness's android. I don't doubt it."

"Thanks."

Cinder rubbed her clammy palm on her pants, listening as Iko's treads got farther away. The text continued to repeat across the screen. It seemed whoever was on the other side of the link had no intention of answering.

A series of clicks startled her, followed by telltale humming. She turned around, propping her knuckles on the gritty floor.

The android's control panel was glowing as the system ran through its routine diagnostics. It was turning back on.

Cinder stood and dusted her hands just as a calm female voice began to emanate from the android's speakers, as if it were continuing a speech that had been rudely interrupted.

"—pected that a man by the name of Logan Tanner, a Lunar doctor who worked under the reign of Queen Channary, first brought Princess Selene to Earth approximately four months after her alleged death."

Cinder froze. *Princess Selene?*

"Unfortunately, Tanner was admitted into Xu Ming Psychiatric Hospital on 8 May 125 T.E., and committed bioelectric-induced suicide on 17 January 126 T.E. Though sources indicate that Princess Selene had been given to another keeper years before Tanner's death, I have thus far not been able to confirm the identity of that keeper. One suspect is an ex-military pilot from the European Federation, Wing Commander Michelle Benoit, who—"

"Stop," said Cinder. "Stop talking."

The voice silenced. The android's head rotated 180 degrees. Its sensor flashed bright blue as it scanned Cinder. Her internal control panel dimmed. The fan in her torso began to spin.

"Who are you?" said the android. "My global positioning system indicates that we are in the 76th Sector of New Beijing. I have no memory of leaving the palace."

Cinder straddled her seat, draping her arms over the back. "Welcome to New Beijing's mechanic suite. Prince Kai hired me to fix you."

The loud humming in the android's torso died down until it was barely discernible, even in the quiet room.

The bulbous head rotated back and forth, scanning its unfamiliar surroundings, then refocused on Cinder.

"My calendar tells me that I have not been conscious for over twelve days, fifteen hours. Did I experience a system crash?"

"Not exactly," said Cinder, glancing over her shoulder at the netscreen. It continued to repeat the same line of text, unable to establish the direct link. "It seems someone installed a comm chip that didn't meld well with your programming."

"I come preinstalled with vid- and text-comm capabilities. A new comm chip would be unnecessary."

"This was for a direct link." Cinder settled her chin on her wrist. "Do you know if it was Prince Kai? If maybe he wanted to be able to get in touch with you without going through the net?"

"I was unaware of any direct communication chip in my programming."

Cinder chewed her lip. Clearly the comm chip had been responsible for the android's sudden malfunction, but why? And if Kai hadn't installed it, then who had?

"When you woke up just now," she said, "you were talking about . . . you have information on the Lunar heir."

"That information was classified. You should not have heard it."

"I know. But I think you were probably communicating it to someone when you were disabled." Cinder prayed that it had been Kai, or someone loyal to him. She doubted that Queen Levana would be too happy to know that the soon-to-be emperor was searching for the rightful heir to her throne.

"Hold still," she said, reaching for her screwdriver. "I'll put your panel back on, and then take you back to the palace. In the meantime, you should download the news broadcasts from the last few days. A lot's happened since you've been out."

Twenty-Two

CINDER COULD HEAR DR. ERLAND'S WARNINGS IN HER HEAD, echoing like a damaged audio file, the entire six miles to the palace.

Queen Levana will stop at nothing to ensure her control, to terminate any resistance. That means killing those who could resist her—people like you.

If she were to see you, she would kill you.

And yet if something were to happen between the apartment and the palace to this android who had real information on the missing Lunar princess, Cinder would never forgive herself. It was her responsibility to get the android back to Kai, safe and sound.

Besides, the palace was a huge place. What were the chances she would run into the Lunar queen, who probably didn't intend to spend much time socializing with the citizenry anyway?

Nainsi was much faster on her treads than Iko, and Cinder had to hurry to keep up with her. But their pace slowed as they discovered that they were not the only citizens on their way to the palace that afternoon. At the base of the cliff, the main road had been blocked off as it left the city behind and became the private drive of the palace, shaded by twisted pines and drooping willows. The winding street was filled with pedestrians making their slow way up the hill. Some walked alone, others in large cliques. Their conversations reached Cinder, irate and determined, arms flying in mad gestures. *We don't want her here. What could His Highness be thinking?* The growing roar of the mob echoed down the road. Hundreds, perhaps thousands, of angry voices chanting in unison.

"No moon queen! No moon queen! No moon queen!"

Turning the last corner, Cinder's gaze fell on the crowd up ahead, filling up the courtyard before the palace's maroon gates and spilling down the street. It was barely contained by a flustered row of security guards.

Signs bobbed over their heads. WAR IS BETTER THAN SLAVERY! WE NEED AN EMPRESS, NOT A DICTATOR! NO ALLIANCE WITH EVIL! Many included the queen's veiled image slashed through with red *X*s.

Half a dozen news hovers circled the sky, capturing footage of the protests for global broadcasting.

Cinder skirted the edge of the crowd, shoving her way to the main gate while trying to shield Nainsi's compact body with her own. But upon reaching the gate, she found it closed and guarded by both humans and androids, standing shoulder to shoulder.

"Pardon me," she said to the closest guard. "I need to get into the palace."

The man stretched his arm toward her, pushing her back a step. "No entrance to the public today."

"But I'm not with *them.*" She placed her hands on Nainsi's head. "This android belongs to His Imperial Highness. I was hired to fix her, and now I'm returning her. It's very important that she be returned to him as soon as possible."

The guard peered down his nose at the android. "Did His Imperial Highness give you a pass?"

"Well, no, but—"

"Does the android have its ID?"

"I do." Rotating her torso, Nainsi flashed her ID code at the guard.

He nodded. "You may enter." The gates were opened, just barely, and it wasn't a breath before the crowd surged forward. Cinder cried out at the rumble of angry voices in her ears and the sudden crush of bodies, shoving her into the security guard. Nainsi rolled through the gate without hesitation, but when Cinder moved to slip through behind her, the guard blocked her with his arm, straining against the crowd. "Just the android."

"But we're together!" she yelled over the chanting.

"No pass, no entrance."

"But I fixed her! I need to deliver her. I need to . . . to collect payment." Even she was put off by the whining in her voice.

"Send your invoice to the treasury like everyone else," the man said. "No one is to be admitted without an issued pass."

"Linh-mèi," said Nainsi from the other side of the iron gate. "I will inform Prince Kai that you would like to see him. I'm sure he can comm you an official pass."

Instantly, Cinder felt the weight of her silliness. Of course she didn't need to *see* the prince. She had delivered the android; her job was done. And she wasn't really going to bill him for her work, anyway. But Nainsi had turned away and rolled off toward the palace's main entrance before Cinder could protest, leaving Cinder trying to come up with a reasonable excuse as to why it was so important to see Kai, something better than the very stupid, very childish reason that first entered her head. She simply wanted to.

The chanting stopped suddenly, making Cinder jump.

The crowd's silence created a vacuum on the street, yearning to fill with breath, with sound, with anything. Cinder looked around, at the dazzled faces turned upward to the palace, at the lowered signs held in limp fingers. A ripple of fear stroked her spine.

She followed the gazes of the crowd up to a balcony that jutted from one of the palace's highest stories.

The Lunar queen stood with one hand on her hip, the other on the balcony's railing. Her expression was stern—bitter—but the look did nothing to dispel her uncanny beauty. Even from afar, Cinder could make out the pale luminescence of her skin, the ruby tinge of her lips. Her dark eyes were scanning the silenced crowd, and Cinder shrank back away from the gate, wanting to disappear behind the empty faces.

But the shock and terror was short-lived. This woman was not frightening, not dangerous.

She was warm. Welcoming. Generous. She should be their queen. She should rule them, guide them, protect them. . . .

Cinder's retina display flashed a warning at her. She tried in vain to wink it away, annoyed by the distraction. She wanted to look upon the queen forever. She wanted the queen to speak. To promise peace and security, wealth and comfort.

The orange light beamed in the corner of her vision. It took Cinder a moment to realize what it was, what it meant. She knew it was out of place. She knew it didn't make sense.

Lies.

She squeezed her eyes shut. When she looked up again, the illusion of goodness had faded. The queen's sweet smile had turned haughty and controlling. Cinder's stomach curdled.

She was brainwashing them.

She had brainwashed *her.*

Cinder stumbled back a step, colliding with a senseless middle-aged man.

The queen's gaze jerked toward them, focusing on Cinder. A wash of surprise flashed over her face. Then hatred. Disgust.

Cinder flinched, wanting to hide. Cold fingers clamped over her heart. She was compelled to run, yet her legs had melted beneath her. Her retina display was drawing confused lines over her vision as if it couldn't stand to look upon the queen's glamour a moment longer.

She felt naked and vulnerable, all alone in the brainwashed crowd. She was sure the earth beneath her feet would open up and swallow her whole. She was sure the queen's gaze would turn her into a pile of ashes on the cobblestoned road.

The queen's glower darkened until Cinder began to feel that, tear ducts or not, she would burst into tears.

But then the queen spun away, her shoulders back as she stormed into the palace.

With the queen gone, Cinder expected the crowd to take up their protests again, even angrier that she had dared show herself. But they didn't. Slowly, as if sleepwalking, the crowd began to depart. Those with signs let them fall to the ground, to be trampled and forgotten. Cinder pulled back against the wall bordering the palace, out of the way as the citizens meandered past.

So this was the effect of the Lunar glamour, the spell to enchant, to deceive, to turn one's heart toward you and against your enemies. And amid all these people who despised the Lunar queen, Cinder seemed to be the only one who had resisted her.

And yet, she *hadn't* resisted her. Not at first. Gooseflesh covered her arms. Her skin ached where it melded with metal.

She had not been entirely immune to the glamour, the way shells were supposed to be.

Worse still, the Queen had seen her, and she had known.

Twenty-Three

KAI DUG HIS FINGERNAILS INTO HIS KNEES WHEN THE chanting of the protestors ceased. Torin turned toward him, their expressions mirrors of surprise, though Torin was quicker to disguise it. The queen's success at calming the crowd had been far too easy; Kai had hoped for at least a hint of struggle from the citizens.

Gulping, Kai morphed his face back into collectedness.

"It is a most useful trick," said Sybil, sitting on the edge of the chaise lounge by the holographic fire. "Particularly when dealing with unruly citizens, which are never tolerated on Luna."

"I've heard that when citizens are unruly, there's usually a good reason for it," said Kai. Torin flashed him a warning frown, but he ignored it. "And brainwashing doesn't exactly seem like the proper solution."

Sybil folded her hands politely in her lap. "*Proper* is such a subjective word. This solution is *effective,* and that can hardly be argued with."

Levana flew back into the parlor with clenched fists. Kai's pulse ratcheted when the queen's glare fell on him. Being in her presence was like sitting in a confined room that was quickly running out of oxygen.

"It would appear," she said, carefully enunciating each word, "that you are in violation of the Interplanetary Agreement of 54 T.E., Article 17."

Kai tried his best to remain neutral under her accusation, but he couldn't keep a twitch from developing above his right eye. "I'm afraid I do not have the Interplanetary Agreement memorized in full. Perhaps you could enlighten me as to the article in question?"

She took a slow breath through flared nostrils. Even then—even with all the hatred and anger smeared across her face—she was stunning. "Article 17 states that no party of the agreement shall knowingly shelter or protect Lunar fugitives."

"Lunar fugitives?" Kai glanced at Torin, but his adviser's face was neutral. "Why would you think we're sheltering Lunar fugitives?"

"Because I've just seen one in your courtyard, along with those insolent protestors. This is not to be tolerated."

Kai stood and folded his arms over his chest. "This is the first I've ever heard of Lunars in my country. Present company excluded, of course."

"Which leads me to believe that you've been turning a blind eye to the problem, just as your father did."

"How can I turn a blind eye to something I've never heard of?"

Torin cleared his throat. "With all due respect, Your Majesty, I can assure you we monitor all spacecrafts both coming to and leaving the Commonwealth. Though we can't deny the possibility of some Lunars being smuggled in under our radar, I can promise that we've done everything in our power to comply with the Interplanetary Agreement. Besides, even if a Lunar fugitive had come to reside in the Commonwealth, it seems unlikely they would choose to risk being discovered by coming to a protest when they knew you would be present. Perhaps you have been mistaken."

The queen's eyes smoldered. "I know my own when I see them, and right now there is one in these city walls." She pointed a finger toward the balcony. "I want her found and brought to me."

"Right," said Kai, "that'll be no problem in a city of two and a half million people. Let me just go dig out my special Lunar detector, and I'll get right on that."

Levana tilted her head back so she could peer down her nose at Kai, even though he was taller than she was. "You do not wish to try my patience with your sarcasm, young prince."

He flexed his jaw.

"If you are incapable of finding her, then I will have a regiment of my own guards dispersed to Earth, and *they* will find her."

"That will not be necessary," said Torin. "We apologize for doubting you, Your Majesty, and are eager to fulfill our country's part of the agreement. Please allow us time to prepare for the coronation and the festival, and we will begin our search for the fugitive as soon as resources allow."

Levana narrowed her eyes at Kai. "Do you intend to always let your adviser make your decisions for you?"

"No," said Kai, allowing a cold smile. "Eventually, I'll have an empress for that."

Queen Levana's gaze softened, and Kai barely bit back his next words. *And it won't be you.*

"Fine," said Levana, turning away and seating herself beside her thaumaturge. "I will expect her, along with any other Lunar fugitives in the country, delivered to Luna one moon cycle after your coronation."

"Fine," said Kai, hoping that Levana would forget this conversation before the time came. Lunars in New Beijing—he'd never heard anything so absurd.

The anger vanished so completely from Levana's face that it seemed the past few minutes had been a dream. She crossed her legs, so that the slit in her sheer dress displayed a swath of milk-white skin. Kai set his jaw and stared out the window, not knowing if he was going to blush or gag.

"Speaking of your coronation," said the queen, "I have brought you a gift."

"How thoughtful," he deadpanned.

"Yes. I wasn't sure if I should save it for the big night, but I've determined that it might give the wrong impression if I were to withhold it."

Unable to deny his piqued curiosity, Kai eyed the queen. "Is that so?"

She inclined her head, auburn curls cascading over her bosom, and extended her fingers toward her second thaumaturge, the man in the red coat. He produced a glass vial, no larger than Kai's pinkie finger, from his sleeve and placed it on Levana's palm.

"I want you to know," said Levana, "that I have a very keen interest in the welfare of the Commonwealth, and watching your struggle with the letumosis disease has been heartbreaking."

Kai dug his nails into his palms.

"You are probably not aware, but I have had a research team dedicated to studying the disease for some years now, and it appears that my scientists have finally discovered an antidote."

Blood rushed to Kai's head. "What?"

Levana pinched the vial between her thumb and forefinger and held it out to him. "This should be enough to cure one adult male," she said, then clicked her tongue. "Awful timing, isn't it?"

The world spun. Kai's fingers itched to reach out and strangle her until his entire arms were shaking.

"Go ahead," said Levana, a persistent warmth behind her gaze. "Take it."

Kai snatched the vial away from her. "How long have you had this?"

The queen's brow arched upward. "Why—it was only confirmed as a true antidote hours before my departure."

She was lying. She was not even trying to hide the fact that she was lying.

Witch.

"Your Highness," Torin said quietly, placing a firm hand on Kai's shoulder. At first gentle, then squeezing—warning. Kai's pulse began to filter the fantasies of murder, but only barely.

Levana folded her hands in her lap. "That vial is your gift. I hope you will find it helpful, young prince. I believe it is in both of our interests to rid your planet of this disease. My scientists could have thousands of dosages prepared by month's end. However, such an undertaking, coupled with six years' worth of work and resources, has put quite a strain on my own country, and so I'm sure you'll understand the need for compensation. *That* will require further negotiations."

Kai's lungs constricted. "You would withhold this? When so many are dying?" It was a stupid question. She'd already withheld it long enough—what was it to her if more Earthens suffered in the meantime?

"You have much to learn about politics. I think you will soon discover that it is all about give and take, my dear handsome prince."

His pulse pounded against his temples. He knew his face had gone red, that his anger was playing right into her game, but he didn't care. How dare she use this as a political bargaining chip? How *dare* she?

Sybil stood suddenly. "We have a guest."

Releasing a pent-up breath, Kai followed Sybil's gaze to the doorway, glad to look away from the queen, and gasped. "Nainsi!"

Nainsi's sensor flashed. "Your Highness, I apologize for my interruption."

Kai shook his head, trying to dispel his surprise. "How—when—?"

"My consciousness has been restored for one hour and forty-seven minutes," said the android. "And I am now reporting for duty. Might I offer my condolences on the untimely loss of Emperor Rikan. My heart is broken from the news."

Kai heard Queen Levana snort behind him. "The idea that a pile of metal could experience emotion is insulting. Send this monstrosity away."

Kai pursed his lips, having a number of choice words to say about *her* heartlessness, but instead he turned to Torin. "Indeed, let me remove this *monstrosity* from Her Majesty's presence and have her reinstated into active status."

He half expected Torin to chastise him for the sorry escape plan, but Torin seemed too relieved that the argument was over. Kai noticed he'd gone pale and wondered how hard it had been for Torin to dominate his own temper. "Of course. Perhaps Her Majesty would like a tour of the gardens?"

Kai glared at Queen Levana, filling the look with loathing, and clipped his heels together. "Thank you for your considerate gift," he said with a short bow.

"It was my pleasure, Your Highness."

Kai left the room with Nainsi at his side. When they had reached the main corridor, he released a guttural scream and slammed his fist into the nearest wall, then fell against it, pressing his forehead against the plaster.

When his breathing was manageable, he turned around, suddenly wanting to cry—from anger, from desperation, from relief. Nainsi was back.

"You can't imagine how happy I am to see you."

"So it appears, Your Highness."

Kai shut his eyes. "You don't even know. The past few days. I was sure our research would be lost."

"All records seem to be intact, Your Highness."

"Good. We need to get back to the search right away—it's more important now than ever."

He struggled to contain the panic clawing at his insides. His coronation was still nine days away. Queen Levana had not been on Earth for twenty-four hours and she'd already turned their alliance negotiations upside down. What other secrets could she reveal before his coronation, when the role to protect his country would truly fall to him?

His head pounded. He despised her—for everything she was, for everything she'd done, for how she'd turned Earth's suffering into a game of politics.

But she was wrong if she expected him to become her puppet. He would defy her for as long as he could, in any way that he could. He would find Princess Selene. Dr. Erland would duplicate the antidote. He wouldn't even dance with Levana at the stupid ball if he could help it—to hell with diplomacy.

Remembering the ball suddenly parted the storm clouds in Kai's thoughts. Opening one eye, he peered down at the android. "Why didn't the mechanic come with you?"

"She did," said Nainsi. "I left her waiting outside the palace. She was not allowed entrance without an official pass."

"Outside the palace? Is she still there?"

"I suspect so, Your Highness."

Kai squeezed the vial in his pocket. "I don't suppose she said anything about the ball? If she's changed her mind?"

"She did not mention any ball."

"Right. Well." Gulping, he freed his hands from his pockets and rubbed his palms down the sides of his pants, realizing how hot his bottled anger had made him. "I really hope she has."

Twenty-Four

CINDER CROUCHED AGAINST THE WALL THAT BORDERED THE palace, the coolness from the stone soaking into her T-shirt. The crowd had gone, the only memory of them left in trampled signs. Even the guards had abandoned the courtyard, though the intricate iron gate remained locked. Two stone *qilins* were perched above Cinder's head, occasionally sending out a magnetic pulse that hummed in her ears.

Her hand had finally stopped trembling. The warnings across her vision had finally disappeared. But the confusion remained, persistent as ever.

She was Lunar. Fine.

She was a rare breed of Lunar, a shell, who couldn't twist the thoughts and emotions of others and was immune to the tampering herself.

Fine.

But then why had Levana's glamour affected her the same as everyone else?

Either Dr. Erland was wrong, or he was lying. Maybe she wasn't Lunar at all, and he'd been mistaken. Maybe her immunity was due to something else.

She released a frustrated groan. Never had the curiosity to know her background, her history, been so intense. She needed to know the truth.

The humming of the gates on their buried tracks startled her. Cinder looked up, spotting a pristine white android rolling toward her on the cobblestones.

"Linh Cinder?" It held out a scanner.

Blinking, she clambered to her feet, braced against the wall for support. "Yes?" she said, extending her wrist.

The scanner beeped and, without having come to a complete stop, the android turned its torso 180 degrees and started rumbling back toward the palace. "Follow me."

"Wait—what?" Her gaze darted fearfully up toward the balcony where the Lunar queen had stood.

"His Imperial Highness has requested a word with you."

Checking her gloves, Cinder cast a look toward the road that would take her away from the palace, back to the safety of being an invisible girl in a very big city. Releasing a slow breath, she turned and followed the android.

The palace's elaborate, two-story entry doors were gilded in gold and nearly blinding with the sun glinting off their sheen as they opened. The lobby beyond was blessedly cool and filled with grand jade sculptures, exotic flowers, the voices and footsteps of dozens of harried diplomats and government employees, combined with the calming song of bubbling water—but Cinder hardly noticed any of it. She was filled with panic at the possibility of finding herself face-to-face with Queen Levana, until she found herself face-to-face with Prince Kai instead. He was waiting against a carved pillar.

He straightened when he saw her and almost smiled, but not one of his brilliant, carefree smiles. In fact, he looked exhausted.

Cinder bowed her head. "Your Highness."

"Linh-mèi. Nainsi told me you were waiting."

"They weren't letting people into the palace. I just wanted to be sure she got to you all right." She tucked her hands behind her. "I hope your national-security issues will be resolved soon." Cinder attempted a lightness in her voice, but Kai's expression seemed to falter.

He dropped his gaze to the android. "That will be all," he said, and waited until the android had disappeared into an alcove by the entrance, before continuing. "I apologize for taking up your time, but I wanted to thank you personally for fixing her."

She shrugged. "It was an honor. I hope . . . I hope you'll find what you're looking for."

Kai's gaze squinted suspiciously, and he glanced over his shoulder as two well-dressed women passed by, one talking animatedly, the other nodding in agreement, neither paying Cinder and Kai any attention. When they had passed, Kai let out a breath and turned back to her. "Something's come up. I need to go talk to Dr. Erland."

Cinder nodded in understanding, perhaps too forcefully. "Of

course," she said, backing away toward the massive doors. "Now that Nainsi's back, I'll just—"

"Would you like to walk with me?"

She paused mid-step. "Excuse me?"

"You can tell me what you found. What was wrong with her."

She wrung her hands, unsure if the tingling on her skin was delight, or something closer to dread. The knowledge of the queen's presence lingered, unavoidable. Still, she found herself fighting down a stupid grin. "Sure. Of course."

Kai seemed relieved as he cocked his head toward a wide corridor. "So . . . what *was* wrong with her?" he said as they made their way through the majestic lobby.

"A chip," she said. "The direct communication chip interrupted her power connection, I think. Removing it was all it took to wake her up."

"Direct communication chip?"

Cinder scanned the people milling around them, none of whom seemed at all interested in the crown prince. Nevertheless, she lowered her voice when she answered. "Right, the D-COMM. Didn't you install it?"

He shook his head. "No. We use D-COMMs for international conferencing, but beside that, I don't think I've ever seen one. Why would someone put one in an android?"

Cinder pressed her lips, thinking of the things Nainsi had been saying when she'd awoken. Nainsi had probably been relaying that same information when she'd gone unconscious, most likely over the direct communication link.

But who had received it?

"Cinder?"

She pulled on the hem of her glove. She wanted to tell him that she knew about his research, that someone else probably knew too, but she couldn't say anything in the middle of the crowded palace corridors.

"Someone must have had access to her, right before she malfunctioned. In order to install the chip."

"Why would anyone install her with a faulty chip in the first place?"

"I don't think it was entirely faulty. It does seem that some data was sent over the link before Nainsi shut down."

"What—" Kai hesitated. Cinder noticed the nervousness in his eyes, the tensing of his posture. He craned his head closer to her, barely slowing his pace. "What kind of information can be sent over direct comms?"

"Anything that can be sent over the net."

"But if someone was accessing her remotely like that, they couldn't . . . I mean, she would have to allow access to any information they received, right?"

Cinder opened her mouth, paused, closed it again. "I don't know. I'm not sure how a direct comm would function in an android, especially one that wasn't equipped for it in the first place. But there's a chance that whoever put that chip in her was hoping to gather information. Possibly . . . specific information."

Kai's gaze was distant as they crossed an enclosed glass

bridge into the research wing. "So how do I find out who put that chip in her, and what they learned?"

Cinder gulped. "I tried to initiate the link, but it seemed to have been disabled. I'll keep trying, but at this point, I have no way of knowing who was on the other end. As for what they learned . . ."

Catching on to the hint in her tone, Kai stopped walking and turned to face her, eyes burning.

Cinder lowered her voice, speaking in a rush. "I know what it is you were looking for. I heard some of the information Nainsi had discovered."

"*I* don't even know what she discovered yet."

She nodded. "It's . . . interesting."

His gaze brightened and he inched toward her, craning his neck. "She's alive, isn't she? Does Nainsi know where to find her?"

Cinder shook her head, fear clawing at her, knowing that Levana was somewhere in these very walls. "We can't talk about this here. And Nainsi will know more than I do anyway."

Kai frowned and stepped back, but she could see his thoughts still churning as he proceeded to the elevator bank and gave directions to the android there.

"So," he said, folding his arms while they waited. "You're telling me that Nainsi has some important information, but some unknown person may also have that information."

"I'm afraid so," said Cinder. "Also, the chip itself was unusual. It wasn't silicon or carbon. It was like no chip I'd ever seen before."

Kai peered at her, brows knit. "How so?"

Cinder held up her fingers as if pinching the chip between them, envisioning it. "Size and shape, it looked just like a normal chip. But it was shimmery. Like . . . tiny gemstones. Pearlescent, kind of."

The color drained from Kai's face. A second later, he shut his eyes with a grimace. "It's Lunar."

"What? Are you sure?"

"Their ships are made out of the same stuff. I'm not sure what it is but—" He cursed, kneading his thumb across his temple. "It must have been Sybil, or her guard. They arrived days before Nainsi broke down."

"Sybil?"

"Levana's thaumaturge. The minion that does all her dirty work."

Cinder felt like a clamp was suffocating her lungs. If the information had gone to this Sybil, it had almost certainly gone to the queen.

"Elevator B for His Imperial Highness," said the android as the doors of the second elevator opened. Cinder followed Kai into it, unable to resist glancing up at the camera on the ceiling. If Lunars had infiltrated a royal android, they could have infiltrated anything in the palace.

She brushed a loose strand of hair behind her ear, her paranoia forcing her to act normal as the doors closed. "I take it things aren't going too well with the queen?"

Kai grimaced as if it were the most painful topic in the world and fell back against the wall. Cinder's heart stirred, watching as his royal demeanor slid off him. She dropped her gaze to the toes of her boots.

"I didn't think it was possible to hate anyone as much as I hate her. She's evil."

Cinder flinched. "Do you think it's safe to . . . I mean, if she put this chip in your android . . ."

Understanding flickered over Kai's face. He looked up at the camera, then shrugged. "I don't care. She knows I hate her. Trust me, she's not trying very hard to change that."

Cinder licked her lips. "I saw what she did to the protestors."

Kai nodded. "I shouldn't have let her face them. Once it gets on the netscreens about how fast she controlled them, the city will be chaos." He folded his arms, scrunching his shoulders up toward his ears. "Plus, she's now under the impression that we're intentionally harboring Lunar fugitives."

Her heart skipped. "Really?"

"I know, it's absurd. The *last* thing I want is more power-hungry Lunars running rampant in my country. Why would I—? *Argh.* It's so *frustrating.*"

Cinder rubbed her arms, suddenly nervous. She was the reason Levana believed Kai was harboring Lunars. She hadn't considered that being noticed by the queen could put Kai in jeopardy too.

When Kai fell silent, she risked a glance at him. He was staring at her hands. Cinder snapped them up against her chest, checking the gloves, but they were fine.

"Do you ever take those off?" he asked.

"No."

Kai tilted his head, peering at her as if he could see right through to the metal plate in her head. The intensity of his gaze didn't mellow. "I think you should go to the ball with me."

She clutched her fingers. His expression was too genuine, too sure. Her nerves tingled. "Stars," she muttered. "Didn't you already ask me that?"

"I'm hoping for a more favorable answer this time. And I seem to be getting more desperate by the minute."

"How charming."

Kai's lips twitched. "Please?"

"Why?"

"Why not?"

"I mean, why *me*?"

Kai hooked his thumbs on his pockets. "So if my escape hover breaks down, I'll have someone on hand to fix it?"

She rolled her eyes and found herself unable to look at him again, staring instead at the red emergency button beside the doors.

"I mean it. I can't go alone. And I *really* can't go with Levana."

"Well there are about 200,000 single girls in this city who would fall over themselves to have the privilege."

A hush passed between them. He wasn't touching her, but she could feel his presence, warm and overpowering. She could feel the elevator growing hot, despite the fact that her temperature gauge assured her it hadn't changed.

"Cinder."

She couldn't help it. She looked at him. Her defenses withered a bit upon encountering the openness in his brown eyes. His confidence had been replaced with worry. Uncertainty.

"200,000 single girls," he said. "Why not you?"

Cyborg. Lunar. Mechanic. She was the last thing he wanted.

She opened her lips, and the elevator stopped. "I'm sorry. But trust me—you don't want to go with me."

The doors opened and the tension released her. She rushed out of the elevator, head down, trying not to look at the small group of people waiting for an elevator.

"Come to the ball with me."

She froze. Everyone in the hallway froze.

Cinder turned back. Kai was still standing in elevator B, one hand propping open the door.

Her nerves were frazzled, and all the emotions of the past hour were converging into a single, sickening feeling—exasperation. The hall was filled with doctors, nurses, androids, officials, technicians, and they all fell into an awkward hush and stared at the prince and the girl in the baggy cargo pants he was flirting with.

Flirting.

Squaring her shoulders, she retreated back into the elevator and pushed him inside, not even caring that it was with her metal hand. "Hold the elevator," he said to the android as the doors shut them in. He smiled. "That got your attention."

"Listen," she said. "I'm sorry. I really am. But I can't go to the ball with you. You just have to trust me on that."

He gazed down at the gloved hand splayed across his chest. Cinder pulled away, crossing her arms over her chest.

"Why? Why don't you want to go with me?"

She huffed. "It's not that I don't want to go with *you*, it's that I'm not going *at all*."

"So you *do* want to go with me."

Cinder locked her shoulders. "It doesn't matter. Because I can't."

"But I need you."

"*Need* me?"

"Yes. Don't you see? If I'm spending all my time with *you*, then Queen Levana can't rope me in to any conversations or . . ." He shuddered. "Dancing."

Cinder reeled back, her gaze losing focus. Queen Levana. Of course this was about Queen Levana. What had Peony told her, ages ago? Rumors of a marriage alliance?

"Not that I have anything against dancing. I can dance. If you want to dance."

She squinted at him. "What?"

"Or not, if you don't want to. Or if you don't know how. Which is nothing to be ashamed of."

She started to rub her forehead, a headache developing, but stopped when she realized her gloves were filthy. "I really, really can't go," she said. "You see . . ." *I don't have a dress. Adri won't allow it. Because Queen Levana would kill me.* "It's my sister."

"Your *sister*?"

She wet her throat and dropped her gaze to the polished

blackwood floor. Even the elevators were exquisite in the palace. "Yes. My little sister. She has the plague. And it just wouldn't be the same without her, and I can't go—won't go. I'm sorry." Cinder was surprised to find the words ringing true, even to her ear. She wondered if her lie detector would have gone off if it could see her.

Kai slipped back against the wall, hair fringing his eyes. "No, I'm sorry. I didn't know."

"You couldn't have." Cinder rubbed her palms down her sides. Her skin had grown hot beneath the gloves. "Actually, there's something . . . I'd like to tell you. If that's all right."

He listed his head, curious.

"I just think she'd like you to know about her is all. Um . . . her name is Peony. She's fourteen, and she's madly in love with you."

His eyebrows rose.

"I just thought that if, by some crazy miracle, she might survive—do you think you could ask her to dance? At the ball?" Cinder's voice chafed her throat as she said it, knowing that crazy miracles didn't happen. But she had to ask.

Kai's gaze burned into her, and he gave her a slow, determined nod. "It would be my pleasure."

She dipped her head. "I'll let her know to look forward to it." From the edge of her gaze, Cinder saw Kai slip a hand into his pocket and ball it into a fist.

"People are probably getting suspicious out there," said Cinder. "The rumors will be spreading like mad." She put an awkward chuckle into the statement, but Kai didn't match it. When she dared to look up at him again, he was staring unfocused at the paneled wall behind her, his shoulders heavy.

"Are you all right?"

He started to nod, but stopped. "Levana thinks she can play me like a puppet." His brow creased. "And it just occurred to me that she might be right."

Cinder fidgeted with her gloves. How easy it was to forget who she was speaking to, and all the things he must have on his mind, things so much more important than her. Even more important than Peony.

"I feel like I'm going to ruin everything," he said.

"You won't." She itched to reach out to him, but held back, wringing her hands. "You're going to be one of those emperors that everyone loves and admires."

"Yeah. I'm sure."

"I mean it. Look how much you care, how hard you're trying, and you're not even emperor yet. Besides." She folded her arms, burying her hands. "It's not like you're alone. You have advisers and province reps and secretaries and treasurers and . . . I mean, really, how much harm can one man possibly do all on his own?"

Kai half laughed. "You're not really making me feel better, but I appreciate the effort." He raised his eyes to the ceiling. "I shouldn't be telling you all this, anyway. It isn't your problem to worry about. It's just . . . you're easy to talk to."

She shuffled her feet. "It is kind of my problem. I mean, we all have to live here."

"You could move to Europe."

"You know, I've actually been considering that lately."

Kai laughed again, the warmth returning to the sound. "If that's not a vote of confidence, I don't know what is."

She ducked her head. "Look, I know you're royalty and all, but people are probably getting really impatient for this ele—" Her breath snagged as Kai leaned forward, so close she was sure for a heartbeat he meant to kiss her. She froze, a wave of panic crashing into her, and barely managed to look up.

Instead of kissing her, he whispered, "Imagine there was a cure, but finding it would cost you everything. It would completely ruin your life. What would you do?"

The warm air enclosed her. So close, she could catch a faint soapy smell coming from him.

His eyes bored into hers, waiting, a tinge desperate.

Cinder wet her mouth. "Ruin *my* life to save a million others? It's not much of a choice."

His lips parted—she had no choice but to look at them and then immediately back into his eyes. She could almost count the black lashes around them. But then a sadness filtered into his gaze.

"You're right. There's no real choice."

Her body simultaneously yearned to close the gap between them and push him away. The anticipation that warmed her lips made it impossible to do either. "Your Highness?"

She tilted her face toward him, the subtlest of movements. She listened to his wavering breath and this time, it was his eyes dropping to her lips.

"I'm sorry," he said. "I'm sure this is horribly inappropriate, but . . . it seems that my life is about to be ruined."

Her brow drew together, questioning, but he didn't elaborate. His fingers, light as a breath, brushed her elbow. He craned his head. Cinder couldn't move, barely managing to wet her lips as her eyes slipped shut.

Pain exploded in her head. Raced down her spine.

Cinder gasped and folded over, gripping her stomach. The world lurched. Acid burned her throat. Kai cried out and caught her as she stumbled forward, easing her onto the elevator floor.

Cinder shuddered against him, light-headed.

The pain was doused as quickly as it had started.

Cinder lay panting, hunched over Kai's arm. His voice began to filter past her eardrums—her name, again and again. Muffled words. *Are you all right? What happened? What did I do?*

She was hot, her hand sweating in the glove, her face burning. Like before, when Dr. Erland had touched her. What was happening to her?

She licked her lips. Her tongue was cotton in her mouth. "I'm all right," she said, wondering if it were true. "It's gone. I'm fine." She squeezed her eyes shut and waited, afraid that the slightest movement would bring the pain back again.

Kai's fingers pressed against her brow, her hair. "Are you sure? Can you move?"

She attempted a nod and forced herself to look at him.

Kai gasped and jerked away, his hand freezing inches from

Cinder's brow. Fear clamped her gut. Was her retina display showing?

"What?" she asked, ducking her face behind her hand, running nervous fingers over her skin, her hair. "What is it?"

"N-nothing."

When she dared meet Kai's gaze again, he was blinking rapidly, confusion filling his eyes.

"Your Highness?"

"No, it was nothing." His lips turned upward, unconvincingly. "I was seeing things."

"What?"

He shook his head. "It was nothing. Here." He stood and coaxed her up beside him. "Maybe we should see if the doctor can squeeze you into his busy schedule."

Twenty-Five

KAI RECEIVED TWO COMMS BETWEEN THE TIME THEY LEFT the elevator and the time they reached Dr. Erland's office—Cinder knew because she could hear the chime from his belt—but he didn't answer them. He insisted on helping her down the hallway, despite her protests that she could walk just fine, despite the curious stares of passersby. Curious stares did not seem to bother the prince half so much as they bothered her.

He didn't knock when they reached the office, and Dr. Erland, upon seeing who had burst in without announcement, did not seem surprised when he saw the prince.

"It happened again," said Kai. "Her fainting, whatever it is."

Dr. Erland's blue eyes switched to Cinder.

"It's gone now," she said. "I'm *fine.*"

"You're not fine," said Kai. "What causes it? What can we do to make it stop?"

"I'll take a look at her," said Dr. Erland. "We will see what can be done to keep it from happening again."

Kai seemed to think this was an acceptable answer, but only barely. "If you need funds to do the research . . . or special equipment, or anything."

"Let's not get ahead of ourselves," said the doctor. "She probably just needs another adjustment."

Cinder clenched her teeth as her lie detector flashed at her. He was lying to the prince again. He was lying to her. But Kai didn't object, didn't question. He sucked in a deep breath and faced Cinder. The expression made her uncomfortable—the look that suggested she was a china doll, easily shattered.

And perhaps a hint of disappointment hung behind it all.

"Really, I'm fine."

She could tell he was unconvinced but had no way of arguing with her. His communicator dinged again. He finally glanced at it, then scowled and shut it off. "I need to go."

"Clearly."

"The prime minister of Africa called a world leaders' meeting. Very dull and political. My adviser's about to have a breakdown."

She raised her eyebrows in a look that she hoped conveyed how much she was all right with him leaving her. After all, he was a prince. The most powerful men and women on Earth had summoned him. She understood.

And yet he was still here, with her.

"I'm *fine,*" she said. "Go away."

The worry in his eyes softened. He spun toward Dr. Erland and pulled something from his pocket, forcing it into the doctor's hand. "I also came to bring you this."

Dr. Erland slipped his spectacles on and held the glass vial up into the light. It was filled with clear liquid. "And this is?"

"A gift from Queen Levana. She claims it's an antidote to letumosis."

Cinder's heart lurched. Her gaze focused on the vial.

An antidote?

Peony.

Dr. Erland's complexion had drained, his eyes widening behind the glasses. "Is that so?"

"It could be a trick. I don't know. Supposedly, it's one dosage—enough for an adult male."

"I see."

"So, do you think you can duplicate it? If it is a cure?"

Dr. Erland drew his lips into a thin line and lowered the vial. "That depends on many things, Your Highness," he said after a long pause. "But I will try my best."

"Thank you. Let me know as soon as you find anything."

"Of course."

Relief loosened Kai's brow. He turned to Cinder. "And you'll let me know if anything—"

"Yes."

"—changes your mind about going to the ball?"

Cinder pressed her lips together.

Kai's smile barely reached his eyes. With a curt bow to the doctor, he was gone. Cinder retrained her gaze on the vial, enclosed in the doctor's fist. Desire coursed through her. But then she noticed the whitening of his knuckles and looked up, finding herself pinned under a stormy glare.

"What do you think you are *doing* here?" he said, planting his free hand on the desk. She started, surprised by his vehemence. "Don't you realize that Queen Levana is here, now, in this palace? Did you not *understand* when I told you to stay away?"

"I had to bring the prince's android back. It's part of my job."

"You're talking livelihood. I'm talking *life*. You are not safe here!"

"For your information that android could be a matter of *life*." She clenched her teeth, refraining from saying more. With a heavy sigh, she peeled the stifling gloves from her hands and slipped them into her pocket. "All right, I'm sorry, but I'm here now."

"You have to go. Now. What if she asked to see the lab facilities?"

"Why would the queen care about your lab facilities?" She claimed the seat opposite Dr. Erland. He stayed standing. "Besides, it's too late. The queen already saw me."

She expected the doctor to explode with this announcement, but instead his frown was quickly replaced with horror. His thick eyebrows drew up beneath his cap. Slowly, he sank down into his seat. "She *saw* you? Are you sure?"

Cinder nodded. "I was in the courtyard when the protests were going on. Queen Levana appeared on one of the upper balconies and she . . . did something. To the crowd. Brainwashed or glamoured them or whatever it's called. They all calmed down and stopped protesting. It was so *eerie*. Like they all just forgot why they were there, that they *hated* her. And then they just left."

"Yes." Dr. Erland set the vial on the desk. "It suddenly

becomes clear how she is able to keep her own people from rebelling against her, isn't it?"

Cinder leaned forward, tapping her metal fingers against the desk. "Here's the thing, though. You said before that shells aren't affected by the Lunar glamour, right? That's why she ordered them—us—to be killed?"

"That's right."

"But it did affect me. I trusted her, as much as anyone else. At least, until my programming kicked in and took control." She watched as Dr. Erland took off his hat, adjusted the brim, and pulled it back over his fluffy gray hair. "That shouldn't have happened, right? Because I'm a shell."

"No," he said, without conviction. "That shouldn't have happened."

He lifted himself from his chair and faced the floor-to-ceiling windows.

A compulsion to reach out and snatch the vial off the desk surged to the tips of her fingers, but Cinder withheld it. The antidote—if it was an antidote—was meant for everyone.

Gulping, she leaned back. "Doctor? You don't seem too surprised."

He raised a hand and tapped his mouth with two fingers before slowly turning toward her.

"I may have misread your diagnostics." *Lie.*

She squeezed her hands in her lap. "Or you just didn't tell me the truth."

His eyebrows knit, but he didn't deny it.

Cinder curled her fingers. "So I'm not Lunar?"

"No, no. You are most definitely Lunar." *Truth.*

She sulked in the chair, disappointed.

"I've been doing some research on your family, Miss Linh." He must have seen her eyes brighten because he quickly held up both hands. "I mean your *adoptive* family. Are you aware that your deceased guardian, Linh Garan, designed android systems?"

"Um." Cinder thought about the plaques and awards sitting on the mantel in Adri's living room. "That sounds kind of familiar."

"Well. The year before your surgery, he unveiled an invention at the New Beijing science fair. A prototype. He called it a bioelectrical security system."

Cinder stared. "A what?"

Standing, Dr. Erland tinkered with the netscreen until a familiar holograph flickered before them. He zoomed in on the representation of Cinder's neck, showing the small dark spot on her upper spine. "This."

Cinder reached for the back of her neck, massaging.

"It is a device that ties in with a person's nervous system. It has two purposes—on an Earthen, it prevents outside manipulation of their personal bioelectricity. Essentially, it makes it so that they are immune to Lunar control. Oppositely, when installed on a Lunar, it keeps them from being able to manipulate the bioelectricity of others. It is as if you were to put a lock on the Lunar gift."

Cinder shook her head, still rubbing. "A lock? On magic? Is that even possible?"

Dr. Erland lifted a finger to her. "It is not magic. Claiming it to be magic only empowers them."

"Fine. Bioelectrical whatever. Is it possible?"

"Evidently so. The Lunar gift is the ability to use your brain to output and control electromagnetic energy. To block this ability would require alteration of the nervous system as it enters the brain stem, and to do that while still allowing full movement and sensation would be . . . it's quite impressive. Ingenious, really."

Jaw dropping, Cinder followed the doctor with her gaze as he slipped back into his chair. "He would have been rich."

"If he had survived, perhaps he would have been." The doctor turned off the screen. "When he unveiled the invention at the fair, the prototype was as yet untested, and his contemporaries were skeptical—and rightfully so. He first needed to test it."

"And for that, he needed a Lunar."

"Ideally, he needed both a Lunar and an Earthen subject—in order to test the two purposes separately. If he found an Earthen subject, I have no idea, but clearly he did find you, and he did install his invention as a means of keeping you from using your gift. This explains why you have not had the use of your gift since your operation."

She bounced her foot, restless. "You didn't misread my diagnostics. You knew this from the start. From the moment you walked into that lab room, you *knew* I was Lunar and I had this crazy lock and—you *knew*."

Dr. Erland wrung his hands. For the first time, Cinder noticed a gold band on his finger.

"What did you do to me?" she said, planting her feet and standing. "When you touched me and it hurt so bad and I passed out and—and then again today. What's causing it? What's happening to me?"

"Calm down, Miss Linh."

"Why? So you can lie to me some more, just like you lie to the prince?"

"If I have lied, it has only been to protect you."

"Protect me from what?"

Dr. Erland steepled his fingers. "I understand you're confused—"

"No, you don't understand anything! A week ago, I knew exactly who I was, *what* I was, and maybe that was a worthless cyborg, but at least I knew that. And now . . . now I'm Lunar, I'm a Lunar who supposedly might have magic but can't use it, and now there's this insane queen who for some reason wants to *kill* me."

SPIKING LEVELS OF ADRENALINE, warned her control panel. **RECOMMENDED COURSE OF ACTION: SLOW, MEASURED BREATHS. COUNTING 1, 2, 3 . . .**

"Please, calm *down,* Miss Linh. It is, in fact, a good thing that you were selected to receive this lock."

"I'm sure you're right. I just *love* being treated like a guinea pig, don't you know?"

"Like it or not, the lock has been beneficial to you."

"How?"

"If you would stop yelling, I would tell you."

She bit her lip and felt her breath stabilizing almost against her will. "Fine, but tell me the truth this time." Crossing her arms, she sat back down.

"Sometimes you are quite unnerving, Miss Linh." Dr. Erland sighed, scratching at his temple. "You see, manipulating bioelectricity comes so natural to Lunars that it's virtually impossible to refrain from using it, especially at such a young age. Left to your own devices, you would have drawn too much attention to yourself. It would have been like tattooing 'Lunar' across your forehead. And even if you *could* have learned to control it, the gift is such a fundamental part of our internal makeup that tempering it can create devastating psychological side effects—hallucinations, depression . . . even madness." He pressed his fingertips together. Waited. "So you see, putting a lock on your gift protected you, in many ways, from yourself."

Cinder stared, eyes boring.

"Do you understand how this was mutually beneficial?" continued the doctor. "Linh Garan had his subject, and you were able to fit in with Earthens without losing your mind."

Cinder slowly leaned forward. *"Our?"*

"Pardon?"

"*Our.* You said, the gift is 'a fundamental part of *our* internal makeup.'"

The doctor drew himself up, adjusting the lapels of his coat. "Ah. Did I?"

"You're Lunar."

He took off his hat and tossed it onto the desk. He looked smaller without it. Older.

"Don't lie to me."

"I wasn't going to, Miss Linh. Only trying to think how to explain in a way that will make you look less accusatory at me."

Setting her jaw, Cinder hopped out of the chair again and backed away from the desk. She stared at him, hard, as if there really might appear a "Lunar" tattoo on his brow. "How can I believe anything you've said? How do I know you're not brainwashing me right now?"

He shrugged. "If I were to go around glamouring people all day, I would at least make myself seem taller, don't you think?"

She frowned, ignoring him. She was thinking of the queen on the balcony, how her optobionics had warned her of a lie even when nothing had been said. Somehow, her brain was able to tell the difference between reality and illusion, even when her eyes couldn't.

Squinting, she jutted a finger at the doctor. "You *did* use your mind control on me. When we met. You . . . you brainwashed me. Just like the queen. You made me trust you."

"Be fair. You were attacking me with a wrench."

Her anger wavered.

Dr. Erland opened his palms to her. "I assure you, Miss Linh, in the twelve years that I have been on Earth, I have not abused the gift once, and I am paying the price for that decision every day. My mental stability, my psychological health, my very senses are failing me because I refuse to manipulate the thoughts and feelings of those around me. Not all Lunars can be trusted—I know that as well as anyone—but you *can* trust me."

Cinder gulped and braced herself on the back of the chair. "Does Kai know?"

"Of course not. No one can know."

"But you work in the palace. You see Kai all the time. And Emperor Rikan!"

A flash of irritation sparked through Dr. Erland's blue eyes. "Yes, and why should this upset you?"

"Because you're *Lunar*!"

"As are you. Should I consider the prince's safety threatened because he asked you to the ball?"

"That's different!"

"Don't be dense, Miss Linh. I understand the prejudices. In many ways, they're understandable, even justified, given Earth's history with Luna. But it does not mean we are all greedy, self-serving devils. Believe me—there is not a person on this planet who would like to see Levana off the throne more than I would. I would kill her myself if I had the power." The doctor's face had gone cherry pink, his eyes blazing.

"All right." Cinder pinched the chair's cushion until she felt the material puncture beneath her steel fingers. "I can accept that. Not all Lunars are devils, and not all Lunars are as easily brainwashed into following Levana. But even of those who wish to defy her, how many of them risk their lives to run away?" She paused, eyeing the doctor. "So why did *you*?"

Dr. Erland moved as if he were going to stand, but after a hesitation, his shoulders sank, deflated. "She killed my daughter."

Truth.

Cinder pulled back.

"The worst part," continued the doctor, "is that had it been any other child, I would have felt it was right."

"What? Why?"

"Because she was a shell." He picked his hat off the desk and analyzed it while he spoke, his fingers tracing the herringbone pattern. "I'd agreed with the laws in the past, thought the shells were dangerous. That our society would fall apart if they were allowed to live. But not *my* little girl." An ironic smile twisted up his lips. "After she was born, I wanted to run away, to bring her to Earth, but my wife was even more devoted to Her Majesty than I had been. She wanted nothing to do with the child. And so my little Crescent Moon was taken away, like all the others." He stuffed the hat back onto his head and squinted up at Cinder. "She would be about your age now."

Cinder came around the chair and perched on the edge of the seat. "I'm sorry."

"It was a long time ago. But I need you to understand, Miss Linh, what it was that someone went through to bring *you* here. To go so far as to hide your Lunar gift—to protect you."

Cinder folded her arms, cowering into herself. "But why me? I'm not a shell. I wasn't in any danger. It doesn't make sense."

"It will, I promise. Listen carefully, as this may be something of a shock to you."

"A shock? You mean all that was just the precursor?"

His eyes softened. "Your gift is returning, Miss Linh. I was able to manipulate your bioelectricity to temporarily overwhelm

Linh Garan's prototype. That's what I did the first day you were here, when you lost consciousness, and the lock on your gift has been irreparably damaged because of it. With practice, you will be able to override the fail-safes on your own, until you are in complete control of your gift again. I understand it is painful when it comes on quickly like it did today, but those instances should be rare, only during times of extreme emotional disturbance. Can you think of anything that may have set it off earlier?"

Cinder's stomach flipped, recalling Kai's closeness in the elevator. She cleared her throat. "What you're saying is that I'm becoming Lunar for real. Magic and all."

Dr. Erland screwed up his lips, but didn't correct her again. "Yes. It will take some time, but you will eventually have all the use of your natural gift that you were born with." He spun his fingers in the air. "Would you like to try and use it now? You may be able to. I'm not sure."

Cinder imagined a spark in her wires, something crackling at the base of her spine. She knew it was probably in her head, self-induced panic, but she couldn't be sure. What did it feel like to be Lunar? To have that kind of power?

She shook her head. "No, that's all right. I'm not ready for that."

A thin smile stretched across the doctor's lips, as if he were faintly disappointed. "Of course. When you're ready."

Hugging her arms around her waist, she inhaled a shaky breath. "Doctor?"

"Yes?"

"Are you immune to letumosis, like me?"

Dr. Erland's held her focus, unflinching. "Yes. I am."

"Then why haven't you just used your own blood samples to find a cure? So many people have died. . . . And the cyborg draft . . ."

The wrinkles on his face softened. "I *have* been, Miss Linh. Where do you think the twenty-seven antidotes we've already been through came from?"

"And none of them worked." She tucked her feet beneath her chair, feeling small. Insignificant—again. "So my immunity isn't the miracle you made it out to be." Her eyes fell on the vial. The queen's antidote.

"Miss Linh."

Meeting the doctor's gaze, Cinder found a glint there. Barely contained giddiness, like the first time she'd met him.

"You are the miracle I was looking for," he said. "But you are right. It was not because of your immunity."

Cinder stared at him, waiting for him to explain. What else could be special about her? Had he actually been searching for the ingenious lock on her magic—Linh Garan's prototype?

Her internal comm pinged before he could continue. She jolted, turning away from the doctor as green text skittered across her eyesight.

COMM RECEIVED FROM NEW BEIJING DISTRICT 29, LETUMOSIS QUARANTINE. LINH PEONY ENTERED FOURTH STAGE OF LETUMOSIS AT 17:24 ON 18 AUG 126 T.E.

"Miss Linh?"

Her fingers trembled. "My sister's entered the fourth stage." Her gaze settled on the vial atop Dr. Erland's desk.

He followed the look. "I see," he said. "The fourth stage works quickly. There isn't much time to lose." Reaching forward, he grasped the vial between his forefingers. "A promise is a promise."

Cinder's heart thumped against her ribs. "But don't you need it? To duplicate?"

Standing, the doctor paced to the bookshelf and pulled a beaker stand toward him. "How old is she?"

"Fourteen."

"Then I think this will be sufficient." He poured a quarter of the antidote into the beaker. Corking the vial, he turned back to Cinder. "You do realize it came from Queen Levana. I do not know what her plan could be, but I know it will not be for the greater good of Earth. This could very well be a trick."

"My sister is already dying."

He nodded and held it out to her. "That is what I thought."

Cinder's stood up and took the vial, cradling it in her palm. "You're sure?"

"On one condition, Miss Linh."

Gulping, she clutched the vial against her chest.

"You must promise me not to come near this palace again so long as Queen Levana is here."

Twenty-Six

PRINCE KAI ARRIVED AT THE MEETING SEVENTEEN MINUTES late. He was met with the disgruntled looks of Torin and four other government officials all sitting at a long table, along with an additional dozen faces peering out from their respective netscreens on the paneled wall before him. Ambassadors from every Earthen country—the United Kingdom, the European Federation, the African Union, the American Republic, and Australia. One queen, two prime ministers, one president, one governor-general, three state representatives, and two province representatives. Text along the bottom of the screens helpfully displayed their names, titles, and country affiliations.

"How kind of the young prince to grace us with his presence," said Torin, as the officials around the table stood to welcome Kai.

Kai waved Torin's comment away. "I thought you could use my guidance."

On the wall of screens, Prime Minister Kamin of Africa grunted most unladylike. Everyone else remained silent.

Kai moved to take his regular seat when Torin stopped him and gestured at the chair at the end of the table. The emperor's chair. Jaw clenching, Kai switched seats. He looked up at the grid of faces—although each of the world leaders was thousands of miles away, staring into their own wall of netscreens, it felt as if their eyes were focused on him, disapproving.

He cleared his throat, trying not to fidget. "Is the conference link secure?" he asked, the question bringing back his concerns over the direct communication chip Cinder had found inside Nainsi. The screens in this room were equipped with D-COMMs so they could hold international meetings without fear of anyone listening in through the net. Had the chip inside Nainsi been put there by one of Levana's cronies for the same reason—secrecy, privacy? If so, what exactly had she learned?

"Of course," said Torin. "The links have been verified for nearly twenty minutes, Your Highness. We were just discussing Earth's relationship with Luna when you deigned to join us."

Kai clasped his hands together. "Right. Now, is that the one where the dominatrix queen throws a tantrum and threatens war every time she doesn't get her way? That relationship?"

No one laughed. Torin's gaze focused on Kai. "Is this timing inconvenient for you, Your Highness?"

Kai cleared his throat. "I apologize. That was inappropriate." He met the faces of the Earth's leaders, watching him from thousands of miles away. He gripped his hands beneath the table, feeling like a child sitting in on his father's meetings.

"Obviously," said President Vargas from America, "the

relationship between Earth and Luna has been strained for many years, and the rule of Queen Levana has only made things worse. We can't put blame on any one party, but the important thing is that we fix it, before—"

"Before she starts a war," finished a province representative from South America, "as the young prince already observed."

"But if the reports on the net are not mistaken," said Governor-General Williams of Australia, "communication between Earth and Luna has begun again. Can it be true that Levana is on Earth *now*? I could hardly believe the news when I heard it."

"Yes," said Torin, as all eyes switched to him. "The queen arrived yesterday afternoon, and her head thaumaturge, Sybil Mira, has been a guest in our court for just over two weeks."

"Has Levana informed you of her purpose for this visit?" said Prime Minister Kamin.

"She claims that she wants to reach a peace agreement."

One of the American Republic reps guffawed. "I'll believe it when I see it."

President Vargas ignored the comment. "Quite suspicious timing, isn't it? So soon after . . ." He didn't finish. No one looked at Kai.

"We agree," said Torin, "but we could not refuse the request when it came."

"It does seem she was always more apt to discuss an alliance with the Commonwealth than any of us," said President Vargas, "but her requests were always unsatisfactory. Have those requests changed?"

Kai watched from the corner of his eye as Torin's chest slowly expanded. "No," he said. "To our knowledge, Her Majesty's requests have not changed. Her aim continues to be a marriage alliance with the Commonwealth's emperor."

Although the faces in the room and on the screens tried to remain static, the discomfort ratcheted around them. Kai gripped his hands so tight that crescent moons were left from his fingernails. He had always despised the diplomacy of these meetings. Everyone thinking the same thing, no one brave enough to say it.

And of course they would all be sympathetic to Kai's fate, and yet glad that it wasn't any of them. They would be angry that Queen Levana could infiltrate any Earthen country with her dictatorship, and yet certain that it would be an improvement over infiltrating Earth with her army.

"The Commonwealth's position," continued Torin, "has also not changed."

This *did* seem to jolt the crowd.

"You won't marry her?" said Queen Camilla of the United Kingdom, the wrinkles on her forehead deepening.

Kai squared his shoulders in defense. "My father was firm in his decision to avoid such an alliance, and I believe his reasons are as applicable today as they were last week, or last year, or ten years ago. I must consider what is best for my country."

"Have you told this to Levana?"

"I have not lied to her."

"And what will be her next move?" said Prime Minister Bromstad of Europe, a fair-haired man with kind eyes.

"What else?" said Kai. "She intends to add more bargaining chips to the pile until we cave."

Stares clashed through the screens. Torin's lips had gone white, his eyes urging Kai to tread lightly. Kai could guess that Torin hadn't intended to mention the antidote, at least until they could plan their next move—but letumosis was a pandemic that affected all of them. They at least had a right to know that an antidote might exist. Assuming Levana hadn't lied to him.

Kai took in a deep breath, splaying his palms out on the table. "Levana claims to have found a cure for letumosis."

The netscreens seemed to crackle with surprise, though the gathered leaders were all too stunned to speak.

"She brought a single dosage with her, and I've passed it off to our research team. We won't know if it's a true antidote until they've had a chance to study it. If it *is* real, then we need to find out if we can replicate it."

"And if we can't replicate it?"

Kai looked at the Australian governor-general. He was older than Kai's father had been by many years. They were all so much older than him. "I don't know," he said. "But I will do what has to be done for the Commonwealth." He enunciated Commonwealth very carefully. True, they were an alliance six countries and a single planet strong. But they all had their own loyalties, and he would not forget his.

"Even then," said Torin, "we can yet hope to make her see

reason and convince her to sign the Treaty of Bremen without a marriage alliance."

"She will refuse," said a state representative from the EF. "We mustn't fool ourselves. She is as stubborn—"

"Of course, the Commonwealth's imperial family is not the only royal bloodline she could harbor hopes of marrying into," said the African state representative. He said this knowing that his own country could not be a choice, as it was not a monarchy. Any marriage bond would be too superficial, too transient. He continued, "I think we should explore all possible options so that we can be sure to have an offer prepared, no matter what Levana decides to do next. An offer that we, as a group, feel would best benefit the citizenry of our entire planet."

Kai had followed the group's attention to Queen Camilla of the UK, who had an unmarried son in his early thirties, closer to Levana's age than Kai was. He noted how passive the queen was trying to appear and had to keep himself from looking smug. It felt nice to turn the tables.

And yet, politically, there was no doubt that Kai was the best option in Queen Levana's eyes. The prince from the United Kingdom was the youngest of three siblings and may never become king. Kai, on the other hand, would be coronated next week.

"What if she refuses anyone else?" said Queen Camilla, lifting an eyebrow that had seen too many youth surgeries over the years. When no one responded to the question, she continued. "I don't mean to raise undue alarm, but have you considered that her reason for coming to Earth might be to secure this alliance through force? Perhaps she intends to brainwash the young prince into marrying her."

Kai's stomach flipped. He could see his unease mirrored in the faces of the other diplomats. "Could she do that?" he asked.

When no one was quick to answer, he turned to Torin.

It took far, far too long for Torin to shake his head, looking frighteningly uncertain. "No," he said. "Perhaps, in theory, but no. In order to keep up the ruse, she could never leave your side. As soon as you were no longer under her influence, you could prove that the marriage wasn't legitimate. She wouldn't risk that."

"You mean we *hope* she wouldn't risk it," said Kai, not feeling very comforted.

"What about Levana's daughter, Princess Winter?" said President Vargas. "Has there been any discussion of her?"

"Stepdaughter," said Torin. "And what should we discuss in regards to the Lunar princess?"

"Why can't we form a marriage alliance with her?" said Queen Camilla. "She can't be any worse than Levana."

Torin folded his hands atop the table. "Princess Winter was of another mother and her father was a mere palace guard. She has no royal blood."

"But Luna might still honor a marriage alliance through her," said Kai. "Wouldn't they?"

Torin sighed, looking like he wished Kai had kept his mouth shut. "Politically, perhaps, but it does not change the fact that Queen Levana is in the difficult position of needing to marry and produce an heir who will continue the bloodline. I do not think she will agree to marry off her stepdaughter so long as *she* requires a suitable marriage arrangement."

"And there is no hope," said the African prime minister, "that the Lunars will ever accept Princess Winter as a queen?"

"Only if you can convince them to give up their superstitions," said Torin, "and we all know how deeply those are ingrained in their culture. Otherwise they will always insist on an heir of the royal bloodline."

"And what if Levana never has an heir? What will they do then?"

Kai slid his gaze to his adviser and raised an eyebrow.

"I'm not sure," Torin answered. "I'm sure the royal family has plenty of distant cousins who would be eager to stake their claim to the throne."

"So if Levana must marry," said the South American representative, "and she will marry only a Commonwealth emperor, and the Commonwealth emperor refuses to marry *her,* what then? We are at a stalemate."

"Perhaps," said Governor-General Williams, "she will make good on her threats."

Torin shook his head. "If her desire were to start a war, she's had plenty of opportunities."

"It seems clear," shot back the governor-general, "that her desire is to be empress. But we don't know what she has planned if you won't—"

"Actually, we do have an idea," said President Vargas, his voice heavy. "I'm afraid we no longer need to speculate if Levana intends to start a war against Earth. Our sources lead me to believe that war is not only likely but imminent."

An uneasy rustle shifted through the room.

"If our theories are correct," said President Vargas, "Levana is planning to move against Earth within the next six months."

Kai leaned forward, fidgeting with the collar of his shirt. "What theories?"

"It seems Queen Levana is building an army."

Confusion swept through the room.

"Certainly the moon has had an army for some time," said Prime Minister Bromstad. "It is hardly news, nor is it controversial. We cannot request that they forgo the keeping of an army entirely, much as we might like to."

"This is not the moon's normal army—soldiers and thaumaturges," said President Vargas, "nor is it like any army we keep on Earth. Here are some photographs that our orbiting operatives were able to obtain."

The president's image faded and was replaced with a fuzzy picture, as if taken from very far away. Satellite photos taken without sunlight. Nevertheless, in the grainy picture, Kai could make out rows and rows of men standing. He squinted, and another picture flickered onto the screen, closer up, showing the backs of four of the men from up above, but, Kai noticed with a shock, these were *not* men. Their shoulders were too wide, too hunched. Their barely discernible profiles too stretched. Their backs were covered in what appeared to be fur.

Another picture came on the screen. It showed a half

dozen of the creatures from the front, their faces a cross between man and beast. Their noses and jaws protruded awkwardly from their heads, their lips twisted into perpetual grimaces. White spots erupted from their mouths—Kai could not see them clearly, could not tell for sure, but they gave him the distinct impression of fangs.

"What are these creatures?" asked Queen Camilla.

"Mutants," answered President Vargas. "We believe they are genetically engineered Lunars. This is a project that we assume has been going on for many decades. We have estimated six hundred of them in this holding alone, but we suspect there are more, likely in the network of lava tubes beneath the moon's surface. There could be thousands—tens of thousands for all we know."

"And do they possess magic?" It was a hesitant question posed by the Canadian province rep.

The picture disappeared, showing the American president again. "We do not know. We have not been able to see them train or do anything other than stand in formation and march in and out of the caverns."

"They are Lunar," said Queen Camilla. "If they are not dead, then they possess magic."

"We have no proof that they kill their ungifted infants," interrupted Torin. "And as exciting as it is to look at these pictures and create wild speculations, we must keep in mind that Queen Levana has not yet attacked Earth, and we have no evidence that these creatures are intended for such an attack."

"What else could they be intended for?" said Governor-General Williams.

"Manual labor?" said Torin, daring anyone to deny the possibility. The governor-general sniffed but said nothing. "We should, of course, be prepared should a war come to pass. But in the meantime, our priority needs to be forming an alliance with Luna, not alienating it with paranoia and distrust."

"No," said Kai, propping his chin on his fist. "I think this is the perfect time for paranoia and distrust."

Torin scowled. "Your Highness."

"It seems you've all missed the very obvious point of those pictures."

President Vargas puffed out his chest. "What do you mean?"

"You say they've probably been building this army for decades? Perfecting whatever science they've used to create these . . . creatures?"

"So it would seem."

"Then why have we only noticed it now?" He waved his hand at the screen where the images had been. "Hundreds of them, standing out in the open as if they have nothing better to do. *Waiting* to have their pictures taken." He folded his arms on top of the table, watching as uncertain expressions turned toward him. "Queen Levana wanted us to see her spook army. She wanted us to take notice."

"You think she's trying to threaten us?" said Prime Minister Kamin.

Kai shut his eyes, seeing the rows of beasts fresh in his mind. "No. I think she's trying to threaten me."

Twenty-Seven

THE HOVER RUMBLED TO A STOP OUTSIDE THE QUARANTINE. Cinder flew out of the side hatch and immediately reeled back, covering her nose with her elbow. Her gut heaved at the stench, rotting flesh intensified by the steamy afternoon heat. Just outside the warehouse's entrance, a group of med-droids were loading dead bodies into a hover to be carted away, their forms bloated and discolored, each with a red slit in the wrist. Cinder looked away, keeping her eyes averted and her breath held as she slid past them into the warehouse.

The sunlight turned from blaring to murky, caught by the green sheeting on the windows along the ceiling. The quarantine had been near empty before; now it was overflowing with victims—every age, every gender. Buffeting fans on the ceiling did little to dispel the sweltering heat or the smell of death. The air was heavy with it.

Med-droids buzzed between the beds, but there were not enough of them to tend to all the sick.

Cinder slipped down an aisle, gasping for shallow breaths against her sleeve. She spotted Peony's green brocade blanket and ran to the foot of the bed. "Peony!"

When Peony didn't stir, she reached out and placed a hand on her shoulder. The blanket was soft, warm, but the bulk beneath it didn't move.

Shaking, Cinder grasped the edge of the comforter and pulled it back.

Peony whimpered, a mild protest, which sent relieved chills across Cinder's arms. She slumped down beside the bed.

"Stars, Peony. I came as soon as I heard."

Peony squinted up at her, eyes bleary. Her face was ashen, her lips peeling. The dark splotches on her neck had begun to fade to lavender beneath the surface of her ghostly skin. Eyes on Cinder, she pulled her arm out from beneath the blanket and spread out her fingers, displaying their blue-black tips and the yellowish tinge of her nails.

"I know, but it's going to be all right." Still panting, Cinder unbuttoned the pocket on the side of her cargo pants and pulled out the glove that normally lived on her right hand. The vial was in one of the fingers, protected. "I brought something for you. Can you sit up?"

Peony pulled her hand into a loose fist and tucked it again beneath the blanket. Her eyes were hollow. Cinder didn't think she'd heard her.

"Peony?"

A ping echoed in Cinder's head. Her display showed an

incoming message from Adri, and the familiar surge of anxiety that came with it clamped Cinder's throat.

She dismissed the message.

"Peony, listen to me. I need you to sit up. Can you do that?"

"Mom?" Peony whispered, spittle collecting at the corner of her lips.

"She's at home. She doesn't know—" *That you're dying.* But, of course, Adri did know. The comm would have gone to her too.

Pulse racing, Cinder bent over Peony and slid her arm beneath her shoulder. "Come on, I'll help you."

Peony's expression didn't change—the blank, corpse stare—but she did let out a pained groan when Cinder lifted her up.

"I'm sorry," she said, "but I need you to drink this."

Another ping, another message from Adri. This time, irritation welled up in Cinder and she shut off her netlink, blocking any more incoming messages.

"It's from the palace. It might help. Do you understand?" She kept her voice low, worried that the other patients might hear, might riot against her. But Peony's gaze remained empty. "A *cure,* Peony," she hissed against her ear. "An antidote."

Peony said nothing, head drooped against Cinder's shoulder. Her body had gone limp, but she was light as a wooden doll.

Cinder's throat felt coated in sand as she stared into Peony's empty eyes. Eyes looking past her, through her.

"No . . . Peony, didn't you hear me?" Cinder pulled Peony fully against her and uncorked the vial. "You have to drink this." She held the vial to Peony's lips, but Peony didn't move. Didn't flinch.

"Peony." Hand trembling, she coaxed Peony's head back. Her papery lips fell open.

Cinder forced her hand to still as she lifted the vial, afraid to spill a single drop. She set the glass against Peony's lips and held her breath, but paused. Her heart was convulsing. Her head felt heavy with tears that wouldn't come. She shook her head, harshly. "Peony, *please.*"

When no sound or air passed through Peony's lips, Cinder lowered the vial. She buried her head into the crook of Peony's neck, gritting her teeth until her jaw ached. Each breath stung as it entered her throat, rank with the stench around her, but even now she caught whiffs of Peony's shampoo from so many days past.

Clutching the vial in her fist, she gently released Peony, letting her slip back onto the pillow. Her eyes were still open.

Cinder slammed her fist onto the mattress. Some of the antidote splashed up over her thumb. Squeezing her eyes until stars flashed before her, she slumped over and planted her face into the blanket. "Dammit. *Dammit.* Peony!" Rocking back on her heels, she sucked in a long, uneven breath and gazed at her little sister's heart-shaped face and lifeless eyes. "I kept my promise. I brought it for you." She barely refrained from shattering the vial in her fist. "Plus, I talked to Kai. Peony, he's going to dance with you. He told me he would. Don't you get it? You *can't* die. I'm *here . . .* I—"

A splitting headache rocked her against the bed. She gripped the edge of the mattress and lowered her head, letting it hang to her chest. The pain was coming from the top of her spine again, but it did not overwhelm her like before. Just uncomfortable heat, like a sunburn on the inside.

It passed, leaving only a dull throbbing behind, and the thought of Peony's blank stare haunting her. She lifted her head and corked the vial with weak fingers, slipping it back into her pocket. Reaching up, she closed Peony's eyes.

Cinder heard the familiar crunch of treads on the dirty concrete and spotted a med-droid coming toward her, no water or damp rags in its prongs. It paused on the other side of Peony's bed, opened its torso, and retrieved a scalpel.

Cinder reached across the bed and clamped her gloved hand over Peony's wrist. "No," she said, louder than she'd intended. Nearby patients lolled their heads toward her.

The android's sensor rose to her, still dim.

Thieves. Convicts. Fugitives. "You can't have this one."

The android stood with its blank white face, the scalpel jutting from its torso. Bits of dried blood clung to the edge.

Without speaking, the android reached forward with one of its free arms and latched onto Peony's elbow. "I have been programmed—"

"I don't care what you've been programmed to do. You can't have this one." Cinder yanked Peony's arm out of the android's grip. The pincers left deep scratches across her skin.

"I must remove and preserve her ID chip," the android said, reaching forward again.

Cinder bent over the bed and plastered her hand against the android's sensor, holding it at bay. "I said you're not getting it. Leave her alone."

The android swung the scalpel up, burying the tip into Cinder's glove. It clanged, metal on metal. Cinder reeled back from surprise. The blade clung to the thick fabric of her work gloves.

Gritting her teeth, she wrenched the scalpel from the glove and jammed it into the android's sensor. Glass shattered. The glowing yellow light flashed out. The android wheeled back, metal arms swinging, loud beeps and error messages spilling from its hidden speakers.

Cinder barreled over the bed and slammed her fist into the android's head. It crashed to the ground, silenced, arms still twitching.

Panting, Cinder looked around. The patients who could were sitting up in bed, blinking glossy eyes. A med-droid four aisles away left its patient and rambled toward her.

Cinder sucked in a breath. Crouching down, she reached into the android's shattered sensor and grabbed the scalpel. She spun back to Peony—the disheveled blankets, the scratches on her arm, the blue fingertips dangling over the side of the bed. Kneeling beside her, she asked for hurried forgiveness while she grasped her sister's fragile wrist.

She spliced the scalpel into the soft tissue. Blood dribbled out of the wound and onto her glove, mixing with years of grime. Peony's fingers twitched when Cinder hit a tendon, making her jump.

When the cut was wide enough, she peeled it open with her thumb, revealing bright red muscle. Blood. Her stomach squirmed but she dug the tip of the blade in as carefully as she could, easing up the square chip.

"I'm so, so sorry," she whispered, setting the mutilated wrist down on Peony's stomach and standing. The grating of the med-droid's treads worked closer.

"Ashes, ashes . . ."

She spun toward the dry, singsong voice, scalpel gripped firmly in one hand, Peony's chip protected in the other.

The small boy in the next aisle shrank back as his dilated eyes spotted the weapon. The nursery rhyme faded away. It took Cinder a moment to recognize him. Chang Sunto, from the market. Sacha's son. His skin now glossy with sweat, black hair matted to one side of his head from sleeping too much. *Ashes, ashes, we all fall down.*

Everyone who was strong enough to sit up was staring at her.

Stealing a breath, Cinder swept toward Sunto. She fished the vial from her pocket and forced it into his clammy fingers. "Drink this."

The med-droid reached the foot of the bed, and Cinder shoved it aside. It toppled to the ground like a fallen pawn. Sunto's delirious eyes followed her without recognition. "Drink it!" she ordered, pulling out the stopper and forcing the vial up to his mouth. She waited for his lips to close around it, and then she ran.

The sun momentarily blinded her as she bolted into the street. Blocked from her hover by the med-droids and two gurneys of dead patients, she spun and ran in the other direction.

She turned a corner and had gone four blocks when she heard another hover overhead, the hum of magnets awakening beneath her pounding feet.

"Linh Cinder," came a booming voice over the speaker, "you

are hereby ordered to halt and be taken peacefully into custody."

She cursed. Were they *arresting* her?

Planting her feet she turned to face the white hover, panting. It was a law enforcement vehicle, manned by more androids. How had they gotten to her so quickly?

"I didn't steal it!" she yelled, holding up her fist with Peony's chip enclosed. "It belongs to her family, not to you or anyone else!"

The hover settled to the ground, its engine still thrumming. An android alighted from a ramp, its yellow light scanning Cinder up and down as it approached her. It held a taser in its prongs.

She shuffled back, her heels kicking up debris on the deserted street.

"I haven't done anything wrong," she said, hands extended toward the android. "That med-droid was attacking me. It was self-defense."

"Linh Cinder," said the machine's mechanical voice, "we have been contacted by your legal guardian in regard to your unauthorized disappearance. You are hereby in violation of the Cyborg Protection Act and have been labeled a runaway cyborg. Our orders are to apprehend you by force if necessary and return you to your legal guardian. If you come peaceably, this infraction will not be recorded on your permanent record."

Cinder squinted, confused. A bead of sweat rolled over her eyebrow as she looked from the android who had spoken to a second android just leaving the hover's ramp.

"Wait," she said, lowering her hands. "Adri sent you?"

Twenty-Eight

THE UNCOMFORTABLE SILENCE OF THE DINING HALL WAS broken only by the clatter of chopsticks against porcelain and the shuffling of servants' feet. Only human servers were present—a concession to Levana's avid distrust of androids. She claimed it went against her people's morals, and the laws of nature, to bestow fake emotions and thoughts on man-made machines.

Kai knew, however, that she just didn't like androids because she couldn't brainwash them.

Sitting opposite the queen, Kai found himself struggling not to look at her—it was both a temptation and a repellent, and both feelings irritated him. Torin was beside him, and Levana was flanked by Sybil and the second thaumaturge. The two Lunar guards stood against the walls. Kai wondered if they ever ate.

The emperor's seat at the end of the table would remain empty until the coronation. He did not want to look at that empty chair, either.

Levana made a grand, flourishing gesture, drawing everyone's attention to her, though it resulted in nothing more than taking a sip of tea. Her lips curled as she set the cup down, her gaze meeting Kai's. "Sybil tells me your little festival is an annual occurrence," she said, the cadence of her voice swooning like a lullaby.

"Yes," Kai said, lifting a shrimp wonton between his chopsticks. "It falls on the ninth full moon of each year."

"Ah, how lovely for you to base your holidays on the cycles of my planet."

Kai wanted to scoff at the word *planet* but sucked it back down into his throat.

"It is a celebration of the end of the Fourth World War," said Torin.

Levana clucked her tongue. "That is the problem with so many little countries on a single globe. So many wars."

Something splattered on Kai's plate. He looked down to see that the wonton's filling had been squeezed from its wrapper. "Perhaps we should be glad the war happened, then, and forced the countries to conglomerate as they did."

"I hardly think it harmed the well-being of the citizenry," said Levana.

Kai's pulse throbbed in his ears. Millions had died in World War IV; whole cultures had been devastated, dozens of cities reduced to rubble—including the original Beijing. Not to mention the countless natural resources that had been destroyed through nuclear and chemical warfare. Yes, he was quite sure some harm had come to the citizenry's well-being.

"More tea, Your Highness?" said Torin, startling Kai. He realized he'd been gripping his chopsticks like a weapon.

Grumbling inwardly, he sat back, allowing a servant to refill his cup.

"We can give credit to the war for bringing about the Treaty of Bremen," said Torin, "which has thus far been beneficial to all countries in the Earthen Union. We hope, of course, to see your signature on the document someday soon, Your Majesty."

The queen's lips tightened against her teeth. "Indeed. The good of the treatise is thoroughly discussed in your history books. And yet, I cannot help but feel that Luna—a single country ruled by a single government—provides an even more ideal arrangement. One that is fair and beneficial to all inhabitants."

"Assuming that the ruling government *is* fair," said Kai.

A flash of contempt set the queen's jaw but almost instantly faded into a serene smile. "Which of course Luna has, as is evidenced by hundreds of years without a single uprising—not even the smallest protest. *Our* history books attest to that."

Shocking. Kai would have grumbled if he hadn't felt Torin's glower upon him.

"It is a testament that every ruler strives for," said Torin.

The servants came forward and whisked away the first course, replacing it with silver tureens.

"My queen is as eager to forge a bond between Luna and Earth as you are," said Sybil. "It is a shame that an agreement could not be reached under the rule of your father, but we are hopeful that you, Your Highness, will be more accepting of our terms."

Kai again strove to loosen his grip, lest he accidentally leap across the table and jab a chopstick into the witch's eye. His father had tried every compromise imaginable to forge an alliance with Luna, except the one thing he could not agree to. The one thing he was sure would signal the end of freedom for his people. A marriage to Queen Levana.

But nobody objected to Sybil's comment. Not even himself. He couldn't get the image from today's meeting out of his head. The Lunar mutations, the army of beast-like creatures. Waiting.

It chilled him not only because of what he'd seen, but of what he could imagine he hadn't seen. If he were right, then Levana had put her army out for show—as a threat. But he knew she wouldn't give her hand away so easily.

So what else was she hiding?

And did he dare risk finding out?

Marriage. War. Marriage. *War.*

The servants simultaneously lifted the silver domes from the trays, releasing clouds of steam scented of garlic and sesame oil.

Kai mumbled a thank-you to the servant over his shoulder, but the words were interrupted by a gasp from the queen. She shoved her chair away from the table. The legs screeched across the floor.

Startled, Kai followed the queen's gaze to her plate. Instead of thinly cut pork tenderloin and rice noodles, the plate harbored a small hand mirror set into a shimmering silver-white frame.

"How dare you?" Levana turned blazing eyes on the servant

who had delivered the meal—a middle-aged woman with fine gray hair. The servant stumbled back, her eyes round as the mirror.

Levana stood so fast her chair tumbled to the floor behind her. A chorus of chair legs creaked on the floor as everyone stood.

"Speak, you disgusting Earthen! How dare you insult me?"

The servant tossed her head, mute.

"Your Majesty—" Kai started.

"Sybil!"

"My Queen."

"This human has shown disrespect. It is not to be tolerated."

"Your Majesty!" said Torin. "Please, calm yourself. We do not know that this woman is to blame. We mustn't jump to conclusions."

"Then she must be made an example of," said Sybil, quite coolly, "and the true perpetrator can thus suffer the guilt, which is often a far worse punishment."

"That is *not* how our system works," said Torin. His face had flushed red. "While you reside in the Commonwealth, you will abide by our laws."

"I will not follow your laws so long as they permit disobedience to flourish," said Levana. "Sybil!"

Sybil rounded the queen's fallen chair. The servant backed away, bowing, muttering apologies and begging for mercy and not knowing what she said.

"Stop it! Leave her alone!" said Kai, rushing toward the servant.

Sybil snatched a knife from the service table and held its handle out toward the woman. The woman took the knife, crying, pleading as she did so.

Kai's jaw dropped. He was both disgusted and mesmerized as the servant turned the blade toward herself, clutching the handle with both hands.

Sybil's beautiful face remained complacent.

The servant's hands trembled and slowly lifted the knife until the glistening edge was poised at the corner of her eye. "No," she whimpered. *"Please."*

Kai's entire body shook as he realized what Sybil meant to force the woman into. Heart racing, he squared his shoulders. *"I did it!"*

The room stilled, silenced, but for the woman's bumbling sobs.

Everyone turned to Kai. The queen, Torin, the servant with the tiny inflamed scratch beside her eyelid, the knife still in her hand.

"I did it," he repeated. He looked at Sybil, who watched him without expression, and then at Queen Levana.

The queen fisted both hands at her sides. Her dark gaze seethed. Her complexion shimmered. In a single, tilting moment, she was hideous, with her ragged breath and sneering coral lips.

Kai ran his dry tongue across the roof of his mouth. "I

ordered the kitchen to put the mirror on your tray." He pressed his arms firmly against his sides to keep them from shaking. "It was meant as a friendly joke. I understand now that it was an ignorant decision, and a joke that would not cross cultural lines, and I can only apologize and ask for your forgiveness." He leveled his gaze at Levana. "But if forgiveness is not in your power, then at least direct your anger toward me and not the servant, who would have had no idea that the mirror was there. The punishment should be all mine."

He had thought the tension bad during the appetizer course, but now he was choking on it.

Levana's breathing returned to normal as her eyes weighed her options. She did not believe him—it was a lie, and everyone in the room knew it. But he had confessed.

She opened her fists, stretching her fingers out against the material of her dress. "Release the servant."

The energy dispersed. Kai felt his ears pop as if the air pressure in the room had changed.

The knife clattered to the floor and the servant stumbled back, crashing into a wall. Her shaking hands flattened over her eyes, her face, her head.

"Thank you for your honesty, Your Highness," Levana said, her tone flat and hollow. "Your apology is accepted."

The crying woman was led away from the dining room. Torin reached across the table, picked up the silver dome, and covered the mirror. "Bring our most honored guest her entrée."

"That won't be necessary," said Levana. "I have quite lost my appetite."

"Your Majesty—" said Torin.

"I will retire to my quarters," said the queen. She was still battling Kai across the table, her eyes cold and calculating, and he unable to look away. "I have learned something valuable about you tonight, young prince. I hope you have learned something about me, as well."

"That you prefer to rule through fear rather than justice? So sorry, Your Majesty, I'm afraid I already knew that about you."

"No, indeed. I hope you noticed that I am capable of choosing my battles." Her lips curved, her beauty returning full force. "If that's what it takes to win the war."

She departed from the room like a feather, as if nothing at all had happened, her entourage falling into step behind her. Only when the guards' clopping feet had drifted down the halls did Kai slump into the nearest seat, head hanging over his knees. His stomach was heaving. Every nerve shook.

He heard a chair being set upright and Torin settle beside him with a heavy sigh. "We should find out who was really at fault for the mirror. If it was someone on the staff, they should be suspended for so long as the queen is staying at the palace."

Kai lifted his head far enough to peer over the table's edge, seeing the towering silver dome in front of the queen's abandoned chair. Inhaling a breath, he reached forward and uncovered the mirror, then grasped its slender handle. It was smooth as glass but sparkled like diamonds when he twisted it in the dim lighting. He had only seen material like that once before. On a spaceship.

Holding the mirror's face toward Torin, he shook his head, disgusted. "Mystery solved," he said, turning the mirror around so that his adviser could see the strange Lunar rune carved into the back of the frame.

Torin's eyes widened. "She was testing you."

Kai let the mirror tip back onto the table. He rubbed his brow with outstretched fingers, still shaking.

"Your Highness." A messenger clicked his heels from the doorway. "I have an urgent message from the Secretary of Public Health and Safety."

Kai tilted his head, squinting at the messenger through his bangs. "Couldn't she send a comm?" he said, checking his belt with his free hand before remembering that Levana had requested no portscreens at their dinner. He grunted and sat up. "What's the message?"

The messenger stepped into the dining room, his eyes bright. "There's been a disturbance at the District 29 quarantine. An unidentified person attacked two med-droids, disabling one of them, and then escaped."

Kai frowned, straightening. "A patient?"

"We're unsure. The only android that would have recorded a good visual was the one that was disabled. Another android caught glimpses of the act from afar, but only of the perpetrator's back. We've been unable to get an accurate ID. The perpetrator didn't seem ill, though."

"Everyone at the quarantines is ill."

The messenger hesitated.

Kai gripped the arms of the chair. "We have to find him. If he has the disease—"

"It appeared to be a female, Your Highness. And there's more. The footage we have shows her speaking to another patient, moments after she attacked the first med-droid. A young boy by the name of Chang Sunto. He was admitted to the quarantine yesterday with stage two letumosis."

"And?"

The servant cleared his throat. "The boy seems to be recovering."

"From what? The attack?"

"No, Your Highness. Recovering from the disease."

Twenty-Nine

CINDER SLAMMED SHUT THE APARTMENT DOOR AND marched into the living room. Adri was sitting stiff beside the hearth, glowering at Cinder as if she'd been waiting for her.

Cinder clenched her fists. "How dare you send for me like some common criminal? Didn't you think that maybe I was in the middle of something?"

"How dare I treat you like a common cyborg, you mean?" Adri folded her hands in her lap. "You are a common cyborg, and one who is under my legal jurisdiction. It is my duty to ensure you don't become a menace to society, and it seemed quite clear that you were abusing the privileges I've allowed you in the past."

"What privileges?"

"I have always allowed you freedom, Cinder, to do as you like, to go where you like. But it's come to my attention you do not respect the boundaries and responsibilities that come with that freedom."

Cinder frowned and drew back. She'd had her own angry

speech repeating in her head the entire hover ride home. She had not been expecting Adri to bite back with a speech of her own. "Is this because I didn't respond to a few comms?"

Adri tucked her shoulders back. "What were you doing at the palace today, Cinder?"

Cinder's heart skipped. "The palace?"

Adri raised a calm eyebrow.

"You've been tracking my ID."

"You've made it necessary to take precautions."

"I haven't *done* anything."

"You haven't answered my question."

Cinder's internal warnings went off. Spiking adrenaline. She sucked down a breath. "I went to join the protests, all right? Is that a crime?"

"I was under the impression that you were in the basement, working, as you were supposed to be doing. To sneak out of the house without permission, without even informing me, to attend some gratuitous parade, and all the while Peony is—" Her voice hitched. Adri lowered her eyes, collected herself, but her voice was thicker when she spoke again. "Your records also show you took a hover ride today, to the outskirts of the city, the old warehouse district. It seems clear to me that you were attempting to run away."

"Run away? No. There is . . . that's where . . ." She hesitated. "There's an old parts store down there. I was going for parts."

"Is that so? And pray tell, where did you get the money for the hover?"

Biting her lip, Cinder sank her gaze to the floor.

"This is unacceptable," said Adri. "I will not tolerate such behavior from you."

Cinder heard shuffling in the hallway. Glancing around the door, she saw Pearl sneaking from her bedroom, drawn to her mother's raised voice. She turned back to Adri.

"After everything that I've done for you," continued Adri, "everything we've sacrificed, you have the gall to *steal* from me."

Cinder frowned. "I didn't steal from you."

"No?" Adri's knuckles whitened. "A few univs for a hover ride I could have overlooked, Cinder, but tell me, where did you obtain the 600 univs in order to pay for your—" Her eyes fell to Cinder's boots, lips curling in a sneer. "—your new *limb*? Isn't it true that that money was reserved for rent and food and household expenses?"

Cinder's stomach clenched.

"I screened Iko's memory. 600 univs in just one week, not to mention toying with the pearls that Garan gave me for our anniversary. It makes me sick to think what else you've been hiding from me."

Cinder squeezed her trembling fists against her thighs, glad, for once, that she'd never told Iko about being Lunar. "It wasn't—"

"I don't want to hear it." Adri bunched her lips. "If you hadn't been out dallying all day you would know that"—her voice rose, bolstered, as if anger alone could keep tears at bay—"that I now have a funeral to pay for. 600 univs would have bought my daughter a respectable plaque, and I intend to get that money back. We'll be selling off some personal belongings in order to afford it, and you will be required to make up your fair share."

Cinder gripped the doorjamb. She wanted to tell Adri that no fancy plaque would bring Peony back, but she didn't have the strength. Shutting her eyes, she planted her brow against the cool wood frame.

"Don't just stand there, pretending to understand what I can be going through. You are not part of this family. You aren't even *human* anymore."

"I am human," said Cinder, quietly, the anger drained out of her. She just wanted Adri to stop talking so she could go to her room and be alone and think about Peony. The antidote. Their escape.

"No, Cinder. Humans cry."

Cinder sank back, wrapping her arms protectively around herself.

"Go ahead. Shed a tear for your little sister. I seem to be all dried up this evening, so why don't you share the burden?"

"That's not fair."

"Not fair?" Adri barked. "What isn't fair is that *you* are still alive while *she* is not. That is not fair! You should have died in that accident. They should have let you die and left my family alone!"

Cinder stomped her foot. "Stop blaming me! I didn't ask to live. I didn't ask to be adopted. I didn't ask to be made cyborg. None of this is my fault! And Peony isn't my fault either, and neither is Garan. I didn't start this plague, I didn't—"

She stopped herself as Dr. Erland's words crashed down on her. Lunars had brought the plague to Earth. Lunars were at fault. Lunars.

"Did you just short-circuit?"

Cinder shook off the thought and threw a silent glare at Pearl before swinging back toward Adri. "I can get the money back," she said. "Enough to buy Peony the most beautiful plaque—or a real tombstone even."

"It is too late for that. You have proven that you have no part in this family. You have proven that you cannot be trusted." Adri smoothed her skirt over her knees. "As punishment for your thievery and for attempting to run away this afternoon, I have decided you will not be allowed to attend the annual ball."

Cinder bit back a wry laugh. Did Adri think she was a fool?

"Until further notice," Adri continued, "you will go only so far as the basement during the week and to your booth at the festival so you can begin repaying me for the money you stole."

Cinder dug her fingers into her thighs, too incensed to argue. Every fiber, every nerve, every wire was trembling.

"And you will leave your foot with me."

She started. "Excuse me?"

"I think it a fair solution. After all, you bought it with my money, therefore it is mine to do with as I please. In some cultures they would cut off your hand, Cinder. Consider yourself fortunate."

"But it's my foot!"

"And you will have to do without it until you can find a cheaper replacement." She glowered at Cinder's feet. Her lip curled with disgust. "You are *not* human, Cinder. It's about time you realized that."

Jaw working, Cinder struggled to form an argument. But legally, the money had been Adri's. Legally, *Cinder* belonged to Adri. She had no rights, no belongings. She was nothing but a cyborg.

"You may go now," said Adri, casting her eyes toward the empty mantel. "Just be sure to leave your foot in the hallway before going to bed tonight."

Fists clenching, Cinder drew back into the hallway. Pearl plastered herself to the wall, eyeing Cinder with disgust. Her cheeks were flushed with recent tears.

"Wait—one more thing, Cinder."

She froze.

"You will find I've already begun selling off some unnecessary items. I've left some faulty parts in your room that were deemed worthless. Perhaps you can find something to do with them."

When it was clear that Adri was finished, Cinder stormed down the hall without looking back. Anger sloshed through her. She wanted to rampage through the house, destroying everything, but a quiet voice in her head calmed her. Adri wanted that. Adri wanted an excuse to have her arrested, to be rid of her once and for all.

She just needed time. Another week, two at the most, and the car would be ready.

Then she really would be a runaway cyborg, but this time, Adri wouldn't be able to track her.

She stomped into her bedroom and slammed the door,

falling against it with a hot, shaking breath. She squeezed her eyes. One more week. *One more week.*

When her breath had begun to settle and the warnings in her vision disappeared, Cinder opened her eyes. Her room was as messy as ever, old tools and parts scattered across the grease-stained blankets that made up her bed, but her eyes immediately landed on a new addition to the mess.

Her gut plummeted.

She knelt over the pile of worthless parts that Adri had left for her to find. A beat-up tread punctured with pebbles and debris. An ancient fan with a crooked blade. Two aluminum arms—one that still had Peony's velvet ribbon tied around the wrist.

Clenching her jaw, she started sorting through the pieces. Carefully. One by one. Her fingers trembled over every mangled screw. Every bit of melted plastic. She shook her head, silently pleading. Pleading.

Finally she found what she was searching for.

With a dry, grateful sob, she crumpled over her knees, squeezing Iko's worthless personality chip against her chest.

BOOK Four

The prince had the stairway smeared with pitch,

and when Cinderella tried to run away,

her left slipper got stuck.

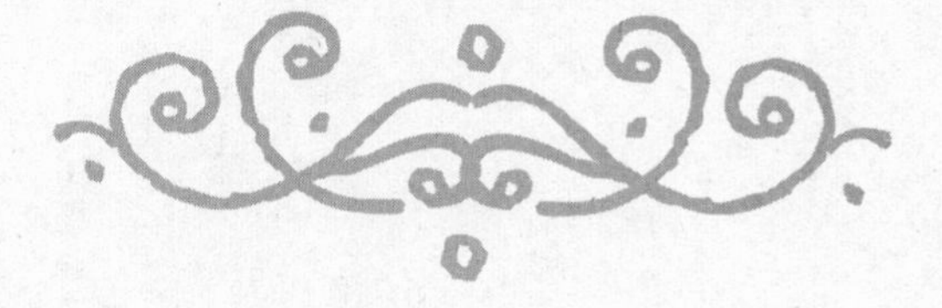

Thirty

CINDER SAT INSIDE HER BOOTH, CHIN CUPPED IN BOTH palms, watching the huge netscreen across the crowded street. She couldn't hear the reporter's commentary over the chaos, but she didn't need to—he was reporting on the festival that she was stuck in the middle of. The reporter seemed to be having a lot more fun than she was, gesturing wildly at passing food vendors and jugglers, contortionists on miniature parade floats and the tail end of a passing lucky dragon kite. Cinder could tell from the hubbub that the reporter was in the square just a block away from her, where most of the events took place throughout the day. It was a lot more festive than the street of vendor booths, but at least she was in the shade.

The day *would* have been busy compared to market days—lots of potential customers had sought prices on broken portscreens and android parts—but she had been forced to turn them all away. She would be taking no more customers in New Beijing. She would not have been there at all if Adri hadn't forced her to come, dropping her off while she and Pearl went shopping for last-minute ball accessories. She suspected that Adri really just wanted to watch as everyone gawked at the limping, one-footed girl.

She couldn't tell her stepmother that Linh Cinder, renowned mechanic, was closed for business.

Because she couldn't tell Adri that she was leaving.

She sighed, blowing a misplaced lock of hair out of her face. The heat was miserable. The humidity clung to Cinder's skin, pasting her shirt to her back. Along with the budding clouds on the horizon, it promised rain, and lots of it.

Not ideal driving conditions.

But that wouldn't stop her. Twelve hours from now, she would be miles outside of the city, putting as much distance between herself and New Beijing as she could. She had gone down to the garage every night that week after Adri and Pearl were in bed, hopping along on homemade crutches so she could work on the car. Last night, for the first time, the engine had roared to life.

Well, more like sputtered to life and spewed out noxious fumes from the exhaust that made her cough like mad. She had used nearly half of the plague-research money Erland had wired her on a big tank of gasoline that, if she were lucky, would carry her at least into the next province. It would be a bumpy ride. It would be a stinky ride.

But she would be free.

No—*they* would be free. Her and Iko's personality chip and

Peony's ID chip. They were going to escape together, like she'd always said they would.

Though she knew she could never bring Peony back, she hoped that someday she would at least find another body for Iko. Some other android shell, perhaps—maybe even an escort with their tauntingly ideal feminine shapes. She thought Iko would like that.

The netscreen changed, showing the other favorite news story of the week. Chang Sunto, miracle child. Plague survivor. He'd been interviewed countless times about his unbelievable recovery, and every time it sparked a little glow in Cinder's silicon heart.

Footage of her mad dash from the quarantines had been played repeatedly on the screens too, but the recording never showed her face, and Adri had been too distracted—by the ball and the funeral that Cinder had not been invited to attend—to realize the mystery girl was living under her own roof. Or perhaps Adri just paid her such little attention that she wouldn't have recognized her anyway.

Rumors abounded about the girl and Chang Sunto's miraculous recovery, and while some had talked of an antidote, no one was coming clean. The boy was now under the surveillance of the palace research team, which meant that Dr. Erland had a new guinea pig to play with. She hoped it would be enough, given that her role as research volunteer was over. She hadn't had the heart to tell the doctor that yet, though, and the guilt clawed at her upon seeing a new monetary deposit every morning.

Dr. Erland had made good on his promises—he'd set up an account ID-linked so that only Cinder could access it, not Adri, and had made almost daily payments from the research and development fund. So far he'd asked for nothing in return. His only comms had been to tell her he was still making use of her blood samples and to remind her not to return to the palace until the queen was gone.

Cinder frowned, scratching her cheek. Dr. Erland had never had the chance to explain to her why she was so special when he was also immune. Her curiosity lingered in the back of her thoughts, but not as strongly as her determination to run away. Some mysteries would have to remain unsolved.

She pulled her toolbox toward her on the table, fishing through it for no other reason than to keep her hands busy. The boredom of the past five days had led her to meticulously organize every last bolt and screw. Now she'd taken to counting, creating a digital inventory in her brain.

A child appeared across her worktable, silky black hair pulled up in pigtails. "Excuse me," she said, pushing a portscreen onto the table. "Can you fix this?"

Cinder cast her bored eyes from the child to the port. It was small enough to fit into her palm and covered with a sparkling pink shell. Sighing, she picked up the port and flipped it over in her hands. She pressed the power button but only gobbledygook filled the screen. Twisting her lips, she smacked the corner of the screen twice on the table. The girl jumped back.

Cinder tried the power button again. The welcome screen beamed up at her.

"Give that a shot," she said, tossing it back to the kid, who stumbled to catch it. The girl's eyes brightened. She flashed a grin with two missing teeth before scurrying into the crowd.

Cinder hunched over, settling her chin down on her forearms and wishing for the thousandth time that Iko wasn't trapped inside a tiny scrap of metal. They would be poking fun at the vendors with their damp, rosy faces, fanning themselves beneath the canopies of their booths. They would talk about all the places they were going to go and see—the Taj Mahal, the Mediterranean Sea, the transatlantic maglev railway. Iko would want to go shopping in Paris.

When a shudder ran through her, Cinder buried her face in her elbow. How long would she have to carry their ghosts around with her?

"Are you all right?"

She jumped and raised her eyes. Kai was leaning against the corner of the booth, one arm propped on the door's steel track, the other hidden behind him. He was wearing his disguise again, the gray sweatshirt with the hood pulled over his head, but even in the sweltering heat, he managed to look perfectly composed. His hair just tousled, the bright sun behind him—Cinder's heart started to expand before she clamped it back down.

She didn't bother to get up, but she did mindlessly tug her pant leg down to cover as many of the wires as possible, once again grateful for the thin tablecloth. "Your Highness."

"Now, I don't want to tell you how to run your business or anything," he said, "but have you considered actually charging people for your services?"

Her wires seemed to be struggling to connect in her brain for a moment before she remembered the little girl from moments before. She cleared her throat and glanced around. The girl was sitting on the sidewalk with her dress stretched over her knees, humming to the music that streamed up from the tiny speakers. Shoppers mulled about, swinging bags against their hips and snacking on tea-boiled eggs. The shopkeepers were busy sweating. No one was paying them any attention.

"I don't want to tell you how to be a prince, but shouldn't you have some bodyguards or something?"

"Bodyguards? Who would want to harm a charming guy like me?"

When she glared up at him, he smiled and flashed his wrist at her. "Trust me, they know exactly where I am at all times, but I try not to think about it."

She picked a flat-head screwdriver from the toolbox and started twirling it over her fingers, anything to keep her hands preoccupied. "So what are you doing here? Shouldn't you be, I don't know. Preparing for a coronation or something?"

"Believe it or not, I seem to be having technical difficulties again." He unhooked the portscreen from his belt and peered down. "You see, I figured it's probably too much to hope that New Beijing's most renowned mechanic is having trouble with *her* port, so I figured there must be something wrong with mine." Screwing up his lips, he whapped the corner of his portscreen on the table, then checked the screen again with a heavy sigh. "Nope, nothing. Maybe she's been ignoring my comms on purpose."

"Maybe she's been busy?"

"Oh, yes, you look completely overwhelmed."

Cinder rolled her eyes.

"Here, I brought you something." Kai put the portscreen away and pulled his hand out from behind him, producing a long, flat box wrapped in gold foil and a white ribbon. The paper was gorgeous, the wrapping job less so.

Cinder dropped the screwdriver with a clatter. "What's that for?"

A flash of hurt crossed his face. "What? I can't buy you a gift?" he asked, in a tone that nearly stopped the electric pulses in her wiring.

"No. Not after I've ignored six of your comms in the last week. Are you dense?"

"So you did get them!"

She propped her elbows on the table, sinking her chin into both palms. "Of course I got them."

"So why are you ignoring me? Did I do something?"

"No. Yes." She squeezed her eyes shut, massaging her temple. She'd thought the hard part was over. She would disappear, and he would go on with his life. She would spend the rest of her life watching as Prince, no, *Emperor* Kai gave speeches and passed bills. As he went on diplomatic missions around the world. As he shook hands and kissed babies. She would watch him marry. She would watch as his wife gave him children—because the whole world would watch it happen.

But he would forget about her. Which is what needed to happen.

How naive of her to think it could be so simple.

"No? Yes?"

She fumbled, thinking it *should* have been easy to blame her silence on Adri, her cruel stepmother who had refused to let her leave the house, but it was not that easy. She couldn't risk giving him hope. She couldn't risk anything that might change her mind.

"It's just that I . . ."

She drew back, knowing she should tell him. He thought she was a mere mechanic, and he was, perhaps, willing to cross *that* social divide. But to be both cyborg and Lunar? To be hated and despised by every culture in the galaxy? He would understand in a moment why he needed to forget her.

More than that, he probably *would* forget her just as quickly.

Her metal fingers jerked. Her right hand was burning hot beneath the cotton.

Pull off the gloves and show him.

She mindlessly reached for the hem, fingering the grease-stained material.

But she couldn't. He didn't know. She didn't want him to know.

"Because you kept going on and on about the stupid ball," she said, cringing at her own words.

He dropped a cursory glance to the gold box in his hands. The tension melted until his arms dropped to his sides. "Stars, Cinder, if I'd known you were going to embargo me for asking you on a date, I wouldn't have dared."

She cast her gaze skyward, wishing he'd been at least a little annoyed with her response.

"All right, you don't want to go to the ball. Got it. I won't mention it again."

She fidgeted with the fingertips of her gloves. "Thanks."

He set the box down on the table.

She shifted uncomfortably, unable to reach for it. "Don't you have something important to be doing? Like, running a country?"

"Probably." Leaning forward, he flattened one hand on the desk and leaned over, straining to see into Cinder's lap. Her heart jolted and she scooted herself closer to the table, thrusting her foot as far out of his line of sight as possible.

"What are you doing?" she asked.

"Are you all right?"

"Fine. Why?"

"You're usually the prime example of royal etiquette, but you didn't even stand up. And I was so prepared to be the gentleman and urge you to sit back down again."

"So sorry to steal *that* proud moment from you," she said, sinking lower in her seat. "But I've been here since dawn and I'm tired."

"Since dawn! What time is it now?" He reached for his portscreen.

"13:04."

He paused with his hand on the gadget at his waist. "Well. It's time for a break then, right?" He beamed. "Might I have the honor of treating you to lunch?"

Panic sparked in the back of her head and she sat up straight. "Of course not."

"Why?"

"Because I'm working. I can't just leave."

He raised an eyebrow at the piles of neatly organized screws on the table. "Working on what?"

"For your information, I'm expecting a big parts order to come in and someone has to be here to receive it." She was proud that the lie sounded so believable.

"Where's your android?"

Her breath snagged. "She's . . . not here."

Kai took a step back from the table and made a show of looking around. "Ask one of the other shopkeepers to look after your booth."

"Absolutely not. I pay money to rent this booth. I'm not just going to abandon it because some *prince* shows up."

Kai inched toward the table again. "Come on. I can't take you to the . . . *B*-word; I can't take you to lunch. Short of my unplugging the processor on one of my androids, this could be the last time we ever see each other."

"Believe it or not, I'd actually kind of resolved myself to that fact already."

Kai rested his elbows on the table, ducking so that the hood concealed his eyes from her. His fingers found a screw, began twisting it between them. "Will you be watching the coronation, at least?"

She hesitated before shrugging. "Of course I will."

With a nod, he used the tip of the screw to scratch beneath his thumbnail, though Cinder couldn't see any dirt beneath it. "I'm supposed to make an announcement tonight. Not at the coronation but at the ball. About the peace negotiations we've been having the past week. It won't be recorded because of Levana's ridiculous no-cameras policy, but I wanted you to know."

Cinder stiffened. "Has there been any progress?"

"I guess you could say that." He peered up at her but couldn't hold the gaze long. Soon he was staring past her, at all the abandoned parts. "I know this is stupid, but part of me felt like if I could come see you today, if I could convince you to go with me tonight, then maybe I could still change things. It's dumb, I know. It's not like Levana cares if I, you know, might have actual feelings for someone." He craned his head again, tossing the screw back onto its pile.

Cinder's entire body tingled at his words, but she gulped, forcing the giddiness away. She reminded herself that this was the last time she would ever see him.

"You mean you're . . ." The words dried out. She dropped her voice. "But what about Nainsi? About the things she . . . the things she knew?"

Kai stuffed his hands into his pockets, the troubled look vanishing. "It's too late. Even if I could find *her*. It couldn't happen today, or even before. . . . And then there's the antidote, and I . . . I just can't wait on that. Too many people are dying."

"Has Dr. Erland learned anything?"

Kai nodded, slowly. "He's confirmed it as a real antidote, but he says they can't duplicate it."

"What? Why?"

"I guess one of the ingredients is only found on the moon. Ironic, huh? And then there was the boy who recovered last week, and Dr. Erland's been running tests on him for days, but he's being very secretive about it. He says I shouldn't get my hopes up that the boy's recovery could lead to any new discoveries. He hasn't said it outright, but . . . I'm getting the impression that the doctor is losing hope of finding an antidote anytime soon. An antidote other than Levana's, at least. It could be years before we make anymore headway, and by that time . . ." He hesitated, eyes haunted. "I just don't know that I could watch so many people die."

Cinder lowered her gaze. "I'm so sorry. I wish there was something I could do."

Kai pushed himself back from the table, standing again. "Were you still thinking about heading to Europe?"

"Oh, yes, actually. I kind of was." She sucked in a deep breath. "Do you want to come with?"

He conceded a short laugh and pushed his hair back from his face. "Yes. Are you kidding? I think that's the best offer I've ever had."

She smiled up at him, but it was short-lived. A single blissful moment of pretend.

"I need to get back," he said, peering down at the thin gold-covered box. Cinder had nearly forgotten about it. He nudged it across the table, pushing a neat row of screws along with it.

"No. I can't—"

"Sure you can." He shrugged, seemingly uncomfortable, which was an oddly charming look on him. "I'd thought for the ball, but . . . well, whenever you have the chance, I guess."

Curiosity boiled inside her, but she forced herself to push the box back toward him. "No, please."

He laid his hand firmly over hers—she could feel his heat even through the thick glove. "Take it," he said, and flashed his signature prince-charming grin, as if he were completely unfazed. "And think of me."

"Cinder, here, take these."

Cinder jumped at Pearl's voice and wrenched her hand out from Kai's grip. Pearl swiped an arm across her work desk, sending bits and screws clattering to the pavement, then slammed a stack of papered boxes down in their place.

"Put them somewhere near the back, where they won't get stolen," said Pearl, gesturing airily toward the back of the booth. "Somewhere *clean* if such a place exists."

Heart thumping, Cinder reached for the boxes and pulled them toward her. Her thoughts raced down to her empty ankle, how she would have to limp to the back of the booth, how there would be no way to hide her deformity.

"What, no please or thank you?" said Kai.

Cinder flinched, wishing Kai had already gone before Pearl ruined the last moments she would ever see him.

Pearl bristled. She tossed her long hair over one shoulder as she turned toward the prince, eyes darkening. "Who are you to—" The words disappeared, leaving her lips puckered in surprise.

Kai pocketed his hands and eyed her with barely veiled disdain.

Cinder wrung her fingers into the twine that tied Pearl's boxes. "Your Highness, please meet my stepsister, Linh Pearl."

Pearl's lips parted, jaw dropping as the prince gave her a curt bow. "A pleasure," he said, his tone too sharp.

Cinder cleared her throat. "Thank you again for your generous payment, Your Highness. And, uh, best of luck at your coronation."

Kai's gaze softened as he peeled it away from Pearl. A hint of a shared conspiracy touched the corners of his lips, something too suggestive to go unnoticed by Pearl. He dipped his head to her. "I guess this is good-bye then. My request still stands, by the way, if you change your mind."

To Cinder's relief, he didn't elaborate, just turned and disappeared into the crowd.

Pearl followed him with her eyes. Cinder wanted to as well, but she forced herself to look at the stack of shopping boxes. "Yes, of course," she said, as if the prince's interruption hadn't happened. "I'll just put these on the shelf back here."

Pearl slammed her hand down on top of Cinder's, halting her. Her eyes were wide, disbelieving. "That was the prince."

Cinder feigned indifference. "I fixed one of the royal androids last week. He was just coming to pay me."

A crease formed between Pearl's eyebrows. Her lips tightened. Her suspicious gaze fell down to the thin gold box that Kai had left behind. Without hesitation, she snatched it up.

Cinder gasped and swiped for the box, but Pearl danced out of reach. Cinder had her knee up on the table, prepared to lunge over it, when she realized what a catastrophe that would be. Pulse racing, she froze and watched as Pearl tore the bow and let it drop to the dusty ground, then shredded the gold paper. The box beneath was simple and white, unmarked. She lifted the lid.

Cinder tilted her head up, trying to peer inside as Pearl gawked down at the gift. She could see crinkles of tissue paper and something white and silky. She analyzed Pearl's face, trying to judge her reaction, but could only pinpoint confusion.

"Is this a *joke?*"

Saying nothing, Cinder slowly backed up, lowering her knee off the table.

Pearl tilted the box so Cinder could see. Inside was the finest pair of gloves she could have imagined. Pure silk and shining silver-white. They were tall enough to cover her elbows, and a row of seed pearls along the hems added the simplest touch of elegance. They were gloves fit for a princess.

It did seem like a joke.

A sharp laugh exploded from Pearl. "He doesn't know, does he? He doesn't know about your—about *you.*" She clutched the gloves, ripping them from their tissue bed, and let the box tumble into the street. "What did you think was going to happen?" She waved the gloves at Cinder, the empty fingers wagging helplessly. "Did you think the prince might actually *like* you? Did you think you might go to the ball and dance with him in your pretty new gloves and your—" She scanned Cinder's clothes, the filthy cargo pants, the stained T-shirt, the tool belt strapped around her waist, and laughed again.

"Of course not," said Cinder. "I'm not going to the ball."

"Then what use does a cyborg have of *these*?"

"I don't know. I didn't—He just—"

"Maybe you thought it wouldn't matter," said Pearl, clicking her tongue. "Is that it? Did you think the prince—no—the *emperor* would find it in his heart to overlook all your . . ."—she twirled her hand—"shortcomings?"

Cinder squeezed her fists, trying to ignore the sting of the words. "He's just a customer."

The mocking light died in Pearl's eyes. "No. He's the prince. And if he knew the truth about you, he wouldn't have given you a passing glance."

Resentment flared in Cinder's chest. She leveled Pearl with her own glare. "Which is about as much as he gave you, right?" She wished she'd held her tongue the moment the words were out, but the outrage that flushed over Pearl's face was almost worth it.

Until Pearl threw the gloves to the ground, then grasped the toolbox atop the table and heaved it over on top of them. Cinder cried out at the crash that followed, nuts and bolts skittering halfway across the road. The crowd stopped to stare at them, at the mess.

Pearl angled her nose toward Cinder. Her lips barely creased. "You'd better get that cleaned up before the festival closes. I'll require your help tonight. After all, I have a royal ball to attend."

Cinder's wires were still humming as Pearl grabbed her shopping boxes and marched away, but she wasted no time in hopping over the desk and crouching down beside the toppled toolbox. She turned the box right-side up but ignored the loose parts, reaching instead for the gloves at the bottom of the pile.

They were caked with dirt and dust, but it was the bits of smeared grease that made her heart sink. Cinder draped them over her knee and tried to smooth the wrinkles from the silk, only smearing the oil. They were beautiful. The most beautiful things she'd ever owned.

But if there was one thing she knew from years as a mechanic, it was that some stains never came out.

Thirty-One

IT WAS A LONG WALK HOME. ADRI AND PEARL HAD LEFT THE market without her, anxious to get ready for the ball, which had been a relief to Cinder at first, but after the first mile of walking with her makeshift crutches digging into her underarms and messenger bag banging against her hip, she was cursing her stepmother with each limping step.

Not that Cinder was in any big hurry to get home. She couldn't imagine what preparations she could assist Pearl with, but she didn't doubt they would be designed to torture her. One more evening of servitude. One more evening.

The words propelled her on.

When she finally reached the apartment, she found the hallways eerily quiet. Everyone was either down at the festival or getting ready for the ball. The shouts that could normally be heard behind closed doors had been swapped for girlish laughter.

Cinder tucked the crutches beneath her sore arms and used the wall to guide her to the door.

The apartment seemed empty as she entered it, but she could hear the floors creaking as Adri and Pearl moved around their bedrooms toward the back. Hoping she might be able to make it through the whole evening without seeing either of them, Cinder hobbled to her small room and closed the door behind her. She had just thought to start packing in earnest when someone knocked at the door.

Sighing, she opened it. Pearl was in the hallway, wearing her golden gown, all silk and seeded pearls and a neckline that plunged just how Adri had requested.

"Could you have come home any slower?" she said. "We'll be leaving as soon as the coronation is over."

"Well, I'm sure I could have come home faster, except someone stole my foot."

Pearl glared briefly, then stepped back into the hallway and did a half spin, letting the skirt billow around her ankles. "What do you think, Cinder? Will the prince notice me in this?"

Cinder barely restrained the urge to slime her own filthy hands over the dress. Instead, she peeled off her work gloves and tucked them into her back pocket. "Is there something you needed?"

"Yes, actually. I wanted to ask your opinion." Pearl hitched up her skirt to reveal mismatched shoes on her tiny feet. On her left foot was a small velvet boot the color of fresh milk that laced up her ankle. On her right foot was a gold sandal tied with sparkling ribbons and tiny heart-shaped charms. "Given that you're so close to the prince, I thought I would ask if you think he would prefer the gold slippers or the white?"

Cinder pretended to think. "The boots make your ankles look fat."

Pearl smirked. "The metal plating makes *your* ankle look fat. You're just jealous because I have such lovely feet." She sighed in mock sympathy. "What a shame you'll never know the pleasure."

"I'm just glad you found at least *one* body part that's lovely."

Pearl tossed her hair, a smug grin on her face. She knew that Cinder's jest had no grounding, and Cinder was irritated when the low insult brought her no pleasure.

"I've been rehearsing my conversation with Prince Kai," said Pearl. "Of course, I intend to tell him *everything*." She swayed so her skirt caught the light. "First, I'm going to tell him all about your ugly metal extremities and how much of an embarrassment you are—what a disgusting creature they turned you into. And I'm going to make sure he also realizes how much more desirable *I* am."

Cinder leaned against the door frame. "I wish I would have known about this little crush of yours earlier, Pearl. You know, before she passed away, I was able to obtain a promise from His Highness that he would dance with Peony tonight. I could have asked the same for you, but I guess it's too late for that now. Shame."

Pearl's face flushed. "You shouldn't even say her name," she said, her voice a harsh whisper.

Cinder blinked. "Peony?"

The anger in Pearl's eyes grew intense, overtaking the

childish taunts. "I know you killed her. Everyone knows it was your fault."

Cinder gaped at her, unbalanced by the sudden switch from the immature boasts. "That's not true. I never got sick."

"It's your fault she was at the junkyard. That's where she caught it."

Cinder opened her mouth, but her jaw just hung.

"If it wasn't for you, she would be going to the ball tonight, so don't try to pretend like you would have done her any favors. The best thing you could have done for Peony would have been to leave her alone. Then maybe she'd still be here." Tears were pooling in Pearl's eyes. "And you try to pretend like you cared about her, like she was *your* sister, and that's not fair. She was sick and you were . . . meeting the prince, trying to catch his attention, when you know how she felt about him. It's sick."

Cinder folded her arms, protecting herself. "I know you don't believe this, but I really did love Peony. I do love her."

Pearl sniffed once, loudly, as if to stop the crying before it could overtake her. "You're right. I don't believe you. You're a liar and a thief, and you don't care about anyone but yourself." She paused. "And I'm going to make sure the prince knows it."

The door to Adri's bedroom opened, and she stepped out wearing a white and magenta kimono embroidered with elegant cranes. "What are you two bickering about now? Pearl, are you ready to go?" She eyed Pearl with a shrewd eye, trying to determine if anything still needed work.

"I can't believe you're going," said Cinder. "What will people think, when you're still in mourning?" She knew it was a button she shouldn't push, an unfair comment when she'd heard them both crying through the thin walls, but she was not in a mood to be fair. Even if she'd had a choice, she wouldn't have gone. Not without Peony.

Adri fixed a cold glare on her, lips pulled taut. "The coronation is starting," she said. "Go wash the hover. I want it to look brand new."

Glad she wouldn't be forced to sit through the coronation with them, Cinder made no argument as she grabbed her crutches and headed back for the door.

One more evening.

She turned on her netlink as soon as she reached the elevator, delegating the coronation proceedings to a corner of her vision. It was still the pre-ceremony. A parade of government officials was marching into the palace, swarmed by a sea of journalists and cameras.

She picked up a bucket and soap in the storage room before hobbling toward the parking garage, half listening as the newscaster explained the symbolism behind different elements of the coronation. The embroidery on Kai's robe, the designs in the crests that would be raised when he took his vows, the number of times the gong would be struck when he ascended to the dais, all practices that had been around for centuries, cobbled together from the many cultures that had come together to form the Commonwealth.

The news continuously switched between the festival in the city center to the occasional shot of Kai during his preparations. Only these latter bits snagged Cinder's attention away from the bucket of sudsy water. She couldn't help imagining she was in the palace with him, rather than this dim, cool garage. Kai shaking hands with some unknown delegate. Kai greeting the crowd. Kai trying to steal a private conversation with his adviser. Kai turning toward her, smiling at her, glad she was by his side.

The momentary glimpses of him made Cinder's heart feel soothed, rather than injured. It was a reminder that much bigger things were happening in the world, and Cinder's yearning for freedom and Pearl's taunts and Adri's whims and even Kai's flirting with her did not fit into that bigger picture.

The Eastern Commonwealth was crowning its new emperor. Today, the whole world was watching.

Kai's clothing blended old and new traditions. Turtledoves embroidered across his mandarin collar signified peace and love. Draped over his shoulders was a midnight-blue cloak embroidered with six silver stars, signifying the peace and unity of the six Earthen kingdoms, and a dozen chrysanthemums, signifying the twelve provinces of the Commonwealth and how they would flourish under his reign.

A royal adviser stood beside Kai on the platform. The first rows of the crowd were made up of government officials from every branch and province. But Cinder's eyes were always drawn back to Kai, magnetically latching onto him again and again.

Then a small entourage came down one of the aisles, the last to take their seats—Queen Levana, along with two thaumaturges. The queen was wearing a delicate white veil that draped to her elbows, hiding her face and making her look more like a phantom than a royal guest.

Cinder shivered. She didn't think any Lunars had ever been present at a Commonwealth coronation. Rather than making her feel hopeful for the future, the sight filled Cinder with a lump of anxiety. Because Levana's haughty stance suggested that she belonged there more than any of the Earthen citizens. As if *she* were the one about to be coronated.

The queen and her entourage claimed their reserved seats in the first row. Those seated around them tried, unsuccessfully, to hide their distaste at being so close to her.

Cinder pulled the sopping rag from the bucket and put her apprehension to work, scrubbing Adri's hover to a fine gleam.

The coronation began with a thunder of drums.

Prince Kai kneeled on a silk-covered platform as a slow parade of men and women passed before him, each dropping a ribbon or medallion or jewel around his neck. Each was a symbolic gift—long life, wisdom, goodness of heart, generosity, patience, joy. When all of the necklaces had been placed on him, the camera zoomed in on Kai's face. He appeared surprisingly serene, his eyes lowered but his head held high.

As was customary, a representative from one of the other five Earthen kingdoms had been selected to officiate the coronation in order to show that the other countries would honor and respect the new sovereign's right to govern. They had selected the European Federation's Prime Minister Bromstad, a tall, blond man with broad shoulders. Cinder had always thought that he looked more like a farmer than a politician. He held out an old-fashioned paper scroll that contained all the promises Kai was making to his people when he accepted the role of emperor.

As both of the prime minister's hands gripped either end of the scroll, he spoke a series of vows, and Kai repeated after him.

"I solemnly swear to govern the peoples of the Eastern Commonwealth according to the laws and customs as laid down by generations of past rulers," he recited. "I will use all the power bestowed on me to further justice, to be merciful, to honor the inherent rights of all peoples, to respect the peace between all nations, to rule with kindness and patience, and to seek the wisdom and council of my peers and brethren. All this, I promise to do today and for all the days of my reign, before all the witnesses of the Earth and heavens."

Cinder's heart swelled as she scrubbed the hood. She had never seen Kai look so serious, or so handsome. She feared for him a bit, knowing how nervous he must be, but in that moment he was not the prince who had brought a broken android to the market or almost kissed her in an elevator.

He was her emperor.

Prime Minister Bromstad lifted his chin. "I hereby proclaim you Emperor Kaito of the Eastern Commonwealth. Long live His Imperial Majesty."

The crowd burst into cheers and animated chants of *"Long live the Emperor"* as Kai turned to face his people.

If he were happy at his raised position, it was impossible to tell. His lips were neutral, his gaze reserved as he stood on the dais and the applause of the crowd surged around him.

After a long moment of his own serenity clashing with the tornado of praise, a podium was brought to the stage for the emperor's first address. The crowd quieted.

Cinder dashed water over the vehicle.

Kai stood expressionless for a moment, staring at the edge of the platform, his fingers gripping the podium's sides. "I am honored," he began, "that my coronation coincides with our most revered holiday. 126 years ago, the nightmare and catastrophe that was the Fourth World War ended, and the Eastern Commonwealth was born. It grew out of the unification of many peoples, many cultures, many ideals. It was strengthened by a single enduring belief that together, we as one people are strong. We have the ability to love each other, no matter our differences. To help each other, no matter our weaknesses. We chose peace over war. Life over death. We chose to crown one man to be our sovereign, to guide us, to uphold us—not to rule, but to serve." He paused.

Cinder pulled her focus away from the retina display long enough to give the hover a quick inspection. It was too dark to tell if she'd done a decent job, but she had lost interest in perfection.

Content, she dropped the wet rag into the bucket and sank against the concrete wall behind the row of parked hovers, giving the tiny screen her full attention.

"I am the great-great-great-grandson of the first emperor of the Commonwealth," Kai continued. "Since his time, our world has changed. We continue to face new problems, new heartaches. Though a war between men has not been fought on Earthen soil in 126 years, we now fight a new battle. My father was fighting a war against letumosis, the pestilence that has ravaged our planet for over a dozen years. This disease has brought death and suffering to our doorstep. The good people of the Commonwealth, and all our Earthen siblings, have lost friends, family, loved ones, neighbors. And with these losses, we face loss of trade and commerce, a downturn of economy, worsened living conditions. Some have gone without food because there are not enough farmers to toil the land. Some have gone without heat as our energy supplies dwindle. This is the war we now face. This is the war my father was determined to end, and I now vow to take up that torch.

"Together we will find a cure for this disease. We will defeat it. And we will return our great country to its former splendor."

The audience applauded, but Kai showed no sign of joy at his words. His expression was resigned, dark.

"It would be naive of me," he said when the audience had quieted, "not to mention a second kind of conflict. One no less deadly."

The crowd rustled. Cinder leaned her head back against the cold wall.

"As I am sure you are all aware, the relationship between the allied Earthen nations and Luna has been strained for many generations. As I am sure you are also aware, the sovereign of Luna, Her Majesty Queen Levana, has honored us with her presence for this past week. She is the first Lunar sovereign to step foot on Earth for almost a century, and her presence indicates hope that a time of true peace between us is fast approaching."

The screen panned out, showing Queen Levana in the front row. Her milky hands were folded demurely in her lap, as if she were humbled by the recognition. Cinder was sure she fooled no one.

"My father spent the last years of his life in discussion with Her Majesty in hopes of seeing an alliance to fruition. He did not live to see the result of those discussions, but I am determined that his efforts will live on in me. It is true that there have been obstacles on this road to peace. That we have had difficulties finding a common ground with Luna, a solution that would serve both parties. But I have not given up hope that a resolution can be found." He took a breath, then paused with his lips still parted. His gaze dropped down to the podium. His fingers locked around the edges.

Cinder leaned forward as if she could get a closer look at the prince as he struggled with his next words.

"I will—" He paused again, straightened, and focused his eyes on some distant, invisible point. "I will do whatever needs to be done to ensure the well-being of my country. I will do whatever needs to be done to keep you all safe. That is my promise."

He peeled his hands from the podium and walked off before the crowd could think to applaud, leaving a sprinkle of concerned but polite clapping behind him.

Cinder's heart strangled her as the screen allowed another glimpse of the Lunars in the front row. The veil may have hidden the queen's conceit, but the smug grins on her two attendants could not be mistaken. They believed they had won.

Thirty-Two

CINDER WAITED HALF AN HOUR BEFORE LIMPING BACK TO the elevator. The apartment building had come to life again. She kept herself plastered to the wall, crutches tucked behind her, as her neighbors danced by in their fine clothes. A few pitying glances turned on Cinder as she kept out of their way, careful not to smudge any of the beautiful dresses, but mostly her neighbors ignored her.

Making it to the apartment, she shut the door behind her and listened for a moment to the blissful emptiness of the living room. She ran a mental checklist of everything she wanted to grab, green text scrolling across her vision. In her room, Cinder spread out her blanket and filled it with her few belongings—oil-stained clothes, tools that had never made their way back to the toolbox, silly little gifts that Iko had given to her over the years, like a "gold ring" that was actually a rusted washer.

Both Iko's personality chip and Peony's ID chip were tucked safely in her calf compartment, where they would stay until she found a more permanent home for them.

She shut her eyes, suddenly tired. How was it that with freedom so close on the horizon, she suddenly had the overwhelming desire to lie down and take a nap? All those long nights fixing the car were catching up with her.

Shaking off the feeling, she finished packing as fast as she could, trying her best not to think of the risks she was taking. She would be considered a runaway cyborg for real this time. If she were ever caught, Adri could have her imprisoned.

She kept her hands moving. Trying not to think of Iko, who should have been at her side. Or Peony, who should have made her want to stay. Or Prince Kai.

Emperor Kai.

She would never see him again.

She knotted the blanket corners with an angry tug. She was thinking too much. She just had to leave. One step at a time and soon she would be in the car, and all this would be behind her. Settling the makeshift bag over her shoulder, she hobbled her way back to the hall and down to the labyrinth of underground storage spaces. Limping into the storage room, she dropped the bag onto the floor.

She paused for only a moment to catch her breath before she continued, unlatching the top of the handheld toolbox and shoveling everything off the desk into it. There would be time for sorting later. The standing toolbox that came nearly to her chest was much too big to fit into the car and would have to be left behind. Her gas mileage would have been ruined with all that weight in the back, anyway.

She surveyed the room where she'd spent most of the past five years. It was the closest thing to a home she'd ever known, even with the chicken wire that felt like a cage and the boxes that smelled of mildew. She didn't expect to miss it much.

Peony's crumpled ball gown was still draped over the welder. It, like the toolbox, wouldn't be coming with her.

She moved to the towering steel shelves against the far wall and began rummaging for parts that would be useful for the car or even her own body should anything malfunction, throwing the pieces of miscellaneous junk into a heap on the floor. She paused as her hand stumbled across something she'd never thought she would see again.

The small, battered foot of an eleven-year-old cyborg.

She lifted it from the shelf, where it had been tucked out of sight. Iko must have saved it, even after Cinder had asked her to throw it away.

Perhaps in Iko's mind, it was the closest thing to an android shoe she would ever own. Cinder cradled the foot against her heart. How she had hated this foot. How overjoyed she was to see it now.

With an ironic smile, she slumped into her desk chair for the last time. Pulling off her gloves, she eyed her left wrist, trying to picture the small chip just beneath the surface. The thought brought Peony to mind. Her blue-tipped fingers. The scalpel against her pale white skin.

Cinder shut her eyes, forcing the memory away. She had to do this.

She reached for the utility knife on the corner of her desk, the blade soaking in a tin can filled with alcohol. She shook it off, took a deep breath, and rested her cyborg hand palm up on the desk. She recalled seeing the chip on Dr. Erland's holograph, less than an inch away from where skin met metal. The challenge would be getting it out without accidentally splicing any important wires.

Forcing her mind to quiet, her hand to still, she pressed the blade into her wrist. The pain bit into her, but she didn't flinch. Steady. Steady.

A beep startled her. Cinder jumped, pulling the blade away and spinning around to face the wall of shelving. Her heart pummeled against her ribs as she scanned all the parts and tools that would be left behind.

It beeped again. Cinder's eyes dropped to the old netscreen that was still propped against the shelves. She knew it was disconnected from the net, and yet a bright blue square was flashing in the corner. Another beep.

Setting down the knife, Cinder slinked away from her chair and kneeled before the screen.

On the blue square was scrawled:

DIRECT LINK REQUEST RECEIVED FROM UNKNOWN USER. ACCEPT?

Tilting her head, she spotted the D-COMM chip still inserted in the screen's drive. The small green light beside it glowed. In the shadow of the screen, it looked like any other chip, but Cinder remembered Kai's response when she'd described the chip's shimmery silver material. A Lunar chip.

She grabbed a dirty rag from the pile of junk and pressed it against the barely bleeding wound. "Screen, accept link."

The beeping stopped. The blue box disappeared. A spiral turned over on the screen.

"Hello?"

Cinder jumped.

"Hello hello hello—is anybody there?"

Whoever she was, she sounded on the verge of a breakdown. "Please, oh, please, someone answer. Where is that stupid android? *HELLO*?"

"Hell-o? . . ." Cinder leaned in toward the screen.

The girl gasped, followed by a short silence. "Hello? Can you hear me? Is somebody—"

"Yes, I can hear you. Hold on, something's wrong with the vid-cable."

"Oh, thank heavens," the voice said as Cinder set aside the rag. She set the screen facedown on the concrete and opened the door to its control panel. "I thought maybe the chip had gotten damaged or I'd programmed it with the wrong connection ID or something. Are you in the palace now?"

Cinder found the vid-cable disconnected from its plug; it must have come loose when Adri had knocked it off the wall. Cinder screwed it in and a flood of blue light splattered across the floor. "There we are," she said, righting the screen.

She jolted back when she saw the girl on the other side of the connection. She must have been close to Cinder's age and had the longest, waviest, most unruly mess of tangled blonde hair imaginable. The golden nest around her head was tied in a big knot over one shoulder and cascaded in a jumble of braids and snarls, wrapping around one of the girl's arms before descending out of the screen's view. The girl was fidgeting with the ends, fervently winding and unwinding them around her fingers.

If it weren't for the mess of hair, she would have been pretty. She had a sweet heart-shaped face, giant sky-blue eyes, and a sprinkle of freckles across her nose.

She was somehow not at all what Cinder had been expecting.

The girl looked equally surprised at seeing Cinder and her cyborg hand and dreary T-shirt.

"Who are you?" the girl asked. Her eyes darted behind Cinder, taking in the dim lighting and the chicken wire. "Why aren't you at the palace?"

"I wasn't allowed to go," Cinder answered. She squinted at the room behind the girl, wondering if she were looking at a home on the moon . . . but it did not look like any home at all. Rather, the girl was surrounded by metal walls and machines and screens and computers and more controls and buttons and lights than a cargo ship's cockpit.

Cinder folded her legs, letting her footless calf dangle more comfortably over her thigh. "Are you Lunar?"

The girl's eyes fluttered, as if caught off guard by the question. Instead of answering, she leaned forward. "I need to speak with someone at New Beijing Palace right away."

"Then why don't you comm the palace information board?"

"I can't!" The girl's shriek was so unexpected, so desperate that Cinder nearly fell over. "I don't have a global comm chip—this is the only direct link I've been able to get down to Earth!"

"So you are Lunar."

The girl's eyes widened to near perfect circles. "That's not—"

"Who are you?" said Cinder, her voice raising. "Are you working for the queen? Are you the one who installed the chip in that android? You are, aren't you?"

The girl's eyebrows drew together, but rather than looking irritated at Cinder's questions, she appeared frightened. Even ashamed.

Cinder clenched her jaw against the onslaught of questions and took in a slow breath before asking, steadily, "Are you a Lunar spy?"

"No! Of course not! I mean . . . well . . . sort of."

"*Sort of?* What do you mean—"

"Please, listen to me!" The girl clenched her hands together, as if fighting an internal battle. "Yes, I programmed the chip, and I am working for the queen, but it's not what you think. I've programmed all the spyware that Levana's used to watch Emperor Rikan these past months, but I didn't have a choice. Mistress would kill me if . . . stars above, she *will* kill me when she finds out about this."

"Mistress who? You mean Queen Levana?"

The girl squeezed her eyes tight, her face contorted with pain. When she opened her eyes again, they were glistening. "No.

Mistress Sybil. She is Her Majesty's head thaumaturge . . . and my guardian."

Recognition pinged in Cinder's head. Kai had suspected the queen's thaumaturge of putting the chip in Nainsi in the first place.

"But she's more like a captor, really," the girl continued. "I'm nothing to her but a prisoner and a sla-ave." She hiccupped on the last word and buried her face in a bundle of hair, sobbing. "I'm sorry. I'm so sorry. I'm an evil, worthless, wretched girl."

Cinder felt her heart tug in sympathy—she could relate to being a slave for her "guardian," but she couldn't recall ever being afraid that Adri might actually kill her. Well, other than that time she sold her off for plague research.

She clenched her jaw against the mounting pity, reminding herself that this girl was Lunar. She had helped Queen Levana spy on Emperor Rikan, and on Kai. She briefly wondered if the girl was only manipulating her emotions now, before she remembered that Lunars couldn't control people through the netscreens.

Blowing some hair out of her face, Cinder leaned forward and yelled, "Stop it! Stop crying!"

The crying stopped. The girl peered up at her with big, watery eyes.

"Why were you trying to get a hold of the palace?"

The girl shrank back and sobbed, but the tears seemed to have been startled out of her. "I need to get a message to Emperor Kai. I need to warn him. He's in danger, all of

Earth . . . Queen Levana . . . and it's all my fault. If I'd only been stronger, if I'd only tried to fight, this wouldn't have happened. It's all my fault."

"Stars above, would you *stop crying*?" said Cinder before the girl could dissolve into hysterics again. "You need to get a hold of yourself. What do you mean Kai's in danger? What have you done?"

The girl hugged herself, her eyes pleading with Cinder as if she alone could offer forgiveness. "I'm the queen's programmer, like I said. I'm good at it—hacking into netlinks and security systems and the like." She said this without a hint of arrogance on her wavering voice. "For the last few years, Mistress has been asking me to connect feeds from Earth's political leaders to Her Majesty's palace. At first, it was just court discussions, meetings, document transfers, nothing very interesting. Her Majesty wasn't learning anything that your emperor hadn't already told her, so I didn't think much harm could come of it."

The girl twisted her hair around both sets of knuckles. "But then she asked me to program a D-COMM chip that she could install in one of the royal androids, thinking then she could spy on the emperor outside of the netlinks." She raised her eyes to Cinder. Guilt was scrawled across her face. "If it had been any other android, any android in the entire palace, she still wouldn't know anything. But now she does know! And it's all my fault!" She whimpered and pulled the lock of hair into her mouth like a gag.

"Wait," Cinder held up her hand, trying to slow the girl's rapid words. "What exactly does Levana know?"

The girl pulled the hair out as tears started to slip down

her cheeks. "She knows everything that android knew, everything she'd been researching. She knows that Princess Selene is alive and that Prince—I'm sorry, that Emperor Kai was searching for her. She knows that the emperor wanted to find the princess and instate her as the true Lunar queen."

Dread squirmed in Cinder's stomach.

"She knows the names of the doctors who helped her escape and this poor old woman in the European Federation who housed her for so long. . . . Her Majesty's already sent people to hunt her down, using the information Kai had. And when they find her—"

"But what will she do to Kai?" Cinder interrupted. "Levana's already won. Kai all but said he was going to give her what she wants, so what does it matter now?"

"He tried to usurp her! You don't know the queen, her grudges. She'll never forgive this. I have to get a message to him, to somebody at the palace. He has to know it's a setup."

"A setup? What kind of setup?"

"To become empress! Once she's in control of the Commonwealth, she intends to use her army to wage war on the rest of Earth. And she can do it too—her army . . . this army . . ." She shuddered, ducking her head as if someone had swiped at her.

Cinder shook her head. "Kai wouldn't allow it."

"It doesn't matter. Once she's empress, she'll have no more use of him."

Blood rushed in Cinder's ears. "You think—but she would be an idiot to try to kill him. Everyone would know it was her."

"Lunars suspect she killed Queen Channary *and* Princess Selene, but what can they do about it? They might think of rebellion, but as soon as they're in her presence, she brainwashes them into compliance again."

Cinder rubbed her fingers over her brow. "He was going to announce it at the ball tonight," she murmured to herself. "He's going to announce his intent to marry her." Her heart was racing, thoughts spilling over in her brain.

Levana knew he had been searching for Princess Selene. She would kill him. She would take over the Commonwealth. She would wage war on . . . on the whole planet.

She grasped her head as the world spun around her.

She had to warn him. She couldn't let him make the announcement.

She could send him a comm, but what were the chances he was checking them during the ball?

The ball.

Cinder peered down at her drab clothes. Her empty ankle.

Peony's dress. The old foot that Iko had saved. The silk gloves.

Her head bobbed before she knew what she was agreeing to, and she used the shelves to pull herself to standing. "I'll go," she muttered. "I'll find him."

"Take the chip," said the girl on the screen. "In case we need to contact each other. And please, don't tell them about me. If my mistress ever found out—"

Without waiting for her to finish, Cinder bent over and pulled the chip from its drive. The screen went black.

Thirty-Three

THE SILK DRESS FELT LIKE POISON IVY SLIDING OVER CINDER'S skin. She stared down at the silver bodice with its trim of delicate lace, the full skirt, the tiny seed pearls, and wanted to shrivel inside the gown and disappear. This was not her dress. She was a fake in it, an imposter.

Oddly, the fact that it was wrinkled as an old man's face made her feel better.

She snatched the old foot from the shelf—the small, rusted thing she'd woken up with after her operation, when she was a confused, unloved eleven-year-old girl. She'd sworn to never put it on again, but at this moment it might have been made of crystal for how precious it looked to her. Plus, it was small enough to fit into Pearl's boots.

Cinder fell into her chair and whisked out a screwdriver. It was the most hurried fix she'd ever done, and the foot was even smaller and more uncomfortable than she'd remembered it, but soon she was on two feet again.

The silk gloves felt too fine, too delicate, too flimsy, and she worried she might snag them on some poorly placed screw. At least they too were covered in grease smudges, completing the affront.

She was a walking disaster and she knew it. She'd be lucky if they let her into the ball at all.

But she would deal with that when she got there.

The elevator was empty as she made her way to the parking garage. She rushed toward the abandoned car, the boots clipping awkwardly on the concrete floor as she tried not to trip on the too small foot and sprain her ankle. She could feel it precariously attached at the end of her leg. Not having had time to connect it to her wired nervous system, she felt like she was dragging around a paperweight. She tried to ignore it, thinking only of Kai and the announcement he was supposed to make that night.

She reached the dark corner of the garage, already sweating from her exertion, and knowing it would only get worse once she got out into the city's relentless humidity. Before her, the car was sandwiched between two sleek, chrome-accented hovers. Its awful orange paint was dulled by the garage's flickering lights. It didn't belong.

Cinder knew how it felt.

She slipped into the driver's seat, and the smell of old garbage and mildew embraced her. At least she'd replaced the seat's stuffing and covered it in a scavenged blanket so she didn't have to worry about sitting on rat droppings. Still, she could only imagine what stains the car's frame and floorboards were leaving on Peony's dress.

Shoving her thoughts to the back of her mind, she reached

under the steering column and grasped the power supply and circuit wires she'd already stripped and wrapped. She fumbled for the brown ignition wire.

Holding her breath, she tapped the wires together.

Nothing happened.

A drop of sweat rolled down the back of her knee. She flicked them together again. Again. "Please, please, please."

A spark lashed out from the wires, followed by unhappy clattering from the engine.

"Yes!" She pressed her foot down on the accelerator, revving the engine, feeling the car thrum and rumble beneath her.

Cinder allowed one overwhelming cry of relief, then jammed her foot into the clutch and pulled the transmission out of neutral, reciting the instructions she'd downloaded a week ago and had been studying ever since. How to drive.

Maneuvering out of the garage proved the most difficult part. Once on the road, her way was guided by solar streetlamps and the pale yellow glow from apartment windows—the city's constant light was a blessing, as the car's headlights had been busted out. Cinder was surprised at how rocky the roads were, how much garbage and debris littered the pavement since hovers no longer required an open path. The ride was jerky and harsh, and yet Cinder felt a surge of power with every turn of the wheel, press of the accelerator, rattle of the stick shift, screech of rubber.

A warm breeze blew through the missing back window, tousling Cinder's hair. The clouds had reached the city and hung threateningly above the skyscrapers, casting the evening in a gray shroud. Toward the other horizon, the sky was still wide open and proudly displaying the ninth full moon of the year. A perfect sphere in the blackened sky. A white, ominous eye transfixed upon her. Ignoring it, Cinder floored the accelerator, pushing the car to go faster—to fly.

And it flew. Not smoothly or gracefully like a hover but with all the roar and power of a proud beast. She couldn't help a grin, knowing that she had done this. She had brought this monstrosity back to life. It owed her now and it seemed to know it.

She would have made it, she thought, as the palace came into view, towering over the city atop its jagged cliff. She would have been nearing the city limits by now. Picking up speed. Watching the lights blur past. Racing for the horizon and never looking back.

A splatter of rain hit the cracked windshield.

Cinder gripped the steering wheel tighter as she started up the twisting, winding drive to the palace entrance. There were no hovers to compete with—she would be the last guest to arrive.

She crested the hill, reveling in the rush of escape, of freedom, of power—and then the torrent began. Rain drenched the car, blurring the palace's lights. The sound pounded against the metal and glass. Without headlights, the world disappeared beyond the windshield.

Cinder jammed her foot into the brake pedal.

Nothing happened.

Panic surged through her and she desperately pumped the stiff brake. A shadow loomed against the storm. Cinder screamed and covered her face.

The car collided with a cherry blossom tree, rocking Cinder with a jolt. Metal crunched around her. The engine sputtered and died. The seat belt burned across her chest.

Shaking, Cinder gaped at the storm that surged against the windshield. Wet maroon-colored leaves fell from the overhead branches, sticking to the glass. She reminded herself to breathe as adrenaline coursed through her veins. Her control panel's recommended course of action: take slow, measured breaths. But the breaths choked her as much as the seat belt did, until she reached a trembling hand toward the latch and peeled it off her.

A leak revealed itself along the weather stripping of her door's window, dripping down onto her shoulder.

Cinder fell back against the headrest, wondering if she had the strength to walk. Maybe if she just waited out the monsoon. Summer storms like this never lasted long; it would be a drizzle in a blink.

She held up her sodden gloves and wondered what, exactly, she was waiting for. Not pride. Not respectability. Being soaked could almost be an improvement at this point.

Gasping for a full breath, she pulled at the door handle and kicked with her booted foot to force it open. She stepped out into a downpour, the rain cool and refreshing on her skin. Slamming the door shut, she turned to survey the damage, pushing her hair back off her forehead.

The front end of the car was crumpled around the tree's trunk, the hood folded like an accordion to the passenger-side fender. Her heart broke a little as she looked at the wreckage—all her hard work, destroyed so quickly.

And—the thought occurring a second later—there was her chance for escape. Gone.

Shivering in the rain, she shoved the thoughts aside. There would be other cars. Right now, she had to find Kai.

Suddenly, the rain stopped pounding down on her. She glanced up at the umbrella overhead, then turned around. A greeter was staring at the car wreck with round eyes, his hands gripping the umbrella handle.

"Oh, hi," she stammered.

The man's disbelieving stare found its way to her. Her hair, her dress. He looked more repulsed by the second.

Cinder snatched the umbrella from him and flashed a smile. "Thanks," she said and dashed across the courtyard into the yawning double doors of the palace, dropping the umbrella at the stairs.

Guards dressed in crimson uniforms lined the corridor, directing guests away from the elevator dock and toward the ballroom in the south wing, as if the clinking glasses and orchestral music weren't clear enough. The walk to the ballroom entrance was long and tedious. Cinder didn't know if the guards let their stoic gazes land on her as she passed by, wet boots squishing, and she dared not meet their eyes if they did. All her focus was busy being directed down her wiring into her lump of a foot.

Be graceful. Be graceful. Be graceful.

The music grew louder. The hall was ornamented with dozens of ornate stone statues—gods and goddesses long forgotten. Hidden cameras. Disguised ID scanners. She felt a spark of paranoia, remembering that she still carried Peony's ID chip, stashed away in her leg compartment. She imagined alarms blaring and lights flashing when they realized that she had two ID chips inside her—which would be suspicious, if not outright illegal—but nothing happened.

Emerging from the hallway, she found herself at the top of a grand staircase that cascaded into the ballroom. A row of guards and servants flanked the stairs, their faces as unreadable as those in the hall. The high ceiling had been hung with hundreds of crimson paper lanterns, each one glimmering with rich, golden light. The far wall was lined with floor-to-ceiling windows that overlooked the gardens. Rain pummeled the glass, almost louder than the orchestra.

The dance floor had been set up in the center with round tables surrounding the space. Each table was bedecked with lavish orchid centerpieces and jade sculptures. The walls of the room were lined with folding silk screens hand painted with designs of cranes and tortoises and bamboo, ancient symbols of longevity that hinted at a single defining message: Long live the Emperor.

From her vantage point, she could see the entire room, thriving with vibrant silks and crinolines, rhinestones and ostrich plumes. She sought out Kai.

He wasn't hard to find—dancing. The crowd parted for him

and his partner, the most beautiful, most graceful, most divine woman in the room. The Lunar queen. Cinder couldn't stifle a gasp of bewilderment at the sight of her.

Her stomach flipped, the momentary awe turning to revulsion. The queen held a poised smile, but Kai's expression was as unfeeling as stone as they waltzed across the marble floor.

Cinder stepped back from the stairs before the queen noticed her. She scanned the crowd, convinced that Kai had not made his announcement yet, or the atmosphere in the room wouldn't be so jolly. Kai was fine. He was safe. All she had to do was find a way to speak with him, somewhere private, and tell him the queen's plans. Tell him the queen knew about his search for her niece. Then it would be up to him to put off accepting the queen's terms until—

Well, Cinder knew nothing could put Queen Levana off forever without convincing her to start the war she'd been threatening for so long.

But maybe, just maybe, Princess Selene could be found before that happened.

Letting out a slow breath, Cinder stepped out of the massive doorway and ducked behind the nearest pillar, stumbling on her tiny foot. Gritting her teeth, she glanced around, but the nearby guards and servants remained as disinterested as a concrete wall.

Cinder plastered herself against the column, trying to smooth back her hair so she could at least pretend to be fitting in.

The music ceased and the crowd began to applaud.

She dared to peer down at the dance floor and saw Kai and Levana parting ways—he with a stiff bow and she with the grace of a geisha. As the orchestra started again, the entire ballroom joined in the dancing.

Cinder followed the queen's glossy brunette curls heading toward a staircase on the other side of the room, the crowd parting eagerly before her. She scanned for Kai again, and found him heading in the opposite direction—toward her.

Holding her breath, she inched away from the protective column. This was her chance. If only he would look up and see her. If only he would come to her. She could tell him everything and then slip away into the night and no one would ever have to know she'd been there at all.

She bunched the silver gown up in her fists, her eyes boring holes into the emperor's head, willing him to look up. Look up. *Look up.*

Kai froze with a look of mild perplexity, and Cinder thought with a jolt that she'd succeeded—had she just used her Lunar gift?

But then she noticed a spot of gold beside Kai, a frilly sleeve brushing his arm. Her breath caught.

It was Pearl, brushing her fingertips against Kai's elbow. She was full of dazzling smiles and fluttering lashes as she dipped into a curtsy.

Stomach clenching, Cinder sank back against the pillar.

Pearl started to talk, and Cinder monitored Kai's expressions as her pulse pounded in her ears. At first, he only attempted a weary smile, but soon there was confusion. Surprise. An uncertain frown. She tried to guess what Pearl was saying: *Yes, I am the girl from the festival this morning. No, Cinder is not coming. We wouldn't disrespect this momentous occasion by allowing my ugly cyborg stepsister to attend. Oh—didn't you know she's cyborg?*

Cinder shuddered, her eyes glued to the two of them. Pearl was going to tell Kai everything, and there was nothing she could do but watch and wait for the horrible moment when Kai realized he'd been flirting with a cyborg. He would want nothing more to do with her. He wouldn't want to hear her excuses. She would be forced to stumble after him to tell him the reason she'd come, feeling like the disgrace she was.

Someone cleared his throat, and Cinder jumped out of her growing anxiety, nearly twisting her ankle. One of the servants had evidently gotten tired of standing motionless and impartial and was now looking her over with barely veiled revulsion.

"I beg your pardon," he said, with a tightness to his voice. "I must scan your ID."

Cinder instinctively pulled her hand away from him, pressing her wrist against her stomach. "Why?"

His eyes darted to the row of guards, ready to call on them to have her escorted out at any moment. "To ensure you're on the guest list, of course," he said, holding up a small handheld scanner.

Cinder pressed her back into the pillar, nerves humming. "But—I thought every citizen in the city was invited."

"Indeed, they are." The man grinned, looking almost gleeful

at the prospect of *dis*inviting the girl before him. "But we must ensure that we are receiving those who responded to their invitations. It's a security measure."

Gulping, Cinder glanced out toward the dance floor. Kai was still being hounded by Pearl, and now Cinder could see Adri hovering not far off, looking primed to jump into the conversation should Pearl say anything to embarrass her. Pearl had not dropped her shy, flirtatious charm. She stood with her head bowed and one hand gingerly pressed against her collarbone.

Kai still looked perplexed.

Goose bumps racing up her arms, Cinder turned back to the courtier and attempted to channel Peony's cheerful innocence. "Of course," she said. Holding her breath, she stretched out her arm. She was concocting a number of excuses, justifications—her RSVP must have gotten mixed up with someone else's, or perhaps there was confusion as her stepmother and sister had already arrived without her, or—

"Ah!" The man jolted, his eyes staring at the small screen.

Cinder tensed, wondering what her chances were of knocking him out with a quick blow to the head without any of those guards noticing.

His bewildered eyes took another turn over her dress, her hair, and then returned to his screen. She could see the internal struggle as his smile slowly turned up, attempting politeness. "Why, Linh-mèi, what a pleasure. We are so glad you could join us tonight."

Her eyebrows shot up. "You are?"

The man gave her a stiff bow. "Please forgive my ignorance. I'm sure His Imperial Majesty will be glad you've arrived. Please, step this way, and I will have you announced."

She blinked, dumbly following his arm as he stepped toward the stairs. "Have me what?"

He tapped something into his portscreen, before glancing back at Cinder. His gaze swooped over her again as if he couldn't believe what he was about to do, but his polite smile didn't fade. "All personal guests of His Imperial Majesty are duly announced, as recognition of their import. Of course, they don't usually arrive so . . . late."

"Wait. Personal guests of . . . oh. Oh! No, no, you don't have to—"

She was silenced by the blare of recorded trumpets through invisible overhead speakers. She ducked at the sound, eyes widening, as the short melody faded. At the last trill of the horns, a majestic voice boomed through the ball room.

"Please welcome to the 126th Annual Ball of the Eastern Commonwealth, a personal guest of His Imperial Majesty: Linh Cinder of New Beijing."

Thirty-Four

THE BALLROOM TEMPERATURE SPIKED AS HUNDREDS OF faces turned toward Cinder.

Perhaps the crowd would have turned away a moment later, indifferent, if they hadn't found the emperor's personal guest to be a girl with damp hair and mud splatters on the hem of her wrinkled silver dress. As it was, the gazes halted, pinning Cinder to the top of the stairs. Her mismatched feet stuck to the landing as if concrete had hardened around them.

She looked at Kai, his jaw hanging as he took her in.

He'd expected her to come the entire time. He'd reserved a spot for her as his personal guest. She could only imagine how he was regretting that decision now.

Beside him, Pearl's face had begun to burn beneath the glowing chandeliers. Cinder looked at her stepsister, at Adri, took in their speechless mortification, and reminded herself to breathe.

It was already over for her.

Pearl had almost certainly told Kai that she was cyborg.

Soon, Queen Levana would see her too and know she was Lunar. She would be taken, maybe killed. There was nothing she could do about it now.

But she had taken the risk. She had made the decision to come.

It would not go to waste.

She squared her shoulders. Lifted her chin.

Gathering up the full silk skirt, she fixed her gaze on Kai and made her way slowly down the steps.

His eyes softened into something almost like amusement, as if such a ragged appearance was all one could expect from a renowned mechanic.

A murmur rippled through the crowd and as the heel of Cinder's boot hit the marble floor with forced precision, the sea of gowns began to shuffle aside. Women whispered behind their hands. Men craned their necks to catch the hushed gossip.

Even the servants had stopped to watch her, holding trays of delicacies aloft. The scent of garlic and ginger clouded around them, twisting Cinder's stomach into knots. She realized suddenly how famished she was. All the preparations for running away had left little time for eating. Coupled with her anxiety, it almost made her feel faint. She did her best to ignore it, to be strong, but nervousness was expanding through her taut muscles with every step. Her pulse was a drumbeat inside her head.

Every eye swept over her, mocking her. Every head turned to whisper, rumors already taking flight. Cinder's ears rang, picking snatches of conversation—A *personal guest? But who is she?*

And what is that stuff on her dress?—until Cinder adjusted the audio interface, silencing the words.

Never in her life had she been so glad she could not blush.

Kai's lips twitched, and though he still looked baffled, he did not look angry or disgusted. Cinder gulped. As she got nearer, her arms burned to wrap around herself, to cover her filthy, wrinkled, water-stained dress as best she could, but she didn't allow them. It would have been futile, and Kai didn't care about her dress.

If anything, he was probably trying to discern how much of her was metal and silicon.

She kept her head high, even as her eyes stung, even as panic filled her vision with warnings and precautions.

It was not her fault he had liked her.

It was not her fault she was cyborg.

She would not apologize.

She focused only on walking, one thudding step after another, as the crowd parted before her, then closed again in her wake.

But before she reached the emperor, a figure pushed out of the crowd and into her path. Cinder froze, halted by the seething glare of her stepmother.

She blinked, dumbfounded, as reality stumbled in on the still, silent moment. She'd forgotten that Adri and Pearl were there.

Blotchy red cheeks showed through Adri's translucent white makeup, and her chest was heaving beneath the modest neckline of her kimono. The confused tittering hushed, pushing the questions toward those in the back of the crowd who couldn't see what was happening but could no doubt feel the tension expanding around them.

Adri's hand snatched forward, capturing Cinder's skirt in her fist. She shook the material. "Where did you get this?" she hissed, her voice low as if she were afraid of causing more of a scene than Cinder already had.

Setting her jaw, Cinder stepped back, whipping the dress away from her stepmother. "Iko saved the dress. Peony would have wanted me to have it."

Behind her mother, Pearl gasped, her hands flying to her mouth. Cinder glanced at her and found Pearl looking down at her feet with horror.

Cinder shuddered, imagining her cyborg leg visible for all to see, until Pearl pointed at her feet and shrieked, "My boots! Those are my boots! On *her*!"

Adri's eyes narrowed. "You little *thief.* How dare you come here and make a mockery of this family." She jutted her finger over Cinder's shoulder toward the grand staircase. "I command you to go home this instant before you embarrass me further."

"No," she said, clenching her fists. "I have as much right to be here as you do."

"What? *You?*" Adri's voice started to rise. "But you're nothing but a—" She caught her tongue, even now unwilling to share the mortifying secret about her stepdaughter. Instead, she raised her hand over her shoulder, palm flat.

The crowd gasped and Cinder flinched, but the strike did not come.

Kai stood beside her stepmother, one hand firmly wrapped around Adri's wrist. Adri turned to him, her face burning with anger, but the look quickly fell away.

She shriveled back, stammering. "Your Majesty!"

"That is enough," he said, his voice gentle but stern, and released her. Adri shrank into a pathetic curtsy, head bobbing.

"I am so sorry, Your Majesty. My emotions—my temper—this girl is . . . I am sorry she has interrupted . . . she is my ward—she should not be here . . ."

"Of course, she should." There was a lightness to his words, as if he believed his presence alone could dissolve Adri's hostility. He fixed his gaze on Cinder. "She is my personal guest."

He glanced around over the heads of the shocked audience, toward the stage where the symphony had gone silent. "This is a night for celebration and amusement," he said loudly. "Please, let the dancing resume."

The band started, shakily at first, until music again filled the ballroom—Cinder could not recall when it had died out, but her hearing was still dulled to the swarming noise around her.

Kai was looking at her again. She gulped and found that she was shaking—with anger and terror and nerves and the sensation of being captured by his brown eyes. Her mind was blank, not sure if she wanted to thank him or turn away and keep yelling at her stepmother, but he didn't give her a chance to do either.

Kai reached forward and took her hand, and before she realized what was happening, he had plucked her away from her stepmother and stepsister and taken her into his arms.

They were dancing.

Heart hammering, Cinder pried her gaze away from him and looked over his shoulder.

They were the only ones dancing.

Kai must have noticed it too, for he floated his hand briefly away from her waist, gesturing to the gawking crowd, and said in a tone that was part encouragement, part command, "Please, you are my guests. Enjoy the music."

Awkwardly, those nearby traded glances with their own partners, and soon the floor was filling with bustled skirts and coattails. Cinder risked glancing toward where they had abandoned Adri and Pearl—they were both standing still amid the shuffling crowd, watching as Kai expertly guided Cinder farther and farther away from them.

Clearing his throat, Kai murmured, "You have no idea how to dance, do you?"

Cinder fixed her gaze on him, mind still reeling. "I'm a *mechanic.*"

His eyebrows raised mockingly. "Believe me, I noticed. Are those grease stains on the gloves I gave you?"

Mortified, she glanced at their intertwined fingers and the black smudges on the white silk gloves. Before she could apologize, she felt herself being gently pushed away and spun beneath his arm. She gasped, for a moment feeling light as a butterfly, before she stumbled on her undersized cyborg foot and fell back into his embrace.

Kai grinned, coaxing her back to arm's length, but he didn't tease her. "So. That's your stepmother."

"Legal guardian."

"Right, my mistake. She seems like a real treasure."

Cinder scoffed and her body started to ease. Without sensation in her foot, it felt like trying to dance with a ball of iron soldered to her ankle. Her leg was beginning to ache from carrying it, but she resisted the urge to limp, picturing ever-graceful Pearl in her ball gown and heels, and wished her body into conformity.

At least her body seemed to be memorizing the pattern of the dance steps, making each movement slightly more fluid than the last, until she almost felt as if she knew what she were doing. Of course, the tender pressure of Kai's hand on her waist didn't hurt.

"I'm sorry about that," she said. "About her, and my stepsister. Can you believe they think *I'm* the embarrassment?" She made it sound like a joke, but she couldn't help analyzing his response, bracing for that moment when he asked her if it were true.

If she really were cyborg.

Then, as his smile started to crumble, she realized the moment had come far too soon, and she desperately wished she could take the comment back. She wished they could go on pretending forever that her secret was still safe. That he still did not know.

That he still wanted her to be his personal guest.

"Why didn't you tell me?" Kai said, his voice lowering even though the noise of laughter and tapping heels had filled the air around them.

Cinder opened her mouth, but her words snagged in her throat. She wanted to refute Pearl's claim, to call her a liar. But what would that get her? More lies. More betrayal. The fingers of her metal hand tightened on his shoulder, the hard, unforgiving confines of the limb. He didn't flinch, just waited.

She wanted to feel relief now that they had no more secrets. But that wasn't entirely true either. He still didn't know she was Lunar.

She opened her mouth again, unsure what she was going to say until the faint words came to her. "I didn't know how."

Kai's eyes softened, little wrinkles forming in their corners.

"I would have understood," he said.

Almost imperceptibly, he inched closer, and Cinder found her elbow crawling up his shoulder in a way that felt impossibly natural. Still, he did not back away. Did not shudder or tense.

He knew, but he wasn't disgusted? He would still touch her? Somehow, unbelievably, he still even, maybe, liked her?

She felt she would have cried if it had been an option.

Her fingertips tentatively curled around the hair at the back of his neck, and she found that she was shaking, sure he would push her away at any moment. But he didn't. He did not pull away. Did not grimace.

His lips parted, just barely, and Cinder wondered if maybe she wasn't the only one having trouble breathing.

"It's just," she started, running her tongue across her lips, "it isn't something I like to talk about. I haven't told anyone who . . . who . . ."

"Who didn't know her?"

Cinder's words evaporated. *Her?*

Fingers stiffening, she eased them out of his hair and settled her palm back on his shoulder.

The intensity in his gaze melted into sympathy. "I understand why you didn't say anything. But now I feel so selfish." His jaw flexed, his brow turned up with guilt. "I know, I should have guessed after you told me she was sick to begin with, but with the coronation and Queen Levana's visit and the ball, I just . . . I guess I forgot. I know that makes me the biggest jerk in the world, and I should have realized that your sister had . . . and why you were ignoring my comms. It makes sense now." He drew her closer, until she could almost lay her head on his shoulder, but she didn't. Her body had gone rigid again, the dance steps forgotten. "I just wish you would have told me."

Her gaze shifted over his shoulder, focusing on nothing. "I know," she murmured. "I should have told you."

She felt as though all her synthetic parts were squeezing together, crushing her inside.

Kai didn't know.

And yet to have felt the comforting presence of acceptance, only to be confined by secrecy again, was even more unbearable than lying to him to begin with.

"Kai," she said, shaking herself from the misery that threatened her. She pushed back to arm's length, returning them to the acceptable distance of strangers—or of a mechanic dancing with her emperor. For the first time, Kai missed a dance step, eyes blinking in surprise. She ignored the guilt scratching at her throat.

"I came here to tell you something. It's important." She glanced around, ensuring that no one could hear them. Though she caught a few jealous scowls targeting her, no one was close enough to hear over the music, and the Lunar queen was nowhere to be seen. "Listen. You can't marry Levana. No matter what she wants, no matter what she threatens."

Kai flushed at the queen's name. "What do you mean?"

"She doesn't just want the Commonwealth. She's going to start a war with Earth either way. It's just that being empress here will pave the way for her."

It was his turn to look around, simultaneously molding his look of panic into cool indifference, though up close, Cinder could see the worry in his eyes.

"And there's more. She *does* know about Nainsi . . . about what Nainsi found out. She knows you were trying to find Princess Selene, and she's taken the information you found and is hunting her down now. She has people out looking for her . . . if they haven't found her already."

Eyes widening, Kai looked back at her.

"And you know," she continued, not allowing him to interrupt, "you *know* that she won't forgive you for trying to find the princess." She gulped. "Kai, as soon as you marry her, and she has what she wants . . . she's going to kill you."

The color drained from his face. "How do you know all this?"

She took in a deep breath, somehow exhausted from getting all the information out, as if she'd only reserved enough energy to bring her to this moment. "The D-COMM chip I found in Nainsi. There was this girl, its programmer . . . ugh. It's complicated." She hesitated, thinking she should give the chip to Kai while she had the chance. He may be able to get more information out of the girl, except in her hurry to leave for the ball, she'd stashed it in her calf compartment. Her gut sank. To retrieve it now would be to reveal herself to Kai and everyone around her.

She gulped, shoving aside the rising distress. Was saving her own pride more important to her?

"Is there somewhere we can go?" she asked. "Away from the crowd? I'll tell you everything."

He glanced around. In their dancing, they had traveled almost the entire length of the ballroom, and now they stood before a set of massive doors that opened out onto the royal gardens. Beyond the steps, a willow tree was weeping from the heavy rain, a koi pond nearly overflowing. The pummeling of the storm came in waves, almost drowning out the noise of the orchestra.

"The gardens?" he said, but before he could move, a shadow fell across them. Glancing up, Cinder saw the unhappy expression of a royal official, looking at Kai with lips so tight they'd started to go white. He did not acknowledge Cinder.

"Your Majesty," he said, his face drawn. "It is time."

Thirty-Five

CINDER LOOKED UP AT THE MAN, HER LINK TO THE NET database informing her that he was Konn Torin, royal adviser. "Time?" she said, turning back to Kai. "Time for what?"

Kai stared at her, part apologetic, part afraid. Her gut twisted.

Time to seal the fate of the Eastern Commonwealth.

"No," she hissed. "Kai, you can't—"

"Your Majesty," said Konn Torin, still without deigning to meet Cinder's eye. "I have allowed you your freedom, but it is time to put an end to this. You are embarrasing yourself."

Kai let his gaze fall, before shutting his eyes altogether. He rubbed at his brow. "Just a moment. I need a moment to think."

"We do not have a moment. We have been over this time and again—"

"There's new information," Kai said, his tone harsh. Konn Torin's face darkened, and he cast a suspicious glare at Cinder. She shivered at the disapproving frown—for once, this was hatred directed at her not because she was a cyborg, but because she was a normal girl, unworthy of the attention of the emperor.

For once, she couldn't disagree.

If the understanding showed on her face, the adviser ignored it. "Your Majesty. With all due respect, you no longer have the luxury of being a lovesick teenager. You have a duty to fulfill to your people now."

Dropping his hand, Kai met Konn Torin's gaze, his eyes hollow. "I know," he said. "I will do what is best for them."

Cinder gathered up the material of her skirt in both hands, hope stirring inside of her. He understood her warnings. He understood the mistake he would be making if he agreed to marry Levana. She had succeeded.

But then he turned toward her, and the hope shattered at seeing the helplessness etched in deep lines across his brow.

"Thank you for warning me, Cinder. At least I won't be going into this blindly."

She shook her head. "Kai. You *can't*."

"I don't have a choice. She has an army that could destroy us. An antidote that we need. . . . I have to take my chances."

Cinder stumbled back as if his words had landed the blow that he had protected her from before. He was going to marry Queen Levana.

Queen Levana would be empress.

"I'm sorry, Cinder."

He looked as crushed as Cinder felt, and yet while her body became heavy and immoveable, Kai somehow found the strength to turn away with head lifted and start walking toward the platform at the far end of the ballroom, where he would announce his decision to those who had gathered.

She searched her brain for anything she could do to change his mind. But what else was there?

He knew Levana would still start a war. He knew Levana would probably try to kill him after the wedding. He probably knew about more cruel and evil deeds she'd committed than Cinder did, and none of it made a difference. Somehow, he was still naive enough to think that more good than bad could come from the union. He would not stop it from happening.

The only other person who had the power to stop the marriage alliance was the queen herself.

A fist clenched over Cinder's heart.

Before she knew what she was doing, she was storming after Kai. She grabbed his elbow and spun him back around to face her.

Without hesitating, Cinder wrapped her arms around his neck and kissed him.

Kai froze, his body as tense as an android's against her, but his lips were soft and warm. Though Cinder had intended for it to be a short kiss, she found herself lingering. Hot tingles coursed through her body, surprising and scary but not unpleasant, surging like electricity through her wires. This time, they did not overwhelm her. This time, they did not threaten to burn her from the inside out.

The desperation melted and, for the briefest of moments, the ulterior motives were gone. She found herself kissing him for no other reason than she wanted to. She wanted him to know that she wanted to.

She didn't realize how badly she wanted Kai to kiss her back until it became quite clear that he wouldn't.

Cinder pried herself away. Her hands lingered on his shoulders, still shaking from the raw energy inside her.

Kai gaped at her, lips left hanging open, and though Cinder's gut reaction was to back away and apologize profusely, she swallowed it down.

"Perhaps," she said, testing her voice before raising it loud enough that she was sure the crowd would hear her. "Perhaps the queen will not accept your proposal, once she finds out you're already in love with me!"

Kai's eyebrows rose higher. "Wha—?"

Beside him, the adviser took in a hissing breath, and a series of gasps and rustles passed through the crowd. It occurred to Cinder that the music had stopped again as the musicians stood and tried to get a look at what was happening.

A burst of jovial, tittering laughter split through the awkwardness. The sound, though filled with the sweetness of a child's giggle, sent a chill down Cinder's spine.

Pulling her hands away from Kai's neck, she slowly turned. The crowd followed the noise as well, swiveling in unison like puppets on strings.

And there was Queen Levana.

She was leaning against one of the columns that flanked the doorway to the gardens, holding a goblet of gold wine in one hand and pressing the fingers of the other against her smiling red lips. Her figure was perfection. Her posture could not have been more poised had she been carved from the same stone as the pillar. She wore a royal blue dress that shimmered with what were probably diamonds yet gave the very distinct impression of stars in an endless summer sky.

The orange light blinked beside Cinder's vision. The queen's glamour, the endless lie.

In addition to the queen, a Lunar guard stood just within the doorway, stark red hair swept up from his brow like a candle flame. A man and woman dressed in the distinctive uniforms of royal thaumaturges also lingered nearby, awaiting their mistress's order. Every one of them was strikingly beautiful and, unlike their queen, their beauty didn't seem to be an illusion. Cinder wondered if that was a requirement for serving the Lunar throne—or if she just happened to be the only Lunar in the galaxy who hadn't been born with brilliant eyes and flawless skin.

"How charmingly naive," said the queen, followed by another spill of laughter. "You must misunderstand my culture. On Luna, we consider monogamy to be nothing more than archaic sentimentality. What do I care if my husband-to-be is in love with another . . ."—she paused, her dark eyes sweeping over Cinder's dress—"woman?"

Terror wrapped around Cinder's throat as the queen's eyes seemed to pierce right through her. The queen knew she was Lunar. She could tell.

"What does concern me," continued Queen Levana, her voice a sweet lullaby that sharpened with her next words, "is that it appears my betrothed has fallen in love with an insignificant shell. Am I mistaken?"

The thaumaturges nodded in agreement, their eyes fixed on Cinder. "She certainly has the smell of one," said the woman.

Cinder wrinkled her nose. According to Dr. Erland, she wasn't actually a shell, and she wondered if the woman was making that insult up to mock her. Or maybe she was smelling the gasoline fumes from the car.

Suddenly, her netlink recognized the woman, and Cinder forgot about the affront. She was the diplomat who had been in New Beijing for weeks, whose picture had been all over the news feeds, though she'd never paid her much attention.

Sybil Mira, head thaumaturge to the Lunar queen.

Mistress Sybil, the girl had said over the D-COMM chip. This was the woman who had forced her to make the spy equipment, who had put the chip in Nainsi.

Cinder tried to relax, surprised that her control panel hadn't short-circuited with all the adrenaline coursing through her veins. What she wouldn't have given for a weapon, even a measly screwdriver to protect herself with—anything other than this useless foot and slight silk gloves.

Kai abandoned Cinder, marching toward the queen. "Your Majesty, I apologize for this disruption," he said, Cinder only catching his words as she adjusted her audio interface. "But we need not make a scene in front of my guests."

The queen's charcoal eyes flashed with the warm ballroom light. "It seems you're perfectly capable of making a scene without my help." Her smile turned to a playful pout. "Oh, dear, it seems that I'm more hurt than I thought I was by your fickleness. I believed *I* was to be your personal guest tonight." Again, her eyes caressed Cinder's face. "You *can't* think her prettier than me." She reached out a fingernail and traced it along Kai's jaw. "My dear, are you *blushing*?"

Kai slapped Levana's hand away, but before he could respond, she turned toward Cinder and her expression filled with disgust. "What is your name, child?"

Cinder downed a painful gulp, barely forcing her name from her throat. "Cinder."

"Cinder." A condescending laugh. "How fitting. Ashes. Dirt. *Filth.*"

"That's enough—" started Kai, but Levana breezed past him, the sparkling dress swaying over her hips. She held her wine glass aloft, as if prepared to compliment the prince on such a pleasant dinner party.

"Tell me, Cinder," she said, "what poor sapling Earthen did you steal that name from?"

Cinder's hand went to her wrist and gripped the silk glove and flesh that concealed her ID chip, barely sore from the small incision she'd made earlier. A weight settled in the pit of her stomach.

The queen sniffed. "You shells," she said, her voice rising for the crowd. "You think you're so clever. So you stole a chip from a dead Earthen's wrist. So you managed to slip into the government's system. So you think you pass as human, that you can exist here without any repercussions. You are fools."

Cinder clenched her jaw. She wanted to explain that she had no memory of being anything *but* Earthen—anything but cyborg. But who would she be pleading her case to? Certainly not the queen. And Kai . . . Kai, who was tossing glances between her and the queen, trying to fit the puzzle pieces of Levana's words together in his head.

The queen turned back to the emperor. "Not only harboring Lunars but also cavorting with them. I am disappointed in you, Your Majesty." She clucked her tongue. "The fact that this girl lives within your borders proves that you are in violation of the Interplanetary Agreement. I take the blatant disregard of such a statute quite seriously, Emperor Kaito. In fact, it could warrant a call to war. I insist that this traitor be taken into captivity and returned to Luna immediately. Jacin?"

A second Lunar guard stepped out of the crowd, equally handsome to the others, with long blond hair and serious ice-blue eyes. Without warning, he grasped Cinder's wrists, pinning them behind her. She gasped, her gaze flying wildly toward the gathered audience as alarmed cries rippled through it.

"Stop!" Kai rushed toward Cinder and grabbed her elbow. He tugged her toward him and she stumbled, but the guard did not loosen his grip.

The guard pulled Cinder back again and her arm, made slippery by the silk gloves, was torn from Kai's grip. She found herself plastered against the Lunar. His chest was solid behind her and a faint hum buzzed in her head, like static electricity in her hair.

Magic, she realized. Bioelectricity humming inside him. Could everyone hear it from so close, or was this another sign of her awakening gift?

"Let her go!" Kai said, appealing to the queen. "This is absurd. She isn't a fugitive—she isn't even Lunar. She's just a mechanic!"

Levana quirked one slender eyebrow. Her glittering eyes surpassed Kai, staring into Cinder with a gaze both beautiful and cruel.

Warmth was building in Cinder's spine, steady and growing hot. She feared a meltdown. The pain would come, and she would collapse and be useless.

"Well, Cinder?" said Queen Levana, swirling the pale wine. "It seems you've been keeping secrets from your royal superiors. Do you wish to refute my claim?"

Kai turned to her, and she could sense his desperation, even if she couldn't look at him. She focused only on the queen, her jaw aching with hatred.

She was glad that no tears would betray her humiliation. Glad that no blood in her cheeks would betray her anger. Glad that her hateful cyborg body was good for one thing as she clutched onto her shredded dignity. She leveled her glare at the queen.

Her retina display began to panic, noting her increased levels of adrenaline, her racing pulse. Warnings were flashing before her, but she ignored them, surprisingly calm.

"If I had not been brought to Earth," she said, "I would be a slave under your rule. I will not apologize for escaping."

In the corner of her gaze, she saw Kai's face fall, eyes widening as the truth became undeniable. He had been courting a Lunar.

A cry rang out from the trembling crowd. A round of gasps, a soft thud. Adri had fainted.

Gulping, Cinder squared her shoulders.

"I want no apologies," said Levana, flashing a wicked smile. "I only want to see the wrongs of your life righted, swiftly and surely."

"You want to see me dead."

"How bright she is. Yes, I do. And not just you, but all those like you. You shells are a threat to society, a danger to our ideal culture."

"Because you can't brainwash us into worshipping you like everybody else?"

The queen's lips tightened, hardening like plaster on her face. Her voice fell, chilling the room. A sudden burst of rain behind her shook the windows.

"It is not only for my people, but for all Earthens as well. You shells are a plague." She paused, a lightness returning to her eyes, as if she might laugh. "Quite literally it seems."

"My Queen," said the dark-haired woman, "refers to your so-called blue fever that has wreaked such havoc on your citizens. And, of course, your own royal family . . . may Emperor Rikan rest in—"

"What does that have to do with anything?" said Kai.

The woman tucked her hands into the bell-shaped sleeves of her ivory coat. "Hadn't your brilliant scientists drawn that conclusion yet? Many ungifted Lunars are carriers of letumosis. They brought it to Earth. They continue to spread it, without concern, it seems, for the lives they are taking."

Cinder shook her head. "No," she said. Kai turned to her, unconsciously taking a step away. She shook her head more harshly. "They don't know they're doing it. How could they? And, of course, the scientists have figured it out, but what can they do, other than try to find a cure?"

The queen laughed sharply. "Ignorance is your defense? How trite. You must see the truth, the fact that you *should* be dead. It would be so much better for everyone if you were."

"And for the *record*," said Cinder, her voice rising, "I'm not a shell."

The queen smirked, unconvinced.

"That's enough," said Kai. "I don't care where she was born. Cinder is a citizen of the Commonwealth. I will not have her arrested."

Levana did not tear her gaze from Cinder. "Harboring a fugitive *is* grounds for war, young emperor. You know this."

Cinder's visibility dimmed as her retina cascaded a nonsensical diagram over her eyesight. She slammed her eyes shut, cursing. Now was not the time for a brain malfunction.

"But perhaps," said the queen, "we can reach some sort of a compromise."

Cinder opened her eyes. The darkened film remained, but the muddled diagram was gone. She focused on the queen just in time to see a cruel tilt of her lips.

"This girl seems to think you *love* her, and here is your chance to prove it." She coquettishly dipped her lashes. "So tell me, Your Majesty, are you prepared to bargain for her?"

Thirty-Six

“BARGAIN,” SAID KAI. “FOR HER LIFE?”

“Welcome to the world of true politics.” Levana took a sip of her wine. Despite her blood-red lips, no mark was left on the glass.

“This is not the time or the place to be having this discussion,” he said with a barely restrained growl.

“Isn’t it? It seems to me that this discussion involves every being in this room. After all, you want peace. You want to keep your citizenry safe. They are both admirable goals.” Her gaze slid to Cinder. “You also want to save this hapless creature. So be it.”

Cinder’s heart thudded, her eyesight flickering as she refocused it on Kai.

“And you?” said Kai.

“I want to be empress.”

Cinder squirmed against the guard. “Kai, no. You can’t do it.”

He turned back to her. His eyes were turbulent.

“It won’t make a difference,” Cinder said. “You know it won’t.”

"Silence her," ordered Levana.

The guard clamped a hand over her mouth, pulling her hard against his chest, but he could not keep her eyes from pleading. *Don't do it. I'm not worth it, you know that.*

Kai paced to the doorway. He gazed out at the raging storm for a moment, shoulders quaking, before he turned and swept his gaze over the ballroom. The ocean of color, silk and taffeta, gold and pearls. The frightened, confused faces around him.

The annual ball. 126 years of world peace.

He released a strangled breath and pulled his shoulders taut. "I thought I'd made my decision quite clear. Only hours ago, I told my country that I would do anything to keep them safe. Anything at all." He opened both palms, pleading, toward the queen. "I acknowledge readily that you are more powerful than all Earthen kingdoms combined, and I have no desire to test our forces against yours. I also recognize that I am ignorant in the ways of your culture and your people, and I cannot condemn you for the way you have governed them. I trust you have always had the best interests of your people at heart." He met Cinder's gaze. His shoulders became rigid. "But it is not the way that I will have the Commonwealth governed. We must have peace, but not at the expense of freedom. I cannot—I will not marry you."

The air sucked out of the room, low rushed whispers scattering in the crowd. Relief swelled in Cinder, but it was squashed when Kai met her gaze, and he could not have looked more miserable. He mouthed, simply, "I'm sorry."

She wished she could tell him it was all right. She understood. This was the decision she'd wanted him to make from the start, and nothing would change that.

She was not worth starting a war over.

Levana's lips were pinched, her face static but for the slow drawing back of her ears, the almost imperceptible clenching of her jaw. Cinder's retina scanner flickered madly in the corner of her sight, scrolling through numbers and bits of data, but she ignored it like she would an annoying gnat.

"You have made your decision?"

"Yes," said Kai. "The girl—the fugitive will be held in our prison until your departure." He lifted his chin as if reconciling himself to the decision. "I have meant no disrespect, Your Majesty. I do wish with all my heart that we can continue our discussions for an acceptable alliance."

"We cannot," said Levana. The glass in her hand shattered, sending bits of crystal cascading to the hard floor. Cinder jumped, a chorus of screams burst from the crowd as they drew back, but the Lunar guard seemed immune to the outburst. "My requirements were made quite clear to your father, as they have been made quite clear to you, and you are a fool to deny them." She tossed the glass's thin stem at the column. Wine dribbled from her fingertips. "Do you insist on denying my requests?"

"Your Majesty—"

"Answer the question."

Cinder's retina scanner lit up, as if a spotlight had been dropped down on the queen. She gasped. Her knees collapsed, and she slumped against the guard, who jerked her back upright.

She shut her eyes, sure she was imagining things, then opened them again. The diagram realigned. Lines pinpointing the exact angles of Levana's face. Coordinates showing the placement of her eyes, the length of her nose, the width of her brow. A perfect illustration overlaid the perfect woman—and they were not the same.

Cinder was still gawking at the queen, trying to make sense of the lines and angles that her scanner was showing her, when she realized that the arguing had ceased. Her reaction had been so abrupt that everyone's attention had returned to her.

"Stars," she whispered. Her scanner was seeing beyond the illusion. Unscathed by the Lunar glamour, it knew where the true boundaries of the queen's face were, the imperfections, the inconsistencies. "It really is an illusion. You're not beautiful."

The queen paled. The world seemed to have frozen around the diagrams in Cinder's gaze, the tiny points and measurements revealing the queen's greatest secret. She could still see the queen's glamour, her high cheek bones and full lips, but the effect was hidden beneath the truth of the diagram. The longer she stared, the more data her display gathered, gradually filling in Levana's true features.

She was so entranced with the slow revealing that she didn't notice Levana curling her long fingers at her side. It was not until an electric current seemed to shimmer in the air that Cinder snapped her focus away from the scribblings in her vision.

The queen flexed her fingers. The guard pulled away, releasing Cinder's wrists.

Planting her feet, Cinder barely caught herself from toppling forward—at the same time that her hand reached back, as if with a mind of its own, and snatched the gun from the guard's holster.

She stiffened, feeling the heavy gun so abruptly, unexpectedly in her steel hand.

Her finger slipped over the trigger as if it were an extension of her. The gun felt comfortable in her palm. But it shouldn't have. She'd never held one before.

Her heart thudded.

Cinder lifted the gun, pressing the barrel against her own temple. A shuddering cry escaped her. A strand of hair clung to her parched lips. Her eyes darted to the left, unable to see the gun or the traitorous hand holding it. She looked at the queen, the crowd, Kai.

Her whole body was shaking, but for the confident arm holding the gun poised to kill her.

"No! Leave her alone!" Kai rushed for her, grasping her elbow. He tried to yank it away, but she was immobilized, solid as a statue. "Let her go!"

"K-Kai," she stammered, terror seizing her. She urged her hand to drop the gun, urged her finger to pull away from the trigger, but it was useless. She squeezed her eyes shut. Her head throbbed. INCREASING LEVELS OF ADRENALINE. CORTISONE. GLUCOSE. HEART RATE INCREASING. BLOOD PRESSURE INCREASING. WARNING, WARNING . . .

Her finger twitched, briefly, then solidified again.

She imagined what the gun would sound like. She imagined the blood. She imagined her brain shutting down, feeling nothing. BIOELECTRICAL MANIPULATION DETECTED. INITIALIZING RESISTANCE PROCEDURE IN 3 . . . 2 . . .

Her finger slowly, slowly pulled down on the trigger.

Fire exploded in her spine, racing along her nerves and wires, slithering down the metal braces in her limbs.

Cinder screamed and forced the gun away from her head. Arm straight, barrel pointed at the ceiling. She stopped fighting it. Pulled the trigger. A chandelier shattered above her, glass and crystal and sparks.

The crowd screamed and surged for the exit.

Cinder crumpled to her knees and doubled over, cradling the gun against her stomach. Pain tore through her, blinding her. Fireworks burst in her head. It felt as if her body were trying to dispel all her cyborg parts—explosions and sparks and smoke tearing at her flesh.

Kai's voice over the tumult in her ears made her realize that the pain was subsiding. She felt hot to the touch, like someone had thrown her into a kiln, but the pain and heat had moved to her exterior, to her skin and fingertips rather than eating her up inside. She opened her eyes. White dots speckled her gaze. Her display was flashing red warnings. Diagnostics scrolled through the corner of her vision. Her temperature was too high, her heart rate too high, her blood pressure too high. Some foreign substance had invaded her blood that her system did not recognize and could not dispel. Something is wrong, her programming screamed at her. *You are sick. You are ill. You are dying.*

But she did not feel like she was dying.

Her body felt so hot she was surprised she didn't incinerate the fragile dress. Sweat sizzled on her brow. She felt different. Strong. Powerful.

On fire.

Shaking, she sat back on her heels and stared at her hands. The left glove had started to melt, forming patches of gooey, silky skin on her white-hot metal hand. She could see electricity sizzling across the steel surface, but she couldn't tell if it was her human or cyborg eyes detecting it. Or maybe, not human. Not cyborg.

Lunar.

She raised her head. The world was covered in a cool gray mist, as if everything had frozen—except for her. Her body was beginning to cool. Her skin paling, her metal dulling. She tried to cover her metal hand, stupidly, in case Kai had been too blinded by the flash to notice it.

She caught the queen's eye. Levana's rage seemed to hiccup when their gazes met. The queen gasped and drew back a step. For a moment, she looked almost afraid.

"Impossible," she whispered.

Cinder called forth every nanobyte of strength she possessed in order to stand, and pointed the gun at the queen. She pulled the trigger.

The red-haired guard was there. The bullet hit him in the shoulder.

Levana didn't even flinch.

Cinder's brain caught up with her body as blood dripped over the guard's armor.

Cinder dropped the gun and ran. Knowing the frenzied crowd was impenetrable, she barreled toward the nearest exit, the massive doors that led into the gardens. Past the guard, past the queen, past her entourage, glass crunching beneath her stolen boots.

The hollow echo of the stone patio. A puddle splashing onto her legs. The fresh, cool smell of rain that had turned to a drizzle.

The stairway stretched before her. Twelve steps and a Zen garden, a towering wall, a gate, the city—escape.

On the fifth step, she heard the bolts snap. The wires tore loose, like tendons stretched to the max. She felt the loss of power at the base of her calf, sending a blinding warning signal up to her brain.

She fell, screaming, and tried to block her fall with her left hand. A shock of pain jolted up her shoulder and into her spine. Metal clattered against stone as she crashed down to the gravel pathway.

She lay sprawled on her side. Holes frayed her glove where she'd tried to catch her fall. Blood stained the beautiful cream-colored silk over her right elbow.

She struggled to breathe. Her head felt suddenly heavy, and she let it slump against the ground, little pebbles digging into her scalp. Her roaming eyes squinted up at the sky, where the storm had fizzled out but for a foggy mist that clung to Cinder's hair and lashes, refreshing against her hot skin. The full moon sought to break through the cloud cover, burning a slow hole above her as if it planned to swallow up the whole sky.

Movement drew her eye back to the ballroom. The guard who had been holding her reached the stairs and froze. Kai was beside him a second later and screeched to a halt, grasping the railing to stop himself.

His eyes drunk her in—a gleam of metal fingers, the wires sparking at the end of her battered metal leg. His jaw fell, and he looked momentarily as if he might be sick.

More pounding at the top of the stairs. The man and woman appeared in their thaumaturge uniforms, and the guard she'd shot, undeterred by his oozing wound. Kai's adviser and, finally, Queen Levana herself. Her glamour had returned full force, but all her beauty could not hide the fury contorting her features. Gathering her sparkling skirt in both hands, she moved to stomp down the steps toward Cinder, but the lady thaumaturge stopped her with a gentle hand and gestured up to the wall of the palace.

Cinder followed the movement.

A security camera was on them—on her. Seeing everything.

The last remnants of strength fled from Cinder, leaving her exhausted and weak.

Kai crept down the stairs as if sneaking up on a wounded animal. Stooping, he picked up the rusted cyborg foot that had fallen out of the velvet boot. His jaw flexed as he studied it, perhaps recognizing it from the day they'd met at the market. He would not look at her.

Levana's lip curled. "Disgusting," she said from the doorway, safely hidden from the camera's view. Her words were loud and unnaturally forced compared to her usual lilting voice. "Death would be merciful."

"She wasn't a shell after all," said Sybil Mira. "How did she hide it?"

Levana sneered. "It matters not. She'll be dead soon enough. Jacin?"

The blond guard descended a single step toward Cinder. He was holding his gun again, the one Cinder had dropped.

"Wait." Kai stole down the remaining stairs until he stood on the pathway before her. It seemed he had to force himself to meet her gaze, and he flinched at first. Cinder could not read him, the ever-changing mix of disbelief and confusion and regret. His chest was heaving. He tried to speak twice before words would come, quiet words that would never leave Cinder's head.

"Was it all an illusion?" he asked.

Pain lanced through her chest, squeezing the air out of her. "Kai?"

"Was it all in my head? A Lunar trick?"

Her stomach twisted. "No." She shook her head, fervently. How to explain that she hadn't had the gift before? That she couldn't have used it against him? "I would never lie—"

The words faded. She had lied. Everything he knew about her had been a lie.

"I'm so sorry," she finished, the words falling lamely in the open air.

Kai peeled his eyes away, finding some place of resignation off in the glistening garden. "You're even more painful to look at than she is."

Cinder's heart shriveled inside her until she was sure it would stop beating altogether. She reached her hand to her cheek, feeling the damp silk against her skin.

Setting his jaw, Kai turned back to the queen. Cinder stared up at the back of his crimson shirt with the peaceful turtledoves embroidered along the collar. One hand still clutched her cyborg foot.

"She will be taken into custody," he said, with little strength behind his words. "She will be imprisoned until we can decide what to do with her. But if you kill her tonight, I swear I will never agree to any alliance with Luna."

The queen's glare darkened. Even if she agreed, Cinder would eventually be given back to the moon. And as soon as Levana had her in her power, a noose would be put around her neck.

Kai was buying her time. But probably not much.

What she couldn't fathom was why.

Cinder watched the queen fight with her temper, knowing she could kill both her and Kai in a blink.

"She will be my prisoner," Levana finally conceded. "She will be returned to Luna and tried under our judicial system."

Translation: She would die.

"I understand," said Kai. "In return, you will agree not to wage war against my country or planet."

Levana tilted her head up, looking down her nose at him.

"Agreed. I will not wage war against Earth for *this* infraction. But I would tread lightly, young emperor. You have tried my patience greatly this night."

Kai took in a single breath, dipped his head at her, and then stepped aside as the Lunar guards trudged down the steps. They lifted Cinder's broken body off the gravel path. She tried her best to stand, peering at Kai, wishing she could have just one moment to tell him how sorry she was. One breath to explain.

But he didn't look at her as she was dragged past him. His eyes were locked on the dirty steel foot clasped in both hands, his fingertips white from gripping it too hard.

Thirty-Seven

SHE LAY ON HER BACK, LISTENING TO THE STEADY TAPPING of her metal fingers against the white resin floor of her white resin prison cell. Of all the thoughts that should have been taking up her mind, a single moment seemed captured in her thoughts, stuck on endless repeat.

Market day, the humid air, the smell of Chang Sacha's sweet rolls permeating the city square. Before any of this had happened—before Peony had gotten sick, before Levana had come to Earth, before Kai had asked her to the ball. She was just a mechanic, and he was the prince with all the charms she pretended to be immune to. And he was there, before her, while she tottered on a single foot and tried to calm her rapidly beating heart. How she could barely meet his gaze. How he leaned forward, forced her to see him, smiled.

There.

That moment. That smile.

Again and again and again.

Cinder sighed and changed the tempo of her tapping fingers.

The net was rife with vids from the ball. She had watched exactly 4.2 seconds of the footage via her netlink—her in her dirty ball gown tumbling down the steps—before shutting it off. The footage made her look like a madwoman. Surely, every human on Earth would bid her good riddance when Queen Levana claimed her and took her back to Luna. For her "trial."

She heard the guard's footsteps, muffled, on the other side of the cell door. Everything around her was white, including the brilliantly bleached cotton jumpsuit they'd put her in when she'd been forced to discard Peony's destroyed gown and the bits of silk glove that hadn't already been melted or ripped away. They hadn't yet bothered to turn out the eye-straining lights either, leaving her restless and exhausted. She was beginning to wonder if it would be a relief when the queen came for her, if maybe she would at least be allowed a moment's sleep.

And she'd only been there for fourteen hours, thirty-three minutes, and sixteen seconds. Seventeen seconds. Eighteen.

The door clunked, startling her. She squinted at the tiny window that had opened up in the door, seeing the shadow of a man's head on the iron gate. The back of his head. None of the guards would look at her.

"You have a visitor."

She propped herself up on her elbows. "The emperor?"

The guard snorted. "Yeah, right." His shadow disappeared from the grate.

"Kindly open the door if you would," said a familiar voice in a familiar accent. "I must speak with her in private."

Cinder climbed to her one foot, leaning against the glass-smooth wall.

"She's under top security," said the guard. "I can't let you go in. You must speak with her through the grate."

"Don't be ridiculous. Do I look like a threat to security?"

Cinder hopped to the window and bounced on her toes. It *was* Dr. Erland, holding a pale linen bag. He still wore his lab coat, with the tiny silver spectacles on his nose and wool hat on his head. Though he had to crane his head back to meet the guard's eye, his stance was undaunted.

"I am the leading scientist of the royal letumosis research team," said Dr. Erland, "and this girl is my prime test subject. I require blood samples from her before she leaves the planet." He whipped a syringe out of the bag. The guard staggered back in surprise before folding his arms over his chest.

"I have my orders, sir. You'll have to obtain an official release from the emperor to be allowed entrance."

Dr. Erland let his shoulders slump and tucked the syringe back into the bag. "All right. If that's protocol, I understand." But instead of turning away, he fiddled with the cuffs of his sleeves, his expression momentarily darkening, before he flashed another grin at the guard. "There, you see?" he said, his voice sending an odd ripple down Cinder's spine. The doctor continued, the cadence of his words as soothing as a song. "I have obtained the necessary release from the emperor." He swooped his hands toward the cell door. "You may open the door."

Cinder blinked as if to clear cobwebs from her mind. It

seemed Dr. Erland meant to get himself arrested as well, but then the guard turned toward her with a dazed expression and swiped his ID before the scanner. The door opened.

Cinder stumbled back, catching herself on the wall.

"Thank you kindly," said the doctor, entering the cell without turning his back on the guard. "I'll ask that you give us a bit of privacy. I won't be but a minute."

The guard shut the door without argument. His footsteps echoed off down the corridor.

Dr. Erland turned around and snatched a breath when his bright blue eyes fell on Cinder. His lips parted momentarily before he turned his head away and squeezed his eyes shut. When he opened them again, the look of amazement had softened over his features. "If there were ever any doubt, it is gone now. It may do you good to practice controlling your glamour."

Cinder pressed a hand against her cheek. "I'm not doing anything."

The doctor cleared his throat uncomfortably. "Don't worry. You'll get the hang of it." He cast his gaze around the cell. "Quite the predicament you've gotten yourself into, isn't it?"

Cinder lifted her finger toward the door. "You have to teach me that trick."

"It would be an honor, Miss Linh. It's really quite simple. Focus your thoughts, twist your subject's thoughts toward you, and clearly state your intent. Internally, of course."

Cinder frowned. It didn't sound simple at all.

The doctor waved away the look. "Don't worry. You'll find it comes quite naturally when you need it, but we haven't time for lessons. I must be quick before anyone's suspicions are raised."

"*My* suspicions are raised."

He ignored her, his gaze sweeping down Cinder's form—the white jumper, bulky and loose over her slender frame, the metal hand dinged and scratched from her fall, the multicolored wires that dangled from the cuffed pant leg.

"You've lost your foot."

"Yeah, I noticed. How's Kai?"

"What? Aren't you going to ask how I am?"

"You look fine," she said. "Better than usual, actually." It was true—the fluorescent light of the cell took ten years off his features. Or more likely, she realized, it was the lingering effects from using his Lunar gift on the guard. "But how is *he*?"

"Confused, I think." The doctor shrugged. "I do believe he was a bit smitten with you. To find out you were, well . . . it was a lot to take in, I'm sure."

Cinder ran a frustrated hand through her hair, tangled from fourteen hours of nervously bunching it up in her fists. "Levana forced him to choose. Either marry her or hand me over. Otherwise she said she would declare war based on some law about harboring Lunars."

"It seems he made the right decision. He will be a fine ruler."

"That's not the point. Levana won't be satisfied with his decision for long."

"Of course not. Nor would she have let you live for long had he chosen the marriage. She very much wants you dead, more than you realize. Which is why she must believe that Kai has done everything in his power to keep you confined and is willing to give you over to her as soon as she returns to the moon—which won't be long now, I think. Otherwise there could be some horrible consequences for him . . . and the Commonwealth."

Cinder squinted at him. "It seems to me like he *is* doing everything he can to keep me confined."

"Indeed." He twiddled his thumbs. "That complicates matters, doesn't it?"

"What do you—?"

"Why don't we sit? You cannot be comfortable standing on one foot like that." Dr. Erland sank down onto the cell's single cot. Cinder slid down the wall opposite him.

"How is your hand?"

"Fine." She flexed her metal fingers. "The joint on my pinky is busted, but it could be worse. Oh, and hey—" She gestured at her temple. "No hole in my head. I'm still happy about that."

"Yes, I've heard how the queen attacked you. It was your cyborg programming that saved you, wasn't it?"

Cinder shrugged. "I guess so. I received some message about bioelectrical manipulation, right before I . . . I'd never gotten that message before, not even around your glamour."

"It was the first time a Lunar had made you *do* something, other than simply believe or feel something. And it seems your programming worked just as it was meant to—another impressive decision by your surgeon, or perhaps it was Linh Garan's prototype that did it. Either way, Levana must have been caught quite off guard. Although I suspect the fireworks display you put on may not have endeared you to many Earthens."

"I didn't know how to control it. I didn't know what was happening." She pulled her knees up to her chest. "It's probably a good thing I'm in here. There's nowhere out there I would fit in, not after that." She gestured to some nonexistent place beyond the white walls. "Good thing Levana's going to put me out of my misery."

"Is she, Miss Linh? That's a shame. I was hoping you would have inherited more gumption from our people."

"Sorry. I seem to have lost my gumption when my foot fell off during a live netfeed."

The doctor wrinkled his nose at her. "You worry so much about such silly things."

"Silly?"

Dr. Erland smirked. "I came down here for a very important reason, you know, and we haven't got all day."

"Right." Cinder grumbled as she rolled up her sleeve and extended her arm toward him. "Take as much blood as you want. I won't be needing it."

Dr. Erland patted her elbow. "That was a ruse. I am not here for blood samples. There will be Lunars in Africa to test if I need them."

Cinder let her arm sink back into her lap. "Africa?"

"Yes, I am going to Africa."

"When?"

"In about three minutes. There is much work to be done, and it will be difficult to complete it in a jail cell, so I've decided to go to where the first cases of letumosis were documented, in a small town east of the Sahara Desert." He spun his fingers through the air, as if gesturing at an invisible map. "I hope to find some carrier hosts and convince them to become a part of my research."

Cinder unrolled her sleeve. "So why are you here?"

"To invite you to join me there. When it's convenient, of course."

Cinder scowled. "Gee, thanks, Doc. I'll check my calendar to see when I'll be available again."

"I hope you will, Miss Linh. Here, I have a gift for you. Two gifts, in fact." Dr. Erland reached into the bag and pulled out a metal hand and a metal foot, both gleaming beneath the bright lights. Cinder's eyebrows shot up.

"State of the art," said Dr. Erland. "Fully accessorized. Plated with 100 percent titanium. And look!" Like a child with a new toy, he fidgeted with the hand's fingers, revealing a hidden flashlight, a stiletto knife, a projectile gun, a screwdriver, and a universal connector cable. "It's a pillar of usefulness. The tranquilizer darts are stored in here." He opened a compartment on the palm, revealing a dozen skinny darts. "Once your wiring synchronizes, you should be able to load it with a simple thought."

"That's . . . fantastic. Now when I'm on the chopping block, I can at least take a few bystanders down with me."

"Exactly!" He chuckled. Cinder frowned, irritated, but Dr. Erland was too busy ogling the prostheses to notice. "I had them made especially for you. I used your body scan to make sure I had the right dimensions. If I'd had more time, I could have done a skin graft, but we can't have everything, I suppose."

Cinder took the parts when he handed them to her, inspecting their craftsmanship with trepidation.

"Don't let the guard see those, or I really will be in trouble," he said.

"Thanks. I sure am excited to wear them for the last two days of my life."

With a sly grin, Dr. Erland cast his gaze around the small cell. "Funny, isn't it? So much advancement, so much technology. But even the most complicated security systems aren't designed with Lunar cyborgs in mind. I guess it's a good thing there aren't many of you around, or we might have a reputation for jailbreaks."

"What? Are you crazy?" Cinder said, voice dropping to a harsh whisper. "Are you suggesting that I should try to *escape*?"

"In fact, I am a little bit crazy these days." Dr. Erland scratched at his lined cheek. "Can't be helped. All that bioelectricity with nowhere to go, nothing to do. . . ." He sighed whimsically. "But no, Miss Linh, I am not suggesting you should *try* to escape. I am saying you *must* escape. And you must do it soon. Your chances for survival will drop drastically once Levana comes for you."

Cinder leaned back against the wall, sensing the start of a headache. "Look, I appreciate that you care about me, I really do. But even if I could find a way out of here, do you realize how livid Levana would be? You yourself said there will be horrible consequences if she doesn't get what she wants. *I* am not worth starting a war over."

His eyes brightened behind the spectacles. He looked young for a moment, almost giddy. "Actually, you are."

She cocked her head, squinting at him. Maybe he really was mad.

"I tried to tell you when you were in my office last week, but you had to run off to see your sister—ah, and I am sorry about your sister, by the way."

Cinder bit the inside of her cheek.

"Anyway, you see, I had your DNA sequenced. It informed me not only that you are Lunar, not only that you are *not* a shell, but also something of your heritage. Your bloodline."

Cinder's heartbeat quickened. "My family?"

"Yes."

"And? Do I have one? My parents, are they . . ." She hesitated. Dr. Erland's eyes had saddened at her outburst. "Are they dead?"

He pulled his hat off. "I'm sorry, Cinder. I should have gone about this a better way. Yes, your mother is dead. I do not know who your father is or if he is alive. Your mother was, shall we say . . . known for her promiscuity."

She felt her hopes shrivel. "Oh."

"And you have an aunt."

"An aunt?"

Dr. Erland squeezed the hat in both hands. "Yes. It's Queen Levana."

Cinder blinked at him.

"My dear girl. You are Princess Selene."

Thirty-Eight

SILENCE FILLED THE STERILE WHITE AIR BETWEEN CINDER and Dr. Erland, filled the fogginess in Cinder's head. The confusion did not leave her face. "What?"

The doctor reached forward and put his hand over Cinder's. "You are Princess Selene."

She jerked away from him. "I don't—what?"

"I know. It seems unbelievable."

"No, it seems . . . that's impossible. Why would you joke about this?"

He smiled softly and patted her hand again. Which is when Cinder realized that her vision was clear. No orange light was plaguing her.

The breath left her. Her gaze fell to the empty wires poking out from her ankle.

"I know it will take time for you to come to terms with this," said Dr. Erland, "and I wish I could be here to help you through it. And I will. I will tell you everything you need to know when you get to Africa. But now, it is imminent that you understand why you cannot let Levana take you. You are the only one who can dethrone her. Do you understand?"

She shook her head, dazed.

"Princess—"

"*Don't* call me that."

Dr. Erland wrung the hat in his lap. "All right. Miss Linh, listen to me. I have been searching for you for so many years. On Luna, I knew the man who brought you to Earth and performed your surgery. I tracked him down in an attempt to find you, but by then he'd already started to lose his mind. All I could get out of him was that you were somewhere here, in the Commonwealth. I knew I was looking for a cyborg, a teenager—and yet there were so many times when I thought I would go crazy myself before finding you. Before being able to tell you the truth. And then you were there—suddenly—in my lab. A *miracle*."

Cinder raised a hand, cutting him off. "Why? Why did they make me a cyborg?"

"Because your body was too badly damaged in the fire," he said, as if the answer were obvious. "Your limbs could not have been rescued. It's amazing you were able to survive at all, and that you've managed to stay hidden for all these—"

"Stop. Just stop." Cinder flexed her beat-up prosthetic hand before folding it around the fingers of the brand-new limb the doctor had brought her. Her eyes darted around the cell, her breath coming in short gasps. She shut her eyes as a wave of dizziness washed over her.

She was . . .

She was . . .

"The draft," she whispered. "You set up the draft to find me. A cyborg . . . in the Eastern Commonwealth."

Dr. Erland stirred, and when she dared to look up again, guilt had filled his eyes. "We've all had to make sacrifices, but if Levana isn't stopped—"

Releasing the new prosthesis, Cinder covered her ears and buried her face against her knee. The draft. All those cyborgs. So many people convinced that it was the right thing. That it was better them than humans. Once a science project, always a science project.

And he'd only wanted to find her.

"Cinder?"

"I'm going to be sick."

Dr. Erland pressed a hand to her shoulder, but she shook it off. "Nothing that has happened is your fault," he said. "And now I've found you. We can begin to make it right again."

"How can I make anything right? Levana's going to kill me!" Gasping, Cinder lifted her head. "Wait. Does she know?"

Her memory answered her first—Levana at the top of the stairs, frightened. *Furious.* She hid her face again. "Oh, my stars, she does know."

"Your glamour is unique, Cinder, so much like Queen Channary's. Levana would have known right away who you are, although I doubt anyone else has figured it out yet, and Levana will try to keep it hidden as long as she can. Of course, she will waste no time in killing you. I am sure they are planning their departure even at this moment."

Cinder's mouth grew dry.

"Look at me, Cinder."

She obeyed. And though the doctor's eyes were breathtakingly blue and filled with pity and almost even comforting, she somehow knew that he was not doing anything to manipulate her mind. This was just an old man who was determined to dethrone Queen Levana.

An old man who had somehow placed all his hopes on her.

"Does Kai know?" she whispered.

Dr. Erland shook his head, sadly. "I cannot approach him so long as Levana is present, and this is not something I can send via a comm. She will have taken you before I have a chance to see him. Besides, what could he do?"

"If he knew, he would release me."

"And risk Levana turning her wrath against his entire country? Levana would find a way to kill you long before you had any hope of taking back the throne. Kai would be a fool to do something so rash, not without a plan."

"But he deserves to know. He's been looking for her. For … he was looking for …"

"Many people have been looking for you. But finding you and being able to reinstate you as queen are two very different goals. I have planned this moment for a long time. I can help you."

Cinder gawked at him as panic gripped her lungs. "Reinstate me as queen?"

The doctor cleared his throat. "I understand you are frightened right now, and confused. Do not think too much. All I'm asking is that you find a way out of this prison. I *know* you can do that. Then come to Africa. I will guide you through the rest. Please. We cannot let Levana win."

She couldn't respond, couldn't even begin to fathom what he was asking of her. A princess? An heir?

She shook her head. "No. I can't. I can't be a queen or a princess or—I'm nobody. I'm a cyborg!"

Dr. Erland folded his hands together. "If you won't let me help you, Cinder, then she will have already won, won't she? Soon Queen Levana will take you away. She will find a way to marry Kai and become empress. She will wage war against the Earthen Union and, I have no doubt, be victorious. Many will die, the rest will become slaves, just like us Lunars. It is a sad fate but unavoidable, I suppose, if you are not willing to accept who you truly are."

"That isn't fair! You can't just throw this on me and expect me to be able to do anything about it!"

"I don't, Miss Linh. All I expect is for you to find a way out of this prison and come meet me in Africa."

She stared at him, mouth agape, as those words gradually seeped into her brain.

Escape from prison.

Go to Africa.

It seemed almost simple when he said it like that.

The doctor must have seen something change in her

face for he lightly tapped her wrist again, then stood with the groans of old joints growing older. "I believe in you," he said as he reached the doorway and rapped on the grate. "And whether or not he knows it right now, Kai believes in you too."

The cell door opened, Dr. Erland tipped his hat to her, and he was gone.

Cinder waited until two sets of footsteps had ricocheted down the corridor before shuddering and collapsing over her knees, folding her hands over her ears. Her brain was downloading information faster than she could sort it: old articles about the princess's disappearance, interviews with conspiracy theorists, images of the scorched rubble of the nursery where her burned flesh had been found. Dates. Statistics. The transcript of Levana's coronation as the crown passed to her, next in line for the throne.

Princess Selene's birth date. 21 December 109 T.E. She was almost a month younger than she'd always believed. It was a small fact, an insignificant fact, and yet for a moment she had the distinct impression that she had no idea who she was anymore. No clue who she was supposed to be.

And then came the cyborg draft. All the names of those who had been drawn flashed before her. Their pictures, their ID numbers, their birth dates, the dates they'd been pronounced dead, honorably, for their sacrifice for the good of the Commonwealth.

She heard a clock ticking inside her head.

Cinder's breath came in jagged gasps as the information

flooded her brain. Panic churned in her stomach. Bile seeped into her mouth, burning as she swallowed it down.

Queen Levana would come for her, and she would be executed. That was her fate. She'd been resolved to it. She'd been prepared for it. Not to be an heir. Not to be a queen or a savior or a hero.

It would be so simple to let it happen. So simple not to fight back.

Amid the jumbled information clattering through her head, her thoughts landed again on that same quiet moment captured in time.

Kai's carefree smile at the market.

Huddling in a ball, Cinder cut off the netlink.

The noise silenced. The images and videos snipped to black.

If she didn't try to stop Levana, what would happen to Kai?

Though she tried to block out the question, it continued to plague her, echoing in her thoughts.

Maybe Dr. Erland was right. Maybe she had to run. Maybe she had to try.

She felt for the prosthetic limbs in her lap and wrapped her hands around them. Lifting her head, she looked up at the grate in the prison door. The guard had never closed it.

A tingle passed down her spine. A strange new electricity was thrumming beneath her skin, telling her she wasn't just a cyborg anymore. She was Lunar now. She could make people see things that weren't there. Feel things they shouldn't feel. Do things they didn't mean to do.

She could be anyone. *Become* anyone.

The thought both sickened and frightened her, but the resolve made her calm again. When the guard returned, she would be ready.

As her hands stopped shaking, she slid the stiletto knife out from the new titanium-plated finger and maneuvered the blade against her wrist. The cut was still fresh where she'd started to remove her ID chip before, so they would not be able to track her. This time, there was no hesitation.

Soon, the whole world would be searching for her—Linh Cinder.

A deformed cyborg with a missing foot.

A Lunar with a stolen identity.

A mechanic with no one to run to, nowhere to go.

But they would be looking for a ghost.

Acknowledgments

I've been lucky to be surrounded by a wealth of lovely and supportive people who've helped me turn a crazy idea into the book you're holding now.

My deepest gratitude goes to my agent, Jill Grinberg. It's impossible to express how lucky and honored I feel to be represented by such a rock star. I'm also grateful to the rest of my agency team, Cheryl Pientka and Katelyn Detweiler, for all their work, dedication, and enthusiasm.

So many fathomless thanks go to my editor, Liz Szabla, my publisher, Jean Feiwel, and everyone at Feiwel and Friends. The excitement they've shown for *Cinder* has been truly mind-boggling. I couldn't have asked for a more amazing group of advocates.

Thanks are due to my online friends, fellow bloggers, and Sailor Moon fandom geeks, who've encouraged me every step of the way. In particular, I'd like to thank my early readers for offering input, suggestions, critiques, honesty, support, and the occasional fangirling: Whitney Faulconer, Tamara Felsinger, Jennifer

Johnson, Rebecca Kihara, and Meghan Stone-Burgess. Also, thanks to the Circlet critique group for helping me tweak that so-important first chapter into submission, including Naomi Boyd, Dominique Samantha Dulay, Jelena Radosavljevic, and Steve Tara.

I want to send a particularly *gigantic* thank you to Gina Araner and Jennifer S. De Mello, Ph.D., for helping with my questions on genetics, mutations, and bioelectricity, and filling my head with all sorts of useful vocabulary. I'm also immensely grateful to Paul Manfredi, Ph.D., for his assistance with Chinese honorifics.

Of course, none of this would have been possible without the constant support from my closest friends and family. Mom and Dad, thanks for letting me have all those books when I was growing up, and for letting me sit on the computer and write silly stories during summer vacations when I probably should have been pulling weeds. Big brother Jeff, thanks for a healthy obsession with Star Wars. Sister-in-law Wendy, thanks for appreciating my snark when no one else does. Cousin Lucy, thank you for being a fellow book lover, and for all the wine. Uncle Bob, thanks for taking me and a VW Bug full of teenage girls to anime conventions and instilling in me a hearty respect for cosplay. Best friends Leilani Adams and Angela Yohn, thank you for all the coffee and gossip—, I mean, *work*-dates.

Finally, thanks to my fiancé, Jesse—who will be my husband by the time he reads this—for bringing me coffee in bed every morning, for telling me to go back to my office when I hadn't hit my daily word quota, and, mostly, for believing in me. I think it's safe for you to read it now.

Turn the page for

Cinder

bonus materials. . . .

Questions for the Author
Marissa Meyer

© Kali Raisl

WHAT WAS YOUR INSPIRATION FOR *CINDER*? HOW DID YOU COME UP WITH THE IDEA?

In early 2008, I entered a short story contest with a futuristic retelling of *Puss in Boots*, in which Puss was a robotic, talking cat trying to convince a plain schoolgirl that she was really a lost princess. I had so much fun writing it that I thought it would be fun to write an entire series of futuristic fairy tales, so I started brainstorming different sci-fi twists on my favorite stories. Then, as I was drifting off to sleep one night, I had the lightbulb moment: Cinderella, as a cyborg! The plot for the entire series started to click together after that.

WHERE DID YOU WRITE *CINDER*? WHAT IS YOUR DREAM "ROOM OF YOUR OWN"?

Much of *Cinder* was written on the bus. When I worked in Seattle, I would have an hour commute each way, which was premium writing time! I also love going to cafes and restaurants, but I mostly write at home these days—in bed, on the couch, in my office, or if the weather is nice, out on our front porch.

My dream writing room would have a floor-to-ceiling wall of books, a fireplace, and a big picture window with a view of either a woodland lake or snow-capped mountains. Ah, to dream . . .

WHAT HAS SURPRISED YOU THE MOST ABOUT THE PUBLISHING PROCESS, SO FAR?

How up and down it is, as far as the influx of news and happenings. After the book deal came through, there was an immediate rush of editorial to-dos and foreign sales and the like, and then there were months and months of silence. Then overnight, there was a new rush of promotional and publicity happenings. I was expecting it all to be much more balanced, but I am learning to appreciate the slow times. That's when the writing gets done, after all.

DID YOU HAVE ANY SAY IN THE JACKET DESIGN?

My publisher sent me an early cover concept that was very similar to the final cover—I loved it! I think they would have humored me if I'd had any big complaints, but I didn't, so there wasn't much say to be had.

CINDER IS A MECHANICAL GENIUS. DO YOU HAVE ANY EXPERIENCE WITH MECHANICS? IF NOT, HOW DID YOU DO YOUR RESEARCH?

I have absolutely NO experience with mechanics, although I certainly learned a lot about cars and engines while writing this book! Luckily, I have two men in my life who do know about these things—my husband, Jesse, and my older brother, Jeff—so I was able to take a lot of my questions to them. My husband has worked on cars since he was a teenager and is currently in the process of rebuilding a 1930 Ford Model-A Sedan. When I was writing *Cinder*'s junkyard scene, he and I crawled beneath an old Ford Mustang so he could show me what the engine compartment looked like from underneath, what the different parts are called, and how they all work together to make the car move. He also read many of the technical portions of the book and corrected me where things were blatantly wrong.

Then there's my brother who, in addition to being a full-fledged mechanic himself, is also a huge *Star Wars* fan, so he was able to loan me some books on fictional spaceships and scientific theories. Those were helpful for coming up with the terminology for some of the higher technology like hovercars and, in the later books, spaceships.

WHAT WAS YOUR FAVORITE PART OF THE WORLD-BUILDING PROCESS?

I loved having the freedom to create my own East-meets-West fusion in the Eastern Commonwealth. I chose the Asian setting partly because of the history of the Cinderella tale (many scholars believe that the first recorded version comes to us from 9th-century China), but also because I was a huge fan of anime as a teenager, which translated into an interest in Asian cultures in general.

With the travel, communication, and technology we have today, we're already seeing the lines between East and West beginning to blur, with people from both cultures adopting the fashions and trends of the other. So I took that idea and ran with it, and had a lot of fun bringing in foods, names, language elements, fashion, symbolism, and traditions from all over Asia, as well as some Western influences, such as the old-fashioned ball gowns.

(I should also credit Joss Whedon's *Firefly*, which took a similar East-meets-West approach to its world-building, and was inspirational for this series on many levels.)

IF YOU COULD ONLY CHOOSE ONE, WOULD YOU RATHER HAVE ANDROIDS EXIST, OR HAVE A COLONY ON THE MOON? WHY?

Androids, definitely! While a colony on the moon could be neat, I suspect it would be fairly exclusive to scientists and engineers and their families, maybe with some vacation homes for the very rich. But androids, if mass-produced, could become as commonplace as computers—and just think how useful they would be! It would be like returning to the days of butlers and hired help, except at the end of the day, it would be okay to tuck them away in a closet. Unless, of course, their artificial intelligence matches that of our dear friend Iko, in which case they could become as much a friend as an appliance.

WHICH CHARACTER DO YOU MOST IDENTIFY WITH IN *CINDER* AND WHY?

Probably Peony. She's giggly and chipper and has a mad celebrity crush on Prince Kai. If I was fourteen years old and living in the Eastern Commonwealth, I would be just like her!

HOW ARE YOU LIKE (OR UNLIKE) CINDER?

Like: We share the same sarcastic sense of humor. After my mom finished reading the book, the very first thing she said to me was, "Well, I see where she gets her sarcasm from." Hardy har har.
Unlike: Cinder is very talented at fixing things, whereas I am very talented at telling my husband when something is broken.

WE LOVE IKO! WHAT AND/OR WHO WAS YOUR INSPIRATION FOR HER?

I haven't the faintest idea! I love Iko too, but as with a lot of my characters, I don't feel like I can take full responsibility for her. She just rolled onto the scene and started saying awesomely hilarious things. An android with a girlish crush on the prince and an obsession with high fashion wasn't a part of my original plan for the series, but she's become one of my favorite characters.

IF YOU HAD TO REPLACE PART OF YOUR BODY WITH A CYBORG PART, WHICH WOULD IT BE?

I think a cyborg hand would be awesome. Two totally random talents I've always envied are spinning coins or poker chips over your fingers, and breaking an egg single-handedly. A cyborg hand could probably accomplish both of those quite easily! Although, whether it could break the egg without getting any shell involved is questionable.

WHAT WOULD YOU WEAR TO THE BALL?

The biggest, poofiest, frilliest ball gown I could find.

WOULD YOU WEAR HEELS OR BOOTS TO THE BALL?

Heels. Very sexy heels. Though yes, I would probably regret it by the end of the night.

WOULD YOU RATHER BE A PRINCESS OR MECHANIC?

Who says one can't be both?

WHO'S MORE ATTRACTIVE, A PRINCE OR A MECHANIC?

A mechanic. I like men with useful skills. Running a country? Psh. Fixing that weird sound in the engine? Yes, please!

WHAT WERE YOU LIKE AS A TEEN?

A geek! I loved reading and writing even then, and I remember sitting in the back of my classes so I could write fan fiction in my spiral notebooks. Somehow, I still managed to get good grades though. I also loved anime—my best friend and I used to sneak into the anime club at our local college, which the college students just loved (note the sarcasm)—and, of course, I was completely boy-crazy. But who isn't?

WHAT ARE YOUR FAVORITE MEMORIES OF READING AS A . . .

CHILD: Being completely absorbed in *The Hobbit* during a camping trip with my grandparents. Everyone else wanted to go swimming, but I just wanted to stay at the campsite and read.

TWEEN: We read a super-abridged version of *Les Misérables* in seventh grade and I was fascinated by how all the different characters' lives entwined and entangled with each other in such a complex story. I think it gave me something of an obsession for stories with big casts of characters.

TEEN: I was really into graphic novels as a teen, but this was before all the American publishers picked up on the trend, so my best friends and I would take the bus up to the International District in Seattle to buy graphic novels in Japanese, then come back home and spend hours looking up translations on the Internet. Some favs were *Sailor Moon*, *Rurouni Kenshin*, and *Fushigi Yuugi*.

ADULT (SO FAR): My honeymoon. We went to Maui and my husband and I spent hours and hours reading by the pool, cocktails in hand—paradise indeed! I read six books during the trip: *Divergent*, *The Faerie Ring*, *Lola and the Boy Next Door*, *My Life Undecided*, *Entwined*, and *Magic Under Glass*.

DO YOU HAVE ANY OTHER FAVORITE RETELLINGS OF FAIRY TALES?

One of my all-time favorites is *Ella Enchanted* by Gail Carson Levine. It's such a fun and romantic book, and gives a really clever twist to the Cinderella story. I also enjoyed the recent books *Entwined* by Heather Dixon (The Twelve Dancing Princesses) and *Enchanted* by Alethea Kontis (The Frog Prince . . . with about a dozen other fairy tales thrown in for good measure). On a darker note, I think Gregory Maguire did an amazing job with both *Mirror Mirror* (Snow

White and the Seven Dwarfs) and *Confessions of an Ugly Stepsister* (Cinderella again), and I really loved the modern-day Little Red Riding Hood twist in Jackson Pearce's *Sisters Red*.

IS THERE A TEACHER OR MENTOR WHO INSPIRED YOU TO WRITE?

I had quite a few teachers who were really encouraging, but one in particular—Suzanne Rahn, my children's lit professor in college—really motivated me to keep writing. I remember one assignment where we were asked to write the first chapter of a would-be fairy tale retelling novel (ironic?) and I started writing a retelling of *East of the Sun and West of the Moon*. Afterwards, the professor told me she believed my writing was strong enough to be published, which meant so much to me.

IF YOU WEREN'T A WRITER, WHAT WOULD YOU BE?

An aspiring writer.

WHY A YOUNG ADULT NOVEL, AND WHY NOW?

I love the rush of first love and self-discovery that you get in YA novels, and the idea that even society's "weakest links," as children and teens are often thought to be, can still change the world. There's also so much exploration happening in YA right now, from science fiction and dystopian to horror and thrillers and fantasy, and the audience is really open to reading and experiencing new types of fiction.

WHAT ARE THE TOP THREE PIECES OF ADVICE YOU'D GIVE TO A WRITER WHO HAS JUST FINISHED HER FIRST YOUNG ADULT NOVEL, AND NOW WANTS TO GET PUBLISHED?

1. Get a good beta reader, or a group of beta readers. A knowledgeable reader will be able to pinpoint areas where your writing and storytelling are weak and give ideas for improvement. And yes, you really do have to revise—no first draft is perfect.

2. Learn as much as you can about the querying and publishing process. The Internet is filled with resources—what agents do and how submissions work and what happens when you get a book deal, etc. The more informed you are, the better.
3. Don't get discouraged. Many writers have written a dozen novels before getting an agent, or queried for years and years and then been on submission for years after that before getting a book deal. Just do the best you can and, when you can't do any more, start writing the next book.

THE LUNAR CHRONICLES IS A QUARTET. CAN YOU TELL US A LITTLE ABOUT WHAT WE CAN EXPECT FROM THE REST OF THE SERIES? (NO SPOILERS PLEASE!)

The first question I always get asked is, "Will we be seeing more of Cinder?" She is left in something of a lurch at the end of Book One, so I am happy to say that YES, there will be much more Cinder and Kai (along with other returning characters) throughout the whole series. You will also meet three new fairy-tale-inspired heroines: *Scarlet* (Little Red Riding Hood), *Cress* (Rapunzel), and *Winter* (Snow White). They all have their own problems to solve and fears to conquer, but they do have one thing in common: their mutual enemy, Lunar Queen Levana. As their stories align, they must join forces if they're to have any hope of ending her tyranny.

SQUARE FISH

DISCUSSION GUIDE

CINDER
by Marissa Meyer

Discussion Questions

1. What parallels can you draw between *Cinder* and the Cinderella fairy tale? What is the symbolism behind the glass slipper, the pumpkin carriage, the ball? Is there a fairy godmother in *Cinder*, and if so, who is it?

2. What does it mean to be human? Is it primarily physiological? Cultural? Emotional? What do you think could have led to cyborgs being perceived as less than human in Cinder's world? What about Lunars, who evolved from a human colony? What real-world parallels can you draw between the discrimination against cyborgs and Lunars to that of race, disability, and class?

3. Cinder has many unique abilities—the ability to detect lies, to download information directly into her head, to overlay her eyesight with helpful diagrams, etc. What kinds of abilities might we want to develop from future technology? What cyborg skill would you like to have today?

4. In Cinder's future, Earth has been conglomerated into six countries who have formed an alliance called the Earthen Union. Though Cinder lives in Asia (the Eastern Commonwealth), there is much evidence of Western influence (ex., the ball gowns that are made for Peony and Pearl). Do you think this mixing of cultures is a believable result of the Earthen Union? How do you foresee cultures changing (or not) as a result of the increased communication and travel we have access to today?

5. Propaganda is used as a political tool both by Luna (ex., Sybil's claim that the history of peace on Luna is a result of the totalitarian regime) and the Eastern Commonwealth (ex., being selected as a cyborg draft subject is an "honor"). When is it justified for a government or institution to use propaganda? When should the people of a society question what information they're given?

6. Dr. Erland compares the arrival of Lunars and the spread of letumosis to rats carrying the bubonic plague to Europe and the Spanish conquistadors bringing smallpox to the Native Americans. Do you think these are accurate comparisons? Why or why not?

7. What is the importance of beauty (real or deceptive) in Cinder's world? Compare the perceived beauty and/or ugliness of Queen Levana and Cinder and how this has affected how they're treated by those around them. How is this similar or different from the way beauty is treated today?

8. In chapter 24, Prince Kai asks Cinder, "Imagine there was a cure, but finding it would cost you everything. It would completely ruin your life. What would you do?" Both Kai and Cinder face decisions that could result in sacrificing their own lives for what they perceive as a greater good. Do you believe that a person is obligated to sacrifice themselves for the sake of many? How does self-sacrifice compare to the imposed sacrifices made by cyborg draft subjects?

9. Was it right for Cinder to try to deliver the antidote to Peony first, even though there were others who also needed it? Was it right for Dr. Erland to offer her first access to the antidote? What would you have done in either situation?

10. Marissa Meyer got the idea for implanted ID chips when she saw a religious propaganda flier warning people against imbedded computer chips that would signal the coming of the apocalypse. In Cinder's world, ID chips are so necessary to everyday life that to be without one is to stop existing on some level. What would be some of the benefits of having such an ID chip implanted in your body? What are some potential dangers?

11. What are your thoughts on Kai's reaction when he discovered that Cinder is both a cyborg and a Lunar? How do you think he would have reacted if Cinder had told him the truth earlier in the book? Can you speculate how his feelings might change (toward Cinder, Lunars, or the cyborg draft) after the shock has worn off?

12. Each book in the Lunar Chronicles will be inspired by a different fairy tale. Can you spot references to any tales besides Cinderella within *Cinder*?

Scarlet Benoit's grandmother is missing, gone under mysterious circumstances. So when Scarlet encounters Wolf, a street fighter who may have information as to her grandmother's whereabouts, she is loath to trust him. But as it turns out, there are many things Scarlet doesn't know about her grandmother, or the grave danger she has lived in her whole life.

As Scarlet and Wolf unravel one mystery, another quickly develops when Cinder, the cyborg mechanic, returns in

SCARLET SPOTTED GILLES BEHIND THE HOT TOP, LADLING béchamel sauce on top of a ham sandwich. She walked around to the other side, yelling to get his attention, and was met with annoyance.

"I'm done," she said, returning the scowl. "Come sign off on the delivery."

Gilles shoveled a stack of *frites* beside the sandwich and slid the plate across the steel counter to her. "Run that out to the first booth and I'll have it ready when you get back."

Scarlet bristled. "I don't work for you, Gilles."

"Just be grateful I'm not sending you out to the alley with a scrub brush." He turned his back on her, his white shirt yellowed from years of sweat.

Scarlet's fingers twitched with the fantasy of chucking the sandwich at the back of his head and seeing how it compared to the tomatoes, but her grandma's stern face just as quickly infiltrated the dream. How disappointed she would be to come back home only to find that Scarlet had lost one of their most loyal clients in a fit of temper.

Grabbing the plate, Scarlet stormed out of the kitchen and was nearly bowled over by a waiter as soon as the kitchen door swung shut behind her. The Rieux Tavern was not a nice place—the floors were sticky, the furniture was a mismatch of cheap tables and chairs, and the air was saturated with grease. But in a town where drinking and gossiping were the favorite pastimes, it was always busy, especially on Sundays when the local farmhands ignored their crops for a full twenty-four hours.

While she waited for a path to clear through the crowd, Scarlet's attention landed on the netscreens behind the bar. All three were broadcasting the same news footage that had filled up the net since the night before. Everyone was talking about the Eastern Commonwealth's annual ball, where the Lunar queen was a guest of honor and where a cyborg girl had infiltrated the party, blown up some chandeliers, and tried to assassinate the visiting queen . . . or maybe she'd been trying to assassinate the newly coronated emperor. Everyone seemed to have a different theory. The freeze-frame on the screens showed a close-up of the girl with dirt smudges on her face and strands of damp hair pulled from a messy ponytail. It was a mystery how she'd ever been admitted into a royal ball in the first place.

"They should have put her out of her misery when she fell on those stairs," said Roland, a tavern regular, who looked like he'd been bellied to the bar since noon. He extended a finger toward the screen and mimed shooting a gun. "I'd have put a bullet right through her head. And good riddance."

When a rustle of agreement passed through the nearest patrons, Scarlet rolled her eyes in disgust and shoved toward the first booth.

She recognized Émilie's handsome street fighter immediately, partly due to an array of scars and bruises on his olive skin, but more because he was the only stranger in the tavern. He was more disheveled than she'd expected from Émilie's swooning, with hair that stuck out every direction in messy clumps and a fresh bruise swelling around one eye. Beneath the table, both of his legs were jogging like a windup toy.

Three plates were already set out before him, empty but for splatters of grease, bits of egg salad, and untouched slices of tomato and lettuce.

She didn't realize she'd been staring at him until his gaze shifted and collided with hers. His eyes were unnaturally green, like sour grapes still on the vine. Scarlet's grip tightened on the plate and she suddenly understood Émilie's swooning. *He has these eyes . . .*

Pushing through the crowd, she deposited the sandwich on the table. "You had le croque monsieur?"

"Thank you." His voice startled her, not by being loud or gruff as she'd expected, but rather low and hesitant.

Maybe Émilie was right. Maybe he really was shy.

"Are you sure you don't want us to just bring you the whole pig?" she said, stacking the three empty plates. "It would save the servers the trouble of running back and forth from the kitchen."

His eyes widened and for a moment Scarlet expected him to ask if that was an option, but then his attention dipped down to the sandwich. "You have good food here."

She withheld a scoff. "Good food" and "Rieux Tavern" were two phrases she didn't normally associate with each other. "Fighting must work up quite an appetite."

He didn't respond. His fingers fidgeted with the straw in his drink and Scarlet could see the table beginning to shake from his bouncing legs.

"Well. Enjoy," she said, picking up the dishes. But then she paused and tipped the plates toward him. "Are you sure you don't want the tomatoes? They're the best part, and they were grown in my own garden. The lettuce too, actually, but it wasn't wilted like this when I harvested it. Never mind, you don't want the lettuce. But the tomatoes?"

Some of the intensity drained from the fighter's face. "I've never tried them."

Scarlet arched an eyebrow. "*Never?*"

After a hesitant moment, he released his drinking glass and picked up the two slabs of tomato and shoved them into his mouth.

His expression froze mid-chew. He seemed to ponder for a moment, eyes unfixed, before swallowing. "Not what I expected," he said, looking up at her again. "But not horrible. I'll order some more of those, if I could?"

Scarlet adjusted the dishes in her grip, keeping a butter knife from slipping off. "You know, I don't actually work—"

"Here it comes!" said someone near the bar, spurring an excited murmur that rippled through the tavern. Scarlet glanced up at the netscreens. They showed a lush garden, flourishing with bamboo and lilies and sparkling from a recent downpour. The red warmth of the ball spilled down a grand staircase. The security camera was above the door, angled toward the long shadows that stretched out into the path. It was beautiful. Tranquil.

"I have ten univs that say some girl's about to lose her foot on those stairs!" someone shouted, followed by a round of laughter from the bar. "Anyone want to bet me? Come on, what are the odds, really?"

A moment later, the cyborg girl appeared on the screen. She bolted from the doorway and down the stairs, shattering the garden's serenity with her billowing silver gown. Scarlet held her breath, knowing what happened next, but she still flinched when the girl stumbled and fell. She crashed down the steps and landed awkwardly at their base, sprawled across the rocky path. Though there was no sound, Scarlet imagined the girl panting as she rolled onto her back and gawked up at the doorway. Shadows cut across the stairs and a series of unrecognizable figures appeared above her.

Having heard the story a dozen times, Scarlet sought out the missing foot still on the stairs, the light from the ballroom glinting off the metal. The girl's cyborg foot.

"They say the one on the left is the queen," said Émilie. Scarlet jumped, not having heard the waitress approach.

The prince—no, the emperor now—crept down the steps and stooped to pick up the foot. The girl reached for the hem of her skirt, tugging it down over her calves, but she couldn't hide the dead tentacle wires dangling from their metal stump.

Scarlet knew what the rumors were saying. Not only had the girl been confirmed as a Lunar—an illegal fugitive and a danger to Earthen society—but she'd even managed to brainwash Emperor Kai. Some thought she'd been after power, others riches. Some believed she'd been trying to start the war that had so long been threatened. But no matter what the girl's intentions were, Scarlet couldn't help a twinge of pity. After all, she was only a teenager, younger than Scarlet even, and she looked wholly pathetic lying at the base of those stairs.

"What was that about putting her out of her misery?" said one of the guys at the bar.

Roland jutted his finger toward the screen. "Exactly. I've never seen anything so disgusting in my life."

Someone near the end leaned forward so he could look around the other patrons at Roland. "I'm not sure I agree. I think she's kind of cute, pretending to be all helpless and innocent like that. Maybe instead of sending her back to the moon, they should let her come stay with me?"

He was met with robust laughter. Roland thumped his palm on the bar, rattling a mustard dish. "No doubt that metal leg of hers would make for a real cozy bedmate!"

"Swine," Scarlet muttered, but her comment was lost in the guffaws.

"I wouldn't mind the chance to warm her up!" someone new added, and the tables rattled with cheers and amusement.

Anger clawed its way back up Scarlet's throat and she half slammed, half dropped the stack of plates back onto the booth's table. She ignored the startled expressions around her and shoved through the crowd, circling to the back of the bar.

The bewildered bartender watched on as Scarlet pushed some liquor bottles out of the way and climbed up onto the counter that stretched the length of the wall. Reaching up, she opened a wall panel beneath a shelf of cognac glasses and plucked out the netlink cable. All three screens went black, the palace garden and cyborg girl vanishing.

A roar of protest bellowed up around her.

Scarlet spun to face them, accidentally kicking a bottle of wine off the bar. The glass shattered on the floor, but Scarlet barely heard it as she waved the cable at the incensed crowd. "You all should have some respect! That girl's going to be executed!"

"That girl's a Lunar!" someone yelled. "She *should* be executed!"

The sentiment was enforced with nods and someone lobbing a crust of bread at Scarlet's shoulder. She planted both hands on her hips. "She's only sixteen."

written by

Marissa Meyer

"ARE YOU READY TO MEET YOUR NEW FAMILY?"

She tore her gaze away from the window, where snow was heaped up on bamboo fences and a squat android was clearing a path through the slush, and looked at the man seated opposite her. Though he'd been kind to her throughout their trip, two full days of being passed between a hover, a maglev train, two passenger ships, and yet another hover, he still had a nervous smile that made her fidget.

Plus, she kept forgetting his name.

"I don't remember the old family," she said, adjusting her heavy left leg so that it didn't stick out quite so far between their seats.

His lips twisted awkwardly into an expression that was probably meant to be reassuring, and this ended their conversation. His attention fell down to a device he never stopped looking at, with a screen that cast a greenish glow over his face. He wasn't a very old man, but his eyes always seemed tired and his clothes didn't fit him right. Though he'd been clean-cut when he first came to claim her, he was now in need of a razor.

She returned her gaze to the snow-covered street. The suburb struck her as crowded and confused. A series of short one-story shacks would be followed by a mansion with a frozen water fountain in its courtyard and red-tiled roofs. After that, a series of clustered town houses and maybe a run-down apartment complex, before more tiny shacks took over. It all looked like someone had taken every kind of residence they could think of and spilled them across a grid of roads, not caring where anything landed.

She suspected that her new home wasn't anything like the rolling farmland they'd left behind in Europe, but she'd been in such a foggy-brained daze at the time that she couldn't remember much of anything before the train ride. Except that it had been snowing there, too. She was already sick of the snow and the cold. They made her bones ache where her fleshy parts were connected to her steel prosthetics.

She swiveled her gaze back toward the man seated across from her. "Are we almost there?"

He nodded without looking up. "Almost, Cinder."

Enfolding her fingers around the scar tissue on her wrist, she waited, hoping he would say something else to ease her nerves, but he didn't seem the type to notice anyone's anxiety above his own. She imagined calling him *Dad*, but the word was laughably unfamiliar, even inside her head. She couldn't even compare him with her real father, as her memory had been reduced to a blank slate during the intrusive surgeries, and all she had left of her parents was their sterile identity profiles, with plain photos that held no recognition and a tag at the top labeling them as **DECEASED**. They'd been killed in the hover crash that had also claimed her leg and hand.

As confirmed by all official records, there was no one else. Cinder's grandparents were also dead. She had no siblings. No aunts or uncles or friends—at least, none willing to claim her. Perhaps there wasn't a human being in all of Europe who would have taken her in, and that's why they'd had to search as far as New Beijing before they found her a replacement family.

She squinted, straining to remember who *they* were. The faceless people who had pulled her from the wreckage and turned her into *this*. Doctors and surgeons, no doubt. Scientists. Programmers. There must have been a social worker involved, but she couldn't recall for sure. Her memory gave her only dizzy glimpses of the French countryside and this stranger sitting across from her, entranced by the device in his hands.

Her new stepfather.

The hover began to slow, drifting toward the curb. Its nose hit a snowbank and it came to a sudden, shuddering stop. Cinder grabbed the bar overhead, but the hover had already settled down, slightly off-kilter in the packed snow.

"Here we are," said the man, eyes twinkling as the hover door slid open.

She stayed plastered to her seat, her hand still gripping the bar, as a gust of icy wind swirled around them. They'd arrived at one of the tiny shack houses, one with peeling paint and a gutter that hung loose beneath the weight of the snow. Still, it was a sweet little house, all white with a red roof and enough dead branches sticking up from the ground that Cinder could almost imagine a garden come springtime.

The man paid the hover with a swipe of his wrist, then stepped out onto a pathway that had been plowed down to a sheet of ice. The door to the house opened before he'd taken a step and two girls about Cinder's own age came barreling down the front steps, squealing. The man crouched down on the pathway, holding out his arms as the girls launched themselves into him.

From her place inside the hover, Cinder heard the man laugh for the first time.

A woman appeared inside the doorway, belting a quilted robe around her waist. "Girls, don't suffocate your father. He's had a long trip."

"Don't listen to your mother, just this once. You can suffocate me all you like." He kissed his daughters on the tops of their heads, then stood, keeping a firm grip on their hands. "Would you like to meet your new sister?" he asked, turning back to face the hover. He seemed surprised at the empty pathway behind him. "Come on out, Cinder."

She shivered and pried her hand away from the safety bar. Sliding toward the door, she tried to be graceful stepping out onto the curb, but the distance to the ground was shorter than she'd expected and her heavy leg was inflexible as it crunched through the compact ice. She cried out and stumbled, barely catching herself on the hover's doorframe.

The man hurried back toward her, holding her up as well as he could by the arm, one hand gripping her metal fingers. "It's all right, perfectly natural. Your muscles are weak right now, and it will take time for your wiring to fully integrate with your nervous system."

Cinder stared hard at the ground, shivering both from cold and embarrassment. She couldn't help finding irony in the man's words, though she dared not laugh at them—what did integrated wiring have to do with being perfectly natural?

"Cinder," the man continued, coaxing her forward, "this is my eldest daughter, Pearl, and my youngest, Peony. And that is their lovely mother, Adri. Your new stepmother."

She peered up at his two daughters from behind a curtain of fine brown hair.

They were both staring openly at her metal hand.

Cinder tried to shrink away, but then the youngest girl, Peony, asked, "Did it hurt when they put it on?"

Steady on her feet again, Cinder pried her hand out of the man's hold and tucked it against her side. "I don't remember."

"She was unconscious for the surgeries, Peony," said the man.

"Can I touch it?" she asked, her hand already inching forward.

"That's enough, Garan. People are watching."

Cinder jumped at the shrill voice, but when she looked up, her "stepmother" was not looking at them, but at the house across the street.

Garan. That was the man's name. Cinder committed it to memory as she followed Adri's gaze and saw a man staring at her through his front window.

"It's freezing out here," said Adri. "Pearl, go find the android and have her bring in your father's luggage. Peony, you can show Cinder to her room."

"You mean *my* room," said Pearl, her lip curling as she began to shuffle back toward the house. "I'm the oldest. I shouldn't have to share with Peony."

To Cinder's surprise, the younger girl turned and latched on to her arm, tugging her forward. She nearly slipped on the ice and would have been embarrassed again, except she noticed that Peony's feet were slipping around too as she pulled Cinder ahead. "Pearl can take the room," she said. "I don't mind sharing with Cinder."

Adri's face was taut as she looked down at their intertwined elbows. "Don't argue with me, either of you."

Condensation sprang up on Cinder's steel hand as she went from the chilled air to the house's warm entryway, but Peony didn't seem to notice as she led her toward the back of the house.

"I don't know why Pearl's upset," she said, shouldering open a door. "This is the smallest room in the house. Our bedroom is much nicer." Releasing Cinder, she went to pull open the blinds on the single small window. "But look, you can see the neighbor's cherry tree. It's really pretty when it blooms."

Cinder didn't follow her to the window, instead casting her gaze around the room. It seemed small, but it was larger than the sleeper car on the maglev train and she had no prior bedrooms to compare it with. A mattress sat in the corner with blankets tucked neatly around its sides, and a small dresser stood empty on the nearest wall.

"Pearl used to have a netscreen in here, but Mom moved it into the kitchen. You can come watch mine whenever you want to, though. Do you like *Nightmare Island*? It's my favorite drama."

"Nightmare Island?" No sooner had Cinder said it than her brain started streaming data across her vision. A POPULAR DRAMA AIMED AT TEENAGE GIRLS THAT INCLUDES A CAST OF THIRTY-SIX YOUNG CELEBRITIES WHO ARE CAUGHT UP IN LIES, BETRAYAL, ROMANCE, AND THE SCHEME OF A CRAZED SCIENTIST WHO—

"Don't tell me you've never heard of it!"

Cinder scrunched her shoulders beside her ears. "I've heard of it," she said, blinking the data away. She wondered if there was a way to get her brain to stop doing that every time she heard an unfamiliar phrase. It had been happening almost nonstop since she'd woken up from the surgery. "That's the show with the crazed scientist, right? I've never seen it, though."

Peony looked relieved. "That's fine, I have a subscription to the whole feed. We'll watch it together." She bounced on her feet and Cinder had to tear her gaze away from the girl's excitement. Her gaze landed on a box half-tucked behind the door. A small pronged hand was hanging over the edge.

"What's this?" she said, leaning forward. She kept her hands locked behind her back.

"Oh, that's Iko." Abandoning the window, Peony crouched down and scooted the box out from the wall. It was filled with random android parts all jumbled together—the spherical body took up most of the space, along with a glossy white head, a sensor lens, a clear bag filled with screws and program chips. "She had some sort of glitch in her personality chip and Mom heard that she could get more money for her if she sold her off in pieces rather than as a whole, but nobody wanted them. Now she just sits here, in a box."

Cinder shuddered, wondering how common glitches were in androids. Or cyborgs.

"I really liked Iko when she was working. She was a lot more fun than that boring garden android." Peony picked up the thin metal arm with the three prongs and held it up so that the fingers clicked together. "We used to play dress-up together." Her eyes lit up. "Hey, do *you* like playing dress-up?"

Adri appeared in the doorway just as Cinder's brain was informing her that "dress-up" was A GAME OFTEN PLAYED BY CHILDREN IN WHICH COSTUMES OR ADULT CLOTHES ARE USED TO AID IN THE PROCESS OF IMAGINATION . . .

Obviously, she thought, sending the message away.

"Well, Cinder?" said Adri, tightening her robe's belt again and surveying the small room with a pinched face. "Garan told me you wouldn't want for much. I hope this meets your expectations?"

She looked around again, at the bed, the dresser, the branches that would someday bloom in the neighbor's yard. "Yes, thank you."

Adri rubbed her hands together. "Good. I hope you'll let me know if you need anything. We're glad to share our home with you, knowing what you've been through."

Cinder licked her lips, thinking to say thank you again, but then a small orange light flickered in her optobionics and she found herself frowning. This was something new and she had no idea what it meant.

Maybe it was a sign of a brain malfunction. Maybe this was a glitch.

"Come along, Peony," said Adri, stepping back into the hall. "I could use some help in the kitchen."

"But Mom, Cinder and I were going to—"

"*Now*, Peony."

Scowling, Peony thrust the android arm into Cinder's hand and followed after her mother.

Cinder held up the limb and shook it at their backs, making the lifeless fingers wave good-bye.

SIX NIGHTS AFTER SHE'D ARRIVED AT HER NEW HOME, Cinder awoke on fire. She cried out, tumbling off the mattress and landing in a heap with a blanket wrapped like a tourniquet around her bionic leg. She lay gasping for a minute, rubbing her hands over her arms to try and smother the flames until she finally realized that they weren't real.

A warning about escalating temperatures flashed in her gaze and she forced herself to lie still long enough to dismiss it from her vision. Her skin was clammy, beads of sweat dripping back into her hair. Even her metal limbs felt warm to the touch.

When her breathing was under control, she pulled herself up onto weak legs and hobbled to the window, thrusting it open and drinking in the winter air. The snow had started to melt, turning into slush in the daytime before hardening into glistening ice at night. Cinder stood for a moment, reveling in the frosty air on her skin and entranced by how a nearly full moon turned the world ghostly yellow. She tried to remember the nightmare, but her memory gave her only fire and, after a minute, the sensation of sandpaper in her mouth.

Shutting the window, she crept toward her bedroom door, careful not to trip on the bag of secondhand clothes Pearl had begrudgingly given to her the day before after her father had lectured her about charity.

She heard Adri's voice before she reached the kitchen and paused, one hand balancing her on the wall as her body threatened to tip toward its heavier left side.

As she strained to hear, Adri's voice grew steadily louder, and Cinder realized with a jolt that Adri wasn't *speaking* louder, but rather something in her own head was adjusting the volume on her hearing. She rubbed her palm against her ear, feeling like there was a bug in it.

"Four months, Garan," Adri said. "We're behind by four months and Suki-jiě has already threatened to start auctioning off our things if we don't pay her soon."

"She's not going to auction off our things," said Garan, his voice a strange combination of soothing and strained. Garan's voice had already become unfamiliar to Cinder's ear. He spent his days out in a one-room shed behind the house, "tinkering," Peony said, though she didn't seem to know what exactly he was tinkering with. He came in to join his family for meals, but hardly ever talked and Cinder wondered how much he heard, either. His expression always suggested his mind was very far away.

"Why *shouldn't* she sell off our things? I'm sure I would in her place!" Adri said. "Whenever I have to leave the house, I come home wondering if this will be the day our things are gone and our locks are changed. We can't keep living on her hospitality."

"It's going to be all right, love. Our luck is changing."

"Our luck!" Adri's voice spiked in Cinder's ear and she flinched at the shrillness, quickly urging the volume to descend again. It obeyed her command, through sheer willpower. She held her breath, wondering what other secrets her brain was keeping from her.

"*How* is our luck changing? Because you won a silver ribbon at that fair in Sydney last month? Your stupid awards aren't going to keep food on this table, and now you've brought home one more mouth—and a *cyborg* at that!"

"We talked about this . . ."

"No, *you* talked about this. I want to support you, Garan, but these schemes of yours are going to cost us everything. We have our own girls to think about. I can't even afford new shoes for Pearl and now there's this creature in the house who's going to need . . . what? A new *foot* every six months?"

Shriveling against the wall, Cinder glanced down at her metal foot, the toes looking awkward and huge beside the fleshy ones—the ones with bone and skin and toenails.

"Of course not. She'll be fine for a year or two," said Garan.

Adri stifled a hysterical laugh.

"And her leg and fingers can be adjusted as she grows," Garan continued. "We shouldn't need replacements for those until she reaches adulthood."

Cinder lifted her hand into the faint light coming down the hallway, inspecting the joints. She hadn't noticed how the knuckles were fitted together before, the digits nestled inside each other. So this hand could grow, just like her human hand did.

Because she would be stuck with these limbs forever. She would be cyborg forever.

"Well how *comforting*," said Adri. "I'm glad to see you've given this so much thought."

"Have faith, love."

Cinder heard a chair being pushed back and backed up into the hallway, but all that followed was the sound of running water from the faucet. She pressed her fingers over her mouth, trying to feel the water through psychokinesis, but even *her* brain couldn't quench her thirst on sound alone.

"I have something special to reveal at the Tokyo Fair in March," Garan said. "It's going to change everything. In the meantime, you must be patient with the child. She only wants to belong here. Perhaps she can help you with the housework, until we can get that android replaced?"

Adri scoffed. "Help me? What can she do, dragging that monstrosity around?"

Cinder cringed. She heard a cup being set down, then a kiss. "Give her a chance. Maybe she'll surprise you."

She ducked away at the first hint of a footstep, creeping back into her room and shutting the door. She felt that she could have wept from thirst, but her eyes stayed as dry as her tongue.

"HERE, YOU PUT ON THE GREEN ONE," SAID PEONY, TOSSING a bundle of green and gold silk into Cinder's arms. She barely caught it, the thin material slipping like water over her hands. "We don't have any real ball gowns, but these are just as pretty. This is my favorite." Peony held up another garment, a swath of purple and red fabric decorated with soaring cranes. She strung her bony arms through the enormous sleeves and pulled the material tight around her waist, holding it in place while she dug through the pile of clothes for a long silver sash and belted it around her middle. "Aren't they beautiful?"

Cinder nodded uncertainly—although the silk kimonos were perhaps the finest things she'd ever felt, Peony looked ridiculous in hers. The hem of the gown dragged a foot on the floor, the sleeves dangled almost to her knees, and street clothes still peeked through at her neck and wrists, ruining the illusion. It almost looked like the gown was trying to eat her.

"Well, put yours on!" said Peony. "Here, this is the sash I usually put with that one." She pulled out a black and violet band.

Cinder tentatively stuck her hands into the sleeves, taking

extra care that no screws or joints caught the fine material. "Won't Adri be mad?"

"Pearl and I play dress-up all the time," said Peony, looping the sash around Cinder's waist. "And how are we supposed to go to the ball if we don't have any beautiful dresses to wear?"

Cinder raised her arms, shaking the sleeves back. "I don't think my hand goes with this one."

Peony laughed, though Cinder hadn't meant it to be funny. Peony seemed to find amusement with almost everything she said.

"Just pretend you're wearing gloves," said Peony. "Then no one will know." Grabbing Cinder by the hand, she pulled her across the hall and into the bathroom so they could see themselves in the mirror. Cinder looked no less absurd than Peony, with her fine, mousy hair hanging limp past her shoulders and awkward metal fingers poking out of the left sleeve.

"Perfect," said Peony, beaming. "Now we're at the ball. Iko used to always be the prince, but I guess we'll have to pretend."

"What ball?"

Peony stared back at her in the mirror as if Cinder had just sprouted a metal tail. "The ball for the peace festival! It's this huge event we have every year—the festival is down in the city center and then in the evening they have the ball up at the palace. I've never gone for real, but Pearl will be thirteen next year so she'll get to go for the first time." She sighed and spun out into the hallway. Cinder followed, her walking made even more cumbersome than usual with the kimono trailing on the ground.

"When I go for the first time, I want a purple dress with a skirt so big I can hardly fit through the door."

"That sounds uncomfortable."

Peony wrinkled her nose. "Well, it has to be spectacular, or else Prince Kai won't notice me, and then what's the point?"

Cinder was almost hesitant to ask as she followed flouncing Peony back into her bedroom—"Who's Prince Kai?"

Peony spun toward her so fast, she tripped on the skirts of Adri's kimono and fell, screaming, onto her bed. "*Who's Prince Kai?*" she yelled, struggling to sit back up. "Only my future husband! Honestly, don't girls in Europe know about him?"

Cinder teetered between her two feet, unable to answer the question. After twelve whole days living with Peony and her family, she already had more memories of the Eastern Commonwealth than she had of Europe. She hadn't the faintest idea what—or who—the girls in Europe obsessed over.

"Here," said Peony, scrambling across her messy blankets and grabbing a portscreen off the nightstand. "He's my greeter."

She turned the screen on and a boy's voice said, "Hello, Peony." Cinder shuffled forward and took the small device from her. The screen showed a boy of twelve or thirteen years old wearing a tailored suit that seemed ironic with his shaggy black hair. He was waving at someone—Cinder guessed the photo was from some sort of press event.

"Isn't he gorgeous?" said Peony. "Every night I tie a red string around my finger and say his name five times because this girl in my class told me that will tie our destinies together. I know he's my soul mate."

Cinder listed her head, still staring at the boy. Her optobionics were scanning him, finding the picture in some database in her head, and, this time, she expected the stream of text that began to filter through her brain. His ID number, his birth date, his full name and title. Prince Kaito, Crown Prince of the Eastern Commonwealth.

"His arms are too long for his body," she said after a while, finally picking up on what didn't feel right about the picture. "They're not proportionate."

"What are you talking about?" Peony snatched the port away and stared at it for a minute before tossing it onto her pillow. "Honestly, who cares about his arms?"

Cinder shrugged, unable to smother a slight grin. "I was only saying."

Harrumphing, Peony swung her legs around and hopped off the bed. "Fine, whatever. Our hover is here. We'd better get going or we'll be late for the ball, where *I* am going to dance with His Imperial Highness, and *you* can dance with whoever you would like to. Maybe another prince. We should make one up for you. Do you want Prince Kai to have a brother?"

"What are you two doing?"

Cinder spun around. Adri was looming in the doorway —again her footsteps had gone unnoticed and Cinder was beginning to wonder if Adri was really a ghost that floated through the hallways rather than walked.

"We're going to the ball!" Peony said.

Adri's face flushed as her gaze dropped down the silk kimono hanging off Cinder's shoulders. "Take that off this instant!"

Shrinking back, Cinder instantly began undoing the knot that Peony had tied around her waist.

"Peony, what are you thinking? These garments are expensive and if she got snagged—if the lining—" Stepping forward, she grabbed the collar of the dress, peeling it off Cinder as soon as the sash was free.

"But you used to let Pearl and me—"

"Things are *different* now, and you are to leave my things alone. Both of you!"

Scowling, Peony started unwrapping her own dress. Cinder bit the inside of her cheek, feeling oddly vulnerable without the heavy silk draped around her and sick to her stomach with guilt, though she wasn't sure what she had to be guilty about.

"Cinder."

She dared to meet Adri's gaze.

"I came to tell you that if you are to be a part of this household, I will expect you to take on some responsibilities. You're old enough to help Pearl with her chores."

She nodded, almost eager to have something to do with her time when Peony wasn't around. "Of course. I don't want to be any trouble."

Adri's mouth pursed into a thin line. "I won't ask you to do any dusting until I can trust you to move with a bit of grace. Is that hand water resistant?"

Cinder held out her bionic hand, splaying out the fingers. "I . . . I think so. But it might rust . . . after a while . . ."

"Fine, no dishes or scrubbing, then. Can you at least cook?"

Cinder racked her brain, wondering if it could feed her recipes as easily as it fed her useless definitions. "I never have before, that I can remember. But I'm sure . . ."

Peony threw her arms into the air. "Why don't we just get Iko fixed and then *she* can do all the housework like she's supposed to?"

Adri's eyes smoldered as she looked between her daughter and Cinder. "Well," she said, finally snatching up the two kimonos and draping them over her arm, "I'm sure we'll be able to find *some use* for you. In the meantime, why don't you leave my daughter alone so she can get some of her schoolwork accomplished?"

"What?" said Peony. "But we haven't even gotten to the ball yet."

Cinder didn't wait to hear the argument she expected to follow. "Yes, stepmother," she murmured, ducking her head. She slipped past Adri and made her way to her own room.

Her insides were writhing but she couldn't pinpoint the overruling emotion. Hot anger, because it wasn't her fault that her new leg was awkward and heavy, and how was she to know Adri wouldn't want them playing in her things?

But also mortification because maybe she really was useless. She was eleven years old, but she didn't know anything, other than the bits of data that seemed to serve no purpose other than to keep her from looking like a complete idiot. If she'd had any skills before, she had no idea what they had been. She'd lost them now.

Sighing, she shut her bedroom door and slumped against it.

The room hadn't changed much in the almost two weeks since she'd come to call it home, other than the cast-off clothes that had been put into the dresser drawers, a pair of boots tossed into a corner, the blankets bundled up in a ball at the foot of her bed.

Her eyes landed on the box of android parts that hadn't been moved from their spot behind the door. The dead sensor, the spindly arms.

There was a bar code printed on the back of the torso that she hadn't noticed before. She barely noticed it then, except that her distracted brain was searching for the random numbers, downloading the android's make and model information. Parts list. Estimated value. Maintenance and repair manual.

Something familiar stirred inside her, like she already knew this android. How its parts fit together, how its mechanics and programming all functioned as a whole. Or no, this wasn't familiarity, but . . . a connectedness. Like she knew the android intimately. Like it was an extension of her.

She pushed herself off the door, her skin tingling.

Perhaps she had one useful skill after all.

IT TOOK THREE DAYS, DURING WHICH SHE EMERGED FROM her room only to sit for meals with her new family and, once, to play in the snow with Peony while Adri and Pearl were at the market. Her metal limbs had frosted over with cold by the time they were done, but coming inside to a pot of green tea and the flush of shared laughter had quickly warmed her back up.

Adri had not asked Cinder to take on any household chores again, and Cinder imagined it seemed a lost cause to her stepmother. She stayed hopeful though, as the jumble of android pieces gradually formed into something recognizable. A hollow plastic body atop wide treads, two skinny arms, a squat head with nothing but a cyclops sensor for a face. The sensor had given her the most trouble and she had to redo the wiring twice, triple-checking the diagram that had downloaded across her eyesight, before she felt confident she'd gotten it right.

If only it worked. If only she could show it to Adri, and even Garan, that she wasn't a useless addition to their family after all. That she was grateful they'd taken her in when no one else would. That she wanted to belong to them.

She was sitting cross-legged on her bed with the window open behind her, allowing in a chilled but pleasant breeze, when she inserted the final touch. The small personality chip clicked into place and Cinder held her breath, half-expecting the android to perk up and swivel around and start talking to her, until she remembered that she would need to be charged before she could function.

Feeling her excitement wane from the anticlimactic finale, Cinder released a slow breath and fell back onto her mattress, mentally exhausted.

A knock thunked against the door.

"Come in," she called, not bothering to move as the door creaked open.

"I was just wondering if you wanted to come watch—" Peony fell silent and Cinder managed to lift her head to see the girl gaping wide-eyed at the android. "Is that . . . Iko?"

Grinning, Cinder braced herself on her elbows. "She still needs to be charged, but I think she'll work."

Jaw still hanging open, Peony crept into the room. Though only nine years old, she was already well over a foot taller than the squat robot. "How . . . *how?* How did you fix it?"

"I had to borrow some tools from your dad." Cinder gestured to a pile of wrenches and screwdrivers in the corner. She didn't bother to mention that he hadn't been in his workshop behind the house when she'd gone to find them. It almost felt like theft and that thought terrified her, but it wasn't theft. She wasn't going to keep the tools, and she was sure Garan would be delighted when he saw she'd fixed the android.

"That's not . . ." Peony shook her head and finally looked at Cinder. "You fixed her by yourself?"

Cinder shrugged, not sure if she should be proud or uncomfortable by the look of awe Peony was giving her. "It wasn't that hard," she said. "I had . . . I can download . . . information. Instructions. Into my head. And I figured out how to get the android's blueprint to go across my vision so I could . . ." She trailed off, realizing that what she'd been sure was a most useful skill was also one more strange eccentricity her body could claim. One more side effect of being cyborg.

But Peony's eyes were twinkling by the minute. "You're kidding," she said, picking up one of Iko's hands and waggling it around. Cinder had been sure to thoroughly grease it so the joints wouldn't seize up. "What else can you do?"

"Um." Cinder hunched her shoulders, considering. "I can . . . make stuff louder. I mean, not really, but I can adjust my hearing so it seems louder. Or quieter. I could probably mute my hearing if I wanted to."

Peony laughed. "That's brilliant! You'd never have to hear Mom when she's yelling! Aw, I'm so jealous!" Beaming, she started to drag Iko toward the door. "Come on, there's a charging station in the hallway!"

Cinder hopped off the bed and followed her to a docking station at the end of the hall. Peony plugged Iko in and, instantly, a faint blue light started to glow around the plug.

Peony had raised hopeful eyes to Cinder when the front door opened and Garan stumbled into the hallway, his hair dripping. He wasn't wearing his coat.

He started when he saw the girls standing there. "Peony," he said, short of breath. "Where's your mother?"

She glanced over her shoulder. "In the kitchen, I thi—"

"Go fetch her. Quickly, please."

Peony stalled, her face clouding with worry, before hurrying toward the kitchen.

Intertwining her fingers, Cinder slid in closer to the android. It was the first time she'd been alone with Garan since their long trip and she expected him to say something, to ask how she was getting along or if there was anything she needed—he'd certainly asked that plenty of times while they were traveling—but he hardly seemed to notice her standing there.

“I fixed your android,” she said finally, her voice squeaking a little. She grabbed the android’s limp arm, as if to prove it, though the hand did nothing but droop.

Garan turned his distraught gaze on her and looked for a moment like he was going to ask who she was and what she was doing in his house. He opened his mouth but it took a long time for any words to form.

“Oh, child.”

She frowned at the obvious pity. This was not a reaction she’d expected—he was not impressed, he was not grateful. Thinking he must not have heard her correctly, she went to repeat herself—no, she’d *fixed* the android—when Adri came around the corner, wearing the robe she always wore when she wasn’t planning on going out. She had a dish towel in her hand and her two daughters trailing in her wake.

“Garan?”

He stumbled back, slamming his shoulder hard into the wall, and everyone froze.

“Don’t—” he stammered, smiling apologetically as a droplet of water fell onto his nose. “I’ve called for an emergency hover.”

The curiosity hardened on Adri’s face. “Whatever for?”

Cinder pressed herself as far as she could into the wall, feeling like she was pinned between two people who hadn’t the faintest idea she was standing there.

Garan folded his arms, starting to shiver. “I’ve caught it,” he whispered, his eyes beginning to water.

Cinder glanced back at Peony, wondering if these words

meant something to her, but no one was paying Cinder any attention.

"I'm sorry," said Garan, coughing. He shuffled back toward the door. "I shouldn't even have come inside. But I had to say . . . I had to . . ." He covered his mouth and his entire body shook with a cough, or a sob, Cinder couldn't tell which. "I love you all so much. I'm so sorry. I'm so, so sorry."

"Garan." Adri took half a step forward, but her husband was already turning away. The front door shut a second later, and Pearl and Peony cried out at the same time and rushed forward, but Adri caught them both by their arms. "*Garan!* No—you girls, stay here. Both of you." Her voice was trembling as she pulled them back, before chasing after Garan herself, her night robe swishing against Cinder's legs as she passed.

Cinder inched forward so she could see the door being swung open around the corner. Her heart thumped like a drum against her ribs.

"GARAN!" Adri screamed, tears in her voice. "What are you—you can't go!"

Cinder was slammed against the wall as Pearl tore past her, screaming for her father, then Peony, sobbing.

No one paused. No one looked at Cinder or the android in their hurry for the door. Cinder realized after a moment that she was still gripping the android's skeletal arm, listening. Listening to the sobs and pleas, the *No*s, the *Daddy*s. The words echoed off the snow and back into the house.

Releasing the android, Cinder hobbled forward. She reached

the threshold that overlooked the blindingly white world and paused, staring at Adri and Pearl and Peony, who were on their knees in the pathway to the street, slush soaking into their clothes. Garan was standing on the curb, his hand still over his mouth as if he'd forgotten it was there. His eyes were red from crying. He looked weak and small, as if the slightest wind would blow him over into the snowdrifts.

Cinder heard sirens.

"What am I supposed to do?" Adri screamed, her arms covered in goose bumps as they gripped her children against her. "What will I do?"

A door slammed and Cinder looked up. The old man across the street was on his doorstep. More neighbors were emerging—at doors and windows, their gazes bright with curiosity.

Adri sobbed louder, and Cinder returned her attention to the family—her new family—and realized that Garan was watching *her.*

She stared back, her throat burning from the cold.

The sirens became louder and Garan glanced down at his huddled wife, his terrified daughters. "My girls," he said, trying to smile, and then a white hover with flashing lights turned the corner, screaming its arrival.

Cinder ducked back into the doorway as the hover slid up behind Garan and settled into the snow. Two androids rolled out of its side door with a gurney hovering between them. Their yellow sensors flashed.

"A comm was received at 1704 this evening regarding a

victim of letumosis at this address," said one of the androids in a sterile voice.

"That's me," Garan choked—his words instantly drowned out by Adri's screaming, "NO! Garan! You can't. You can't!"

Garan attempted a shaken smile and held out his arm. He rolled up his sleeve and even from her spot on the doorstep Cinder could see two dark spots on his wrist. "I have it. Adri, love, you must take care of the girl."

Adri pulled back as if he'd struck her. *"The girl?"*

"Pearl, Peony," Garan continued as if she hadn't spoken, "be good for your mother. Never forget that I love you so, so very much." Releasing the hard-won smile, he perched himself uncertainly on the floating gurney.

"Lie back," said one of the androids. "We will input your identification into our records and alert your family immediately of any changes in your condition."

"No, Garan!" Adri clambered to her feet, her thin slippers sliding on the ice and nearly sending her onto her face as she struggled to rush after her husband. "You can't leave me. Not by myself, not with . . . not with this *thing!*"

Cinder shuddered and wrapped her arms around her waist.

"Please stand back from the letumosis victim," said one of the androids, positioning itself between Adri and the hover as Garan was lifted into its belly.

"Garan, no! NO!"

Pearl and Peony latched back on to their mother's sides, both screaming for their father, but perhaps they were too afraid of the androids to go any closer. The androids rolled themselves back up into the hover. The doors shut. The sirens and the lights filled up the quiet suburb before fading slowly away. Adri and her daughters stayed clumped together in the snow, sobbing and clutching each other while the neighbors watched. While Cinder watched, wondering why her eyes stayed so dry—stinging dry—when dread was encompassing her like slush freezing over.

"What's happened?"

Cinder glanced down. The android had woken up and disconnected herself from the charging station and now stood before her with her sensor faintly glowing.

She'd done it. She'd fixed the android. She'd proven her worth.

But her success was drowned out by their sobs and the memory of the sirens. She couldn't quite grasp the unfairness of it.

"They took Garan away," she said, licking her lips. "They called him a letumosis victim."

A series of clicks echoed inside the android's body. "Oh, dear . . . not Garan."

Cinder barely heard her. In saying the words, she realized that her brain had been downloading information for some time, but she'd been too caught up in everything to realize it. Now dozens of useless bits of information were scrolling across her vision. *LETUMOSIS, ALSO CALLED THE BLUE FEVER OR THE PLAGUE, HAS CLAIMED THOUSANDS OF LIVES SINCE THE FIRST KNOWN VICTIMS OF THE DISEASE DIED IN NORTHERN AFRICA IN MAY OF 114 T.E. . . .* Cinder read faster, scanning until she found the words that she feared, but had somehow known she would find. TO DATE, THERE HAVE BEEN NO KNOWN SURVIVORS.

Iko was speaking again and Cinder shook her head to clear it. "—can't stand to see them cry, especially lovely Peony. Nothing makes an android feel more useless than when a human is crying."

Finding it suddenly hard to breathe, Cinder deserted the doorway and slumped back against the inside wall, unable to listen to the sobs any longer. "You won't have to worry about me, then. I don't think I can cry anymore." She hesitated. "Maybe I never could."

"Is that so? How peculiar. Perhaps it's a programming glitch."

She stared down into Iko's single sensor. "A programming glitch."

"Sure. You have programming, don't you?" She lifted a spindly arm and gestured toward Cinder's steel prosthetic. "I have a glitch, too. Sometimes I forget that I'm not human. I don't think that happens to most androids."

Cinder gaped down at Iko's smooth body, beat-up treads, three-fingered prongs, and wondered what it would be like to be stuck in such a body and not know if you were human or robot.

She raised the pad of her finger to the corner of her right eye, searching for wetness that wasn't there.

"Right. A glitch." She feigned a nonchalant smile, hoping the android couldn't detect the grimace that came with it. "Maybe that's all it is."

Thank you, bloggers, for all your support!

One Librarian's Book Reviews, Hippies, Beauty, and Books...Oh My!, The Romance Bookie, Nicole's YA Book Haven, When I Grow Up, SarawithnH, A Reader of Fictions, The Reading Fever, Esther's Ever After, Simply Stacie, Damsel Chronicles Didi's Blog, Reading With My Eyes Shut, Up in the Bibliosphere, Writers Write, Right?, Blook Girl, Curse of the Bibliophile, Red Reader, The Book Worm Hole, Popcorn Reads, Krazy Elf's Bookshelf, Sapphyria's Book Reviews, FantYAstic Volumes, Jo's Book Corner, The Passionate Bookworm, Please Another Book, Fuzzy Coffee Books, Jess Resides Here, So many books, so little time, Stacked, Book Love 101, The Bookworm, Joie De Lire, Novel Reveries, The Reads4Tweens, Coffee. Novel Read, A Reader's Loves Books, The Forsythia, Rae Gun Poetry to Prose, Geek Girl's Book Blog, Mermaid Vision Books, My 5 Monkeys, Rondo of a Possible World, Cozy Up With a Good Read, Hooked on Books

Lost Amongst the Shelves, Bookshelves Anonymous, Just a Lil' Lost, Shelf Talkers Anonymous, Life. Love, Another Adventure, Alexa Haunting of Orchid Ramblings, Sonder Books, Speculating on SpecFic, Inkblots & Teastains, Liyanaland, Bananas for Books, Book Labyrinth, Geo Librarian, Fairy Layers, Radiant Reads, Winter Haven Books, Scattered Pages, Skyway Avenue, Novel Thoughts, Kristina's World of Books, Life: Merging, Citrus Reads

The Intergalactic Academy, Books from Bleh to Basically Amazing, Reading Vacation, My Bookish Ways, Bookalicio.us, The Fable Faerie, Manga Maniac Cafe, A Backwards Story, Laura's Review Bookshelf, Bibliophilic Monologues, Novel Novice, Mermaid Vision Books, The Book Rat, Almost Grown-Up, Working for the Mandroid, The Book Cellar, Ramblings of a Wannabe Scribe, No More Grumpy Bookseller, A Glass of Wine, A Library of My Own, Dead Tossed Waves, Cuddlebuggery Book Blog, SciFiChick, Just a Girl Geek, The Book Lantern, Blue Egg Books , Into the Hall of Books, Novels by G. Donald Cribbs, The Librarian Writer, Starting the Next Chapter, Ms. Martin Teaches Media, Ashley Loves Books, Two Chicks on Books, Fiktshun, Reading on the F Train, The AP Book Club, Books of Love, The Reading Lair, Me on Books, Bloggers[heart] Books, Words Are Things, The Reading Geek, The Order of Writing, Penmanship Smitten, The Book Life, IB Book Blogging, Were My First Friends

Compulsive Reader, RavenFic Reviews, From Slush to Pulp, whatchYAreading?, The Fuma Files, Hughes Reviews, Emily's Reading Room, Confessions of a Vi3tBabe, Melissa's Eclectic Bookshelf, Silver Sleep, Amira's Book Reviews, Emilie's Book World, YA Bluewater, Writer in progress, The Potter People, Sable Caught, Books and Sensibility, Nyx Book Reviews, Kimba the Caffeinated Book Reviewer, Turning the Pages, Midnight Bloom Reads, Tea and Text, Think Banned Thoughts, Writer Alina, Jaime's Book Blog, V's Book Life, Ink Spot Plot, My Bookshelf, Bec's Blog, bibliophilesisters, Radiant Shadows, Musings of a Book Lover, The Write Path, Anna Banana Smoothie, Bites, My Book Diaries, Paper Cuts, Carina's Books, Book Adventures, The Shangri La of Books, I Read to Relax!, Lauren's Crammed Bookshelf, Leeanna Me, Sisters Grimm Bookshop, Lost at Midnight Reviews, Burn Bright, Michelle & Leslie's Book Picks

© Kali Raisl

Marissa Meyer lives in Tacoma, Washington, with her husband and three cats. She's a fan of most things geeky (*Sailor Moon*, *Firefly*, color-coordinating her bookshelf . . .), and has been in love with fairy tales since she was a kid, something she doesn't intend to ever grow out of. She may or may not be a cyborg. *Cinder*, her first novel, debuted on the *New York Times* bestseller list. Visit Marissa on the Web at marissameyer.com.